ALSO BY CAROLINA DE ROBERTIS

FICTION

The Invisible Mountain
Perla

TRANSLATION

Bonsai, by Alejandro Zambra
The Neruda Case, by Roberto Ampuero

THE GODS OF TANGO

THE GODS OF

Tango

◆

Carolina De Robertis

◆

ALFRED A. KNOPF
New York 2015

THIS IS A BORZOI BOOK
PUBLISHED BY ALFRED A. KNOPF

www.aaknopf.com

Knopf, Borzoi Books, and the colophon are registered trademarks of
Penguin Random House LLC.

Library of Congress Cataloging-in-Publication Data
De Robertis, Carolina.
The gods of tango / Carolina De Robertis. — First edition.
pages ; cm
"This is a Borzoi book."
ISBN 978-1-101-87449-3 (hardcover) — ISBN 978-1-101-87450-9 (eBook)
1. Violinists—Fiction. 2. Gender identity—Fiction. 3. Buenos Aires (Argentina)—
History—20th century—Fiction. I. Title.
PS3604.E129G63 2015   813'.6—dc23   2014023450

Jacket image: Mary Evans Picture Library
Jacket design by Stephanie Ross

Manufactured in the United States of America
First Edition

For Luciana

And all things conspire to keep silent about us, half
out of shame perhaps, half as unutterable hope.

—Rainer Maria Rilke

Convert the outrage of the years into music.

—Jorge Luis Borges

Since the house is on fire, let us warm ourselves.

—Italian proverb

Contents

THE GODS OF TANGO

Dante died a happy man, although a strange one, known for living with a coffin in his house. The gossips of Montevideo had spent years speculating about the reason for the coffin. He's a vampire. He's mad. He's terrified of death. He keeps his violin in there, under a witch's spell, that's why your soul breaks open every time he plays, the old bastard. But as for the true reason, they could never begin to guess.

His last moment came in the kitchen, a sudden blurring of his heart, as if a giant paintbrush had pierced his chest and smeared its inner walls with white. He couldn't breathe; he reached for the table's edge and grasped only air. Something clattered far away. It was not pain, exactly, just a pressure that urged him to collapse into himself, almost sweetly, plunging all his secrets into rubble. His last thought was not of secrets, or of music, or of God, or even of the woman who had flooded his life with joy. It was of Cora. Cora, my darling, *carissima*, come closer. Are you here? Take my hand. If there is light then steer me to it. If there is not, I'm not afraid, not if there is you. You. There you are. Radiant. As you were before it all began.

He reached for Cora's hand and Cora smiled and opened her mouth and out poured an explosion of light.

PART ONE

◆

Think of Nothing, Think of Home

Leda arrived in Argentina on February 4, 1913, on a steamship that only twenty days before had made Italy disappear, swallowed by that ravenous monster called the horizon. On her last morning on board, she dressed with care and latched her trunk tightly so that nothing, no sleeve, no village dust, no errant memory could spill out when the porter came to carry it to the deck. Then she sat in silence for a while. Her bunkmate, Fausta, had left her bedclothes tousled and unkempt. No doubt she was already on deck, craning for a glimpse of Buenos Aires. If Leda didn't find her in the crowds, she might never see her again, a strange thought after twenty nights of sharing quarters with a woman who wasn't kin, whom she'd never met before the voyage. Strangers. Strangeness. These two things filled the crossing to América. She wondered what her mother would say if she were here, in this stuffy little room with her. Here you are, then, or It smells like a sty in here, or For God's sake, Leda, straighten your hat. She told herself that she would see her mother again one day, as well as her father and cousins and uncles and aunts and her great-grandmother's ceaseless dragonfly hands—though none of it was true: in the years and continent to come, Leda would see many things that would astound her, break her into pieces, and reassemble her in shapes she hadn't known a human soul could inhabit, but she would never see her family again.

She was sitting on the trunk that had accompanied her from home. So few things stowed away inside it. Folded dresses. A cluster of books. A jar of olives cured by the baker's wife. Hazelnuts wrapped in burlap. Her father's violin, passed down for generations, gone from Italy for the first time, a gift for her new husband.

It was her grandfather who'd told her the tale of this particular violin, over and over, as if the telling could stave off loss, as if the weight and scope of human history were not found in books or in those mythic universities in Rome and Naples that no one in their village had ever actually seen but, rather, were encoded in objects like this one, a violin touched by hundreds of hands, loved, used, stroked, pressed, made to outlive its owners, storing their secrets and lies. Imagine, said her grandfather: this very violin belonged to the King of Naples until 1501. Oh, it's true, don't you doubt it. How long it was in the royal family, nobody knows. But there is no question that, whoever it belonged to before, it did belong to Federico d'Aragona, the last King of Naples of the Trastámara line. He was a quiet, kindly man never meant to face the kinds of forces that he did—two nations, Spain and France, vying for his throne; a lineage still shaking from the too-brief reigns of his father, brother, and nephew before him. Are you following, Leda? He tried to rule but all it takes is for your enemies to join forces with your unlucky stars and then suddenly there you are, encircled, nowhere to run, and what is there left for you to do? I'll tell you what's left, a simple choice. Either you can die right there or you can flee to another land and start a new life with nothing but your skin and what's inside of it. That's what Federico did: he fled. Right into exile. Not freely, mind you, but as a prisoner flanked by soldiers. But before he left, before the soldiers came for him, he opened his bedroom window, stood overlooking the sprawling lands of Naples, and played his violin. He played a dirge that seemed to rise straight from the red core of the earth. The only person who heard it was a count who later told anyone who would listen that it was the saddest and most beautiful song he ever heard in his life. When the king had finished playing, he gave the count the violin.

You keep it, he said. I'm done with music.

The count protested at first. But what about your sons?

King Federico only shook his head. The violin has to stay.

Whether or not the king ever played another violin during his years of French exile is unknown, a detail lost in the folds of time, so, Leda, I can't give you that piece of the story. But the count kept the violin and passed it down within his family, which eventually, in 1815, sold the instrument to my great-grandfather in order to pay off debts, and my great-grandfather received, along with the thing itself, the story of the King of Naples's dirge, which of course gave the instrument a higher value (whether or not it was actually true, Leda thought as she listened, but she said nothing since it was clear that her grandfather would not harbor a drop of doubt). And so the hands of the king had played this very violin, on that last day of Naples's independence as a kingdom all its own. What exactly did he play, that Federico? How did the song sound? We'll never know. That's what happens to melodies: they get lost in the air. Just like memories. And the body. Memories and melodies and the body dissolve after we die. A musical instrument is not like the body, not at all; like the soul, it carries on.

Leda went up to the deck. It was a hot, humid day, and beads of sweat clung to the foreheads of men, who far outnumbered women on the ship, and who were mostly young, though few as young as her own seventeen years. There was hope in their wide gazes and a frenetic anticipation about them; 368 tightly strung human wires. The women were mostly wives on their way to meet their husbands in Buenos Aires, just like Fausta (and like me, Leda thought, remember, remember, I'm a wife too). The deck burst with people, just as it had the day they'd left Naples. There were no longer any lazy card games with which to kill the hours. Boredom had sloughed overboard into the sea. Everybody was on their feet, crowded against the rail, craning their necks in the direction of land.

Argentina. She pressed into the throng, toward the rail. To her right, a young woman murmured a rosary. To her left, a man in his forties was drying his tears, while the younger man beside him smoked a cigarette with indifference or, Leda thought, a convincing performance of indifference. His demeanor seemed the most theatrical of all. She smelled sweat and tobacco and the hopeful tang of cologne. In front of her, three or four chaotic rows ahead, two men were exclaiming to each other about the land they saw.

"*Che bella*. Beautiful."

"Yes. Beautiful."

Again and again they said it, as though repetition would solidify the truth of the phrase, make it strong enough to sustain them as they disembarked. Their voices wove through the wails and murmurs in the crowd. She gently jostled forward. A man in front of her moved away, apparently having seen enough, and she slunk into his space before it could close, before anyone could notice. She was starved for the sight of land, not just any land, but this land—Buenos Aires, her new home. Over the past three weeks, she had spent many hours alone at these rails, staring out at endless ocean, trying to imagine what Buenos Aires would be like. Over and over she tried to picture the city, but her mind's eye could conjure only the lush tropical ferns and trees of the Botanical Garden, where Dante had taken a photograph of himself when he'd first arrived, to send to the family back home. It had been passed around the table at Sunday lunch, to clucks of admiration and bemusement.

He's really there, in Argentina.

He looks happy.

He looks too skinny.

Look at those parrots, they're big enough to eat him!

Don't be ridiculous, Mario. Those are fake. Just painted wood.

How can you be so sure?

I have eyes in my head.

You don't know anything, you idiot.

I was just—

No fighting today, for the sake of God, Leda's mother said.

How about we let his bride take a look?

That's right! Leda, do you want to see?

The photograph arrived in Leda's hands. In it, Dante stood sur-rounded by strange ferns with enormous fronds and two garish par-rots that, although she believed her brother's insistence to the contrary, seemed intensely alive. His mouth curled into a smirk, and a cigarette dangled from his hand, unlit. *I own this place,* his posture seemed to say. Of course, just because that was the place where he'd found a photog-rapher to take his portrait didn't mean the whole city looked that way. She knew this; at least part of her knew this. But the image still glowed in her mind.

Now, on the steamship, she wondered how it would be with Dante, tonight, her first time. How he would touch her, and for how long. Whether it would hurt or give her joy, the way it did for brides in bal-lads. Whether she would think of the white figs in their orchard, how they glistened when you pressed your fingers into them. Whether she would think of nothing. Whether she would think of home.

A cluster of men in front of her had had their fill of the approaching land, and when they moved, she stepped forward to the rail and leaned against it. Wind whipped her face and stung her nostrils with saline air. She feared the wind might tear her blue hat right off her head, despite the several pins she'd used to place it, and losing the hat—the finest thing she'd ever worn, with real pearls stitched on, *fit for a bride,* her mother had said—would be unbearable, so she reached up and gripped it with both hands. The throng around her seemed to melt away (as it surely did for everyone else: 368 Italians, all wandering their own private visions of Argentina in their minds) as her eyes roved the distant city, Buenos Aires, lying low across the water. The buildings were still so small that she could not discern anything about them, except, of course, that they existed—that while she and her compatriots still had no idea what they would find when they disembarked, they would at least find something, a true place that might show them what they'd ridden across

the open ocean for; that the Américas were more than some fable con-
cocted by ship lines and ticket agents and relatives with their carefully
calibrated letters home, even if seeing that the Américas exist does not
at all reveal the true mystery, a mystery much harder to resolve, namely,
what the Américas actually are.

Leda stood for a long time, watching Buenos Aires glide toward her,
and, because she did not yet dare to imagine its buildings, how she would
fit inside and between them, she pictured herself in that garden with
Dante, strolling past exotic ferns and sleeping curled together beneath
them as they might under the wings of a great forgiving swan.

Leda's wedding had been quick and simple, finished before the tang of
communion bread could fade from her mouth. Since bride and groom
were on different continents, they were married by proxy, with Dante's
father, her uncle Mateo, standing in at the altar for his son. Leda wore
a simple linen dress she'd borrowed in haste from a cousin. It was too
short for her—Leda was the tallest girl in Alazzano—and bunched awkwardly at the hips, but overall, with white carnations in hand and hair
and her mother's borrowed pearls at her throat, she looked enough like
a bride to satisfy the throng of relatives and the melancholy priest. She
would have worn her mother's bridal gown, as was the custom, but there
was no time to tailor it since Leda was to marry immediately and board a
ship to Argentina the following day, and though her mother in her youth
did not yet have the formidable girth she did now, she did have curves
back then that her wedding dress made clear, a voluptuousness that put
Leda's hipless, flat-chested form to shame. *How could I have given birth
to a girl with nothing on her?* her mother would sometimes say. They both
knew the answer; on her father's side, there had been two great-aunts
famous for their tall and sexless forms. They lived their entire lives as
spinsters. People called them the Nails because of their long thin bodies, harsh temperaments, and tendency to stick together as though they

belonged in the same box. As Leda stood at the altar, listening to the
murmurs of the priest, she thought she could palpably feel her mother's
relief that her daughter was getting married and therefore saved from
life as a Nail, though she could not tell whether her mother's relief out-
weighed the sorrow of losing that same daughter to an unknown country far away. Ever since Dante's letter had arrived, *send Leda, I am ready,*
the air around Mamma had been sharp and heavy as an impending slap.

"For richer or for poorer?" the priest said.

"*Sì,*" said Zio Mateo.

"*Sì,*" said Leda, and her voice echoed from the vaulting ceiling, making the saints shiver in their alcoves.

The vows continued. Zio Mateo did not look at her. He had always
had an impenetrable mind. He was the kind of man who seemed to live
somewhere other than inside his own face. At family gatherings he
either brooded in silence or launched long impassioned monologues that
no one dared interrupt. Now that she was marrying his son, she could
not read his expression, it had no message for her, no blessing and no
unblessing, just a slightly bored acceptance, as though he were fulfilling
a minor legal duty in whose outcome he was not invested. As though he
did not think about his younger son in Argentina, did not wonder about
the sweat and noise of Dante's days, the slow push of his nights, the
married life he was about to start. As though he'd grown tired of his role
as patriarch and this ceremony didn't matter, had no weight inside him
except as a burden. The weary, beleaguered patriarch doing his duties
at the altar. But he was a lie, an impostor, it disgusted her to give her
vows to him, this man who had set in motion a family curse so strong
that not even death could break it, a family curse that now could mar
her marriage before it even began. She reminded herself that he was just
a stand-in for the husband to whom she was actually binding her life,
but the revulsion remained, knotting her stomach, darkening the wide
church air.

It was winter, an unusual time for a wedding, and when the party of

fifteen or so walked down the church steps onto the plaza, cold air pricked
Leda's face. She had imagined that the world might look different than
it did when she first entered the church, that it might glow with some
secret light to which only married people were privy, that her eyes might
have gained the power to glimpse some hidden texture of the world that
might make it more comprehensible, more able to align with the world
she carried inside. Countless times she had been told *you'll understand
when you're grown up*—and here it was, the threshold of womanhood.
But the spell hadn't worked. The world was the same. Her brother Tommaso was talking, as always, making her father laugh, but she could not
follow what they were saying to each other. Papà's arm was interlocked
with hers, and she was comforted by this, her father's gentle touch,
almost timid, a lost bird. *I swear it's true,* her brother said, *it hit him right
in his youknowwhere.* Her father laughed again, perhaps a bit too hard, a
sound forced from his throat. Her mother walked behind them, emanat-
ing chaos. The three little ones swarmed around her, along with other
children and their mothers. What were the women talking about? She
picked out the words *grandson* and *oranges* and *never ever ripened.* Their
voices rose and fell in melodious, competing waves. Zio Mateo and his
oldest son, Mario, walked in front, silent. The wedding party crossed
the plaza, their steps echoing on the same cobbles as always, rounded,
gray, slightly uneven, stones her ancestors had walked across to go to
mass, or play chess, or wash clothes in communal tubs, ever since the
first known Dante Mazzoni had fled his native Puglia in 1582—after sid-
ing with the French Bourbons in a failed attempt to overthrow Spanish
rule, which left him suddenly on the wrong side of the law—and settled
here in Alazzano, a tiny village in a valley of figs and ghosts and olive
groves. Now the Mazzoni family owned half the land around the village,
and yet was crushed by debt and other demons that were making the
youngest generation slowly disappear, some overseas, some into oblivion. Although it was not accurate to say the Mazzoni family owned the
land. It was one single member who owned it. Zio Mateo. Leda's father

was the younger brother, Ugo, owner of nothing, not even of the house he lived in by the grace and generosity of the brother who had inherited everything and thanks to whom her family, Ugo's family, could eat and farm and breathe.

What experts we are at hiding poison, she thought as the wedding party reached the door of Mateo's house, Palazzo Mazzoni, the largest house in the village. His wife, Crocifissa, had set out the tablecloths, plates, and silverware hours before, and now she and the other women vanished into the kitchen. Leda tried to join them but her aunts glared at her and blocked the door.

"Where do you think you're going?"

"Not today."

"Not in that dress, you don't."

The living room smelled of rosemary chicken, tomato sauce, and freshly baked sweet cakes. The men settled down to smoke, the children went outside to play, and Leda found a chair in a corner, though she would have liked to join the children in the dirt. She fixed her gaze on the oil painting that hung over the fireplace, of a vineyard beneath a clear blue sky. At one edge of the vineyard, an unusually tall fig tree caught sunlight in its leaves. She remembered that tree. It used to stand at the edge of Zio Mateo's land, at its border with that of a neighbor, Don Paolo. They had disputed over their property line, a fight they'd inherited from their grandfathers. In particular, Don Paolo had wanted the rights to the fig tree, whose fruits were his mother's favorite. After a long battle, a local judge had decided in Zio Mateo's favor, though Don Paolo's mother would spread the rumor that the judge had been bribed. Once he'd won the settlement, Mateo had taken an ax and cut down that fig tree with his own hands, because he wanted to, because he could. And then nobody in the entire village could enjoy its fruits ever again. In the painting, however, the tree's broad leaves continued to reach upward, their five sections resembling fingers splayed open to the air.

Leda shifted her weight restlessly. This living room made her think, how could it not, of Cora, who used to live here, who used to call this home. How could there be a wedding day without her?—especially since it was Cora's brother she was marrying. Cora her soul-cousin, her almost-sister who'd opened the world to her when they were very small, before the nightmare, when their spirits were so large they could have eaten the whole sky and called it breakfast, licked their fingers and been ready for more, Cora who'd seemed to understand the world from the inside in a secret way that Leda was hungry to know also, who'd brushed Leda's hair and warmed her milk when Mamma was too tired to notice, who'd sung her the lullabies that mothers sing for girls, who'd taken her to the river to fetch water and shown her how to brave the shallows, ankle-deep, calf-deep, even thigh, she was so bold, Cora, bright as hellblaze on a Lenten night, skirts hitched up in heedless fists, and laughing. Leda, two years younger, stood at the shore, scared to wade too deep, staring at her feet through the cold translucent river as it ran and ran and kissed her skin and Cora splashed her and said *Go on, go on, what's a little water in your skirts?* Cora teacher of secrets, such as how to pluck a chicken (soften its skin, she said, so the feathers are glad to slide out; they don't fight you if they're warm enough; dip the bird in boiling water and let heat work its magic, then get a good grip, strip it bare) and also how to read. She read aloud to Leda on winter evenings in this very living room, in that dark-honey voice of hers that made each syllable sound delicious. She loved the books that chronicled journeys most of all. The *Odyssey*. The *Inferno*. *A History of Joan of Arc*. In the end she'd put the volumes down and started to tell the stories in her own words, a mix of telling them from memory and embellishing the bones. Odysseus unlashed himself and swam out to the sirens. Joan escaped from prison before she could be burned. The road through the inferno became riddled with the dead of their own village, the grocer's wife, the long-gone priest, their ancestors whose names still bristled on the pages of records in the church. Even hell could seem appealing to a village girl itching for adventure, a village girl like Cora. Listen, Leda, she'd said, imagine traveling to places where you recognize nothing, not even your own face. Just imagine. And Leda did imagine. When Cora was nine, at the stone washing tubs on the village plaza, she learned about the bleeding of women. Leda was seven then. They say it hurts, Cora whispered, and Leda was terrified. Don't worry, Cora said. It'll happen to me first, and by the time it's your turn I'll know how to help you. But it didn't happen that way. By the time Leda's blood came, Cora was gone.

Within an hour, the wedding party had swelled with guests. The entire 107-person population of the village seemed to have come, as well as a few guests from the two nearest villages up the mountain, Monte Rosso and Trinità. As there was no groom to speak to, everybody wanted to talk to Leda, congratulate her, and ask questions about Argentina that she could not begin to answer. The married women formed a knot around her that refused to be undone.

"Are you ready? You've packed everything?"

"She'd better have. The carriage comes at dawn."

"At dawn!"

"Your trunk must be full to the brim."

"Is it cold there in winter?"

"No no, Giovanna, it's summer there now—incredible, no?—so when she gets there it'll be warm."

"Ah!"

"Even if it isn't warm, Dante will soon get the heat going for her."

Laughter.

"Poor bride, already married but she still has to wait."

"It'll be worth it."

"Oh yes. Don't worry, Leda."

"Take it from us: you'll be just fine."

More laughter.

"Leda, I brought you hazelnuts from my orchard. For you and Dante to eat together when you arrive."

"How romantic. He can crack them open for you."

"Heh, heh, heh."

"I didn't mean it that way."

"But he'll still do it."

"Do what?"

"I have to explain it to you?"

"Don't you know anything?"

"That's not funny."

"Now, ladies."

"Well, she's always—"

"No fighting, now."

"Leda, here, I have something for you too: olives from last year's harvest. For your Dante."

"Our Dante."

"Yes, our Dante, he'll always be our Dante. Remember when he got caught stealing your oranges? What was he, five?"

"Four."

"Santa María. What a precocious boy."

"Unstoppable, that one. Even when he was up to no good."

"Especially then."

"Well, he never gave *me* any trouble. He always had a pleasant word when he came to the bakery. '*Sì, signora. Per favore, signora.*' A little gentleman."

"Until he became a very tall gentleman."

"Nothing little about him now, I'll bet. Heh, heh."

"That's not for you to know, you crow."

"You're lucky, Leda."

"You'll be just fine, Leda."

"You two will build quite a kingdom for yourselves in Argentina."

"Not for nothing that the country's named after silver."

"Just don't forget us."

"You will write, won't you?"

"Of course she will."

She didn't say a word and no one asked her to. Night had fallen and the women's faces flickered in the light of kerosene lamps. The musicians had been playing across the room, but they had taken a break to smoke and their flutes and violins lay silent on their chairs. Leda's fingers itched to pick up one of the violins, as she had when she was a child, mimicking her father's hands along the neck, plucking the strings, discovering notes, hiding so that no one would stop her, stealing time, chasing melodies with which her father used to flood the living room, before, before. The women were eating second and third helpings of cake, and white powdered sugar smudged their lips. They were smiling with their mouths, but only some were smiling with their eyes. Leda felt strange, as though everyone, including herself, were acting out a tacitly agreed upon theater script from which the most important lines had been erased. Unsaid words infused the air; she could not decipher their meaning. She felt a sudden terror at the thought of not seeing these faces every day. What would the world be without them in it, these women who were pressed around her now, giving her laughter and olives and assurances and other things they would not name aloud—what were those things? a kind of hunger, a dull knife—as though they wanted to take the journey with her, as though their souls longed to flee across the ocean as stowaways in a corner of her trunk. I can't carry so much, she thought, I can't pack these secret parts of you. She felt alone. But this was what she'd wanted, wasn't it? For four years now she'd longed for escape. At thirteen, she'd begun to dream of packing a bundle of bread and clothes and trekking to Naples, on foot, or begging rides in carriages. But of course she could not. She knew the dangers of the road, of the city. She had also imagined climbing Vesuvius and hurling herself down its great black throat. But Vesuvius was far, how could she get there? Two weeks after her fifteenth birthday, Dante had offered another way out. He had announced his plan to leave for the New World over Sunday lunch with the family, and the afternoon sun had shot through the grape trellis to streak his face as he spoke. Afterward, she had slipped him a note, *meet me under the tall olive tree behind our house at nine o'clock.*

When she arrived that night, he was already there. He stood in the light of a half-moon.

"Not here," she said. "We have to go in."

She slunk under the slender cupola of branches and gestured for him to join her. Now they were sheltered from prying eyes, though still not entirely safe. He waited for her to start the conversation.

"When are you leaving?" she asked.

"In three weeks."

"Why Argentina?"

"Why not Argentina?"

She fidgeted. "Are you excited?"

"I don't know. I think so."

"Scared?"

"No," he said, too quickly.

She wondered what he was running away from, whether there was more than the second son's empty pockets and the lure of change. His sister's death. The things he'd seen before that in dark corners of his home. "I would be. Excited, I mean."

"Not scared?"

"Maybe. A little."

They were silent. His shadow so black and whole against the leaves.

She gathered her courage. "Send for me," she said, "if you want a wife."

He made an odd sound, sharp air through teeth. There was so little moon beneath the leaves. She waited. Then he said, "You'd come?"

"I'd come."

He was quiet for a very long time, a card player studying the unexpected hand he'd just been dealt. "We would be gone a very long time."

"Yes."

"Probably forever."

"Yes. I know."

"And there would be a long wait before I could send for you. Months, maybe more."

"I understand."

He seemed to be gazing at her now, though she couldn't be sure in the near dark. "You'd wait for me?"

She was restless; she didn't want to wait; if migration was the only way to push open the confines of her world, then she wanted it to happen now, she wanted to embark right along with Dante, cross the ocean and begin scraping her destiny out of foreign rock. But he was asking something different. About the other village boys. Resisting them would be no sacrifice at all. "Yes. I'll wait."

Dante was silent again. Now that her eyes had adjusted to the dark, she could make out the contours of his face. He was studying her closely. Seeing her in an entirely new way. "Leda," he said and took her hand.

"Dante."

"Are we engaged?"

"Do you want to be?"

"Yes. I do." He didn't sound certain. He sounded as though he were trying to persuade someone sitting just above them in the branches. He said it again, more firmly. "I do. I want a wife, somebody who knew me here at home. I want you to be with me where I'm going."

He stroked her palm with his thumb, gently, waking her skin. He was a good man. He was Cora's brother. This was what Cora would have wanted, wasn't it, for them to launch out into the world together, expanding it through their sheer insistence on life, on youth, risk, escape, if only she were here to see it and perhaps she was, her spirit hovering near them, watching with a happiness that could wash Leda clean of guilt. And wash Dante, too, if he shared her guilt over Cora. She thought he must. She longed to ask. She did not dare. "In that case," she said, "we're engaged."

In the weeks that followed, before his departure, they met every night under the olive tree. By then the engagement had been established, Papà had given his reluctant blessing—though her mother would not speak to her for a week, she acted as though Leda weren't there, as though her daughter had already disappeared into another world so unreachable it might as well not exist—but even so the night meetings were illicit, more than the etiquette of courtship was designed to bear. And yet no one ever stopped them. Perhaps the fact that they were cousins increased the trust that Dante would remain a gentleman; perhaps they were given looser rules as a way to soften the harsh separation that lay ahead. With every night that passed, Dante seemed more steadfast in his resolve, as though he were a scrupulous student assigned the task of falling in love. In that dark leafy chapel, Leda let him kiss her, stroke her body through her clothes, and, after a few more nights, touch her naked breasts for as long as he wished, first standing, then him kneeling before her, and then, in the final week, both of them on the ground. His touch soothed her. It made her feel ripe and strong. The moon stitched a lace of light through the branches that weakened with every passing night. On their last night together, there was no moon, and their bodies plunged through darkness. His hands and mouth were on her breasts, and he hardened against her, as he did each night, he made no attempt to hide it from her anymore and in fact he pressed it against her thigh through their clothes as though it had something to say. Its shape filled her with alarmed curiosity, what did it look like? what did it want? what if somebody walked by and heard his ragged breath? His body seemed to burn with a question she could not answer. He rubbed harder against her thigh, she didn't stop him, she didn't know how to stop him or even whether she wanted to or not, she kept her legs closed and he did not try to open them but his hands grew forceful on her breasts and he was louder now and biting her, what is this, she thought, what is this, my cousin made beast and now his body goes taut, push, silence. His weight rested against her. She held him. She felt starved for something—for what?

A kind of knowledge.

She longed to know how that had felt to him, what it was like inside his skin.

They were quiet for a while, and then he said, "I can't wait for you to join me."

"If you work hard, it won't be long."

"I will. Of course I will."

And he did.

Or so she gathered from his letters, which for a year and nine months brought brief trickles of his life in Argentina that made her long to also hear the rest of it, the raw silent parts, every bit of the great river of things unsaid. She didn't sleep on her wedding night. By the time she and her family arrived home, there was only an hour and a half left before the carriage would arrive to take her and Papà to Naples, where her ship would depart in the evening. The instant they entered the house, Mamma disappeared into her bedroom and closed the door. All night she had barely looked at Leda, and on the walk home she hadn't said a word.

Tommaso and her father had carried her two smallest brothers home in their arms, sleeping soundly, while her seven-year-old sister, Margherita, had stumbled home on her own feet, holding Leda's hand, insisting in a plaintive voice that she wasn't tired, though as soon as Leda tucked the covers to her chin, the child was lost in dreams.

Leda returned to the kitchen, a dim room dominated by a wooden table the family always crammed around to eat. Tommaso and her father stood by the stove, awkwardly, as if awaiting instructions from a long gone fire.

"The boys are asleep?"

"Like stones," said Tommaso.

He looked tired. They hadn't spoken at the party and now it was too late for a last laugh or quarrel, a loss she couldn't bear to measure.

"Tomorrow, then," Papà said.

"Not tomorrow," said Tommaso. "Today."

Papà looked at Leda sadly.

"You make a nice bride," Tommaso said, for once without a trace of irony.

She startled at the compliment. "Not so bad for your big sister?"

He smiled but wouldn't look at her. "No."

And then they dissolved from each other, each to their own room—

Tommaso to the boys' room, Papà to Mamma, Leda to the little room she shared with Margherita—without a word, not even good night, as if the air were too laden with goodbyes already. Leda stood for a moment beside her bed, dreading sleep.

"Leda?" her father's voice at the door.

"Come in."

He entered with the black violin case, the sight of which shocked her, since for the past five years it had languished in a locked trunk that she'd tried and failed to force open with a hairpin just so she could give the instrument a little air, a little light, a drop of oil to smooth its strings as her father had taught her to do when she was a young girl because it wasn't the violin's fault, what had happened to Cora, it was an unfair punishment for an innocent instrument to be locked away, and she would have given it a few moments of relief if she'd only been a more competent thief. He hadn't taught her to steal, her father. Only to polish the curved body and rub resin along the horsehairs, taut in their bow. She loved to do it, loved to imagine it made her part of what happened when her father played, the way the sky itself became an open canvas begging to be painted with his music. He played Scarlatti, Donizetti, folk songs, drinking songs, *tarantelle*, tunes he improvised himself and never put to words. The violin gave voice to what his lips did not. She used to watch, hungry, intensely curious, wishing he would teach her instead of Tommaso, whose lessons were an exercise in frustration, as Tommaso had no desire to learn. And yet Papà insisted on teaching him, on trying to make him the next musician in the family. It was not that women had never played; Leda knew, because she'd found a history of music on her father's bookshelf, that noble ladies had played the violin for centuries, in Naples, in Rome. But she was neither noble nor a Roman lady, and, in their village, women's hands were needed for cooking and sewing and cleaning. When men played at parties, women served the coffee and washed pots. When men practiced, women darned their shirts. It was a waste of time to teach a girl a skill she wouldn't be able to use or, worse, would indulge in instead of doing her chores—as Leda had done. In those years before they lost Cora, before her father locked the violin away in grief and guilt (above all, guilt, she thought, was what made him stop playing, blood on his hands, they all felt Cora's blood on their hands, or so it seemed to Leda: her whole family changed when Cora died, grew more bitter and fragile and shut, and her father above all seemed to crumple beneath the weight of it, he should have done something, he was a man after all, or wasn't he?, he'd loved his niece Cora and how could he have left her to—or at least that's what Leda thought her father felt, she couldn't be sure, these things all went unspoken), before all that, she'd studied her brother's lessons with ferocity, hovering in the doorway of the living room or sitting in the corner pretending to be immersed in her sewing as she memorized every word of her father's instruction. Then, later, she'd steal the violin outside and practice every detail he'd described, studying the strings and notes, adjusting her posture in the way he'd told Tommaso to do, repeating the melodies of *tarantelle* over and over until they flowed from her hands, hot with secrecy, alone among the stern olive trees.

"A wedding gift," her father said, quietly, so as not to wake her little sister. "Give it to Dante."

She stared at him.

"Let it bring you both a little beauty."

The King of Naples, writhing in his four-hundred-year-old grave. She should say no. It seemed a sacrilege for the instrument to leave Italy. But was it any less of a sacrilege for it to stay here, silent?

Her father pushed the violin toward her and her hands gripped the case before her mind could decide. Still she couldn't speak. They stood awkwardly for a moment, the air thick between them, and then he was gone.

She could not bring herself to open the case and look at the violin. Not yet. She put it in the trunk, sat down on her bed, and tried not to think, tried to rein in the unbroken horses of her thoughts. Here she was: a bride on her wedding night. With no groom to do the things that were supposed to be done. She closed her eyes. It was as dark behind her eyelids as it was inside the room. She let her mind loosen its moorings and float out into the great night world, where it soared, strangely, to Mount Vesuvius, visible from the hills beyond her village, presiding over the earth like a green-mantled king. When she was a girl and had a rare slice of time all to herself with no peas to shell or water to carry or hens to pluck, she would scale the hills just to stare out at the landscape, at the volcano, searching for some hint of the deadly fire inside it, the red-hot ferocity that had destroyed the ancient city of Pompeii. It was her grandfather who had told her the story of Pompeii. Her nonno, her mother's father, had rarely missed the chance to tell a good tale, and liked none better than the one of that great city which some years ago (that was how he put it, *some years ago,* as though the story had been handed down only a generation or two) had been buried by the volcano's eruption. Thousands died, he said. It was terrible, so sudden. Women caught naked in their baths never again put on a robe. Children fighting over a wooden doll never had the chance to make amends. Husbands on their way home lost the chance to kiss their wives ever again. All of them were buried in mid-stride, mid-scuffle, mid-lather of their lovely thighs. Can you imagine? All that life and heat and dreaming packed inside them and then—*whoosh!*—they were nothing. They were dead. It can happen that quickly, *cara Leda.* That's the thing about life. We think we are so strong, we think we are so real, but there are things that are much more real than us, and stronger, and we forget about them until it's too late and they're burying us in ash. Her grandfather's tales of old Pompeii stretched on and on, sometimes for hours, until that paralyzed and buried city became more alive in Leda's mind than her own village. He would tell his stories on the shaded patio just beyond their kitchen door, on long summer evenings, as dusk gathered gently around them and as she shelled hazelnuts or peas. As Leda's hands moved from bowl to bowl, she would see legions of ghosts, with penetrating clarity.

Charioteers raising whips over glistening horses. Children squabbling over that ill-fated toy, one of them, a bully, grasping it with both hands, while three others reached for it with arms that would never arrive. And women in their baths. Nonno always managed to include these women in their baths. In old Pompeii, he explained, there were maidservants to pour water over ladies, to wash their bodies, their backs, their breasts. They would be relishing the cool water against their summer-hot bodies, naked in marble tubs, dreaming, if they were maidens, of their wedding nights, of what would happen on those future occasions after all of the festivities were done. He told it that way, with the part about the wedding nights, only when he'd drunk more wine than usual. But Leda could never shake the image of these young women, naked in the water, soaping their bodies, dreaming of a first bout of lovemaking that was never to arrive. She would think of them as she sat by the river, or lay alone in bed—and she thought of them now, on her wedding night: her body flushed strangely as she pictured an ancient bathtub right in front of her, a naked maiden arching her back with her eyes closed, raising her breasts toward the ceiling, shivering at the touch of imaginary hands, oblivious to her fast-approaching death.

When she finally opened her eyes, light crept in through the window, fresh and tentative. Her travel dress still lay neatly on the trunk. Margherita stirred gently in her sleep. Outside, a sparrow launched a lover's quarrel with the dawn, and, from the kitchen, she heard the sounds of her mother making coffee. She changed clothes, clasped her hair into a bun, and went to help Mamma, who did not greet her and did not look up. She smelled tart, like smoldering wood and restless sleep. Leda wanted to memorize the smell, to stash it in her mind along with the exact shape of her mother's body in the kitchen, the space it had occupied for so many years that without her the room would surely implode. Just as the coffee began to percolate on the stove, Mamma turned to her and said, "I can't." Leda waited for her to go on, but Mamma only stared at her with liquid and terrifying eyes, those same eyes that had summoned instant obedience from her when she was a child, could make her feel as though the most hidden parts of her were suddenly laid bare. Until this moment, it had not occurred to Leda that Mamma might be anguished on this day. She was always so tired, harsh with her oldest, the daughter, Leda, who could never do enough or be a good enough girl or ease the edge of bitterness in Mamma, the suffering of the two failed pregnancies and the stillborn that came after Tommaso and wore out her body and probably, Leda now thought, wore her heart out as well, so that she was spent by the time the little ones came, and didn't seem to care about Leda, didn't notice her except to criticize or make sure the chores were done. Or so Leda had thought before this look, this moment. She knew nothing about her mother's heart; she'd assumed it to be closed, exhausted by life, indifferent to her. Only now, moments before leaving, did she grasp that she might have been wrong.

"Mamma," she said. She stood, knife in hand, arrested over a loaf of bread.

"I can't," Mamma said again. "You pour the coffee." And then she walked out of the front door and up the path away from the street, toward the river.

Tommaso and Papà rose and drank coffee and ate toast and Mamma did not come back. Tommaso chattered about the party last night, who had drunk too much, laughing at his own quips. He seemed nervous; he tended to chatter more when he was nervous, a trait that had always grated on Leda, though now it simply made her see the boy in him. The delicate boy who sang to the chickens and cried for hours when first forced to slaughter them. He'd groomed his hair carefully this morning, the way he did for special occasions, dipping the comb in grape-seed oil and forming a perfect part. She tried not to think about never seeing him again. She tried not to think of her mother at the river, and was still pushing the image from her mind when the carriage arrived.

And then they were all outside: Leda, her father, Tommaso, and the children, who'd been shaken out of their beds and gathered in a blurred, obedient mass to say goodbye, still wearing their crumpled party clothes from the night before. Together, the coachman and her father lifted the trunk up into the carriage. She kissed each of the boys, who understood nothing, and then Margherita, who clung to her neck as though it were the mast of a sinking ship. Tommaso kissed her and for once had nothing to say. Her father reached out his hand to help her up into the carriage. Still no sign of Mamma. How could she leave without kissing her mother goodbye? But she had no choice, Mamma had run away by her own will and if she went to look for her in the woods she might not find her in a whole day's searching, might still be scaling hills riddled with undergrowth when the ship pulled out of Naples this evening. She had to leave. All the goodbye kissing was done, and Leda had her hand on the door of the carriage, already halfway in. Her father took her gently by the arm and helped her up, then entered and sat beside her. She looked down at Tommaso and the children through the window of the raised cabin. They looked very small.

"*Ciao, Leda!*" the boys called. "*Ciao,* good luck in América!"

Their tone was light, jubilant. As though América were a village just past Naples.

They waved at her as the coachman stirred the horses into motion. She waved back until they were out of sight.

Her father held her hand. She closed her eyes and pretended to sleep. The hard clop of horses' feet against cobblestones gave way to the soft thud of packed earth, which told her that they were out of the village now, no longer in Alazzano but on the dirt roads that led up toward Trinità and through it, until they widened into the long straight road northwest toward Naples. And Naples was closer with each hoofbeat. She wanted to watch the road change, but if she opened her eyes Papà would know she was awake and might try to talk to her. She couldn't stand the thought of what he might say. So she kept her eyes closed and followed the contours of the land in her mind. The slopes and curves. The infinite shades of green. The rumble of the carriage lulling her into a voluptuous cloud that held her suspended in its folds but she was not asleep, she was not dreaming, it was really true that she was now inside a carriage with her father as they rode a long band of golden dust through stark air toward a great void.

She woke to the din of voices. She was leaning against her father and had left a trail of spit on his coat sleeve. He had not noticed; he was staring out the window at a crowded street. Naples. Her first time there. Every building was taller than she'd imagined possible. Here was a church whose façade seemed carved straight out of the imagination of crazed angels: tall arches, cherubs wailing at beheaded saints, balconies lined with decadent pillars. Here was a fountain filled with nymphs, their thin robes clinging to their breasts as they lilted toward the water, captured in stone, arrested in motion. And everywhere, people; the scent of horseshit and sweat and rotting melon rinds; men in hats and women with baskets and vendors with laden carts, all crowding the sidewalk with such force that she couldn't understand how they wove past each other, how they knew where they were going, how they found space between the bodies of others to move their own. Would she ever learn to walk like that? A man was hawking fish, he had the best catches from the morning, his fish, his fish, you should buy it now, if your husband died with this fish in his belly he'd die happy. Milk, milk, another man had milk, and if you had it any fresher you'd be sucking from the teat. The people on the street walked without slowing down, their eyes focused far ahead as though they could see the future and were striding right toward it.

The carriage paused at an intersection. At the corner stood a woman in a dress of that bright red color women were never allowed to wear, or so Leda had believed for as long as she could remember. Could this color possibly be considered decent in Naples? But it was not only the color. The cut of the dress dipped dangerously and bared the woman's pale, freckled shoulders. If flesh itself could laugh. A terrible sight. Leda could not wrench her eyes away. The woman was standing still, and, when a man slowed to look at her, she smiled and let him look. Leda was looking, too, although the woman could not see her, and for an instant she pictured opening the carriage door and stepping out without a goodbye to her father, without retrieving her belongings, out toward the red woman and into the great river of Napoletanos, an insane act since it could only lead to the gutter and even worse things that awaited young women who abandoned their trunks and patient faraway grooms to dive alone into the large and dangerous arms of a city. What a shocking thought, where had it come from? *Behave yourself,* her own mind said in her mother's voice; and then, right after it, Cora's voice, *Go on, go on, what's a little water in your skirts*—and then she could not think anymore, she was in the river with Cora and Cora was screaming, dying, she was going to drown right along with her but she had to live, she had to live, she would not go in, she would not dive out of this carriage into the river of Napoletanos or get close to the red woman; the man on the street who'd looked at the woman had now walked off and the woman was alone again, her dress a bloody stain on the crowd, and the carriage drove on with Leda still inside it, still a good wife, a sane girl, a lady. The red woman disappeared, and Leda expunged the hazards and sharp edges from her mind.

"We're almost there," her father said.

They spent two hours at the port, waiting for the steamship, watching the throng of people grow around them, more people than Leda had ever seen gathered in one place, several villages' worth of people crushed onto the platform. How could so much of Italy leave its own land for the Américas? Who would be left? Of course, some of the people in the port, like her father, were not leaving but were here to bid their loved ones a last goodbye: there was the close-clasping mother, the last-chance-to-give-instructions father, the relatives clustered like human fortresses about to crumble, the men smoking and all talking at once, the women weeping lavish tears, the milling, the cold, the patting of backs again and again, the undercurrents of dread and longing for the parting moment when the goodbyes would finally be done. Her father must feel that way too. Their conversation had petered out. He must be tired. He was standing because the few benches on the platform were occupied by elders, and he'd insisted on letting her sit on her trunk. She unwrapped the brown paper packets of bread, cheese, and olives she'd packed that morning.

"Come, Papà, sit down with me to eat."

"I am fine standing."

"No—there's room for both of us here."

"You sit, Leda."

She stood up. "I won't sit unless you sit with me."

He did not look her in the eye. "You've always been stubborn."

They sat beside each other on the trunk, eating slowly, looking out at the boats and ships, the city hugging the shoreline and, after the buildings gave way, Vesuvius. From this vantage point the mountain seemed to keep watch over the city, a kind of guardian, or warden, or both.

The cold penetrated her dress. She pulled the shawl close around her.

The steamship began to approach along the water, large and strong and armored with hard gray metal. Somehow the sight of the ship made distance seem more visceral, more daunting.

Papà was also staring at the ship.

"It's bigger than I thought it would be," she said.

"Bigger than they look in the posters."

"Big enough to get lost in."

"You won't get lost," he said and took her hand, his eyes still on the steamship.

His touch surprised her, and for a moment she wanted nothing more than to stay here, on this shore with her father. For years now she had been furious at him, for his defeat, the sad hunched shoulders; but today the slouch of him merely inspired a desperate tenderness. His body was the only barrier between her and the cold wind that swept in across the water. His hand was callused and worn but the tips of his fingers had grown soft again and lacked the little tough spots they had had when he still played the violin, the skin hardened by a thousand notes of music. The ship arrived at the dock, sounding a long and hollow moan. The crowd around them prickled with excitement. A porter came to take her trunk. She and Papà both stood, bereft of their seat.

"Leda, *carissima*," Papà said.

She turned and quickly wished she hadn't. He was crying. He made no sound and no attempt to wipe the wetness from his face. She looked away.

"I should board," she said.

He nodded, put his arm through hers, and walked her to the gang-plank. They pressed toward it, people all around them, and her father held tightly to her arm so as not to lose her in the crowd. Then, before she knew it, she was at the plank and the moment she'd been running from was here, her father's last touch, she was going to simply break away but then his arms enveloped her so tightly it was hard to breathe.

"Remember us," he said into her ear as the crowd pressed her up the walkway.

She stepped up the gangplank toward the deck and, she thought, toward América, toward Dante, her cousin, her groom, and now that her steps were not on solid earth but on a long board suspended diago-nally in the air, she felt that she had finally become an emigrant. An in-between, she thought as her feet reached the deck. A wife, but uncon-summated, and on neither Italian nor South American land. I am what is not possible—which makes everything possible, like a leak in the dam of time. The thought both confused and thrilled her. She no longer knew what her own mind was saying.

The crowd pressed toward the rail to wave their kerchiefs in goodbye to their loved ones on land.

"Alfredo, do you see me? Alfredo!"

"Goodbye, goodbye!"

"Mamma, Mamma—don't forget me—"

Leda joined the crowd and craned her neck, but by the time she reached the front she could not find Papà among the people left on land. Perhaps he'd decided to leave without saying goodbye, or else the multitude had made him small, he was just a second son from Alazzano after all—and in that moment she hated them, all of them, every single one of the Italians waving at the dock, for shrinking her father. She waved her kerchief at the volcano. Voices rose and crashed around her, interweaving their cries of *God keep us safe* and *Pater noster* and *Amalia, ciao, Amalia!* and *my God the water so much water* and *Ciao! Ciao, Italia!* until one man began a well-known *tarantella* that spread across the crowd and soon it seemed all three hundred and something Italians were singing it in unison, and Leda sang along, too, having known the song since childhood, a Neapolitan song about love that has no hope and no end.

The coast receded at a startling pace. Water unfolded long and blue all around the ship like an infinite quilt made by the Fates, or at least two of them, the spinner and the weaver, with no third sister to cut and stop the thread. How vast the ocean. Could the world really hold it? Would the world itself explode? But the great liquid cloth kept unfolding.

She slept terribly that night, unaccustomed to the motion of the ship and wrenched out of her dozes by her bunkmate Fausta's vomiting, and her own. Nothing had prepared her for the effect of the night sea on the body, the whorl of her insides when she lay down. Fausta, a matronly and grave-faced woman about ten years her senior, vomited first, flooding the floor. Before she could rise to clean it up, Leda did it for her, using the sheets from her own bed to dispatch the mess. She bundled the dirty sheets in the hall outside their door. The pile joined other crumpled heaps of linens scattered along the hall. The stench was overpowering. She returned to the room.

"I'm sorry," Fausta said from her bare mattress.

Fifteen minutes later, Leda vomited into her chamber pot. The smell filled the tight space, there was no escaping.

"You all right?" said Fausta.

"I will be."

"I can't take twenty nights of this."

"You won't. It'll get easier, you'll see."

"How do you know it'll get easier?"

"Because it has to."

It was an unfounded assertion, invented on the spot, yet it seemed to comfort Fausta. Her eyes closed and the muscles of her face relaxed. She had the square, strong-jawed face of a woman born to grow old early, Leda thought. That evening, when they'd first met, she had told Leda about her husband, who had been in Buenos Aires for ten years now; he had left Italy after they'd been married for one year in which they'd hoped but failed to have a baby, and when he'd left to *make América,* as they say, to make his fortune, he'd promised to return very soon, after a year, two at most, with money and a new foundation for the family they'd raise. But he didn't return. The years dragged on. Finally Bruno wrote a letter saying that it would be better for her to come and join him in Buenos Aires. She balked, at first. She wrote back, *I don't want to go, I can't imagine, can't you please come home?* He wrote back, simply, *No.* It was the shortest letter she received from him in all their years of separation, devoid of explanations or even the usual expressions of love. And now, here she was, already twenty-eight years old and childless, crossing the ocean to meet him in a strange new land. And are you glad to be going? Leda had asked her. Of course I am, Fausta had said, that is to say, I want to stay in Italy, but what I want more is to be with my husband, and to start my family before it's too late.

She had seemed so sure of herself, as she said it. She had spoken in the tone of a nun who didn't question her faith in God.

Now, Fausta had fallen back asleep. Leda shifted her body on her stripped bed and thought about water and land and the impossibility of human crossings. We are not made for a journey like this one, she thought. These modern ships go against what we are. She wondered how it had been for Dante, during his crossing, whether he had slept the first night, whether he'd needed bowls. She would have to ask him when she arrived. She had so very many things to ask him.

When Leda finally drifted off to sleep, she dreamed of Vesuvius. She was climbing the side of the mountain. Her feet were bare, and they bled as she walked, but she did not slow down. *I will arrive.* The walk seemed endless and her belly churned with nausea. Suddenly she was at the highest point, right at the lip of the crater. She bent down toward the blackness. It was vast and seemed to have no end. She stared down, petrified. Something flickered in the depths, a pale spark, two sparks, three: the lights of lamps at windows; and then it came into view, Alazzano itself, her village trapped in the crater, and she too high to reach it or get burned by its fires.

Now, on her arrival day, she stood at the rail and watched Buenos Aires grow larger. The waters of the port teemed with ships, and the docks teemed with people. Argentinos. People who inhabited this city's streets, slept in its beds, listened to its everyday secrets. And somewhere on that dock, Dante. How would he look? How would it be between them? She checked her hat again with her hand. The pins were solid, the pearls still in place. It gave her strength to face this moment, to have such a delicate thing on her head, though she also feared that she would not be able to live up to the womanhood it demanded of her. So far she had succeeded, at least, in transporting it intact across the ocean. This had been her mother's charge: *don't let anything happen to your hat.* It had been her mother's hat, the best one she owned, even before she'd sewn on a strand of real pearls, so that, Mamma said, no matter how exhausted or worn Leda looked after the journey, she would have one thing befitting the dignity of the moment, because you have to look your very best when you arrive in Buenos Aires, you don't want him to think you've fallen, even if you're tired. Not to mention, Mamma added as she stitched, that you'll be a bride without a gown. Leda thought about this now as she leaned against the rail: a bride without a gown. Those words made it sound as though she were arriving naked, stepping off the boat with her elegant blue hat and nothing else, vulnerable, shamed. The image stung her. Perhaps Mamma had meant for it to sting.

The ship made contact with the port. *Clank.* The yoke of land. Leda felt a rush of excitement around her. Three hundred and sixty-eight Italians pressed their way toward the gangplank to taste their first encounter with Argentina. A small cluster of men walked up the gangplank and boarded the ship, uniforms starched, buttons gleaming. Three of them wore stethoscopes.

"Form two lines, please, and have your documents ready."

The crowd obeyed. Leda joined a line, trying to edge toward the front, but the men's bodies pushed her out of the way. Her heart beat loudly in her chest. Her skin was lined with sweat from the humid air. The line snaked back and forth along the deck, and from where she stood it was impossible to see the docks below the ship. She took out her handkerchief and wiped her face; she had to look fresh and healthy for the officials, so they could have no reason to deny her entry. Of course, from everything she'd heard, there was no reason to worry. Argentina was promoting immigration. They wanted workers. They did not take the old, sick, or unsound of mind. She was young and healthy, though she'd lost weight from motion sickness and her frame had become even skinnier than before. Her bones jutted. She wiped her face again. She hoped there would be no problems. As for soundness of mind, she sometimes doubted that she had it, as she had always been strange, off-kilter to the rhythms of those around her, but surely that was not a reason to be denied the Américas. She was very good at hiding her strangeness. The line inched forward. She would be standing here a long time. She was hungry and hot. Dante must be close now, just down the gangplank on the dock, waiting for her. She wondered what was going through his mind. What he would think when he first saw her. Would he see how thin she was? Would he want her less than before? She squared her shoulders and stood tall. Dante, she thought, it's too late to return me. We are going to start our family, our home, our children—she had not thought much about the children, though she knew they were part of it, inevitably, a few hazy forms around the dinner table, though not too many, not a large brood please, she had seen too many women, including her mother, buried in their own progeny—and it shall be good. We will lose the old nightmares and launch new dreams.

There was Fausta, in the line snaking in the opposite direction, ahead of her. She wore a gray, loose-cut dress, and her stout body slouched forward slightly. Leda waved and smiled, and Fausta nodded back, but tightly, sternly, as though this were a dangerous time for pleasantries. Her face was closed, formal, nothing like the openness of that one night halfway through the trip when they lay and talked for hours, in the dark, because neither of them could sleep, sharing hopes for the next chapter of their lives—their hopes more than their fears: Fausta's hope that she would be able to find the thyme, coriander, basil, and oregano she needed to cook properly, Leda's hope that her new house would have a window overlooking a tree by which she could sit and sew (or read, she thought, but all she said was *sew*), her hope that Dante would not have changed too much.

And if he has? Fausta said.

Then—I don't know.

He's still your husband, Fausta said firmly. You owe him your respect.

No matter what?

No matter what.

Leda stirred in the darkness, adjusting her body in a vain attempt to get comfortable on the lumpy bed. Are you worried about whether Bruno has changed?

No.

Leda wondered at the confidence in Fausta's voice. Ten years is a long time, she said.

You were seven years old ten years ago.

Yes.

So what can you possibly understand?

Leda shrank from the thorn in those words. You must love him very much, she said more softly.

Of course I do.

Fausta said this with a vehemence that bordered on a warning. Leda thought it best to change the subject. Tell me more about how you'll use the basil, she said.

The New World basil will be sweet and tart and plentiful, I will grow it on the windowsill the way we did at home, it will brighten my sauces and sing in my salads and if we're ever sad I'll pass a sprig under our noses, we'll be cured. Listen, Leda, there are bound to be demons in this city: if they ever arrive at your house, use basil. Eat it. Smell it. Cover bad things with it. Dip a sprig in water and sprinkle it into every corner, and sing a song, any song, the happier the better, so the evil eye will go away. Will you remember?

I will.

Now, as they stood in the blazing sun waiting for their test, Leda envied Fausta the strength of her conviction, her unwavering love, her trust that even if her husband had changed, her own formidable devotion would dissolve the intervening years like salt in a cup of water. Perhaps marriage could contain such magic.

Though even dissolved salt, for all that it vanished from sight, still left traces that stabbed the tongue.

There she goes, thought Fausta, that girl like a steel rod hiding in the skin of a rabbit, who jumps at the slightest knock on the door and yet can vomit all night and rise up the next day with vigor, and not only that, but also help a stranger through her sickness the way she did for me on the very first night, she cleaned up the mess on the floor as though it were nothing, as though it were her own. It was kind of her. A kind girl. A strange girl. Look at her, standing there with that expression of amazement on her face, as though she doesn't know how she got here to the deck of this ship, or perhaps how she arrived to live inside her own skin, a question to which no one knows the answer except perhaps the priests, and even if they do, who's to say it's right?

Blasphemy. I didn't think that!

The girl. She's so young. How will she fare here? And me, me, what will happen to me? Ten years, the girl said to me the night that I came dangerously close to spilling out the secret, as we lay near each other in the dark, ten years is a long time. And what I wanted to say back to her, but didn't say, was this: ten years in the course of a young woman's life is everything—absolutely everything—her one chance at passion and fertility and grasping at some fistful of the happiness in the world and if you misuse those years they'll either wither like a putrefying rose or explode and tilt you into horror. I should know. The line on the deck moved forward several paces. There must have been a group of easy approvals or denials, waved on through. Leda's line advanced in the opposite direction, and now she was out of sight. Fausta crossed herself. She had no reason to think that she wouldn't be admitted into Argentina, but still, every muscle in her body was tense. If they didn't let her in she wouldn't know whether to panic or applaud.

Oh, but it was too hot, how the sun bore down. And not just down, but how the heat hung around them, thick and inescapable. Even with all her wiping of face and neck, she would be sweaty when she first saw Bruno. He would be sweaty as well, no doubt; at home, on days this hot, he'd soak through the handkerchiefs she folded neatly into his pockets. She washed them every summer night and had three ready for him every morning. She'd made the handkerchiefs herself out of torn shirts, there was no buying such luxuries, but she was a good wife, back then, she embroidered the edges into elegance. How would Bruno look today? How had he changed? His letters had grown cold. Terse. Businesslike. She had heard tales, legends really, of emigrants whose very souls were chilled by life in the New World. In Salerno, she'd had a neighbor whose uncle had returned after thirty years in the mines of Florida. Everybody had always called him Vampata—Blaze—because, when he left as a young man, he'd had so much energy he seemed constantly on the brink of bursting into flames. But when Vampata came home, he was dull as ash, a trudging shell of a man. He never smiled or said a word, only nodded or shook his head in response to questions. He worked in his nephew's forge all day and kept to himself the rest of the time. The word *vampata*, in her neighborhood, acquired a new meaning. It came to be used for anything that had the life drained out of it. Don't marry that boy, his mother will make you a *vampata* with her harangues. Come on, smile, what's wrong with you, *vampata?* This country is a *vampata* now, that's why the young men all want to leave; who wants to start their life out in a wasteland?

The line shuffled forward again. Closer and closer. Bruno, she thought, if your fire has died I will not accept it. I'd have to kill you, and slowly, with a dull fork. You're the only thing I have here in this place and if you don't give me a baby before it's too late I will never forgive you for the lost years. That girl I shared a room with, she thinks that I can't wait to see you, I've played the role of dutiful wife and convinced everyone of my performance, nobody sees my fury. You were supposed to come home more prosperous than before. You were supposed to give me a life, motherhood, a future that could be endured. I waited for you for one year, then two. Obediently. Only at three years did I grow hopeless, and, Bruno, you must know, from your years in América, what it is to be alone, the toll on the body and its hungers, perhaps worse for men because their hungers are so strong but it cannot be that women do not have them. Look at me. Am I the only woman who has known savage lust? Am I a malformed woman? This is what I've asked myself on a thousand and one nights, how God could misshape me the way He did, how He could put so much terrible desire in a woman's body and then send her husband across the ocean and leave her in his parents' house, to wait, untouched, alone. How can you blame me for what happened? For the afternoons in the back of the grocer's shop, on his sacks of beans and wheat? But of course you would. And that is why I've prayed and prayed that when I see you I'll succeed in hiding the truth so that you, my husband, a stranger to me now, won't detect betrayal in my face. I didn't do it to betray you, Bruno, but to be faithful to myself, to my wretched self, which was threatening to die without some touch, and the grocer, your uncle, he gave me that touch, his hands on my naked waist were the hands of a conjurer, he brought me back to life, I came to crave him as I crave the air. Everybody thought that it was good when I took the job there, helping him with his stores, let her contribute a little to her keep, they said, and anyway it'll do her good to get out of the house. And they were right.

But then the two. The horror of the two.

She was almost at the front of the line. They were waving people through even faster now, she could see the Argentinean doctor looking in the mouth and ears of each man, putting his stethoscope to each heart to listen for what it carried from one continent to another, then removing it quickly, satisfied that, after three seconds, he'd heard enough. She prayed for a safe passage and for Bruno to make love to her that night and for God to hear the clamor of their bodies and in His infinite mercy send them a child. A son or daughter would redeem her life and give her proof of God's forgiveness. If a child didn't come it would be proof of His rage. Because her body knew how to conceive: this she knew without a doubt. One. Two. A shout of light inside her and the blood not flowing. The sachet of herbs from the cobbler's wife was so bitter, so small. The tea from it stung her throat night after night—she brewed it when all her in-laws had gone to sleep—and then blood roared from her and the grocer was angry that she wouldn't come to the back of his store for three weeks and wouldn't tell him why. He thought she didn't want him anymore. Am I too old for you? he said. He was not too old, his touch was ageless in its wanting, his sex always firm with joy and ready for her as it was not, he said, for his wife anymore. He had four children and he was her husband's uncle; of course he would not want to know about the teas, the bleeding, and the deep-in-the-night tears for an innocent soul who could not could not come to earth because its destiny would be shattered from the start. And so she told him nothing, even when she returned to him and to their afternoons of pleasure so intense they made her glimpse the golden edges of the underworld. They always made love in perfect silence, attuned to the slightest noise from the shop. Silence gave their movements more ferocity. One afternoon they accidentally broke open the sack of flour that was beneath them, and because the grocer didn't realize it he kept on thrusting and she sank and sank and sank into the whiteness. The second time Fausta went to the cobbler's wife, a year after the first, the old woman looked at her with mournful disgust and said, Fausta, I do not give this cure to the same person twice.

Please, said Fausta, you have to help me.

You can die from this, you know.

Please, please.

You can't go on this way.

I won't.

Promise me.

I promise, Fausta said without thinking.

You know that I am not a gossip, said the cobbler's wife. I'm the only woman in this whole city who can hold a secret. But if you break this promise and go back to that man, then I will tell two women, and by night all of Salerno will know.

At that moment something inside of Fausta died. She was trapped. She had nowhere to run. If she did not make the promise she would give birth to a disgrace that would swallow her whole, as well as her husband, both of their families, and a new baby doomed to live forever in the shadow of its mother's crime.

There was more blood this time, and far more pain. She did not die. But it was the end of her life. She lay in bed for four days, despite her mother-in-law's diatribe: you lazy girl, how sick can you really be, what about us? What about your job?

I want to leave my job.

You what?

I want to leave the grocery store.

But why on earth?

I . . .

Did you fight with my brother?

. . . yes.

Fausta, you can't stop working. With all the food we put on the table for you? My brother can be harsh, but I will talk to him.

Her mother-in-law went to the grocery store that very day and everything was arranged. When Fausta returned to work, the grocer did not look at her. They spoke only of the essentials and never of what was already becoming a figment of the past. Soon he was unlovered by time, reduced to being her boss, her uncle by marriage, how had she ever desired that graying man?

That is when she began to age. Her body became matronly, thick waist, heavy hips. Her passion closed in on itself until it vanished altogether. She lived that way, a goodwife, half-dead, for three more years, hoping for nothing except the tenuous dream of Bruno's return. But then the letter came telling her to come to the New World, and now she was here at the gate of the Américas, a dozen paces from the gatekeepers. The doctor would not hear the hidden cemeteries of her heart. He would not see, on examining her teeth, the unsaid words haunting her mouth. How many secrets were being smuggled, on this day, into the New World? She looked out at the dock, with its wooden awning under which she could hear the roil of a gathered crowd (Bruno surely among them). The awning had no label, but it seemed to her that it should wear a gargantuan sign emblazoned with the words LAST HOPE, because that was what this place was to so many of the people on this ship, you could see it on their faces full of hunger, and why else would they have come?

She was next in line. The man in front of her stepped forward and opened his mouth for the doctor. Fausta tried to imagine her own future, as a trick to calm her nerves. She would have—how many children? Was there still time for three? Boys, all boys, and they'd distract her from the sorrows of daily life, they'd redeem the ones who had to die. She was getting nervous now; these thoughts weren't helping. She shifted her tactic to picturing the future of that girl Leda. She was lucky, that girl, she had it all ahead of her; a pristine canvas; as young as Fausta had been when she married. She could see Leda's vibrant future stretching out before her. Four children, maybe five. A long marriage that might have its torrential fights but ultimately would become solid and happy, a bulwark against the world. Joy in her role as a mother; and, one day, many years from now, that Leda girl—no longer a girl—would take her whole big family back to Italy, where she would watch her great-grandchildren play in the orchards of her youth.

As she stepped forward and opened her mouth for the physician, Fausta held these predictions in her mind like talismans.

Leda had no trouble with the doctor's exam. It was perfunctory, and went by with surprising speed. The examination of her papers was equally smooth. The men were quick and businesslike, there were so many people to admit to their nation, all in a day's work.

She stepped onto the gangplank. Below her lay the dock, a long platform packed with people whose faces tilted eagerly upward to receive their wives or cousins or nephews or neighbors from Italia, their voices raised in wails of joy and chanted names—*Francesco! Emilia! Alessandro! Vito!*—as though the calling were a kind of invocation, as though their loved ones could appear here from Italia on the power of the crowd's voices alone. The migrants on the gangplank surged with a current of excitement, and she was not Leda, in that moment, but a single drop in a river pouring from ship to dock with a force of its own, longing to merge with a new soil, unified in its direction, down, down, down. She searched the crowd with her eyes. A swarm of faces looking up at her, then quickly past her, at the rest of the immigrants slowly pouring down the gangplank, she was not their arrival—*Paolo! You've arrived! Paoooolooo*—though the faces were Italian, as were the words they called out—*Blessings of all the saints! A joy a joy*—she listened keenly for Dante's voice, but could not hear it.

Her foot touched land. It was a concrete slab, not yet the feel of Argentina's earth, but it thrilled her. Three men from behind her excused themselves as they walked past, directly to the warehouse that held their baggage, there was no one waiting for them and they would make their own way. They would take their baggage to the Hotel de Inmigrantes, a place that Argentina had designed especially for immigrants who arrived with nowhere to stay, where they would receive room and board for five days while they began to look for work—a help, surely, but still she pitied them, so alone, so far from home.

To her left, two brothers found each other. They wept and laughed and slapped each other's backs.

Just beyond them a man was greeting his wife with a long and tight embrace, they were swaying and murmuring to each other, no longer at the port of Buenos Aires but in a private universe all their own.

Dante, where was Dante. She looked and looked but could not find him. She wove through the crowd in search of him, pushing past the many bodies. It was too loud, there were too many voices shouting their excitement, her fellow emigrants were scattering and no longer part of a merged river, she was alone. She began to feel afraid. Was it possible that he was late, or had forgotten the day she was coming? Or that he was playing a trick as he sometimes liked to do, when they were children, crouching behind a rock when Cora went to call him in for dinner, making her climb the hill in search of him when all the while he was just at the edge of the garden?

She stood against a wall, from which she could watch the remaining immigrants disembark. The crowd dissipated. Her husband was not there.

She had no idea what to do. She would do nothing. She would wait for Dante to come.

Soon only a small cluster remained on the dock. A stranger had been watching her, a young man whose clothes were worn but clean. His glances made her nervous. She stood up straight and tried to look dignified, pure, a married woman with somewhere to go. The excitement of arrival had disappeared, replaced with a kind of horror at the sheer size of Argentina, its vast unknown expanse, and she here at the lip of it, alone, female, easy prey.

The stranger approached her, hat politely pressed against his chest.

"Signora di Mazzoni?"

She turned to him, blankly. She had never been called a *signora* before, and for a strange instant she thought he was confusing her with her mother. "Yes."

"I'm here to receive you. I'm a friend of your cous——your husband, Dante."

"Yes? Where is he?"

"I am truly sorry, *signora*. Dante is dead."

A Corner of the Possible

The stranger's name was Arturo. He said he would take her home.

At first, he tried to explain everything, to tell her the story of what happened to Dante, but his words came out jumbled and Leda could not make sense of them, something about a mistake, a hero, the Buenos Aires port—nothing made sense, the very dock she stood on had become the outer edge of chaos, the air around her rioted, broken, too bright. All she could say was, I'm sorry, I don't understand you, I don't understand. And so he gave up and suggested that they get her trunk and go home. She followed him to the warehouse where the baggage was held, not a woman walking, but a ghost of herself, a shadow.

Her trunk was not difficult to find, as they were the last to arrive. The customs official who inspected it had a bulbous nose and a quick smile. When he found the olive jar from the baker's wife, he grinned. He said something in Spanish, shaking his head, then opened the jar and put an olive in his mouth. Leda did not understand him, though the bones of his words were familiar. Listening to Spanish was like listening to someone speak her native tongue through murky water.

"He says you can't bring them into the country," Arturo said.

She should not have cared, it shouldn't have mattered, but in that moment Leda felt as though the man were taking her last scrap of Alazzano, of her old life; and this so he could have it for himself, this man who didn't even speak Italian and could not possibly care about the distant valleys of Campania or about lost cousins, first one, now all of a sudden two. It was not that she wanted to eat the olives herself—in that moment she couldn't imagine eating ever again—but she wanted to keep them close, intact. She felt as though the customs official were eating a green piece of Dante's body. But she could not speak or move. She stood watching as the man put another olive in his mouth. His face lit with satisfaction as he ate it. He said something to Arturo. Arturo spoke back, and, though Leda couldn't understand everything, she could understand various words, inflected as they were with Italian sounds: *husband* and *died* and *come from Italia,* then something else, then *only.*

The official studied Leda with new interest.

Arturo said something else, with the word *exception* and the last syllables inflected politely upward, in the tilt of a question. Asking the man to let her keep the olive jar.

The customs official ate a third olive. Then he said another thing, more slowly, drawled out. The word *young,* then *alone,* and then more sounds punctuated with a slow shake of the head that was at once mournful and shot through with a thread of pleasure.

She had missed something. Arturo's back straightened, a hunter on alert. His answer had steel in it: *not alone,* he said, and here he spoke with such deliberation that she understood him clearly. *She has me. I was a friend of her husband's.*

The customs official's tone became unmistakably mocking. He spoke rapidly, and somewhere in the middle she thought she discerned the word *lucky.*

Arturo's mouth grew tight and he opened it as though about to speak. He glanced at Leda, who pretended that she hadn't understood anything. Her blank expression seemed to comfort him. *Yes, sir,* he said.

The customs official closed the lid of the olive jar and waved his hand. The olives would stay, but they were free to go.

Outside the warehouse, Arturo lifted her trunk onto a wheeled cart and led her to the street, where they boarded an enormous public carriage with no horses to pull it. A tram, Arturo called it. A young man who was also boarding helped Arturo hoist the trunk up into the main car. Arturo's hand was warm and damp when he helped her up the three stairs. He insisted that she sit on her trunk, to be comfortable, though her knees pushed up against his knees and the calves of other men, all standing around her and holding a pole above their heads. It was mostly men on the tram, and the few women had seats. The sharp smell of sweat overpowered the air. The posture of the standing men, with their arms high to grasp the pole, struck her as very strange, but she understood the reason for it as soon as the tram lurched and rattled into motion. A new seasickness engulfed her as they began to navigate the city.

"It won't be long now," Arturo said. "We're not far from La Boca, where we live."

The tram lumbered through the crowded streets. Leda's neck grew sore from craning her head toward the open windows, but she could not tear her eyes from what she saw: an intricate maze of buildings so tall they plunged the cobbled alleys into shadows and, inside that maze, men smoking on doorsteps, men shining shoes on overturned buckets, men shouting their wares, men driving carriages and shouting at their horses, men walking so fast, where were they going? and she, where was she going? The air suffocated, thick and hot and rank. Dante. She couldn't absorb the news; it kept rising up and slapping her in the face like that garish children's toy that springs out of its box. It made her face ache, her bones ache, her mind ache. A man got onto the tram wearing strings of garlic draped across his chest, hundreds of heads of garlic, like copious pearls or bullets. Was he selling them? Collecting them? Following some witch's instructions to break a spell? He stood a few paces from her and her nostrils filled with garlic. She closed her eyes. The noises blurred around her. She felt a hand brush the back of her bare neck and jolted awake; don't rest, don't doze; Arturo was in front of her and seemed to have noticed nothing. Behind her faceless hordes of men. She could still feel the fingers on her nape, damp, crawling. She sat tense for the rest of the ride until the tram finally pulled to a stop where Arturo gestured for them to descend.

The street teemed with pedestrians and drawn carriages. The buildings seemed made of an odd combination of materials: wood and metal sheets and corrugated iron, slapped together and brightly painted: red, orange, yellow, blue, green. She smelled fresh-baked bread and horse piss and onions frying on a fire. An old man played a violin on the corner while, at his feet, a small boy rolled cigarettes with the concentration of a priest preparing bread for communion. The song had a vigor that belied the old man's stony face; its melody rose and fell and refused to resolve, roving with a kind of desperate beauty that cut into Leda's heart. What was this music?

She turned to Arturo, but he'd stepped ahead to ask the boy for help with the trunk. They lifted it together, Arturo working hard to make the task look effortless, to hide his exertion. They walked to the middle of the block and stopped in front of the worn red door of a building pressed against its neighbors, so that they looked like one long house. Judging by the distance between this set of doors and the next, her home seemed to have many rooms and two floors—two floors! For this Dante took so long to gather up the money! Why did he think they needed so much? He could have called her over earlier.

"Here we are," Arturo said. "This red door."

"You live nearby?" Leda said.

He looked surprised. "I live here. With you."

She had mistaken his kindness. How could she have been so stupid. She thought quickly: he looked stronger than she was, but she was taller, she could outrun him, but she wouldn't know which way to run.

He saw her expression and went red. "No, no—in another room. With my mother and sisters."

The boy was watching keenly now. Leda tried to ignore his curiosity. "All of you, here? In this same house?"

"There are many of us here. Many families in one building. A *conventillo*. Dante didn't explain?"

"No." She had always imagined, even in the humblest incarnations of her new life, that she and Dante would have a house to themselves. A private space at the end of the world, far from their own family, that was her dream, even if it were a one-room hut with a dirt floor like those occupied by the humblest citizens of Alazzano, the ones who cleaned the homes and stables of landowning families like her own. It had not occurred to her that the space would be immersed in the noise of other families, that their fellow immigrants would crowd into the same refuge. How naïve she had been. *I do not know this place, not even from my dreaming,* she thought as she followed Arturo and the boy through the front door.

They entered a dim foyer. Just beyond it, double doors let out into a long, open patio crammed with washing tubs, tables covered with fabric and other sewing supplies, dilapidated crates, laundry flapping on haphazard lines, women scrubbing and cutting and shelling and sewing and sweeping, and children, children everywhere, playing with wooden spoons, sharpening knives, mending ragged clothes, helping to scrub and cut and shell and sew and sweep, wiping snot from their grimy faces with their hands. They looked up and stared as she stepped into the glaring light.

"Leda!" a round-faced woman called out. She stood, wiped her hands on her skirt, and approached, arms open. She was stout and erect, with an edge of metal in her, like the matrons in Alazzano who could tear a person to shreds with their wagging tongues, though Leda tried not to think of them as she received the woman's customary kiss.

"I'm Francesca," the woman said. "We have been waiting for you!"

All eyes were on her, it was too much, she was so tired. Some were smiling, but others—the children, always the most honest—simply gazed as though she were a fascinating specimen just fished out of the water, the virgin widow, the grieving bride. Some women seemed to look at her with pity, others as though sizing up the wares at a market plagued with thieves. There were so many of them, did they all live here? And without men? But no, it was the middle of the day, the men must be at work. And so there were even more people than this. She smelled urine and stale oil. Arturo had disappeared through one of the many doors that lined the courtyard, carrying her trunk. The courtyard was like the heart of a labyrinth, with doors on every side, no clear way out. Some of the doors were open, others closed. She wondered whether one of them led to her room, if in fact she had a room and was not meant to sleep here in the unroofed center among the crates and washing tubs.

"These are my daughters," Francesca was saying. "Palmira, Diana, and Silvana."

One by one, the three daughters—one Leda's age, two younger—approached and kissed Leda's cheek. The other women in the patio introduced themselves and kissed her and pointed out their children, some of whom kissed her dutifully while others hung back in defiance, and all of their names swam into Leda's mind only to vanish immediately. She could not retain a single word. She hoped her smile was convincing. The women were chattering around her about how pretty she was, how young, how was the boat, how did she feel, until finally Francesca took charge and grasped Leda's arm with all the firmness of a mother. "Come. I'll show you your room."

She had a room. It was the last one on the right. The air inside was thick and hot, unventilated, and then she knew why all the families congregated in the center patio. It wasn't that they lacked their own spaces but that, inside, there was not enough air. Her room contained a wooden table, two chairs, a chipped armoire, a washbasin, and two narrow beds with rusted metal frames and burlap blankets, with an empty chamber pot under one. There was no stove. The walls had long ago surrendered the whiteness of their paint.

Arturo and the neighbor boy were in the corner, where they'd just placed the trunk. Arturo gave the boy a coin and sent him away.

"Sit, sit," Francesca said, drawing out a chair. She exuded authority. Her accent was unfamiliar, though it sounded Northern Italian. From Genoa, maybe, or Milan.

Leda sat.

"You must be hungry," Francesca said. Eyebrows raised in expectation.

"Please, don't trouble yourse——"

"Arturo," Francesca said, "tell Silvana to make the lady a plate."

Arturo nodded and was gone.

"That boy, Arturo. He's got a good heart. You can trust him, and I should know. He's not my son, but I'm the closest thing to a mother that he's got here. Same went for Dante. And for you."

"Thank you," said Leda, because she couldn't think of anything else to say after such pronouncements. And then, stupidly, "I'm Leda."

"Yes, I know."

Francesca studied Leda for a long and silent minute. Leda looked away, at a spot where the paint had peeled from the wall to reveal the wood beneath.

"You must want some time to refresh yourself," Francesca finally said. "I'll leave you. There's water in the jug under the basin."

Then Leda was alone. She stared at the jug. She should use it to wash her hands, her face, but she could not rise. She could not move. The closed door made the air inside untenably thick, but she needed privacy more than she needed physical comfort. Outside, in the patio, she heard the sound of water sloshing in tubs, and the giggling of girls rose above the din of voices. Were they laughing at her? They shushed each other, but kept laughing.

The last time she'd seen Dante, he'd been distracted by the carriage pulling up to his door, the dust on its wheels that whispered of the road to Naples, the approach to his ship, the ocean that awaited him that very night and across which he'd find, if he was fortunate, a place—some crevice in the rock face of the world—that he could call his own. The whole family was gathered at the door of his house to see him off, but he only had eyes for the carriage. The sun bore down on all of them, made them sweat. There was hunger in Dante's eyes, not so different from the hunger she'd seen there during their nights under the olive tree, but stronger. Sharper. In the last minute, he'd accepted the kisses of his father, mother, brothers, sister, uncles, aunts, and cousins until at last he reached Leda. He smiled. His kiss on her left cheek, then her right, was firm and tender.

No goodbyes for you, he said, because we'll be together soon. I'll see you on the other side.

A knock sounded on her door. Arturo entered with Francesca's youngest daughter, who was about nine years old, carrying a glass of wine and a plate of bread, ricotta, and tomato slices drizzled with oil and salt. Leda had not seen fresh tomatoes in two weeks. She could have wept. The girl saw the expression on Leda's face and hurried to set the plate down on the table.

Arturo stood with his hands clasped in front of him. "Do you mind a little company?"

"No," Leda said, although she did. "Please sit down."

Arturo sat in the chair across from her. The young girl stood, hovering awkwardly. Leda understood her predicament: she couldn't leave a young widow alone with a man in her room. There was no third chair at the table. Leda gestured toward her trunk. "Please," she said. "You too."

The girl smiled gratefully and perched on the trunk, a few paces from the table. She was really a wisp of a thing. She had a delicate face that seemed perpetually startled.

Arturo looked uncomfortable. "Please, eat, don't let me stop you."

"I'm not hungry."

"You have to keep your strength up."

She looked down at her plate. The tomato was beautiful, red and damp with its own juice. She wanted to stroke it with her forefinger. But she could not imagine eating. The three of them sat in silence, enfolded by the sounds through the wall, voices, steps, a woman's complaint, a man's whistle.

Finally, Arturo said, "Dante."

She looked at him. He was younger than she'd realized, twenty at most.

"Maybe you'd rather not hear about it until later, until you've had a chance to rest."

Her mouth suddenly tasted sour, but she said, "No. Please tell me."

"He was murdered in cold blood."

She felt the breath trap in her lungs. Her cousin had been an idiot. He'd argued with the wrong man in a bar. He'd gambled away his money to a ruthless man, like his own father might do, digging the hole for his own coffin. Or else he'd walked down a dangerous street and been killed by strangers for the change in his pockets, as she had heard could happen to men in large cities like this one, and like Naples. The blacksmith of Alazzano had a great-uncle who'd bled to death right in the heart of the Neapolitan Spanish Quarter, stripped of his coins, his hat, his shoes, his wedding band, and the gold fillings of his teeth along with the teeth themselves. That is why, the blacksmith used to say, you should never be seduced by the city.

"He died bravely," Arturo said, more forcibly. "Fighting for the liberation of all workers."

She stared at him. She didn't understand; she hadn't heard a word about Argentina being at war.

"Should I tell you the whole story?"

No, she thought, don't tell me, I don't want to hear another word of this, I want you to put me back on that steamship and send me sailing off to nowhere.

"Please," she said. "I'm listening."

There was so much Arturo wanted to tell her, more than he could ever put into words, because he did not trust words the way he trusted silence. He rarely spoke of his own life, had never been asked, by anyone, to forge a narrative from the raw material of his lived days. But now, tonight, here she was right in front of him, his friend's cousin, his friend's bride, this young woman with an expression on her face like a cornered cat, and he had to talk, had to give her the whole full-bodied story, wanted in fact to pour it directly into her mind, as no language in the world was built to do—the whole of it, the luminous with the horrible. No doubt he'd fail. But he had to try. He owed it to Dante, and he even hoped against hope that he could free himself of the nightmares in which Dante appeared to him, mangled and ardent, if only he could sit across from this girl and find a way to turn a lived experience into speech.

He began with the ship from Italy, where he first met Dante. They were both seventeen and both ambitious, two traits that were enough to turn them into friends. They spent long hours playing cards, complaining about the food, chafing with boredom, and looking out over the water dreaming of their new life in América. At least, that's what Arturo dreamed of. He couldn't have said what exactly went through Dante's mind. Dante had a confidence to him, a kind of swagger, that was uncommon in emigrants his age. It was even more surprising considering that Dante had nobody in Buenos Aires and would be staying at the Hotel de Inmigrantes when he arrived, while Arturo had a distant relative, Carlo, who'd promised a place to stay and help finding work. Only later, when their friendship ran deep, would Arturo suspect that Dante's outer confidence was a story he shouted to the world—with his stride, his strong voice, his eyebrows arched with I've-seen-all-of-this-before—so that he himself could hear it and begin to believe it was true.

On one of those slow afternoons, Dante told Arturo about the girl he was going to marry. Her name is Leda, he said.

She's from your village?

She's my cousin, she grew up next door. She's going to wait for me. He said it with the satisfaction of a man prepared to work a long hard day and go home in the evening to bread still hot from the oven.

Arturo looked out over the endless water. It was almost evening, and the sun hung wearily in the sky, its reflection broken over the waves. He wondered what the sun felt at this time of day, whether, in its descent, it longed to stay suspended—a hopeless struggle against gravity—or to sink away in sweet relief. He tried to picture this girl Leda. She appeared before him, beautiful and pure, with flowers in her hair, dipping her cupped hands into a river. Breasts visible at her neckline as she knelt. He envied Dante his certainty. He'd heard about the lack of immigrant women in Buenos Aires, and despaired of ever finding himself a wife, but there was no one back home to send for. He had girl-cousins, but none would wait for him, except perhaps Giulia, who was too silly to be taken seriously; he couldn't picture her cooking a family meal without burning the pots, let alone surviving whatever the New World held in store.

Maybe, Arturo said, you have a sister you could bring over for me. Do you have any sisters?

No, Dante said sharply.

Arturo felt his face grow hot. I was joking, he said, though this was not quite true. I'm sorry.

One is married, said Dante. The other is dead.

The silence between them grew thickly knotted, and Arturo felt the dead sister slide through the space between them, or, rather, he felt her absence, like a gauzy fabric with the power to suffocate. She must have died young; there was more to the story; he would not ever ask again. They gazed out over the long and darkening water as it lunged toward the impossible horizon.

At the Buenos Aires port, Arturo didn't recognize his second cousin's uncle Carlo and walked right past him, still scanning the crowd.

Arturo! It's me, Carlo!

Arturo turned. Carlo had gone gray in the fourteen years since he'd left Italy, and had a scar now from his right ear to his chin. He wrapped Arturo in an embrace so tight that the pain squeezed his eyes shut. Arturo saw the scar on the backs of his own eyelids, enormous, glowing, a great red slash. When he opened his eyes, he caught sight of Dante walking away. He called out. Dante, come back!

Dante turned.

You weren't going to say goodbye?

I'm sorry.

This is my uncle Carlo.

The two men kissed in greeting. Dante looked uncomfortable, and, as often happened, Arturo could not interpret the expression in his eyes. Before his friend could escape again, he told him the address of his new home. Come see us, he said. We might be able to help.

Dante nodded with an indifference that made Arturo think he'd never see him again. They kissed goodbye and left the port with their trunks on wheeled carts, Dante to the Hotel, Arturo and Carlo to the nearest tram station.

When Dante appeared at the conventillo on the fifth day, Arturo was overjoyed. He'd begun to feel shaky in this strange city without his friend's effortless confidence. Even if Dante's swagger was false, it lulled Arturo, flecked his fears with bright spots of calm.

How was the famous Hotel de Inmigrantes?

Dante shrugged. Nothing worth any fame.

I'm glad to see you.

Is there room for me here?

Arturo wasn't sure, but he said, *mio amico,* if there isn't room we'll make some.

He'd been sleeping on the floor of the middle room on the right, which was populated only by single men, and so had come to be called la Camera di Scapolo—the Bachelor Room. When he arrived, six bachelors already slept there: four of them shared two beds, head to toe, and two more slept on the floor, on straw pallets woven by Francesca's daughters across the patio. Arturo slept along the far wall, if you could call it sleep, the restless hours spent prone in that hot airless room. With Dante added, it would be even harder to breathe. But the other bachelors welcomed Dante, in part because one of the men, a brooding Ligurian, would be staking out a room of his own soon with a cousin about to arrive, and in part because there were never enough pesos to go around.

Dante slept beside Arturo, as his brother had when they were little boys. His friend's breaths were a soft slow loop of sound that carried him gently toward sleep.

It wasn't hard for Arturo and Dante to get jobs. One of the men in their room worked for an export company that needed strong young bodies in its warehouse, having just lost a few to illness or death. Side by side, they loaded and unloaded cargo at the docks, eleven hours a day, sweat pouring down their bare backs in the unrelenting sun. They came home streaked with dirt, bones screaming, to a hot dinner from Francesca and her daughters, who fed the bachelors for a small fee. Arturo worked until his back throbbed and blisters riddled his hands and feet. He worked until he started to see—and this he would never admit to a soul on earth—his mother's face, bent over him, cooing a song of comfort, rubbing his worn skin, enfolding him the way she had long ago when he was a little boy and his father had finished beating him and gone to bed. When he was seven, one of the beatings broke Arturo's arm, and it had never set right, always gave him trouble, even now. His mother had tended to him at home rather than calling on the village healer and incurring further gossip on the family. When she'd wiped up all the blood, iced the bruises, and made a rudimentary cast out of old cloth, she embraced him, hummed into his ear, and crushed his face to her breasts. This memory was the warmest thing his mind possessed. *Mamma, Mamma, my arm hurts at the end of every Buenos Aires day. And something else hurts worse, at the center of my chest: it is an empty place that will never be filled as long as I am far from home in a crowded noisy city that never shuts up or slows down.* He had not expected to miss his village the way he did—not the fear, not his father, not the days when there was only a crust or two of bread that his older brother might rip from his hands, but the sun and air and space, the luxurious green. He hungered for trees. He had taken them for granted, like breathing. Now they were gone, replaced by the relentless noise and stink of a city where there was nowhere to be alone, nowhere calm, nowhere pure—though he didn't dare complain. There were young men in his village who would cut off a limb for the chance to come to the Américas, who looked on with envy during his last days after his mamma had shown him the wad of cash she'd miraculously gathered, thanks to skipped meals and relatives and fervent prayers to the Virgin, for his escape. And look at the other men who surrounded him here. Look at Dante, working with grim ferocity, and never a protest in his voice or even in the muscles of his face; that man had a strong will! and goals! and he was going to build something if he had to push his body past its breaking point to do it.

I don't understand, Arturo said. What keeps you going?

They were on their walk home, and for a moment he heard only the round beat of their shoes against stone streets.

Ghosts, said Dante.

What ghosts?

None, no ghosts, don't be stupid, he said quickly. I just want to eat and to raise a family, like everybody else.

This was all he would admit to. But on two separate nights, Arturo had woken to his friend thrashing beside him, caught in a nightmare, talking in his sleep. *No. No. Cora!* The first time, Dante struggled as if under attack. Arturo shook him and whispered as loudly as he dared.

Dante. Dante!

Dante opened his eyes.

You were dreaming. It was a dream.

Dante made a strange, strangled sound.

Do you need something? Water?

No. Sorry I woke you.

Forget about it.

Dante closed his eyes. Arturo didn't know whether he was asleep or pretended to be, but they didn't speak any more that night.

Six weeks passed before it happened again. Arturo shook him awake as he had before, then whispered the question he'd been carrying since the first time. Who is Cora?

Dante was silent for so long that Arturo thought he'd fallen back asleep. Then he said, very quietly, Nobody.

Arturo hesitated. But—

And if you ever say that name to me again I'll beat the lights out of you. Understand?

The darkness seemed to crash in on them, full of claustrophobic shadows. Yes, Arturo said, I understand.

Whatever secrets drove Dante, whatever ghosts he kept hidden, he still had to modify his dreams. When he arrived, he'd planned to wait until he could afford an apartment of his own, however humble, to marry. Over time, he saw how absurd this notion was in a city that had swelled with so many immigrants seeking a chance at life that rents had soared and sharing a conventillo with one bathroom and one kitchen for sixty people or more had become a normal way of life. If he waited for a full apartment, he'd be an old man on his wedding day and his bride would be long past her childbearing years. The best he could hope for was a room of their own: a table, a bed, space along the walls for the children when they came. This became his new goal.

He spent almost two years saving toward it.

In those years, Arturo found the anarchists, or, rather, the anarchists found him. They were everywhere, expounding in cafés, running union study groups, organizing surreptitiously at the warehouse in defiance of company rules. How they talked: their passionate words and ample gestures encompassed a whole golden future with the sweep of a single hand. There were no leaders—they didn't believe in leaders—but at the longshoremen's union, which he soon joined, everyone knew that when Beto spoke, it was time to listen, and that his words would ultimately form the heart of whatever decision was at hand. Beto was a small man, slightly built, who at first impression made you think of an easily startled deer, but when he opened his mouth to talk, his unexpected baritone commanded attention and quickly entranced a room. He peppered his speeches with examples of injustice, rhythmic repetitions, and quotes from a man called Bakunin. If Beto had been born in another time and social class, he might have become a famous poet, or perhaps a confidence man tricking kings into handing over fortunes. He spoke with a force that seemed to rearrange the world—a force that could surely persuade the president himself, if only Beto could have his ear, that the anarchist revolution was around the corner and would transform Argentina, then the globe, and for this reason Arturo wanted Beto to talk and talk forever. Surely these were not dreams, but prophecies. He, Arturo, would help make them happen. He threw himself into helping the union, distributing pamphlets, attending meetings, and marching in protests and rallies where police gunshots often sent him racing to the closest alley. The adrenaline rush of those moments eclipsed the terrible hollow in his chest and the ache of his limbs. He was alive; he was a man; he had a purpose. He did not need authorities to rule him; he could rule himself. When Arturo looked at his world through this lens, its fractured pieces suddenly coalesced into a shape in which he saw himself, reflected, writ large.

During these years, he and Dante went to Lo de Dalia (and this he did not tell the cousin-bride) once or maybe twice a month. Those nights were like diamonds in a pile of gray stones. Every night, before sleep reached out and grasped him in the crowded dark, he closed his eyes and pictured the brothel girls, one after the other, their naked breasts, their spread thighs, their hips in his work-worn hands as he pulled them toward his sex again and again as if by doing so he could bore right to the center of them and leave his loneliness there, so deeply buried that it would not find him the next day. He thought of rich men like the owner of his company who occasionally stalked the warehouse, hands clasped idly behind his back; men like that could afford girls every night. Every night! He imagined himself with a purse full of pesos, striding into the brothel and taking girl after girl or two at once, his sex in that plump blonde with the strange metallic moans, his hand on the breast of the slim girl Dante liked so much, that quiet wisp of a thing who spoke neither Spanish nor Italian and lay silent no matter how hard you fucked her, waiting until you finished to murmur in that pebbled language from a cold and distant land. Or, even better, he'd think of taking the girls away from the brothel's naked stench, to a private room with a clean double bed, satin sheets, mirrors on every wall, and platters of grapes and roast meat burdening a table. They wouldn't eat at first, they'd have time for that later, they'd have obscene amounts of time to spend together in which he'd miraculously find the courage to find out what the women wanted, what they most enjoyed, and see them in their genuine pleasure because, in a fantasy, even this was possible. They'd beg him to do what he most wanted, and he'd comply. When all three were finally sated, they'd lie close and talk in a common language forged by their erotic love, some mystical blend of their various mother tongues with the Spanish of this land. The girls would cradle his head to their musky breasts. He'd talk. In his sated state he'd be as eloquent as Beto himself—another miracle—bending words around his thoughts with ease. Do you know what's coming? he'd ask. The naked girls would feed each other grapes and shake their heads. And he'd paint it for them: a new nation beyond nations. We're going to dismantle all the borders. Patriotism will be shown for what it is, a lie invented by the owning class to undercut the power of workers across the globe. Think of how many of us there are, in Europe, here in América, in Africa—millions and millions of us, separated by borders but bound by our poverty, our dignity, our rights. Where do you come from? Poland? Russia? You come from the people; you are the people. You're exploited too, and you have rights, just like men who work in factories and ports. See, the anarchists, they've understood that from the beginning. Don't you want to fight for liberation? Don't you want to be free? At this, their eyes would light up with recognition and desire, and perhaps they'd reach for him and force him to make love to them again before he could continue, and he'd oblige, and, when they'd all regained their breath, he'd say, it's coming, you know, the revolution. It belongs to all of us. And the two women would curl their warm bodies toward his in assent.

But Arturo's real visits to Lo de Dalia were nothing like that. They consisted of long dull waits and then a frenzied rutting in which few or no words were exchanged. There were always many more men seeking the women's services than there were women to serve them. The brothel was housed in a conventillo, with the same layout as the building where he lived: a courtyard surrounded by doors past which the girls worked three to a room, their beds divided by sheets tacked to the ceiling. He and Dante would wait their turn for an hour or two in the patio, surrounded by other men. A musical trio played for them, a strange new music, city music, American music, tango it was called, sad or bright, fast or languorous, purely instrumental or sung with lyrics about corncobs or ripe figs or other things that got you thinking about what had brought you to the brothel in the first place, made you want it even more. Golden music to defy the filth of conventillo life. Supple music to wake your bones and make them beg for motion. Sometimes the men danced with each other while they waited—practice, they said, in case we actually find a decent girl to court!—facing each other, clasping bodies, improvising a sweep around the room, and Dante and Arturo joined them, Dante leading, his hand firm on Arturo's back like a bird who knows the way home. The guitarist in the trio was Arturo's uncle Carlo (that mad bastard, how had he gone from *cilentano* peasant to bard of brothel tangos? if the relatives back home could see him, oh, what would they say?), accompanied by a flautist and a neighbor, Nestore, on the violin. Nestore mesmerized. He was old but relentless and a wonder on his instrument. His secret, so he said, was a daily tonic of cigars and whiskey. *Epa!* the madam would say, in a voice loud enough to be heard by all the patrons in the courtyard, and perhaps even some of those behind closed doors, Now that's what I call a song. It takes a real man to play a tune like that!

A real man, Nestore would answer, can do a lot more than this, *señora*. I'll be glad to show you any time you like.

The madam would curtsy and flash a smile missing several teeth. The men would laugh and nod their heads or flick ash from their cigarettes or impatiently finger the tin chips they'd been given when they made their purchases, which each would give to the whore like a ticket when his turn finally came. By the time Arturo got inside a room he was drunk on songs and grappa, and then his turn always went by faster than he wanted it to, a blur of limbs, moans, dim light, her open sex all around him and then that sharp good push, a small collapse, perhaps a quick murmur in her foreign tongue, perhaps her silence, time to go.

Then another month of fierce subsistence, longing to return.

The union's demands became ambitious: eight-hour workdays and a raise in pay. Imagine! To rest every day, and survive! Of course the managers refused the terms, walked out of talks. Strike, the workers whispered on the warehouse floor. Strike, they shouted at café meetings, the word itself an incantation.

It's going to be soon, Arturo told Dante one night after dinner, as the Di Camillo girls gathered and washed the plates. In a week at most.

Dante dropped his cigarette on the patio floor and crushed it. I hope not.

It enraged Arturo, his friend's apathy, his blithe dismissal of the dream. How can you say that? Don't you want better pay? Don't you want to be treated better than cattle?

The bosses are the bosses. They won't give up their power.

We'll make them. Beto says—

Beto's an idiot. He can't even hold his liquor.

Arturo tried another tactic. The bosses are nothing without workers. They need us, we'll show them our strength.

Dante looked at him with the patience of a father schooling a child. Arturo. Use your head. Think of the packing plant.

Arturo didn't want to think of the packing plant, where the anarchists' strike had been repressed by the police, with guns, shots, four workers dead. And in any case that wouldn't happen here, not with Beto at the helm. They would win, they had to win, he knew without a doubt because he'd seen it in vivid visions as he lay awake on his pallet in the darkness, visions of Buenos Aires after the revolution, a city in which workers rose each day to work in dignity and decided for themselves when they would start and end their labors, sailors and factory workers and mothers and whores and stevedores, all with their disparate native tongues and myriad homelands alive inside their skin, gathered together to forge a transformed city in which everybody had enough to eat and a ventilated room to call their own, in which workers rose onto rooftops in the mornings to howl their freedom across the city like proud roosters and gathered in the middle of the street at night to dance the unabashed tangos of the people who had once been called the poor. The vision was so marvelous that the world had no choice but to make it true. But he lacked the language to transmit this to his friend. Instead he said, You can't stand on the sidelines.

I just want to live my life.

As a scab? As a traitor to your own kind?

Is that how you think of me?

It's not how I want to think of you.

Dante stared. Arturo hadn't meant his words to come out so harshly—or maybe he had, but hadn't thought they were so capable of wounding. He stared back. Dante was the first to turn away.

That night, they slept with their backs to each other.

Four days later, Arturo joined two hundred men in a picket line outside the warehouse. It was hot already, humid, one of those January dawns where the sky bore down on you like a threat. They stood in front of the warehouse doors, facing the blue and yellow and green and orange houses of La Boca's edge, built with salvaged sheet metal and planks, held together as much by nails as by immigrants' wild hopes. They would guard the entrance against scabs; he expected Dante to be one of them. So he was shocked to see his friend appear suddenly at his side, as if from nowhere, cigarette in hand.

I'm glad to see you, Arturo said.

Dante shrugged.

Vindication. He had done it. He had persuaded one more man to join the struggle. And not just any man, but this man, Dante, a good man, his best friend. The rust-colored warehouse now looked, to him, like an ancient fortress, one they could storm and destroy. Behind him some-where ran the river, blocked by the warehouse but still wet and full and dark with power that was surely on their side. He strained to sense its presence and to call it to arms as he chanted along with the other men, *justice for the workers! We demand our rights!*

Ten minutes later the police arrived, on horseback, riding right into the crowd of protesters. Disperse!

The crowd jostled back, men pushed into other men. A chant struck up and rose over the throng. *Oppressors, oppressors—*

Disperse or we'll shoot!

Oppressors! Arturo shouted, raising his arms.

Dante grasped his arm and wrenched it down. Not so loud. Careful.

How can you say that, *mio amico*? This is the moment!

I want to see you get out of this strike alive.

Arturo shook off his friend's grasp. I'm not a coward, he snapped. Oppressors, he shouted, oppressors!

One of the horses was becoming agitated by the crowd. It stamped and whinnied, raised its front hoofs dangerously close to Beto's head. The officer who rode the horse could not control it—he clenched his crooked teeth in concentration—but no, Arturo saw, that was not it at all: the officer was not trying to calm his horse but riling it up, pulling its bridle, digging his heels into its sides, pressing it into a trap of men. The horse bucked and shivered, searching for a way out. It looked desperate, capable of anything. The officer's gun was cocked and he had the face of a man bent on breaking several bones.

Rage surged in Arturo, red and immense. He was not a helpless boy anymore, he would not stand for it.

He grasped a rock and hurled it at the officer with a shout.

The rock grazed the policeman on the shoulder, and he immediately turned his face and gun toward the source of the rock. Arturo met his small green eyes for an instant before he ducked. The officer fired. The shot hit Dante square between the eyes—and this, too, Arturo did not tell the cousin-bride sitting across the table from him, listening to his story: he said *a shot* but did not say who'd provoked it or where it landed or how Arturo, crouched just centimeters from Dante's face, felt the flecks of blood and skin and shredded bone strike him in a hot spray that had never fully washed off of his skin because it was part of him now, the shredded skin still singed his own; and he had no words to tell the girl across the table how Dante had crumpled like a marionette whose puppeteer had gotten tired and snipped the strings, or how the bullet made a terrible mistake when it exploded Dante's head because it should have killed Arturo, as the policeman knew because he scowled in disappointment before turning toward a new distraction to his left, as Arturo knew from the nights he'd spent up alone thinking not of whores or revolutions but of the crime he was committing by still walking this crude world, as God himself must know up in His heaven where He sat, all-seeing, fearsome, enraged that he, Arturo, was still alive and sitting in this airless room talking to Leda instead of the man who was supposed to meet her, the man she married, the man she surely loved.

Arturo finished. Leda sat silent, staring at the long flame of the lamp. She saw Dante inside it, small, orange-tinged, eyes shut tight, hands clutched to his bleeding chest (or perhaps it hadn't been his chest? Where did the bullet land?). She would have reached her hand into the lamp to save or at least comfort him, but he was unreal, out of reach. Arturo seemed to be waiting for her to speak. He seemed to need something from her, but she didn't know what, and in any case she doubted she could give it. The day had gutted her, there were no words left, no thoughts, nothing but dark.

"You still haven't eaten," he said.

Leda said nothing. Just the thought of eating made her nauseous.

"Francesca will make a scandal if we take this plate back to the kitchen with food still on it. Won't she, Silvana?"

The girl on the trunk nodded, then resumed her absolute stillness.

"That's how she is." Arturo turned back to Leda. "She's going to send in dinner later, too."

"Thank you, but this is more than enough for the night."

"Maybe you'd rather be alone." Arturo gazed into the flame. "But I have two more things to tell you. First, his clothes are in there."

He gestured toward the armoire, whose closed doors suddenly acquired a new aura; they were not ordinary wooden slabs, but gates of death.

"We didn't know whether you'd . . . want them. Of course, you'll probably want the space for your own dresses. If you ever wish for them to be taken away, just let me know and I'll do it."

Leda nodded.

"Not now, then, I assume."

She shook her head. The thought of losing Dante's clothes seemed unbearable.

"Very well. Secondly. This room is paid for you, for the next two months. We took a collection among members of my labor union. No, don't look at me like that—what else would we have done? Dante was a good man and everybody knew it. We all watched him sacrifice to bring you here. And our brothers in the struggle know he gave his life for all of us."

Leda tried to smile.

"So, in any case, you have some time to figure out what you want to do. Whether you want to look for work, or go back home. Do you think you'll go back home?"

There was a strange lilt in his voice, a forced attempt to sound casual. Leda had no idea how to answer him. "I don't know. I don't have the money to go back."

"Your family might send it. Or you could earn it yourself, over time.

But I should also say"—here, again, the pinch in his voice, trying too hard to sound offhand—"that if your father gives his blessing for you to stay here, well, there aren't a lot of unmarried girls, decent ones I mean, here in this city, but there are some. Francesca and her daughters are seamstresses. They might be able to help you find work. Don't you think, Silvana?"

Silvana nodded again.

"*Grazie,*" Leda said. She had said the word so many times in the past few hours that it seemed to have lost all color.

"Well, no need to decide tonight. We should leave you in peace. You must be tired."

Leda nodded.

Arturo looked disappointed. Really, he was like a puppy, she thought. A puppy too bewildered to realize it was lost. She watched him hesitate, then stand. Silvana followed suit.

"Just promise that you'll eat before you sleep," he said.

"I promise."

"Good night, then, Leda. Get some rest. Leave tomorrow to tomorrow, it'll be there waiting."

They left. Leda didn't move for a long time. Then she pushed the plate to the far corner of the table, turned down the lamp, and drank the wine in two fast gulps. She heard the chime and clang of dinner being cooked in the kitchen, the voices of women and girls as they chopped, washed, stirred. She heard men's voices as they arrived home. Shouts. Mumbles. Laughter. She was fortunate to have landed among people who treated her with such generosity. She should be grateful. But she didn't know these people, didn't know how far their goodwill would stretch, what it was made of. She stared at the wall. It was riddled with stains from grease or moisture. She couldn't imagine sleeping. The rest of her night lay before her, empty, insurmountable. Dante, dead. Where was he buried? What a disgrace, she'd forgotten to ask. Loss piled up inside her, along with innumerable fears, of the night outside, the crowded city, the thoughts in her own mind. She wasn't sure that she could face the day to come.

What if she didn't? If she died?

She considered this possibility. It would be an escape. But how? She had no poison. No knife. She could find a knife in the kitchen but wouldn't know where to stab.

She thought of Arturo, who had just buried his friend, now having to bury his friend's bride as well.

She thought of her mother waiting and waiting for a letter from Argentina.

She thought of the violin in the trunk, cast adrift on a foreign continent with no one to pass down its history or give it voice.

The chatter outside her door began to subside. It was a Tuesday night, after all, there was work to be done tomorrow. Her own plans loomed amorphous, indecipherable. She could kill herself or she could look for work. She could talk to Francesca about sewing, take up a needle and show her what she could do. She could walk down the street and hear and see and smell it, try to understand this new city, this Buenos Aires. She could mail a letter to her family, as she had promised them she would do as soon as she arrived. How would she write that letter? What could she possibly say?

She should start trying.

She went to her trunk for pen, ink, and paper, and brought them back to the table. The page was ruthlessly blank. She stared at it for a long time, and when she finally began to write, her hand shook.

Dear Papà and Mamma,
Terrible news—your nephew is gone—he is not here—

No, she thought, that's not right, he is my husband. Before he is their nephew, he is my husband. And the word *gone* is wrong, it's not as if he left on some adventure. She crossed out everything she'd written, drew a line below it, and began again.

Dear Papà and Mamma,

I am sorry to tell you that my husband, Dante, my cousin, ~~was shot in~~ ~~cold blood by a~~ *has passed away,* ~~I am alone and don't know how I will~~

Wrong. Wrong. She crossed everything out, again, and turned over the page. Her pen hovered over it. Nothing came. Zio Mateo seemed to leer at her from the shadows. She tried to imagine him sad for the loss of his son, but could not picture it, when at Cora's funeral, his daughter's funeral, he'd looked on with a face so closed it could itself have been a tomb. She threw her pen to the floor and stared and stared at the blank page, whose whiteness was interrupted by the stains and bulges of crossed-out, decimated lines on the underside, a forest of words in which she could become irretrievably lost.

Cora's corpse appeared two days after she died. The spring floods had swelled the river and made it carry her downstream, to the low bowl of the valley beneath the village. By then, her face was blue and gray and bloated almost beyond recognition. Her undergarments were stuffed with black stones and a single iron crucifix almost twenty centimeters long.

She had escaped from the hut where she'd been living for six months, up the hill from the village, under strict lock and key, far from everyone except a quiet old monk from the nearby Franciscan monastery who came to tend to her. Nobody had dreamed that she would try to escape, let alone succeed. She had clearly planned ahead. When the monk arrived that afternoon with her bread and cheese, she was waiting for him with the iron crucifix in hand, the only heavy implement in her crude room, which, on previous days, the monk had seen her cradle like a baby and sing lullabies to in her babbling mad-girl's voice, and no matter how much he'd scolded her for the blasphemy, he had not succeeded in making her stop. All of this he told Cora's father, Zio Mateo, on the evening Cora went missing. Leda was not in the room when that conversation occurred, but she heard the whispers of it and she could imagine how Zio Mateo had looked when the monk told him about this, sneering with pity and rage the way he did when people failed to do his bidding. So you knew, then, Mateo said to the monk, that she could unfasten it from the wall.

The monk nodded, ashamed.

But you never stripped her room of it.

She had so little, the monk said. I hoped that Christ's presence would help her soul.

Her soul? How does your head feel now, old monk? Had enough of Crazy Cora's soul?

The monk rubbed his scalp and looked penitent. The blow had been swift and unexpected; she had struck his skull from behind as he was setting her plate on the wooden table. He had lost consciousness, and when he recovered it, the girl was gone.

Her two brothers went to look for her. They thought she might be sleeping in the forest, on a bed of leaves, murmuring words wild enough to make the dirt beneath her go insane. She had to be found. She had to be helped. She had to be punished, too, of course, but that part went unspoken. At night, Leda imagined Cora running and running through the valley and then out of it, through forest and over hills and past villages that speckled the earth with their sadly clustered lives, all the way to the foothills of Vesuvius, and Vesuvius would gather her into its black hollow core and find a way to set her free.

But it did not happen that way. It was Dante who found her, Dante who thought to look downriver, thought to trace the trajectory of the drowned. He pulled her corpse from the water, still light enough to gather into his arms despite the extra burden of wet hair and clothes and skin, let alone the stones he did not yet know about. He carried her pressed against his chest, one arm under her knees and the other at her back, as if she were a princess condemned to sleep by an evil spell, though unlike such a princess Cora hung at a stiff and awkward angle and refused to bend or drape or fold. The walk home was laborious. He did everything he could to avoid being seen by village gossips, taking a long, circuitous path through the forest, and entering their house through the back door. None of it made any difference. The news spread quickly and expanded in the telling.

This part, too, Leda could imagine with precision: Dante walking up the hill with a disfigured body in his arms. The sweat on his neck from exertion. The bruised corpse, soggy in a manner never felt among the living. Those last and terrible moments of touch. The need to put her down on the ground to open the back door, if nobody inside saw him coming and opened it for him. The need to report on how he found her, once inside, Dante's voice a dull scrape against the quiet.

The full story was not told and not acknowledged in Leda's house. Cora had not run past the crumpled body of an aging monk, with the focused gait of a murderer. She had not reached the river and filled her pockets and undergarments with stones and even heaven help her with the holy cross itself, all pressed against her nether skin for the express purpose of pinning her underwater. She had not walked into the river with a will to die.

But in the village, it was told and told—in the plaza, at the apothecary's pungent shop, at the public washing tubs, where women gathered to scrub stained sheets without mercy. Tongues burned with the story.

That girl, what a burden she became to her family.

And look where she's ended up.

You know how they found her? A holy *cross*, right in her—can you imagine?

No.

You mean——?

In the name of the Father, the Son, and the Holy Spirit, amen. Disgusting.

A disgrace.

But she was crazy. We have to remember she was wrong in the head.

That girl was possessed by demons.

I heard she howled like a dog when the moon was full.

I heard her eyes turned red as blood when she attacked that poor monk.

She almost killed him.

I heard she tore her own clothes off like a common whore.

Oh, we *all* saw that.

You remember, don't you, poor Sister Teresa—?

Oh sweet María yes.

She's never been the same since, you know.

What she put the nuns through. All of them.

Pffft, that girl, she brought evil spirits down on us.

It's because of her that the woods are haunted.

I still won't walk out there alone.

Nor I.

Nor I.

Bless the nuns, they did their best.

Oh yes, the way they—

—cleared the woods.

Yes.

Of that girl's evil.

For the good of all.

And the girl's mother: how she must have suffered all these years to think her own womb could make such a creature.

No greater horror for a woman.

But her fault after all. What kind of mother breeds a girl like that?

And now, the worst sin. The taking of your own life.

To think that a Mazzoni daughter will be buried outside of church grounds—the shame of it!

But, despite the gossip, Cora was not buried outside church grounds. Zio Mateo made a gift to the church, and the priests quickly agreed with him; yes, yes, you're absolutely right, it was a terrible accident, she fell into the river and how scared she must have been, poor girl, a tragedy, and thank you for your generosity, Don Mateo.

She was buried in a spare ceremony that nobody attended beyond the immediate family. Leda felt the spurn of it and longed to spit in the face of every gossip-woman in the village who did not come. The air was restless that day, full of wind and bluster; four roses abandoned the coffin's surface for a hapless flight between the spindly cemetery trees. The Mazzoni family tomb lay ready, its marble slab pulled aside to reveal the insatiable open mouth of the ground. A small cluster of relatives, all dressed in black, wept dutifully as the priest muttered his prayers. The women clung to their hats and their black veils fluttered restlessly. Leda stared at the coffin and tried to understand how the radiance that had once been her cousin could be enclosed in that box of wood. Not possible. Though that life-joy had long been gone. She remembered Cora two years ago, before the madness, when she was still the girl who shone too brightly and leapt off too-high rocks. That was the Cora she wanted back. That Cora was not in the coffin. She had vanished without dying, an ending worse than death.

Cora's mother wept in silence, face veiled, shoulders shaking. Dante stood beside her but did not move to offer comfort. He looked as though he were struggling to keep his face from breaking into many little pieces. In her mind's eye Leda saw him walking up the hill, carrying his dead sister. And then, without warning, he looked up at Leda and their eyes locked. He knows, she thought with sudden horror. He knows why Cora went mad. He saw, perhaps not everything, but enough. And he hates himself for knowing, for failing. It is that way for me also, she thought at him. Dante took in her gaze and then looked away, at the far boundary of the cemetery, where centuries-old headstones stood impassive in the lucid wind.

That night, Leda lay in bed and tried to speak to her dead cousin. She started slowly. Cora. Cora are you there? My soul-cousin, my almost-sister, where are you? Are you cold? Are you hungry or does that end after you die? I have not forgotten you, *cara, carissima*. I wish you hadn't gone and I am shouting for you to come back but I also know that there is no place for you here—can you hear me?—for two years now there has been no place for you in Alazzano, and now, as of tonight, there is no place for me. I am going to fly away from here as soon as I find a way, and whatever trace of you is still here in this world is coming with me, Cora, I promise you this; stay with me in spirit and I'll take you out of here, together we'll find a small corner of the possible to call home. I should have done it long ago, should have listened when you asked me to run away, forgive me, Cora, please forgive, I didn't understand, but you did, back then, you already understood everything, understood far too much, because of him. He turned our village into hell. He tore the veils of night and dirtied the soft insides of days and I am speaking of your father: because when you went crazy he was not surprised and when you went up to the hut on the hill I was forbidden to come see you, we were all forbidden and we all obeyed him, what traitors we all are, cowering at his every word, he was the only one allowed to visit you—the only one—your own father, Cora, your own father—and everybody pretending it is not that, not that, unbelieving, unseeing, afraid—

She howled these thoughts into the night in utmost silence.

The night responded with a barricade of stars.

Dawn was close, less than an hour away. Her first dawn in Buenos Aires. She still sat in her chair, fully dressed, the room's darkness wrapped around her like a cape. She heard the first stirrings of feet shuffling across the patio to fetch water, she thought, or perhaps to empty chamber pots. Where did the jugs get filled, the pots emptied? So much geography she had yet to learn.

The night's vigil had given her mind a terrible clarity, the bright sharpness of a knife. The facts unfurled in front of her without grace or mercy. Dante was dead. She was a widow, countless kilometers from home. Home itself had not been home in a long time. She had not asked to become a widow, she had had no choice. But, she thought, if this is my fate, let me not surrender, let me learn to stand inside of this new skin.

She lit the lamp and let her eyes adjust to the light. Then she picked up the pen and began again.

Dear Mamma and Papà,

Dante has died. I am sorry to have to give you this news. It was an accident at work, before I arrived, and it all happened quickly, there was no pain. I have a room of my own and good people around me, Napole-tanos and Northerners also. They are very kind.

There is no money to return right now ~~and even if there were, I don't think I want to return~~ *but today I am going to look for work.* ~~I don't want to go back to Italy.~~

~~I don't know whether I want to go back.~~

~~Please don't tell me to go b~~

There is no need to worry. I will write again soon.

She stopped and stared at her own handwriting for a long time. She stared into the flame of the kerosene lamp. Then she wrote:

There is no such thing as going back. I can't see the way forward. I can't see my own face.

The words scared her. She couldn't imagine what they meant. She struck them through and scribbled over them until they had been swallowed by black ink. Then she took out a new page and copied the words that were not crossed out into a fresh letter, folded it, and placed it in an envelope she'd brought from Alazzano. Like a pigeon it would fly back with her message. She, not a pigeon, would remain.

She knew she should sleep but every muscle in her body felt tense. Outside her building lay the maze of the city, the maze of the impending day. Dawn light came in, slowly, slowly, accompanied by the rasping sounds of a city that at no moment of day or night ever went completely quiet, and in that fresh weak light she tried to listen to this city full of wheeling destinies she had not yet begun to imagine. The city could kill her, or it could remake her: the distant chafe and hum of Buenos Aires on the edge of dawn just might be the sound of her life starting.

The Good People of New Babel

It took weeks to grow accustomed to the noise. The clatter and roar never abated, not even at night, not for an instant. She didn't know how to hear herself inside so much sound. Perhaps silence had existed in this city once, long ago, before the immigrants had poured in with their thousands of jostling voices and hands itching for work, routing any last traces of quiet. In the conventillos—which earned their name, she'd learned, from their cramped spare nature, like the convents that house nuns and monks—there was always the clang of water tubs, the drag of crates across scuffed tiles, the bristling duet of a man fighting with his wife, the shout or squeal or hungry moan of children, mothers' reproaches and lullabies and threats, the stampede of boys just back from hawking newspapers on trams, the tired laughter of men having a smoke at the day's end, the gossip of women as they put laundry on the line, the chorus of a family bickering over dinner, scolding the older kids for taking too much bread. On the street, the din thickened with the constant beat of horse hoofs drawing carriages, vendors with handcarts shouting their wares—fresh bread as good as your mother's! shoes! a pan that will drive your wife wild!—the cracks of whips and groans of wheels, women gossiping through windows with neighbors on their way to the market with their baskets, a respite from the strict sphere of home. And each of those homes, she knew, was as raucous inside as her own conventillo, whole families in each room, bachelors sleeping limb to limb, snores penetrating the thin walls. In her village, she could walk all the way to the bakery and hear nothing but wind in the olive trees; on nights when the moon was dark, everything slept in Alazzano, even the dirt. Alazzano also never smelled like this, like sixty-three people sharing two broken toilets into whose pits they poured the contents of their chamber pots in a relentless stream. Nor had she known hunger in Alazzano. Here, although she was lucky to eat every day, more than once in fact, some child or another always hung in her doorway staring at her plate, and she couldn't help giving morsels away.

When she went out, which was not often, she ventured no further than the butcher shop two blocks down, where she made her purchases in accordance with Francesca's precise instructions. The butcher spoke perfect Italian with a Northern accent. He was polite, but he cut meat with a vehemence that made her nervous. She never lingered in the shop. On the way back home, however, she did linger to talk with the bread vendor who peddled his wares from a ramshackle handcart laden with loaves. His name was Alfonso Di Bacco. He wore a frayed sailor's cap at a slant. He was wiry, with weathered skin, and he presided over his post as though keeping the only lighthouse on a rocky shore. The first time Leda approached him, she asked for three round loaves, and, even though Francesca had assured her that morning that the vendor was Italian and would understand her perfectly, she found herself holding up three fingers and pointing at the bread.

The man tipped his cap at Leda. "You honor me with your purchase. I cannot see for so much beauty!"

Leda handed him her pesos, scuffed coins donated by Dante's fellow workers, and the old man stroked them with callused fingers.

"Francesca sent you?"

"Yes."

"You must be Dante's widow."

Leda nodded. Her chest ached. How many people on this street knew her story?

"Terrible, what happened." He clucked his tongue. "I knew Dante. He was a good man. He died for all of us."

Her husband, the anarchist Jesus. She wished the man would hand her the loaves and set her free.

"Well? Go on and pick the ones you want!"

She examined the bread and selected three loaves. They were fresh, the crust just the right balance of crisp and smooth. "Does your wife bake these?"

"My daughter. My wife is dead too."

"I'm sorry." Embarrassed, she rushed to place the last loaf in her basket. The man reached out and grabbed her wrist.

"*Signora,*" he said, "let me give you some advice." He leaned in so close that she could smell his breath, sour milk and stale tobacco. "Be careful in this city. There are many, many men here, not all of them as kind as I am." His mouth smiled but his eyes did not. "A girl like you, pretty and clean, will get many offers. But watch out. Not all onions are sweet once you cut them open."

His gaze was too sharp, Leda could not hold it. She looked down at the brown, bare humps of bread.

"Do you understand me?"

"Yes, *signore.*"

"Well then! Welcome to Argentina. Here, take this loaf too, a gift from me—no, no, take it. For your new home."

As she walked away she couldn't help but see, in her mind's eye, a man being sliced in half like an onion. Ribs and heart and clockwork parts exposed for all to see. The image made a laugh rise up inside her. She turned to look back at the bread vendor, who was watching her and who touched the brim of his sailor's cap, smiling to bare the dark holes where his teeth had been.

On her second day in Buenos Aires, Leda began sewing with the women of the Di Camillo family. They made clothing for a store in a fashionable neighborhood across town that sold shirts for gentlemen. Francesca insisted that Leda join them, and that no, don't be ridiculous, it didn't take work away from them, there was plenty of work to be done.

"Getting enough work isn't the problem." Francesca pursed her lips as though referring to an impossibly behaved child. "The problem is living off the pittance they give you in return."

The three Di Camillo daughters set up their sewing station in the central courtyard six days a week, as soon as the men left for the factories or the port. The men were gone at dawn, all except Carlo, scarred Carlo, who slept during the day and worked at night (Francesca wouldn't say what kind of work the old man did, but she said *work* as though she feared the word would dirty her mouth if it stayed too long, which, of course, made Leda follow Carlo with her gaze—though she studiously pretended not to do so—in those rare moments when he came out of the Camera di Scapolo during the day for a bit of water and then slunk back to his room without saying a thing). Once all the men except Carlo were gone, two sisters cleaned up breakfast (if there had been breakfast; on some days there was nothing, on better days a bit of yesterday's bread or coffee with milk for the men, on good days enough for the women and children too) while the third sister brought out chairs, a slab of wood they placed over two cinder blocks to serve as a table, and burlap sacks filled with fabric, scissors, threads, and the patterns assigned by their employers, designed to help them cut fabric into shapes they'd assemble into shirts and trousers. They spread their supplies over the table and a couple of extra chairs. They set up in a corner that started in the shade and later bore the brutal lacerations of the sun, but there was no moving to follow the shade because the rest of the courtyard burst with running children, wailing babies, sharp-tongued mothers, the endless cooking and washing and piecemeal work of a horde of women and girls from the adjoining rooms. By day the courtyard hummed with women's labor, overrun with it, a fleeting factory that disappeared at night when the men came home.

Within hours of working with the Di Camillo girls, Leda felt enshrouded by their collective concentration. They did all the work by hand as they could not afford a sewing machine. Francesca reigned over her three daughters with prescience. She knew when a stitch was going awry, even if it occurred beyond her peripheral vision. She sensed when a pot in the kitchen needed a girl to run in and stir. She punished her daughters with a slap when they made a mistake or got distracted, but this was seldom necessary, as the girls were already thoroughly trained. They were allowed to talk as long as they kept up the pace of their work.

The oldest sister, Palmira, looked about Leda's age, only she was much more beautiful, with a voluptuous figure, an easy laugh, and eyelashes long enough to whip you when she blinked. Silvana, the youngest, worked quietly to the side, and seemed shrouded in a world of her own, beyond the bounds of chatter. She was the one assigned to the scissors: whenever there was a need for more fabric to be cut, it was she who laid out the patterns, sliced exacting lines, and piled identically shaped pieces on the makeshift table. Diana, the middle girl, seemed about twelve. She was skinny and restless and hated sewing, as she readily proclaimed to Leda within the first hour of work.

"There's nothing duller, is there?" she said, in a low enough voice for her mother not to hear. "Stitch after stitch, they're all the same and by the end of the day your hands are so sore you want to peel your palms off. Honestly, I'd rather do anything else—laundry, cooking, run down to the market for bread."

"And if she doesn't get picked to go on an errand—how she complains!" said Palmira.

Diana looked ready to protest.

"Come on," Palmira said, "you know it's true."

"Maybe it's true," Diana said, grudgingly. "But I have my rights."

"What rights? You've been reading too many anarchist pamphlets."

"I wish," Diana said, and she laughed.

Palmira laughed with her.

"You don't read anarchist pamphlets, then?" Leda asked, eyes on her sewing. This anarchy. The strikes, the riots, the bullet in Dante's chest. There was so much for her to understand about Buenos Aires.

The sisters didn't respond. She looked up; they were staring.

"You can *read*?" said Diana.

"I can."

"My God."

"Who taught you?" Palmira said.

"My father." *And Cora,* she thought, but her cousin's name stuck in her throat.

"And you can write too?"

"Yes."

An amazed silence settled over the girls. They sewed on. Finally, Diana said, "Well then, you can help me write my own anarchist pamphlet. On the rights of middle daughters."

Palmira smiled. "And the eldest daughters?"

"You'll have to ask her for another one."

"What do you think, Leda?"

"Why not?" Leda said. The smell of shit rose up behind her. It must have been one of the little children; a cluster of them was playing with sticks in a bucket, squealing, enraptured with their invented toy. The girls either didn't notice the smell or were inured to it, focused on their work. Leda felt embarrassed, though she wasn't sure why—there was no shame, was there, in knowing how to read and write, she certainly didn't want it to be otherwise. And yet it bit at her, this difference between them. These girls had not grown up the way she had, a landowning family, meat on the table, books in the house. She tried to lose herself in the stitches, taking shelter from her thoughts in the repetitive rhythms of the needle. She made it through several hours without having to speak. However, in the afternoon, when the light began to deepen to a heavy gold and her hands ached with each stitch, right after Francesca announced that in an hour they would put their supplies away and cook dinner, Palmira said, "Leda, tell us about your village."

"Please," said Diana. "We're so bored with each other's stories."

Stitch, stitch. Leda didn't look up. "I don't have any interesting stories."

"There must be something," Palmira insisted. "What is the village called again?"

"Alazzano."

"And how big is it?"

"Not big."

"How many people?"

"About a hundred."

"What! No more than that! You must know everyone."

"Yes."

"I bet that's wonderful."

Stitch, stitch. Light flashed on Leda's needle.

"Not at all like here," Palmira continued. "It's impossible to know everyone in Buenos Aires."

"Especially since we're never allowed to go out," said Diana.

"That's for our own good," said Palmira, "and you know it! Really, Diana."

"Oh, come on. You yourself just said—"

"Let's get back to Leda's story—"

"—that you wish you could go out and meet more men."

"I said no such thing!"

"But it's what you meant."

Palmira poked Diana with her needle, drawing a pinhead of blood.

"Ouch!" said Diana. "Mamma!"

Francesca came out of the kitchen and slapped Diana across the cheek. The cluster of children behind them, who now squatted in a circle shelling beans into a bowl, looked up in unison at the sound of the slap. They watched, faces expressionless. "Stop distracting your sister and get back to work."

"But—"

Francesca raised her hand again. Diana flinched and bowed over her sewing. The children resumed their shelling.

After a few minutes, Palmira said in a low voice, "What about fruits? What grows in your village?"

"Figs," said Leda. "White and purple ones. Hazelnuts. Lemons. Olives, of course, all over the hills."

"I've never even heard of a white fig," said Palmira.

"It's sad," Diana blurted, "what happened to your husband. Shot in the head like that."

Head. Not chest. Leda felt sick, faint, the courtyard tilted dangerously.

Francesca returned, hand raised to strike Diana again.

"No, don't," said Leda. "Please. It's all right."

"It's not all right, she's a rude girl."

"I'm not offended," Leda said.

Francesca looked torn between maternal discipline and the laws of hospitality. She hovered for a moment, then disappeared to the kitchen.

The three sisters sewed in silence for a while.

Leda stared at the white cloth in her hands, now a canvas for broken shards of her cousin's face.

"I'm sorry," Diana said under her breath.

"It's all right," said Leda.

"I heard he was very brave. On that day, I mean."

"Of course he was," said Palmira.

"But you didn't even get to see him once he was your husband." Diana's voice dropped to a whisper. "You didn't get to, you know, sl——"

"*Diana*," Palmira said, needle threatening her sister's arm.

Diana hushed.

"At least you still have time," said Palmira. "You're so young, you can marry again."

"There are many men here looking for wives. Palmira's gotten several offers," Diana said proudly.

"That doesn't matter," Palmira said quickly.

"Yes it does," Diana said. She lowered her voice again. "They won't let her marry until our brother finishes school. We're all working so he can study."

"And for the family."

"Always for the family."

Stitch, stitch. Blinded by white cloth.

"Almost time to pack up," said Palmira.

Leda nodded. Her fingers throbbed and her back ached from crouching over her needle. She wondered how much money this labor would yield, whether it would be enough to purchase her own bread each day, once the money from the collection had run out. She didn't know what to do with the sympathy the girls had extended to her. Suddenly she longed for Alazzano, where every tree and face was familiar, absurd when she'd been so desperate to leave but she couldn't help it, couldn't help picturing the orange groves, the river, the crush of hazelnuts under her shoe, baring their treasure. And yet she didn't want to go back. What did she want, then? Another husband, as these girls were suggesting? The thought made her cringe. Her first task, she thought, was to survive. Her second task: to learn to live with the low buzz of her grief. And after that, to recover her appetite, which had dissolved at Dante's death.

To be hungry again.

She could see no further into the future than that.

That night—after helping cook dinner and eating two bites in her room despite the Di Camillo family's entreaties that she join them, and after Arturo's alarmingly eager attempt to start a conversation when she crossed the courtyard to empty her chamber pot before bed, too much longing in his eyes, as if there were some aching hole in him she was supposed to fill—she lay in the dark, listening to the creaks and murmurs of the conventillo, her neighbors' chatter, the constant stream of life in the surrounding rooms, and let her thoughts transport her back to Alazzano, with its glorious white figs that not everyone in Argentina had ever tasted, just hanging from the branch, wild, beckoning. How she would take them down to dry on long slabs of wood so they could be enjoyed through the long winter, the sweetness of them speaking of the summer just past, honey captured on your tongue.

Her mattress was hard as stone. She turned uneasily and thought of Palmira. There she was under a white fig tree, gazing at the leaves cascading all around her like a crowd of wide green hands. Let me show you, Palmira: see how I reach up and find the ripest figs, the soft ones that are begging for your mouth. She watched Palmira eat the sweet and unfamiliar fruit, watched startled pleasure spread across her face, lips open, eyes wide—but then the air rushed around them and Leda turned and saw Cora, skin blue, hair wet from the river, watching them with a terrible expression on her face.

Cora, Cora, come closer!

What do you think you're doing?

Palmira vanished. Shame a warm brick in Leda's belly. She'd been caught doing something wrong, but what? Stealing fruit? Wandering too far in the night?

She asked to taste the figs. Although this, Leda realized, was not exactly true.

Cora shook her dripping head, like a mother saddened by a wayward child. *Leda. This place is not what you think.*

Leda sat up in bed, covered in sweat. Hot thick air pressed at her from all sides. She felt both thrilled and afraid, though she couldn't have said why. It was hard to breathe and she longed for ventilation, but it would surely be indecent, if not dangerous, to sleep with the door open. She kept it shut and lay awake until sleep rose to maul her in the darkness.

On Saturday night, the men took their baths in a great clatter of metal and hot water, each patiently waiting his turn to scrub and cleanse himself in one of three large tubs behind closed doors. They emerged looking refreshed and slightly bewildered. When the men were done, the women took their turns. By the time Leda's turn arrived the water was gray and clouded, almost as dirty as the floors. Silvana had just stepped out and was drying herself off discreetly in the corner. Leda knew by now to avert her eyes, the best form of privacy in conventillo life. In the tub, she scrubbed as quickly as she could, fighting her revulsion. Afterward, she felt more refreshed than she'd expected. Around one a.m., the men went out together, combed and groomed and buoyant. On Sunday morning, some of them were still straggling home as Leda and the Di Camillo girls rolled out thin sheets of pasta and cut them into precise rows—these Northerners made their linguini thicker than she did, it took getting used to, and there were also the breaks she took to kill roaches in the futile and eternal war against them—and children yelped in protest from the patio as their turn came in the tubs. At nine, Leda and the Di Camillo girls put aside the pasta, changed into their best dresses, and pinned back their hair. The church was just a half block beyond the butcher. It was larger than the village church back home; Leda had never seen so many people in one room in her life. Like the crowd at the port in Naples, only waiting for God rather than for a ship. She fidgeted during mass. She tried to stop. The nape of Arturo's neck was right in front of her, exposed and somehow pure. He was a sweet man, really. Earnest. His prayers were probably sincere and full of hope. Why couldn't she be like that? To keep still she counted the tiny hairs on Arturo's nape, black, delicate, more vulnerable than anything on a man should be.

Even the communion bread tasted different here. Less airy, more tart.

After church, they returned to the conventillo, and the men brought tables and chairs and crates out from their rooms and arranged them together in the courtyard, for a communal lunch. Mimicking a family on Sunday, Leda thought.

There was meat on this day. There was wine on this day. The scent of basil and tomato sauce veiled the smell of filth. Wine bottles circulated around the tables and poured into each cup.

"Signora Chiara, your *bolognese* could drive the archangels to sin."

"My daughters made it this week."

"They are saints."

"It's true, girls, don't blush—your mother has taught you well."

Across the room: "So then I told her, listen, who do you think you're—"

"Such beautiful flowers on the altar today!"

"Lent is coming. Enjoy them while they're there."

"With Lent coming there are a lot of things we should enjoy."

"Oho!"

Laughter.

"Gentlemen! There are girls here!"

"Sorry."

"Oh, Francesca, come on—"

"Because if she tries that with me one more time I'm telling you I'll—"

"Leda! How do you like our Sunday lunch?"

At the sound of her name, the tables went quiet. Leda felt all eyes on her. She should say something, but found she couldn't. Expectation thickened the air.

"Is it as nice as back home?"

"Of course it's not," Francesca said. "Nothing ever is."

It wasn't true—Leda had not felt such warmth and ease at Sunday meals in Alazzano in years—but Francesca's words punctured the mood. The conversation continued more subdued, weighed down by private thoughts of homes far away.

After lunch, the men pushed the tables back into the rooms while the women made coffee. All the chairs and crates remained on the patio. Carlo went out and returned a few minutes later with a neighbor, the same old man Leda had seen on the first day, playing the violin on the street. They were walking arm in arm, like brothers. The old man had his instrument.

As soon as they arrived, the chant began.

"Mu-si-*ca*! Mu-si-*ca*!"

Other bachelors joined in, then Diana, then Palmira, until all sixty-three residents of the conventillo were clapping and chanting, Leda among them, caught up in the collective sound.

Carlo disappeared into his room and returned with his guitar. The chant rose into a cheer, the rhythmic claps into applause, then silence. Carlo sat beside the old man, by the door to the kitchen.

He counted to four.

And then it happened.

Music. It surged out of string and finger in harsh communion, weeping from the terrible pleasure of the bow. Guitar strings shook and deepened the well of sorrow.

Carlo sang. Something about the night clutching his heart, something about a woman, a bad woman, she couldn't quite make out the Spanish. The sound ensnared her. It invaded her bones, urged her blood. She didn't know herself; it now occurred to her that she knew nothing, nothing, nothing about the world, could not have known a thing when she didn't know the world contained this sensation, such sound, such wakefulness, a melody as rich as night.

A tap on her shoulder. Arturo. "Would you like to dance?"

She hadn't noticed that people were dancing. But there they were, scattered on the patio, not in a row or circle but in pairs, face-to-face, the bachelors holding a girl or another man. They glided around the center of the patio.

"I don't know how to dance like that."

"Of course. You've never danced the tango."

Tango. A name for the sound. She repeated it in her mind. *Tan-go.*

"Don't worry, the man leads so it's not too hard for you. Come, let's try."

She didn't want to but couldn't say no. She stood, awkwardly, just as the song ended. Arturo was broad-bodied and exuded a soapy cologne. He clasped one of her hands and placed the other on his shoulder. To her relief, he didn't look her in the eyes as a new song began, slower than the first, and he gently forced her feet back in time. She tensed at first, afraid of colliding with others, feeling herself stumble, but when she relaxed a little the music seemed to gather and take shape inside her body, propelling her, giving her form. The sound rose and fell in waves and she was riding them, with Arturo, suddenly together, were their neighbors watching? what did they think? what did Arturo want from this dance? She could feel his patience with her, the novice, and, underneath that patience, hunger. For comfort. For a woman. For a wife. And it was a way to survive, wasn't it, to marry a sweet-smelling sweet-dancing man and rope your own destiny to his, cross your fingers and pray he doesn't capsize? Just what I need, she thought, another rope, another man. It seemed a horrible thought, unwomanly, but she couldn't help it; all she wanted was to sit and watch that old man's hands on the violin.

Arturo raised her arm into a high salute just as the song ended. She excused herself as gently as she could.

"We could dance another?"

"I'm tired," she lied.

"Of course," he said, looking deflated.

She sat down near the musicians, who played for another hour and a half, which she spent unmoving, transfixed, straining to memorize each motion. In the middle of their performance, the men exhausted their repertoire and started again at the beginning. This gave her a chance to revisit the melodies, to slide her mind along them, to memorize their curves. There it rises. There it falls. There the violin grows bold and carries the music higher, the old man draws the notes out, the bow points at the sky, the old man's gaze is distant while his strings do the wailing. Nestore, his name is Nestore; the dancers call it out to cajole him to keep playing. He complies. He does not look at the dancers, does not acknowledge her, sitting and staring. He is steeped in a private aural world. He drew out longer notes than her papà ever had; he was more forceful with the bow; she hadn't known the violin contained such wildness. She was reminded of the *tarantella,* which skipped along its notes and pulled you upward, out of yourself, *come and play!* But these pieces, these tangos, didn't only lift; they also plunged you downward, deep inside yourself, to the unexamined corners of your heart. *Come,* they whispered, *come and look, see what's here and dance with it, this is music too.*

After the musicians had finally stopped, she helped with the dishes in the kitchen, and with every plate and pot she dried she thought her way back through the tangos, replaying them in her mind so she could memorize their shape. She thought of her father's violin, buried in her trunk under dresses, silent now for years. The gathering continued in the night, but Leda feigned tiredness and retreated to her room. The voices of her neighbors muscled in through the closed door. She changed quickly out of her best Sunday dress, with its petticoats and buttons, and into her loose cotton nightgown. She opened her trunk and dug through the dresses—she still kept them there, while the armoire had remained unopened, undisturbed—to find the instrument case. She placed it on the table. The latches opened willingly. The violin seemed to glow with its own inner light. She caressed it gingerly, searching for the howls and croons that might be latent in its body, its long black neck.

Can I? she tried to ask the instrument. May I?

The instrument lay still and did not respond.

In the small compartment beneath the violin's neck, she found a square of fresh resin for the horsehairs of the bow. *To turn them to silk,* her father used to say. It looked just like the resin he made, back then, from the olive trees behind their house, and which he let her rub along the horsehairs to prepare them for his songs. He must have made this resin in the months before the wedding. Which meant that he'd been thinking about this gift for some time.

Was it possible that he'd suspected this might happen? That he'd given her the violin with the thought that it might end up in her own hands? *For Dante,* he'd said, and certainly Dante had played a little here and there, but it was she who'd shown true passion for the instrument, who'd begged for lessons and been turned down, who'd reveled in the permission to rub resin and oil strings. *Let it bring you both a little beauty,* he'd said. What kind of beauty? That of a listener, or a player? Her father was a kind man, but not a brave one. If he wanted her to break the rules, he would not tell her outright, but perhaps he would sabotage himself, leave the jail key in reach as if by accident and walk away.

She placed the violin under her chin and wrapped her hand around its neck. It had been a long time, six years at least, since she had stolen time alone with her father's instrument, and yet her body fell into place around it with glad ease, remembering the pose, the rush of it. It took more pressure than she remembered to hold the strings down. She decided not to pick up the bow. She could not let herself be heard through the thin walls; she would play silently; she would hear the music with her fingers and her mind.

A tune. The first tune. Where had the old man put his fingers?

Here. Here. Here.

The joy of it. Savage. Terrifying. Music as piracy. Music without sound. One hand mimed the motions of an invisible bow, while the other curved around a neck that it had always loved, had never stopped loving, a sensation as fresh as it was deeply familiar. She was a little girl out in the olive grove, hiding with her father's instrument, surrounded by the smell of damp night dirt. She was an adolescent widow, adrift in a strange land, mapping new music with her body. She played this way for hours until finally she fell asleep with the violin's curves pressed against hers.

The sewing income would not be enough to keep the room. Once the money from the collection at Dante's death was gone—two months, three at most—she'd have to either move or return to Italy. And, Francesca explained to her as they sewed side by side, there was no use in looking for better-paying work. The factory jobs for women had dried up; the labor unions had long stopped fighting for their rights in the workplace, because women took jobs away from men and, also, because women workers weakened the cause, since their fathers and husbands could force them to work during strikes. And so there were no factory jobs for girls. There was domestic work, but you had to speak the language or else the mistress might well not pay you and blame it on the language barrier, pretend not to understand. As for waiting tables, that was now against the law; too many restaurants and bars were places of ill repute, and the women who had been working there were *those* kinds of women, or at least were accused of being *those* kinds of women, of which there were so many in the city that it could have been true. And anyway, it was unseemly for a decent girl to work in such a place—no self-respecting mother would send her daughter to work in one, no matter how desperate they were—so now only men could wait tables. As for *those* women, rumor had it they had plenty of work for better pay than anything else a woman could do, though of course, in the process, they destroyed their mortal bodies and their immortal souls. There had even been one girl who'd lived here in this conventillo who, well, suffice to say, would never be welcome back. And so, that left needle and thread, piecemeal work, which paid only enough to supplement a household, not to support one, which was why every woman with a healthy husband should bow down and thank God every day—and here Francesca stopped, awkwardly, remembering who she was speaking to, realizing her lack of tact. She lowered her head over her work. All three of her daughters felt her embarrassment; even Silvana stood still, scissors open around empty air.

Leda attempted a smile at the girls. Palmira looked down at her needle; Diana glanced at her mother; Silvana smiled back and closed her scissors, *swoosh,* as though to cut the humid air into a shape that could be worn.

Leda kept sewing, stitch, stitch. She was not upset by the reference to widows; she was far more unsettled by the grim news about her pay. She thought about *those* women. The ones who collapsed down the ladder, to the lowest rung of dignity. How much more money did they make than the good women who sewed? What were their lives like? Was it possible that, one day, she'd have to become one of them? She tried to imagine it and felt a bolt of something that was not quite terror, not quite disgust, but a baffled vertigo, the sensation of looking into the abyss below the edge of the known world.

"Now, of course, you could come and live with us, in our room," Francesca said, "as a sister to the girls."

Relief flooded Leda—she would not have to leap. As a sister to the girls. Would she sleep beside Palmira? Would they share a blanket in the winter, as sisters do, huddling to keep warm, feeling the light brush of each other's breath? The thought filled her with heat and panic and something else, impossible to name. Then there was the matter of Francesca, crusader against dirt and vice, a good woman, exemplary, so good it had worn her down to hard bone. Could she stand to live under such a woman's fist?

"You're too generous," Leda said and glanced at Palmira, who was focused on her work. Rebellious hairs escaped her head scarf on gusts of nonexistent wind.

"But," Francesca kept on, "you should go home, Leda. First chance you get. Family is the homeland of the heart."

"I bet you can't wait to go home," Diana said.

Leda nodded and kept stitching, stitching, stitching, and she envied her needle for its ease in knowing where to go. This will be a collar, here is the sleeve, follow the pins and the shirt will come together of its own accord. I am nothing like this needle, she thought. There are no pins to show the way, I'm wandering blind.

Later that afternoon, Leda went out to the market, her small chance of escaping the conventillo by herself. Francesca had warned her very clearly to head right down the block to the stores and vendors, then return quickly home. But she was starved to see more of the city. The conventillo caged her in. She hadn't planned to break the rules and stray, but, after filling her basket with loaves from Alfonso Di Bacco, who extolled her beauty and dispensed paternal advice as he had come to do each day—*where there's life, there's hope; choose neither linen nor a man by candlelight; the best word is the one that goes unspoken*—she stood at the corner and stared down the block at unknown buildings, unseen doors and rooms and lives, carriages pulled by horses clop-clopping their way to places they knew and she did not, their manes gleaming in the late sun before they dove into shadows, and she thought, what harm can it do to walk a little in the light of day? Can it really be so dangerous? She set out down the block, crossed the street, and kept walking. People, streaming everywhere, women in doorways, old men in cafés or pushing ramshackle handcarts, calling out not in Italian but in Spanish, that strange language that sounded like the Italian of an alternate planet. A planet of drunkards, perhaps. Already she understood more glimmers of it, which meant she was either learning Spanish or getting drunk on this place, or both. The streets were crowded with people, innumerable people who'd arrived before her in the land of promise and already staked their space. Land of promise, you have promised too much already to the thousands. She walked on. Her ear caught shreds of other languages. She heard a woman in a doorway speaking sounds unlike anything she'd heard before, at once angular and melodic. For all she knew it could be the tongue of demons or the gods. Further on, children called to their mothers from inside the house, in Spanish, Italian, another unknown tongue. Two girls with baskets walked purposefully past her, gossiping in French. At a café, an old man told a joke in the Neapolitan dialect to a group of men who laughed appreciatively. More Napoletanos. She had imagined, in her brief visit to Naples, that that would be all she'd see of the city, but Naples had followed her across the ocean. It surrounded her. It had invaded Buenos Aires. And isn't that strange, she thought, the way one city can swirl inside another; the way you can be in one country yet carry another country in your skin; the way a place is changed by whoever comes to it, the way silt invades the body of a river. She was that, a speck of silt. The thought thrilled her but it also made her want to weep without reason, or for reasons utterly unknown to her. With every immigrant she passed she longed to stop and stare into his or her face and ask with nothing but her gaze *And you? What are you here for? Why did you come?,* as though just looking at them might unlatch the trapdoors to their hidden stories. And the stories would be infinite, no two alike, burning with hope and loss and vigorous despair, told in more dialects than even God could possibly speak, and yet, she suddenly saw, it was possible that somewhere beneath the surface all their hidden stories held the same thread, a single hum of longing, *I came to live.* Surely this was true for all of them, including her. And, Buenos Aires, tell me, is there any chance that I can forge a space for myself somewhere in the folds of you? (She turned a corner and kept walking.) Will I ever rove these raucous streets with familiarity and with no fear? She walked and walked. The thrum of her feet, the thrum of the city. She felt hypnotized, expanded, and all the things around her—doors, people, brightly painted walls—threatened to tear her open with their sheer existence. She had never felt more awake in her life. The voices of the city blended and poured into her, filling her up, radiant, sweetly fatal, and that was when she understood that whatever this city was, whatever it held, she wanted it. All of it. She wanted Buenos Aires inside her, around her, covering her skin like a film of sweat. She wanted the breath of this city in her lungs no matter the danger, no matter the other story about the good girl who stays locked inside with needle and thread until she can get back to her home village, to hell with that story, she wanted freedom, wanted to taste this place even if it killed her. She felt exhilarated and afraid of her own exhilaration. Was she going mad? Cora, is this how it was for you? She stopped, leaned against a wall, and closed her eyes. Her mind warred between collecting itself and falling even deeper into thrall.

"*Señorita?*"

She opened her eyes. A man stood before her, hat in hand. He had a kind enough face but his gaze was too raw. He said something in Spanish that she did not understand. Then he smiled and placed his hand on her arm. Her skin prickled. She tried to pull away, but his hand followed and gripped her tightly.

Leda tore away from him and ran.

She was lost. One turn, two, and she was on a block she'd never seen before. Old men played dice on the sidewalk, bickering in a strident Italian. They spoke her language but now she was afraid to ask for help, and the thought pushed in before she could stop it, *I want Mamma. Mamma, where are you?* But Mamma was not here, she was unreachable, twenty steamship days away across a great blue ocean of impossible. Leda tried going the other way. Her arm ached from the basket's weight, she shifted it to the other side and kept walking and walking until she reached the end of a street that let out to the port, and there she saw the ships and cargo, men working high up on ladders, hauling crates, sweat beading on their faces, and one of them—Dante!—turned as if to call to her, but no, he was not Dante, his gaze moved blankly on and he wiped his face and resumed his burden. Dante was dead and did not work here anymore. You are alone, Leda. Alone.

It took her another hour to find her way home.

"Where were you?" Francesca scolded as soon as she arrived. "You can't just wander around this city. You don't know what happens to women out there."

That night, Leda couldn't sleep. She tossed and turned, feverish with thoughts. She thought of the city, pulsing beyond the walls of her conventillo, bursting with life and noise and peril. She thought of Palmira, asleep across the hall, covers thrown off her warm body. She thought of Dante and the moment at the port: it was him, it was not him, he would never be at the port again. His absence stabbed her. She wondered what he'd felt when he walked the streets she'd walked today. Whether they'd amazed him as they had her. She longed to ask him. Longed to close the gap between his life and hers.

She went to the armoire and opened its doors for the first time.

His clothes were all there, as promised. Musty air welled toward her, tinged with the scent of mothballs, dry sweat, and decay. At first, she touched the clothing with trepidation, not wanting to disturb its sleep; but then she found herself taking out a pair of trousers, a shirt, a vest, a jacket. She laid them on the bed in the shape of a man. They were empty clothes, nothing more. She touched them again. How had they felt against his skin? And then, before her mind could ask her body what it was doing, she was taking off her nightgown and putting on the shirt, trousers, vest, in an act that would surely scandalize the living if not the dead. Her hips slipped smoothly into the trousers. Her body flushed with hot alarm. What if someone walked into her room now? No, that would not happen. No one ever walked into her room after she retired for the night. Still she could not shake the sense of an unutterable danger. Dante, can you forgive me? Am I violating your memory, or paying it tribute?

It was shocking, how comfortably his clothes fit. The shirt swelled a little over her breasts. It felt strange to have two layers of fabric between her thighs. How different it must be to walk with the sheath of trousers between your legs rather than a crowd of petticoats rustling around them. She tried it, stalking the room, hesitantly at first, then more boldly, imagining how Dante might have strode on his way to work in the mornings, full of muscle and determination, full of hope. And if he passed another man he would not modestly bow his head and avert his eyes, but rather nod to him, chin high, shoulders squared against the world. Wasn't that how men did it? She wasn't sure. She knew how it looked from the outside, this walk of men, but not how it felt from within. She tried it, walked an imaginary street, passed an imaginary man, nodded, not slow-forehead-down, as women did, but quick-chin-up. She felt preposterous, but she also felt something else: a delectable rush.

She took the clothes off, quickly, then stared at them, bunched on the floor. What had she done? She would never do that again. In that instant, with all her soul, she swore that she never would.

She broke the vow the following night.

This time, she put the clothes on slowly, buttoning with fingers still sore from a day's sewing. Then she looked at herself in a hand mirror, tilting it up and down her body in the lamplight. She looked like a man. She felt like a man—or, at least, she felt the way she imagined a man might feel: emboldened, like she could walk all the way to the end of her neighborhood and people would leave her alone. Like she could walk into a café in the middle of the night and the barman would serve her, casually, like she was just a normal customer, like all she was asking for was a damn drink.

But she was not a man. She was a woman.

Wasn't she?

What kind of woman does this thing you're doing right now?

The question rose out of the air and coiled around her. She didn't want to think about the answer but she also didn't want to take off Dante's clothes.

You should take them off. You disgusting girl. Take them off.

She stood still for a long time. Something broke apart inside her. She sensed that the longer the clothes stayed on her body, the more irreparable the change would become. And yet she made no move to take the clothes off. Instead her hands reached for the instrument case and took out the violin.

She played.

The moves were becoming more familiar to her hands. With men's clothes on, her hands moved more smoothly, with more strength and confidence, and this surprised her. It was difficult to keep silent—she longed to hear the motion of her fingers, to test the quality of her sound. But she did not break the silence; the silence was her shield, her refuge. And soon her fingers' music filled her mind and drowned out the hostile voice that had demanded she take the clothes off. The voice slunk into the corners of the room, where it crouched, shrunken in momentary defeat, helpless in the face of silent music.

These became the two pillars of her clandestine ritual: every night she put on Dante's clothes and played the violin in silence. She did it with the fevered secrecy of obsession. Every night her fingers curved further over the strings to better press at one without dampening the others; her arms strengthened as one held up the violin's body and the other stroked the air with an unseen bow; her ear attuned more deeply to the music. Because, when one plays in silence, it is not only the fingers that shape the notes but the ear also, ear as instrument, forging notes and, out of those notes, the curve of melody, with the raw aural material of the mind. On those nights, Leda's mind felt larger than her skull, which she envisioned as a chapel like the La Boca church, a wide space in which she could pull God's secret humming down from heaven or wherever it lurked—the low unbridled wordless song, the absentminded pleasure he took in his own voice—and let it pour down her arms into the violin on which her hands brought the music into the impassive world. Her fingers moved more quickly now, and she could hear the notes in her mind's chapel as if she'd sounded them. The other voice within her, the censoring voice, faded with each time she played. She swayed to remembered melodies, invented melodies, plaintive calls and smooth glissandos and staccato successions that crackled fast as sparks. All this in silence. All this in a silence surrounded by a loud city that was not and yet had to be home.

The old man Nestore played on the street almost every day, but he played at sporadic times, and she never knew whether she'd catch him on her way to the butcher shop or the peripatetic grocer's cart or whether his patch of sidewalk would be empty, missing him, bereft of his sound.

Every day she made an excuse to be able to leave her sewing station and run an errand, but on the first two occasions he was not there. On the third day, she found him playing and rushed to finish her errand as quickly as she could so as to linger nearby for a few minutes. The boy sat beside him on a wooden crate, sharpening kitchen knives on a flat stone. She watched. Men stared at her as they walked by, a young woman lingering alone on the street for no discernible reason. I have my reason, she thought at them, though she studiously avoided their eyes. Nestore was playing a simple melody, four notes repeated over and over, laden with grace and yearning. He did not look up to greet or even acknowledge her. He was absorbed in his music. The boy saw her but seemed unperturbed. The basket of bread grew heavy on her arm, and she thought of going back. Perhaps, in a pause, he would look up and she could catch his eye, start a conversation, ask the question that lay heavy on her tongue. But when he finished, he stood, and the boy rose without being asked, gathered his knives into the crate he'd been sitting on, and gave Nestore his arm to lead him inside. Because Nestore needed to be led. She saw it with a shock: the man was blind. How had she not realized before?

She could not wait for him to notice her.

The next time she saw him on the street, she stepped closer, and waited quietly, again ignoring the looks of passing men, letting the music enfold her—a muscular tune that made her think, strangely, of gullies—listening not just with her ears but with every centimeter of her skin. When the song ended, she put her basket on the ground and clapped.

Nestore raised his face in her direction.

"Beautiful," she said. "I love your music."

"Thank you, *signorina*." He paused. "Or is it *signora*?"

"My name is Leda. I live next door, in the building with the Di Camillos. I've seen you play with Carlo on Sundays."

"Ah! Yes. You're that young widow? Dante's widow?"

So quickly that name, *Dante's widow*, found its way to her and reattached itself. She felt frustrated, though she wasn't sure why, and angry at herself for the frustration. Nestore was smiling at her. His gaze was focused on a point just to the right of her eyes. She wasn't sure how to go on. "I enjoy your playing."

"I enjoy being heard."

"I have a question."

"Do you now."

"Would you teach me?"

He drew back. His smile fell.

"I—I have a violin. It was my husband's."

He turned away from her, down toward the boy, who was shelling peas into a bowl on the ground. The sound of husks breaking open formed a kind of irregular rhythm, *tchk, tchhk.* "You shouldn't ask me that," Nestore said, the way a grandfather admonishes a child.

"Why not?"

"This isn't just any music. It's tango."

"I love the tango."

"You don't know what the tango is," Nestore snapped. "It's no place for women."

"Women dance it, don't they?"

"On the patio of their own conventillo, at Sunday lunch, yes. But the tango gets a lot of other places where, let's just say *ladies* don't."

She wanted to ask about these other places but held her tongue. She needed a good reason. She groped for one, tempered her voice into that of a loyal wife, soft words, the shake of sorrow. "My husband would have wanted me to. He would have hated for the violin to go unused."

"I'm sorry," Nestore said. "About your husband."

She waited.

"But there's nothing I can do about that. Find a man for the violin."

He turned his back to her and started playing again.

Leda stood in place, slightly unbalanced, listening to a light-footed melody that leapt and flashed and that she longed to sink inside of or else break into little pieces before the sound of it broke her. She had exposed something shameful about herself. And there was so much more she had not exposed. If he only knew.

She turned and vanished into her building before the music could end.

She gave up on her idea after that. So she was shocked when, the following Sunday, after the dishes from the communal meal had been cleared and the musicians had been playing for an hour, Nestore called out, "Dante's widow. Is she here?"

The patio went silent. Leda, perched close enough to watch the old man's hands and far enough to seem inconspicuous, could not move or breathe.

"She's here," Palmira said. She'd been dancing with Arturo and still stood near him. "Over to your left."

"Leda," said Nestore.

"Yes."

"Get your instrument."

She rushed into her room and pulled out the violin before fear could rise up and stop her. When she emerged, murmurs enveloped her, tense, distorted.

Do you see—
What is she—
Was it Dante's?
I never saw him with—
Oh yes it was Dante's—
Stolen.
No.
Yes.
How did Nestore know?
She must have—

Shot you know between the eyes—

Francesca was standing close to the musicians now, a stalwart guard. Her disapproval was palpable, a dark glow around her, because, of course, if tango was a netherworld where women should not go, Francesca would be the first to guard the gate. Don't let her stop you, Leda thought, pretend she isn't there. She stood in front of Nestore and plucked a string to tell him where she was. The open note echoed from the walls.

"Copy me," Nestore said.

He played a simple strain, three repeating notes. She tried to copy him, sweeping a bow across strings for the first time in years. The notes rasped and shrieked. Behind her, someone laughed, a woman, flushing Leda with embarrassment. She was glad, at least, that she'd rubbed resin on the bow over the past few weeks, just for the pleasure of it.

"You're out of tune," Nestore said.

"Yes."

"Fix it."

He plucked his strings, one after another, for her to tune her violin to. It took a few tries, and each moment felt infinite. When they were done tuning, Nestore played the same melodic pattern as before. Leda copied it. A little smoother. Not much.

"You've played before?"

Leda shrugged, then remembered he couldn't see her. "No," she said, to avoid a more complicated answer.

Nestore looked skeptical, which gave her a flicker of confidence.

"You put too much pressure at the end of your stroke. Listen."

They kept on, sounding out a couple of tangos on their two violins. Leda had been practicing these very tunes at night, in silence, and now she could bring them to light, adjust her left hand—she'd been too far up the neck on some notes, not far enough on others—and stroke with a real bow, real horsehair, which sang out with a raspy voice flecked with glints of beauty. Around them people shuffled, coughed, whispered sharply to each other. Ignore them. Ignore them. There is only this, all the world condensed into four strings.

"All right, now go," Nestore said. "Back to you, Carlo."

The two men struck up together, and Leda hovered for a moment, glancing at Nestore's skillful hands and then at Carlo's hands on his battered guitar, their aggression on the strings, or was she just imagining it? She didn't dare look into Carlo's face. Behind her, nobody danced. Everyone was staring at Leda. Her whole body went hot from their gazes on her, it was too much. Beneath their stares the violin felt impossibly heavy in her grip. She went to her room and listened through the closed door as the dancing slowly resumed, more subdued than before. She stayed inside until the musicians were gone and she could hear the women cleaning pots in the kitchen. If she didn't come out now, the gossip would surely revolve all the more intensely around her name. She went to the kitchen to help clean.

"Where did you get that thing?" Palmira said. She was drying beside Leda, whose arms were elbow-deep in a tub full of plates and suds.

"I brought it from my village." She thought of adding *for Dante*, but did not. "It was my grandfather's."

"Well, you know," Palmira whispered, leaning so close that Leda felt the girl's breath stroke her ear, "I think you play beautifully."

"Thank you," Leda murmured into the dirty water.

"You should keep playing," Palmira said, "no matter what anyone says."

Leda placed a rinsed plate on the counter between them and let her hand linger on it until Palmira picked it up. For an instant they were touching the same wet object, fused by it. Then the plate left Leda's grip and dove into the folds of Palmira's rag. Leda's ear still stung from the heat of Palmira's breath, those lips so close to her. She would keep playing. No matter what anyone said. She would go to her room tonight and practice those two tunes until their motions were tattooed into her hands. And if Nestore ever let her play with him again, she'd jump at the chance, even if it meant all the murmurs against her in the world. Because she'd had a first taste now of playing aloud in a space full of people and the thrill was enough to live for. Sound is pure power. It floods a room. It can even flood the world beyond a room. You might be locked behind a shut door, unable to get out, but the sound of you can pour right through locks and walls into the great air that lies beyond, where anything that breathes—a dog, a queen, a girl like Palmira—can be penetrated by your sound.

I've made a mistake, Nestore thought that night as he rinsed his face at the washbasin before work—Sunday night at the brothel was almost as busy as the night before, and he expected to come home at dawn with his fingers sore and satisfied from hours on the strings—I will come to regret teaching that girl, that widow-child, that Leda next door. And in front of all those people. Well. How else was he supposed to find her? He'd called her name out at the gathering because he knew she'd be there. But no. That was not the whole truth. He'd enjoyed what happened to the air when he brought her forward, the hush and horror of women and men. He'd especially enjoyed the women's horror. And anyway, it served her right for trying to enter a world that wasn't hers. This way he'd managed to give her what she wanted and punish her at the same time. He'd done it on purpose, because he didn't know how he felt about the girl, or rather, he felt a lot of things toward her: irritation, curiosity, disgust, and something else, what was it? Recognition.

She had a rare ear. He'd known as soon as she started playing, and then he'd better understood why she'd asked. Unfair of God to put an ear like that on a woman.

He'd known only one other person with an ear like that, and that was his father, who was known, in Naples, as Il Magnifico, for his way with the violin. His renown was so great that noble-blooded violinists—the kinds of men who could read not only letters but also notes, who trained at conservatories and played for lavish operas at the Teatro di San Carlo—had been known to brave the Spanish Quarter's dirty crowded streets just to spy the rapid magic of Il Magnifico's hands. Six days a week, Il Magnifico worked in a pawnshop, sweeping the floor and dusting the relics of his neighbors' broken dreams. He played his violin on the street at night, after work, to escape the single room in which he, his wife, and his seven children lived. Nestore, the sixth child, used to sneak down to the street to watch him play. His mother never tried to stop him: it was hot and stuffy in their room, and there wasn't room for everyone or, on many nights, enough bread for every child. He'd crouch in the street and watch his father's hands, straining to memorize their motion, dizzied by the beauty of his sound. Il Magnifico played well-known ballads but also invented songs on the spot, melodies that seemed to weave an aural tapestry out of the chaos of men's banter, women's shouts, baby's wails, men's boasting, women's pleas, men's weeping and laughter and drunken fights.

When Nestore was eight, Garibaldi's army marched into the city, triumphant, and he went out with his brothers to watch. The soldiers moved in tight formation; they were shaggy from nights in the valleys but walked tall and proud; they were erasing the Kingdom of Naples once and for all to make way for a unified Italy. There would be one flag and one rule of law all the way from Trieste to Calabria. A new era had dawned for the people, or so Il Magnifico told his cousins that night.

Bah, said his cousins. That may be true for kings. For us it'll be the same as always.

A year later, Il Magnifico decided his cousins were right. He was just as poor as ever, and so were his neighbors, and so, it seemed, were the country peasants among whom riots sparked without end. Soldiers marched down from the North to quell them and, before long, invaded Naples. In 1862, Il Magnifico went through a transformation. He became convinced that all soldiers were *jettatura* and could curse you with a single look of their evil eye. Only the dead, he proclaimed, could be trusted. The dead began to speak to him in his bed and on the street and through the crumbling stone walls of the neighborhood, whispering mystic axioms, ruthless gossip, and winning lotto numbers. Naturally everyone believed him, at first, about the lotto numbers, as common knowledge had it there were few better experts on the swift turns of fortune than the dead, but after a while his losing streak undermined the authority of his sources. He lost money he didn't have, money he'd borrowed from his boss at the pawnshop. When he couldn't pay it back three men broke his nose and arm and told him to watch out for his family.

My arm, Il Magnifico shouted when he got home that night, his face still caked with blood. I'll never be able to play again.

Play? Mamma shouted back. What about eating? What are we all supposed to eat?

My arm, my arm.

You bastard.

They're going to come for you, and the children.

Oh God.

My arm. My life is gone.

You'll pawn your violin.

No!

Will it be enough?

Il Magnifico shut his eyes and didn't answer.

Children, Mamma said, on your knees, now. Pray to San Gennaro.

All seven children did as they were told. Nestore saw, behind closed eyelids, the decapitated head of his city's beloved patron saint, as well as a vial of his blood, both of which he had seen before when the priests had brought these sacred relics out into the light to celebrate San Gennaro's feast day. The crowd had been large, he'd only spied them from a great distance, but he knew they protected Naples so fiercely that, in 1631, they'd saved thousands from certain death when Vesuvius erupted and lava rushed down the mountain and stopped at the city's border. Still now the head and blood of this powerful saint was all that kept them from being buried alive like the people of old Pompeii, because, as it turned out, the world was always full of burning ash just waiting to destroy you. San Gennaro, save our family. Save my father. Protect us.

The next day, Il Magnifico pawned his violin, walked out of the shop, and immediately took his clothes off on the street corner where he'd always played. He marched, naked, his formidable sex erect and his broken arm hanging at an awkward angle, right out of the Spanish Quarter, toward the Piazza del Plebiscito, where he paraded in front of the Royal Palace until a group of nervous young soldiers shot him thirty-seven times. This was in 1863. Nestore was eleven years old. He never found out what his mamma did to clear their debts with the local mafia, but soon thereafter she gave up completely. She sat all day and stared at the stove as if any moment it might start cooking of its own accord. She didn't flinch when her two older daughters came home with cash they'd earned on their knees in alleys, didn't say a word when her second son disappeared into the dank mazes of the Spanish Quarter and never returned. She stopped listening, stopped eating, and stopped breathing soon enough as if by force of her own will. After Mamma's death, Nestore's older brother became the head of the household; there was often no bread, no water, no kindness. Nestore roamed the city barefoot, a street rat, picking pockets in the plaza, stealing bones from dogs in alleys, eating garbage, eating nothing. He wandered constantly, propelled by hunger and a wordless, formless rage. He took to going down to the port to watch the droves of country folk arriving to take steamships away to the New World. They had almost nothing to take with them, and looked dazed by the city. *Vedi Napoli e poi muori*. See Naples and die. That was the saying, though whether it meant the city was supposedly so grand you could die happy once you'd been there, or whether it meant the place would kill you, Nestore was never sure. All these people, all these Italians, huddled on the dock, tottering up the gangplank, was this a death for them? Was leaving a kind of death, and, if so, was it any worse than staying put in misery? He thought of his mother's vacant gaze, of the unnatural angle of his father's arm. He thought of food, obscene piles of it, meat and fruit and bread slathered in butter. He wondered where were they going, these ragged masses, what was waiting for them across the water, how they would live, what they would eat, what he might eat if he should join them.

He was nineteen years old when he left. In Buenos Aires he found more grime and poverty, though, back then, in 1871, the waves of immigration were just beginning to rise, and the city did not seem crowded, not to him, not compared to Naples. After a few weeks of sleeping on the street, he found a room in San Telmo—a whole room to himself, a luxury of space made possible by the yellow fever that had gripped the southern neighborhoods of the city: San Telmo, San Cristóbal, Montserrat. The rich families that had lived there for generations were frantically abandoning their homes to build new ones in the north. Their empty mansions were quickly becoming conventillos occupied by new immigrants. Nestore was the first poor person to inhabit his room. When he arrived, there were still two rich families on the block, stragglers caught up in planning their escape. They seemed disoriented and offended by their new neighbors, and never greeted them on the street, never even looked at them, as if they did not exist. *You don't know how bad it got during the sickness,* his Italian neighbors told him. *They blamed us for the outbreak, fired us from our jobs, our people wandered the streets without work, sometimes without a home, men died in the street of cold or of the sickness and it took hours for anyone to come for the bodies.* Nestore's room gleamed with gold-leaf wallpaper that had not yet begun to fade. An elaborately carved chest of drawers stood in one corner, wrought with details that must have taken days of sweat and thought and patience to create, all so someone could have a place to store her stockings. In the bottom drawer he found a single bottle of expensive women's perfume. It shook him. Every night, he sprayed a little of the perfume in the air before going to sleep, and lay down on his pallet under the sweet bite of its scent. He imagined the woman to whom it had belonged. She was a young virgin of noble blood, an innocent whose heart had been broken by the rapid deaths of all her sisters. She was the only one who had miraculously survived the plague. On her last night in this house, she had lain in bed in a translucent white nightgown that she'd soon removed so she could feel the night air of La Boca on her skin for the last time, because she would miss La Boca, she would miss her childhood, she was not a little girl anymore. She had lifted her thighs to the moonlight and prayed for health. She was hungry for life. She was hungry for a man. And then in a swift act of magic he closed the gap of space and time between them and appeared beside her, in this very room, and whispered *You're so beautiful, let me show you,* and he made love to her for hours, this noble daughter of Argentina, this girl who saw beyond the terrible things she'd heard about Italians, and she shook with pleasure and amazement as he did all the things he could think of doing to a maiden like that, or so he imagined as he lay alone on his hard pallet, sex in hand.

She became his secret bride. He kept the perfume bottle and summoned her to his side at night long after the scent itself was gone. Over the decades she remained the same, a startled virgin, grateful, voluptuous, perennially pure. He fucked hundreds of whores over the years, thinking of her. She was the only person in the world who truly loved him, who received him with open arms no matter what, the only person he could trust in a city full of people straining to survive.

There was no going back to Naples; nothing waited for him there. He worked at whatever jobs he could. He hauled stones and tanned leather and slashed cows' throats in the slaughterhouses at the edges of the city. He spent what little money he had on liquor and women, to hell with bread. Even when there was no money for drinks or sex, there was music, and sometimes music was enough, especially in Buenos Aires, where music rapped and hummed and pulsed on every corner—you didn't need to go to a bar, in those days: men appeared in alleys, spilled onto sidewalks, and played. Music on the night streets to terrorize the cobblestones. You had to be alert, you had to have your knife and wits about you, but what music: *payadas,* sung by pairs of country men who knew the life of gauchos and horses and lassos and dirt, who battled each other through song, caught up in a duel of wits, brandishing guitars and verses spit from their mouths as drunken crowds cheered them on; *habaneras,* sparked by sailors freshly arrived from Cuba who swarmed the whorehouses and drummed their blood-quickening beats with their knuckles on every surface they could find; *milongas,* those fast joyful songs that could fill a filthy alley with dancers more quickly than honey could draw flies; and *candombe,* the music of black people whose ancestors had come in ships from Africa, shackled, enslaved, and who now lived among the immigrants, as poor as they were, often poorer, with the most incredible music, unlike anything Nestore had ever heard, music played on drums built with cast-off barrels, whose rhythms interlocked to form a tight vast sound. There was no melody. In Europe it would have been called noise. But candombe had a potency that hit him in his belly, and in depths he hadn't known about. And to dance to it. It woke you up. It made you want to be awake again, made you want to live, if not another day, at least another hour, here, like this, right now, inside the drums' collective voice.

The first time he took up a violin and joined the music—some neighbors had gathered in a conventillo courtyard, it was four in the morning, and, drunk, he saw these men as, if not friends, the closest things to friends he'd found—he thought he saw a ghostly decapitated head in the shadows and felt that it was not San Gennaro but Il Magnifico, watching his son with wild bright eyes.

How much had changed since then, since those days when the tango was fresh and young and had a percussive drive and vibrancy, before it passed through the hands of hordes of immigrants, before it got slowed down by the *bandoneón* and the spirit of lament. The bandoneón, that boxy German instrument, accordion-like, made for voluptuous mourning. But the percussive bones of the tango were not entirely gone. They hovered under the surface, stepping, pulsing, tak-tak-takking in this music that was, along with a perfume vial, the only thing that had stayed with him all these years in which he'd lost so many things, even his sight, but not his life. Somehow, to his own surprise, he'd lived and lived, even as the men and music of yesterday kept disappearing in the grind of time. The cataracts had likely helped him live more years; people pitied a blind old man. Without sight, the realm of sound became vivid to the point of piercing. He was one of the few musicians left who recalled the old days of tango, and he shut them up inside himself, shared his memories with no one except through the sound of his violin.

Now, getting ready for work, he called out for the boy, his *lazarillo*, his guide, his surrogate eyes. The boy arrived without delay, touching Nestore's arm lightly to let him know. Reliable, the boy, and he never complained; no doubt he loved his job of escorting an old man to a brothel, and not only for the coin he got to palm for it. That widow-child, she'd never be able to play in the places where he, Nestore, had played. What did she think she was doing? She was a puzzle he couldn't decipher. He wondered whether she was beautiful. Whether she would let him bed her if he was very nice and very helpful. It had been at least thirty years since he'd been with a woman whom he hadn't paid. Nobody wanted a blind old man, not even María, the kindest of all whores, who stroked his brow afterward in a way that made him think of his mamma and almost weep with a blend of gratitude and relief. But even María wanted her pesos just like everybody else.

But he sensed this girl was not as easily swayed. There was something desperate about her, and desperation, he knew, always went one of two ways. It could either make you pliable as water or make you a living weapon. This girl was not pliable. Already the city was honing her into a blade.

And just as well, he thought as he left his conventillo on his lazarillo's arm—because if that widow-child kept going the way she was, pushing edges in a city that contained more edges than anything else, a blade was exactly what she'd need to be.

———

Six weeks after arriving in Buenos Aires, Leda received her first letter from her parents. It was written in her father's hand.

> *Cara Leda,*
> *What a tragedy. We are all wearing black and Dante's mother has not stopped weeping. We are glad that you, at least, are safe and that there have been people to help you.*
> *You must come home as soon as you can. A strange nation is no place for a young unmarried woman. Leda, anything could happen to you. We are gathering money and will send it dispatched on a boat as soon as possible. Use it for your ticket back to Naples. We are waiting for you here.*
> *Embracing you,*
> *Papà and Mamma*

She held the letter in her hands for a very long time, staring at her father's tight and tidy script. It was dusk, and the day's heat still oppressed the air, though outside her half-open door the women were starting to murmur about taking laundry down from the lines, because look at the clouds, just look. Leda still couldn't fathom how a day this hot could end in showers, but she'd seen them happen now, quick hot summer rains, and, in fact, one of them had caught her on the day Arturo took her to visit Dante's burial site, a humble workers' tomb on which her carnations lay damp and sad and fragile, like soiled girls. She felt torn. Part of her was tempted to obey her parents, go home, be wrapped in their embrace. But another, stronger part of her searched for a way out of the letter's confines, as though the sentences formed the bars of a cage and she were a trapped animal stalking for a loose chink through which she might flee.

If she went back, she'd have to be the same girl as before.

It was too late for that. She had tasted small scraps of freedom. She had lived with strangers and carved herself a home. She had worked all day and kept the pay for herself, not handed it to her father, and the money, however paltry, was hers. She had heard the great cacophony of a South American city, walked its streets, felt its infinite anonymity and muscle. She had even worn men's trousers and survived.

She had played the violin.

For four Sundays now, Nestore had called her over and walked her through a few tangos. Not many. Just two or three. His manner was harsh but she didn't care. Her attention was absorbed by those hands. The demonstrations, broken down line by line, would always be of different melodies than the week before. After that, perhaps as a test, he would strike up one he'd already taught her and she played along, Carlo joining in on the guitar. That was when she felt his skill, the bright confidence of his notes, their rich timbre. She made sure to play softly, so that her sound could hover underneath his, shaping itself to it. It was more than just technique that he was giving her. There was something larger, a kind of inheritance, and though she didn't fully know what it was, she felt it ripple out from him to her and absorbed it greedily. There was a gap between what her ear heard and what her fingers could manage, and she found this maddening, but each week that gap seemed to narrow just a little. The sounds she made were on their way to beautiful. Her hands were learning to make a wooden body sing.

Her neighbors had taken to dancing again, despite the unusual sight of a teenage widow playing with men. There was still disapproval, especially from Francesca. And Leda understood: she had broken the delicate equilibrium of good behavior, an equilibrium without which daughters were in danger of receiving the wrong impression and being led astray, perhaps into those worlds where music played all night and girls were torn beyond repair. Francesca had stopped speaking to her, except to discuss errands or plans for dinner, which made their long sewing days feel tense and even more interminable. The Di Camillo daughters did not follow their mother's lead. Palmira seemed to admire her all the more for breaking unspoken rules. She glowed at Leda as they stitched, continued with their banter and stories. Diana wavered between admiration and a kind of caution, which must, Leda thought, be born from a reluctance to receive her mother's wrath. Silvana was as gentle and ethereal with her as ever. Of course, once money ran out, she might be forced to move into the Di Camillos' room, if the invitation still stood (and it might not). Would she then have to capitulate to Francesca, obey her rules, stop bringing out her instrument?

She would rather go back to Italy.

No. That was not true. She would lose much more if she went home.

She could not bear the thought of stuffing herself back into the cloister of home, much less as a seventeen-year-old widow, constrained by black clothes and the most stringent expectations. The village gossips were vicious with widows who failed to seem sufficiently mournful, *Look at her, it's only been two years and my neighbor saw her laugh—out loud!—at the village well, can you imagine?* She did not want to be that kind of widow. She did not want to be a widow at all. Perhaps this made her despicable, but all she wanted was to be the person she became when she was locked up in her room, in Dante's clothes, playing soundless music. This strange new music, this tango, which could sing parts of her soul she'd never spoken. In those late-night moments alone in her room, she was freer than she'd ever been, freer than she'd ever thought a woman could become.

If only, she thought, I could trade music for bread. Then I could survive here without becoming a whore.

But even here in this América, this place of broken rules, such a thing was not possible. Only men played the tango. And she could not.

Unless.

And that is when the thought surged to the surface of her mind. Unless she lived as a man. She could not breathe. Outside, it had begun to rain, though she hadn't realized it until now. The air rushed and sighed as if releasing a dream. In the courtyard, the women were scrambling to take down their laundry; she should help them, she knew, even though the linens weren't hers. But she sat frozen by the thought, a dangerous thought, as dangerous as suicide, perhaps more so.

Water snaked across the threshold of her room, a dark wet guest.

Cora, my almost-sister, tell me, what would you do?

The first stage of Cora's change came on suddenly, and with such quiet that at first the village gossips didn't notice anything, certainly not enough yet to attach the word *Matta*—Crazy—to her name. She was thirteen years old then, Leda almost twelve. Cora stopped leaving her home. At first that was all. Leda waited for her, by the river, in the patio outside her back door where they'd always met to shell beans or stir cream into stubborn butter, but Cora didn't come.

Where is Cora, Mamma? Leda asked.

I don't know.

Can I take the eggs to her house this afternoon?

When Leda went on the errand, Cora's mother stood at the door and reached for the basket of eggs without a word, transferring them brusquely into a wooden bowl. She did not invite Leda in, and though Leda had always entered this house as easily as her own, something in her aunt's bearing kept her at the threshold. She craned her neck in an effort to spy Cora in the kitchen, but her aunt's formidable body blocked the light.

How is Cora?

She doesn't feel well, her mother said. Her voice was like the whip of a horse's tail, batting flies. It was then that Leda realized that Zia Crocifissa had not yet looked her in the face.

Does she have a fever? Can I bring her anything?

She'll be fine. Go home, Leda. She'll come out when she's better.

But Cora did not come out the rest of that week, not even for church or the Sunday family meal that followed. She did not come out for three weeks. When she finally emerged, it was for Sunday mass, where she sat in the front pew, the one with the brass plaque that read LA FAMIGLIA MAZZONI. Leda sat in the pew behind hers, as she was also a Mazzoni but not of the most important branch, and there was not enough room for all of them in the most honored seats. Throughout mass, as they stood and sat and kneeled to the familiar Latin prompts of the priest, Leda stared at the back of Cora's head, covered in white cloth, and willed her to turn around and meet her eyes, but she did not. Even when the time came to leave the pew and line up for communion, Cora kept her gaze down, a picture of piousness that was nothing like the vibrant girl Leda knew her to be, too bigmouthed for her own good, or so some said of her, full of song and protest and tall tales. After mass, at the family meal, Leda tried and failed to catch Cora's gaze. Cora kept her eyes on her plate. She did not laugh at any of the jokes that Dante or Tommaso told. She did not rise to help her mother when it came time to gather dishes from the table, retreat to the kitchen, and leave the men and boys to smoke and talk. Leda, hands freighted with dishes, looked over at the table in surprise. Cora was the only girl still there.

Cora's father, Mateo, glared at her. Get up and take my plate.

Cora did not move. She stared at the tablecloth.

Cora, Mateo said. Take. My. Plate.

Now all the men and boys were silent. The plates were heavy in Leda's arms, but she could not move. Even the clang of pots in the kitchen had stopped, and the only sound was the sharp plea of birds in the olive trees.

I'll take it, Papà, Dante said and rose to reach for his father's plate.

Mateo raised his hand to strike Dante, but his oldest son, Mario, was faster: he leapt from his seat and pushed his younger brother down into his seat. Dante pushed back at him, and the two brothers wrestled for a few moments, but Mario was not only taller and stronger but more ruthless; he cut the fight short with a punch that sounded across the courtyard and made the birds go quiet.

All this time, Cora had sat so still that she had not even seemed to blink.

Leda looked over at her own father, hunched at the table with a blank look on his face. He, too, had not moved. He almost gave the impression of being elsewhere, not at this table, transported by his own cowardice. In that moment Leda hated him more than she'd ever thought possible.

Now, Cora, Mateo said, you have five seconds to take my plate.

Leda could feel every mind in that courtyard counting in silence.

One. Two. Three.

Four.

Cora rose and took her father's plate, along with her own and Dante's, and carried them to the kitchen.

Mateo sat back and dabbed the edges of his mouth with his napkin.

As if she'd been waiting for this moment to make her entrance, Cora's mother emerged with a tray bearing a bottle of grappa and an army of small glasses for the men.

Leda found Cora in the kitchen. She was washing already. Leda picked up a towel and began to dry. They were silent for a long time.

Are you all right? Leda finally said.

Cora shrugged.

You're feeling better? You're not sick anymore?

It seemed that she had said the wrong thing. Cora turned away from her, toward her tub of dirty water.

Do you want to go to the river when we're done?

Cora shook her head. I'm tired.

After that, Leda stopped trying, and the two of them worked in silence. When the dishes were all clean and put away, Cora disappeared into her room.

It took three more weeks for Leda to persuade Cora to spend some time alone with her. It was a Sunday, after the family meal. They went to their favorite place by the river.

Leda took off her shoes. Come wade with me!

Cora shook her head.

Leda stood, unsure, then walked in anyway. The water was cold and tightened the skin of her feet. She tried to think of something that would cheer her cousin. Tell me a story.

I don't want to.

Please? We can do any one you want. The Inferno. Diana and Actaeon. Old Pompeii.

You already know them, so what's the point?

She said it harshly, and Leda could not help but recoil. Cora looked at her, and for the first time in two months she let Leda meet her gaze and did not look away. Leda searched Cora's eyes for traces of the girl she'd been before, for clues to what had changed in her, was it the woman's blood? already? more painful than they'd thought?

When Cora spoke again, her voice was gentle. You know what, since you know the stories so well by now, you should pick one and tell it to me.

Leda hesitated. This was a steep reversal to the roles they'd always had. She'd always been the listener, never the teller. But she stepped out of the river, back onto the grass, and began.

She decided against the Inferno, and told instead about old Pompeii, where before the eruption people had lived full-blooded lives: men built houses and painted frescoes in the courtyards of the rich, portraying Athena on her throne, Actaeon ripped to shreds by dogs, Poseidon dreaming up an earthquake while sea nymphs wove spells into his hair; women married, gave birth, and chased down the neighbor boys who climbed the garden walls to steal fruit, cuffing their ears without mercy; girls pined for suitors their fathers would never accept; boys wrote maudlin lyrics in the moonlight and cursed their fate as hopeless suitors; children ran through the narrow streets, careful not to drop the eggs in their baskets; children dropped the eggs in their baskets and wept as though the world had ended; men, women, and children alike crushed grapes for wine with enthusiastic feet, certain they would still be alive later to drink it, innocent of the cataclysm that awaited them—except for one young maiden who dreamed of Vesuvius, over and over, shaking and beginning to roar, warning of fire to come. All night in her dreams the mountain roared, but when she woke there was nobody to whom she could tell the dream. Because in ancient Pompeii, Vesuvius was thought to be a mountain like any other. Nobody knew it was a volcano, with a hollow belly and a hidden, deadly power. So who would believe the maiden's dream? Who ever heard of a roaring mountain?

As Leda talked, Cora lay in the grass on her belly, her face hidden in green blades. When she finally lifted her head, her face was caked with dirt. Leda liked her face that way, painted with the brown symbols of an incomprehensible language.

Keep going.

I'm not sure what comes next.

It can be anything.

Leda thought as hard as she could, but before something occurred to her, Cora said, Let's run away.

What?

Let's run off together. Just you and me.

Where to?

I don't know. To Naples. To the sea. Or maybe all the way to Rome.

And do what?

Live, what else?

But how would we live?

Freely.

That wasn't what Leda had meant. She had never heard of two young girls surviving away from their families, without a husband or father to care for them, alone in a large city or on the slope of a volcano. It was not possible. Maybe Cora meant this as the seed of another story, one that she should follow into imaginative flights—but it was too late. Cora had sat up and begun to wipe the dirt from her cheeks.

Forget it, you're right, it's stupid.

They never talked about it again. It was the last day they talked at all. With everything that happened next, the words *let's run away* would come to haunt Leda's nights and shake her awake in bed to demand she open her eyes and meet their stare.

———

The quick summer rain subsided soon after nightfall, but Leda could not sleep. She played her violin in silence until her fingers throbbed, then lay in bed and stared into the dark, cradling her instrument against her chest. The dangerous thought had sunk its teeth into her mind and would not let her go. The next day, she drank it with her breakfast coffee, stitched it into every sleeve and collar, stepped to its rhythm on her walk to buy bread.

She thought about how she would do it. Make a new life as a man. An unnatural act, unheard of, a magician's sleight of hand—or even more than hand: a sleight, if such a thing existed, of the whole body.

To disappear from your own life. To reappear into another one.

An impossible thought.

And yet, if there was any place in the world where it could be possible, that place had to be América. Land of self-creation. Of rootlessness. Of New Babel. Not that Buenos Aires didn't have its walls and rules. But still, perhaps, in a city that held so much noise and anonymity, so many émigrés with so many cultures and tongues, surely mad things could make their way into reality.

As she sat in the patio and numbed her fingers with stitch and needle, she considered what life as a man could afford her. Other jobs. There was much more work out there for men. And the ability to walk down the street, at any time of day or night. What sort of work might she do? She didn't have the strength to work at the docks, like Dante and the men she'd seen the other day, straining under the hot sun, chests bare and muscled. She could never be that. But there were factories. Shops. Even places where men were paid to play music, as Carlo and Nestore did. How could she find out where they went?

Then there was the problem of convincing the world she was a man. Not an easy challenge. If she failed she'd be in a danger so severe that she didn't dare to think about it—though the images arose, a knot of men, outraged, drunk, stronger than she, prepared to beat the transgression out of her, or worse. She had no reason to think it would be otherwise. Just last month one of the bachelors in her conventillo had been beaten to a pulp in a bar brawl, and though the women nursed him to health without a second thought, their judgment was clear: he'd failed to protect himself, he was too gentle and should expect nothing less. As for women themselves, they deserved protection in this city, but not when they crossed lines: look at that girl Francesca mentioned, who used to live here, who was turned out for becoming a prostitute, and to hell with what happened to her next. No. She couldn't fail. She took stock of what she had. A low voice. Small breasts. Narrow hips. Height. Long limbs, long torso. Who would ever have thought that her physique could prove an asset, this same shape that her mother had bemoaned, *how will you ever carry a baby in that body, you're like a tube, things will move in and out of you but never stay and grow the way they should*. And then there was her face: lean, angular, not soft as a woman's ought to be (look at Palmira, bent over her sewing, the lovely curves of her cheeks). Leda's own face was dominated by a nose that jutted out with undeniable vigor, a beak of a nose, with a stubborn knot in the middle of its slope. The nose of a man, some would say. Not delicate at all. Fearsome.

The light had grown heavy and golden with the passing of the day. It settled on the white cloth in her hands like honey. Her fingers hurt. She wanted to stick her needle into something—anything—her own flesh if necessary—so she could be rid of sewing, so her fingers could spring free.

Could she do it?

If she set out as a man, alone and hidden, nothing but herself and Buenos Aires and the violin, what would she find? What would she become?

She burned to find out.

Three weeks later, the money arrived from Italy. She did not buy a ticket with the cash, as the accompanying letter instructed. Instead, she folded it up and hid it in the case of her violin.

The next step: cut off her hair.

The wig shop was not difficult to find. Alfonso Di Bacco had told her about it, though it pained him—truly *pained* him, he insisted, to his *heart*—that she should feel the need to resort to such extremes.

"Keep your hair and I'll give you free bread."

"Thank you, Don Alfonso, but I have to do this."

"You have no other choice?"

She shook her head, and his face was so mournful, so swept up in her tragedy, that guilt stabbed her. Surely it was a sin to hide the truth from a good man.

The wig shop was run by a Genovese man with doleful eyes who put her hair into two braids and sliced them off so quickly that tears of shock stung her eyes. All those years—all seventeen years of her life—of growth, all cut away in an instant, dumped on a heap of amputated braids behind the counter like a common unmarked grave. Ashes to ashes, braid to dust.

"If you want to get some shape to that," the Genovese man said, not unkindly, "my brother-in-law has a barbershop down the block."

I am dead, she thought as she held her hand out for the money and walked directly to the barbershop. I am dead, she thought as she gazed at the image in the mirror when she sat down in the barber's chair. The barber was portlier than his brother-in-law, with receding gray hair and the red nose of a hard drinker; he was missing the smallest finger of his left hand. To her relief, they were alone in the shop, which smelled of lavender, camphor, and sweat. Leda asked him to cut her hair like a man's.

"Are you sure?" the barber asked, astonished.

She nodded.

"Because I could—"

"Like a man's," she said, more firmly this time, meeting his eyes in the mirror.

The barber squared his jaw and folded his arms over his chest. This was going to be harder than she thought.

She pulled out her photograph of Dante. "This," she said, "is my husband, may he rest in peace. All I ask is that you give me hair like his."

The barber stared at the picture. "Dead?"

"Yes."

"How long?"

"Three months." And then, seeing her advantage, she added, "He was nineteen years old."

"So young! How did he die?"

"The police shot him. At a workers' strike."

The barber sucked his teeth mournfully. He held the photograph to the light. "Handsome."

"Yes."

"I had an aunt who was widowed young. She never wore a cheerful color or face again. She was almost thirty when it happened—while you, you look almost like a child." He shook his head. "You shouldn't marry your grief."

"That's not what I'm doing."

The barber eyed her, and for a grim instant she thought he might ask her what, in fact, she was doing. But then he handed back the photograph and reached for his scissors. "Migration is a cruel whore," he said and set to cutting.

Leda hoped that Dante's soul, wherever it was and may it truly rest as she had said in peace, would forgive her for having used his photograph like a joker at a gambling table. Perhaps, she thought as she closed her eyes, surrendering to the scissors, he would even understand what she'd done, the need to run, the urge to be free at any cost.

"Well then," the barber finally said, "what do you think?"

She stared at herself in the mirror. A man-woman stared back at her. With hair like Dante's. Nothing soft about its angles. Nothing pretty at all.

Alarm rushed through her. Her femininity, gone. Without it she felt ugly, worthless—and yet somehow elated, lifted to an unknown and dizzying plane.

She paid the barber and stood.

"Don't get lost," he called to her as she left the shop.

The question *what am I?* looped through her mind as she walked home. Answers roared in from all sides, from the walls of buildings, the slit of sky above her.

You're a beast.

An aberration.

A mistake of nature.

A woman possessed by demons.

And then another voice rose up inside her, brash and unexpected: that may be true, but if it is, then let the demons have their song!

The women of the conventillo gave her looks of pity. Even Francesca's scowl softened, a little; she knew, after all, the sorrows of female survival. Look at the young widow, running out of pesos, selling her hair to keep from turning to the streets. This when all they could see was a kerchief around her head; if they could see the cut she'd gotten, then what looks would she get? She didn't dare think about it.

"You really did it?" Palmira whispered to her at the stove. "You really cut it all off?"

"Yes."

"Your hair was beautiful. Your best feature."

Leda said nothing, listening for the unsaid ending of that sentence, *and without it you'll be ugly, no one will want you.*

"I can't imagine." Palmira washed two green peppers and handed them to Leda. "You're braver than I."

Leda took the damp peppers and began to dice them. Her knife moved briskly. Palmira is wrong, she thought; I'm not brave at all. Brave and desperate are not the same thing. As she chopped, she considered how she'd execute the last stage of her plan. Could she test her disguise, sneak out in men's clothes for an hour or two and see how the world responded? No. Too risky. There was only one sliver of time, at three thirty in the morning, when everyone was either away or asleep, so she'd be trapped out on the streets with no way of coming home unseen. She'd have to do it all at once. Tonight. Put on Dante's clothes, gather up her most essential things, and walk out once and for all. Walk—where? To the edge of La Boca and beyond it, into a neighborhood where nobody knew who she was, and where she'd be known, from that moment forward, only as a man. Beyond La Boca, the rest of Buenos Aires waited, untouched, as yet unknown, each neighborhood a world unto itself, especially for womenfolk, who never went very far, and it was women who posed the greatest threat to her as they were the most likely to look closely, most likely to wag their tongues. And so when she arrived in the next neighborhood over (what was it called? even this she didn't know) she would seek out a room, then a job, and then, if she was very lucky, a place to play the violin.

She excused herself from dinner that night and went to the pawnshop down the block, across from the butcher, where she sold her pearled blue hat. She would have liked to bring her dresses, too, for more cash in her pocket—the more cash the better for a leap like this—but could not think of how to do so without raising too much suspicion.

At midnight, alone in her room, she put on Dante's clothes. This time, she used a bedsheet to bind her breasts down first. Shocking, how much they flattened under pressure. How malleable her body seemed to be.

One in the morning. She combed her hair. Recombed it. Her hair grew slick and shiny with the olive oil she'd taken from the kitchen, as did the comb, which was the only thing of Cora's she'd been able to steal out of her room after she died. Had she used too much oil? Too little? She'd have to learn the way men did it. And she'd have to buy some grape-seed oil, so she didn't smell like a salad—the thought made her smile. She thought of her brother Tommaso, grooming in the mornings, his comb's thin wooden teeth gleaming in the new light. She pictured his face, how he would look if he saw her now. Disbelief. Disgust. No, no, push the thought away, I am sorry Tommaso but I can't let you into this moment. She wiped her hair with a cloth and reshaped it. Better. It was almost alarming, how much she looked like a man.

Two in the morning. Nothing left to prepare. No one stirred anymore, and Carlo had left for work, but she was afraid to leave quite yet; she had heard people across the hall shuffle to the spigot for water around this hour. Not that they couldn't get up at three or five or any moment in between. No hour was completely safe. She crossed her hands. Uncrossed them. Should she play? She felt too nervous. Instead, she took out the violin and held it, traced its curves, took a little comfort in its beauty.

She wondered what had gone through Cora's mind in those last moments as her lungs and vision filled with water. Cora, she thought into the stark night air, I owe you this, a true escape, a break in the walls, come with me, I'm reaching for you, we'll do it this time, finally run away.

Three in the morning. Leda rose. She left a note for her neighbors on the table in her room—*you've been kind to me, I'll always be thankful*—and slipped out in the middle of the night, taking nothing but the suit on her back, her pesos, a few of Dante's clothes in a potato sack, Cora's comb, and the King of Naples's violin. She left behind the trunk she'd brought from Italy, with its empty folded dresses, vestiges of a woman who no longer walked the earth.

PART TWO

◆

Noise and Blades and Death and Also This

She walked to the west, out of La Boca, and wandered foreign streets as they slowly lost their grasp on the night. Men hovered in doorways and on crumbling balconies. She willed herself to look them in the eyes. They did not stare at her in horror or surprise; a quick assessment and the gaze moved on. Whatever they were looking for in her face, they seemed satisfied. Nobody knew who she was, nor did anybody want to know. Was she walking too much like a woman? Or exaggerating the bravado of men? She couldn't tell. She felt larger than her own body, almost floating. The night air wrapped its warmth around her. She didn't dare stop walking. The potato sack hung over her shoulder; her violin swung gently at her side, an anchor, the only thing yoking her to the earth.

Light spread gently over Buenos Aires. A new neighborhood unfolded around her, worn old mansions pressed together on cobbled streets. She felt drawn to it; the men she saw leaving for work in the early dawn seemed like workers, immigrants, like those in La Boca. Children stirred behind shuttered windows, bickering in Italian. She crossed the plaza more than once, doubling back, returning, tracing a wide lasso through the streets. Her eyes stung from lack of sleep and her body felt taut. More men began to fill the sidewalks, walking quickly, some in pairs or groups, others silent and alone. Two workers in factory uniform approached her on the sidewalk. The shorter man was speaking in Spanish, too quickly for her to understand. The taller man was shaking his head with mournful appreciation, as though the tale were at once terrible and engaging. The short man stopped and spit in the street. Just like that. Gathered and spit a fast bullet of saliva onto the cobblestones. Then he wiped his face with his sleeve and kept talking, the tall man listening as if nothing had happened.

She'd seen men spit on the street before, but this time it dizzied her, the freedom of vulgarity. The man's ease with it. He had made it look so natural. As though the whole world were his spittoon.

It took her two more blocks to gather up the courage to try it herself. She looked around. The sidewalk had become crowded with men on their way to work. She was almost invisible among them. Draw the shoulders back. Cheeks taut. Spit.

Nobody saw, or seemed to care. The saliva made a dark mark on the cobbles. *How unladylike,* she could hear her mother say. And if her mother were here she'd surely grasp her by the ear and drag her off the street in shame. But she was not here. Only I am here, Leda thought. Alone with this city and I will spit in its streets when I choose.

She walked until the morning sun was high enough to break up the shadows of tall buildings and she could no longer deny her need for sleep. She listened for Italian-speaking voices, and approached a grave matron, a boulder of a woman, who was dumping a bucket of dirty water in the street.

"*Buongiorno, signora,*" she said, in a low voice, reveling in the sound—her own male voice!—and at the same time scared that it didn't sound right, that it would give her away. "I'm looking for a place to rent."

"We're full," the woman said, without looking up, irritated, as though she'd answered the question so many times that she was sick of the routine. "There's nothing, not even a corner."

"I see," Leda said. "Sorry for the bother."

She had already begun to walk away when the woman called out, "Young man."

It took an instant for Leda to register that she was the young man in question. She turned.

"Where are you from?"

"Campania."

"There's a group of Neapolitan men down the block, next to the grocer."

Leda thanked the woman and walked on, elated at having survived her first conversation. She tried the entrance beside the grocer—tall ornate double doors that suggested a grandeur lost in time—where a young mother with one child on her hip and another burying its face in her skirts told her that there was in fact a bachelor room that likely had space, but all the men were away at work right now and they'd have to make the decision, could he come back that night at nine o'clock?

She didn't trust herself out in the city, without sleep, until nightfall. Nor would she be safe closing her eyes anywhere in the streets. She thought fast. "I've been working all night, *signora*. I'm very tired. Is there any corner where I could rest my head for a peso?"

The woman eyed her more steadily. "A whole peso?"

Leda hoped her offer made her sound more generous than desperate. "A whole peso."

"You'd have to pay up front."

"Of course."

The woman stared at Leda as though she were a beast with two heads, and Leda braced herself to bolt if needed. But then the infant, indifferent to these proceedings, began clawing at the woman's shirt, trying to uncover her breast. The woman slapped the infant's hand back and shrugged. "You can have my room for a few hours. Come with me."

Leda followed the woman down a hall and through the courtyard to a small room where an old man sat in the corner, drinking grappa. He was missing his right leg. His right pant leg flopped emptily below the knee. He glared at Leda and the young mother as they came in.

"He's just going to sleep here for the day, Nonno," the young mother said in a scolding voice. "And he's paying, a peso no less, so don't you give him any trouble." She nodded at Leda. "Don't worry. He's harmless."

"Thank you."

"You're welcome. The peso."

Leda paid the woman, who fingered the coin.

"What did you say your name was?"

"Dante." The only name she could imagine herself answering to.

"Well then, sleep well, Dante," the woman said and left.

Leda lay down on the bed, not daring to get under the rumpled covers with the old man's hostile eyes on her. Was he examining the shape of Leda's body? Could he possibly suspect? A false move and she could die. The room smelled of stale garlic and urine, and every muscle in her body felt tense. The old man's eyes ran over her again, and she realized that it wasn't her body he was staring at but the violin case. She wrapped her arms around it and took a deep breath. Old man, she thought, just try to steal my instrument, you'll see how fast I wring your wrinkled neck with my bare hands. What a thought to have about a cripple. She was ashamed of it, of who she was becoming, but she still kept her arms wrapped tightly around the violin. She closed her eyes and lay awake for a long time, peering at the old man every once in a while, until she saw that he'd dozed off and she finally descended into sleep.

When she woke, it was almost dark, and the laborers were home. They sat on wooden crates in the courtyard, smoking, talking, twenty or so men in their undershirts or no shirts at all, taking relief from the day's heat. I will never be able to strip like that, Dante thought, acutely aware of the sweat soaking her armpits and the torn sheet wrapped tight around her chest. She wished she'd wiped her forehead before coming out, so she could appear more comfortable in her shirt and vest.

The men eyed her, neither smiling nor hostile. "So you're the new kid."

She nodded, bracing herself for questions.

A tall man with a scraggly beard offered her a cigarette. She put it in her mouth and accepted his light. The smoke scratched at her lungs with unexpected strength. She tried to suppress her cough but failed.

"What, don't tell me you've never smoked before!"

"What are you, an altar boy?"

A laugh rippled across the courtyard. Dante felt herself flush. She took another drag of her cigarette and willed her lungs to cooperate, this time with more success.

"That's the ticket."

"More like it."

"Men don't smoke where you're from?"

Dante shrugged, at a loss for an answer.

"Don't talk much, do you?"

She shrugged again. The attention hollowed her with fear.

"You must be a country boy."

There, she nodded.

"Where from?"

"Campania."

The men brightened; almost all of them were from Naples and the surrounding province of Campania, which, here in América, was enough for them to claim her—or him, as they thought—as one of their own. Once they'd established where her village was, and that no one there was from the same place, the focus shifted away from her, to good-natured banter about whose home neighborhood or town was best. When dinner came, it was harder than she'd thought it would be to let the women serve her along with the other men. She ate her spaghetti and stale bread in the courtyard, with the other single men and a few married ones who hadn't left to accompany their families in their respective rooms. The young mother who'd given her a bed that day brought her a glass of wine, and she tried to refuse it, as she already had to pee and had not yet figured out where and how to do it with more privacy than chamber pots afforded.

"What!" one man said, exposing a mouth full of masticated pasta. "No wine for the altar boy?"

"No blood of Christ?"

"Come on, have a little."

She complied. The wine was sharp, with a hint of vinegar. The men toasted with her, and that was when she realized that she'd been welcomed into their room.

When the time came for sleep, she found a space in the middle of the floor and laid her potato sack out as a pillow. The men—there were eight bachelors in all—took turns pissing into a chamber pot and rinsing their faces at the washstand. They undressed in front of each other, keeping their gazes to themselves, but still, she could not join them, nothing for it, she'd have to sleep in her clothes. Dante slipped out and stood in line at the single toilet with a closed door. At least there was this, a lucky step up in the world, a private place to shit. Her bladder ached so much she had to will herself not to shift from one foot to the other. She was afraid the other people in line might hear her and wonder why she hadn't used the chamber pot like all the other men, but fortunately the clatter and voices from the nearby kitchen drowned out the sound. Then, finally, she lay down to sleep on the strip of floor for which she'd pay sixteen pesos a month, and found herself wide awake. She'd slept all day, she was off-kilter; and also, the air rippled with breaths and snores and her own terror that one of them might suspect her lie and come over to feel and test the shape of her body, or simply try to steal the violin out of her arms or the pesos from her pockets, in which case she could lose everything, cash, instrument, her false manhood. It took her hours to fall asleep, and, in the meantime, to stave off thoughts of the future, she ran through all the tangos she knew, letting their rhythms swell and ebb through her body.

The next day, when the men went to work and the women set about chores she didn't dare to offer help with, Dante embarked on a long walk around the neighborhood. San Telmo, it was called. It was different from La Boca in some ways. It was further from the port, and it had none of the clapboard and sheet metal buildings painted in many different colors. All the buildings were tall old mansions that the rich had abandoned to the foreign hordes decades ago, during a legendary bout of yellow fever. Stately houses now crowded with the families of the poor. Bakers and grocers with their wares in wood crates on the sidewalk, and cafés shut down to sleep for the day. And there was a large plaza called Dorrego at the center of the neighborhood, where men came to drink and play dice in the evenings. And yet, for all the differences, the neighborhood was also similar to La Boca in many ways. There was the confluence of languages, overlapping with each other like streams collapsing into the ocean. Vendors trolled the street with their carts, selling bread fresh from their conventillo kitchens or old boots gathered from God knows where. So many ways of scraping out survival in the New World. So much long hard scraping to be done. She walked broad streets and damp alleys. The buildings cast full-bodied shadows across the cobbles, one after another, street after stony street. The green foliage and brown earth of Alazzano were so far away it almost seemed like a dream. Or maybe that had been the waking time and *this* was the dream, this walking in Dante's clothes, answering to Dante's name, in a city so large and crowded it could almost encapsulate a world.

She'd landed with good people. But she could not stay. She realized this two days later, when a bathtub appeared in the bachelors' room and the men began taking turns stripping and stepping calf-deep into water to scrub off the week's detritus and indignities. It was everybody's room and men walked in and out during the baths, to fetch something from their small stashes of possessions, or to prepare for their turn.

"Altar Boy," said Alfredo, the oldest bachelor, who'd been the first to bathe. "You go next."

"No, thanks," she said. She was sitting in the courtyard, rolling her second cigarette in a row. She pictured herself shrinking and disappearing among the shredded leaves, rising to the sky as smoke.

"You may as well take it when it's offered," said Emilio, a wiry young man who thrashed in his sleep. "Next week you'll get stuck with the last bath, when you can't see through the water."

The other men laughed. Leda smiled briefly, but her chest constricted as if the sheet around it were a tightening fist. She could not go in there, could not take a turn, and could not tell them why.

"I'm going out," she said, and she grasped her violin and fled to the street.

She wandered for the next few hours, thinking fiercely. She was furious at herself for not having figured out this dilemma before. Each moment demanded so much attention, all her senses on alert, that she was not preparing for the future. She turned a corner. It was Saturday evening and the streets teemed and hummed. She had to prepare for the future. She could never bathe with the bachelors. But she could not live without bathing, or without changing her clothes, which she had not done for three days. She'd tried to rinse her armpits at the washbasin without removing her shirt, but it wasn't the same, and made her look eccentric, if not outright crazy. Refusing to share the bathtub had made it even worse.

She had no choice but to look for a private place to live, a small miracle for an immigrant.

She began her search immediately. She asked women at windows, old men in doorways drinking *mate*, shopkeepers with dubious smiles. It was such a strange request, a private room, that people looked at her with amazement, no doubt imagining perverse reasons a young man would have to seek such extreme conditions.

It was a grocer who gave her the clue she was searching for.

"Go to La Strega," he said. "She lives around that corner, there, three doors down. The blue door with seven silver nails hammered in beside the doorbell. Don't ask me what the nails are for. They've just always been there, and nobody removes them, even though they have nothing to hold up. La Strega talks to everyone and everyone talks to her. If the place you're looking for exists, she's the one who'll know."

Leda thanked him and walked to the corner, thinking, La Strega! The Witch! A name that conjured up a picture of a hunched woman with a withered face and eels slithering through her hair. How did anyone come to live with a name like that?

But La Strega turned out to be a smiling woman, tall and plump and almost beautiful, old enough to have children her own height but young enough to turn heads on the street. She looked Dante up and down, briskly, then ushered her into the foyer of the conventillo, from which Leda saw a cluster of women and girls taking down linens, men smoking, and small children playing at battle with sticks for swords.

"So. You're looking for what?"

"A private room."

"Hmmm!"

"It can be small. I don't need much. Just a door and walls."

"We don't have anything."

"I'll pay eighteen pesos a month."

La Strega looked shocked. She started to say something, then shut her mouth, gathered herself. "Well. Let's see. You see those stairs?" She gestured across the courtyard, where a narrow flight of stairs rose over the bathroom to the crumbling balcony above. "That door at the top? That's a room, a closet, really. We use it to store things, but I suppose we could clear it out for you."

"Yes."

"Yes?"

"I want the room."

"Wait a minute. You haven't even seen it."

"That's fine."

"It's tiny. Just enough space to lie down and sleep."

"I don't need much."

"And the roaches. It's right over the kitchen. Look, young man, I just want to be honest about everything."

"That door up there, it closes?"

"Yes, of course."

"That's all I need," said Leda.

"Why does it matter so much to you?"

"Because I'm a musician." Strange, bold, to clasp that label to herself.

"I can see that," La Strega said, gesturing toward the violin case.

"So I'd like to practice. If I can close a door then I can play without disturbing my good neighbors."

"You can play in the patio, you know. You don't need a private room to do that."

La Strega tightened her lips and took a good look at Leda, who cringed with panic. What a stupid thing to say. How many musicians were there in San Telmo who practiced in the communal patios of their conventillos, surrounded by relatives and strangers? She reached around in her mind for a better lie, but came up dry.

"You have a secret, don't you?"

The panic grew. She had nowhere to run.

"Well, listen." La Strega bent closer. She smelled like bread and orange rinds. "I don't care. God knows that in this city we all do strange things to survive."

That night, Leda brought her sack of belongings from the other conventillo—the men's disappointment at her departure surprised her—and moved into her room. The place was as tiny as La Strega had said it would be—not a room at all, but a closet—and it stank of mold and rot. There was no bed, just a pallet on the floor, and no window either. The only indication of day or night came from a strip of light under the door. But it was hers. His. Was it for Leda or for Dante? For the woman under her clothes or for the man she was now dreaming into being? It didn't matter. That first night she woke up gasping for air and had to walk out onto the small landing that overlooked the central patio below. The patio was empty and the doors were closed; her neighbors were all asleep. She'd met only a few of them, more tomorrow. She smoked a cigarette, which had quickly become a delectable act, and gazed down at the black and white floor tiles, up at the tentative stars. She thought about stars, about distance, about closed doors and open hands, as her cigarette smoke rose into the night sky and disappeared.

When she went back inside, she slept deeply, alone with the roaches and her violin.

Babel. Now she truly lived in Babel. This conventillo had three rooms bursting with Calabrese, relatives of La Strega's husband; a French family in another room; a quiet childless couple from Spain that piled in with the Calabrese; a network of Lebanese brothers and uncles and wives and children whose exact relationships took weeks for Leda to decipher; and an assortment of single men who spoke to each other in a Spanish inflected with various accents.

Their home was called La Rete. It was the first conventillo that Leda had known to possess a name, and this gave it a distinctive feeling, as though it were its own miniature city inside of the larger one. The atmosphere at La Rete was as friendly as it was chaotic, the courtyard a realm of constant washing, sewing, folding, peeling, fighting, smoking, whittling, chatting, playing, shouting, laughing, whispering as if a lowered voice could pull a magic curtain of privacy around you, which, thanks to the tacit code of conventillo life, it sometimes did. When she felt lonely, Dante sat with La Strega as she scrubbed linens or pots in the courtyard, listening to her stories about Scylla, the small fishing village on the Calabrian coast where she was born, and that, for all its poverty, had made its mark on history as the place where Odysseus had crashed all but one of his ships. According to La Strega's version, that great Greek warrior had been navigating through the narrow strait between the crags of Scylla and the island of Sicily when a terrible monster—some said a witch—attacked them and caused the ships to break apart and men to break their skulls against the rocks. "Homer didn't know this," La Strega said, "but two of those sailors were skewered underwater on a single spear. Their skeletons remained for a millennium." And then she smiled as though describing the sweetest blossoms of her homeland. "As for the Sea-Witch, who lived up on the crags and beat Odysseus, I've never seen her, but they say she never died. We used to leave out figs with bread and honey to appease her."

Dante kept her eyes on La Strega's washing tub. She worked with great efficiency, her hands as skilled as Mamma's or her own. It was difficult to sit and watch a woman work without joining in, wringing out blankets, washing shirts. Her hands were unaccustomed to such stillness. She smoked cigarettes to keep them occupied. Even this, the listening to La Strega's stories, was dangerously un-male of her. But it delighted La Strega to have a new audience. Her mind was bright with bleeding sailors, broken ships, honeyed offerings.

La Strega's name had clung to her ever since she first opened her mouth in Buenos Aires and told the founding tale of her village. At first she didn't like being named for the witch, but then she got used to it, partly because it linked her to Scylla, and partly because she had no other choice: in Argentina, nicknames stuck to people with such strength that their original names often went forgotten. She missed Scylla so much, she told Dante, that the pain of it was physical.

"What do you miss?" asked Dante.

Everything, La Strega told her. The high cliffs whipped smooth by the Mediterranean. The briny smell of the wind. The old stone houses on their narrow streets overlooking the water, perched above it as if constantly collapsing into the sea. The baskets of fish the men brought home on good days, sleek, silvery, eyes glazed from the sight of Death. Above all, the nets that hung everywhere—on walls, across doorways, draped over tables to dry in the sun. La Strega had learned to mend nets the same year she learned to walk. All the girls did. Not only that: in Scylla, all the babies were born into a net—the older women spread it on the ground so that the new mother could lie or stand or squat over it until the baby came. Everybody knew, in Scylla, that it was bad luck to give birth without a net under the woman as she opened. La Strega suspected, though she couldn't prove, that the custom had originated as a kind of protection against the Sea-Witch and her great skill at decimating lives. When she became pregnant in Buenos Aires, she was terrified to give birth without a net, and tried desperately to find or make one, but she and her husband couldn't afford the rope, so she'd had to give birth onto a naked tile floor, not once but four times. To make up for this tragedy, she'd named their home La Rete. The Net. Her best attempt to battle the bottomless threat of the evil eye.

"You use what you have," La Strega said. "To ward off chaos. And chaos is everywhere, it's work that's never finished, like this laundry, like feeding hungry mouths. In Scylla the old people used to say, Odysseus's journey never ends. Well! No one knows that better than immigrants."

People did not eat together at La Rete, separated as they were by gulfs of language, food, and culture. La Strega cooked for bachelors for a modest fee. On Sundays, each group adhered to its own traditions, shedding the pressure to translate every word into Spanish, allowing each mind to rest inside its mother tongue. Sunday lunch was a separate affair, taken in individual rooms or at far-flung tables in the central patio on hot days. And, afterward, no tango and no dancing. Leda tried to hide her disappointment.

She went out searching for the tango. On a Sunday, after lunch, she took a walk in the afternoon light, keeping her ears pricked for music. She found it down the block and around the corner, at a yellow-shuttered window. Violin, guitar, laughter. She stood outside the window for a long time, listening, trying to make herself invisible. The street was empty. April had come, and a cold autumn wind bit at her neck and ears. She turned up her collar and leaned against the wall. They were amateurs, these musicians, with none of Nestore's control—their rhythm was erratic, the guitar a little out of tune—but their enthusiasm made the song beautiful. Violin as lead voice. Violin soaring. Steps of dancers. Steps of someone approaching the front door. She didn't want to be found here, a strange lingering man. She walked on quickly and did not turn back to see who opened the door.

She began taking these walks every Sunday. She learned there was music in many conventillos, after church and food, like the third point in a holy trinity to mark the Lord's Day. Or so it seemed to her. Perhaps nobody else saw the music as part of any trinity, or as part of anything holy for that matter. Perhaps it was just one brief portal of escape from the grind of long days and suffocating nights in crowded buildings so far away from one's familiar land. A respite. A halcyon moment between the battles of the week just past and the ones that lay ahead. Whatever the music meant to people, the people clearly longed for it, turned to it, demanded it, made it sing in the dilapidated buildings they called home. Leda walked the streets and listened at each window for tangos, and, when she found them, she leaned against the wall and soaked them up. She never stayed outside any particular home too long, and she never wandered beyond the few blocks that made up the neighborhood of San Telmo, which in her mind had taken on an almost mythological power to shield her from anyone who might recognize her as Leda (although she thought about them often, and couldn't help wondering whether they thought of her, Palmira, Arturo, Francesca, and, above all, to her surprise, Alfonso Di Bacco, the roaming baker, who stayed with her so vividly that she decided to take his last name).

Valentino, one of the bachelors—a short man with a beak nose and a surprisingly loud laugh—helped her find a job at the cigarette factory where he worked. Twelve-hour days of crushing tobacco in a great machine, so much of it that when she closed her eyes to sleep at night she saw levers pressing over and over into shredded leaves. She stank of raw tobacco and her feet ached from standing all day. But it was work, and, though at four days a week it wasn't enough to pay for her room and La Strega's food, she still had the money her parents had sent her (and how were they? waiting for word? no, don't think about that, don't think about them) to supplement, and, for now, that was enough to buy her time.

This new life brought many freedoms. She could smoke, she could walk the streets at night, she could curse and spit into gutters. She could hold down a job that paid twice as much as anything a woman could do with her clothes on. But there were also new demands. She had to be extremely careful with her posture (head up, shoulders squared) and her gait (long sure strides, no swaying hips). She had to exude confidence, if not outright bravado, at all times. She had to keep her voice carefully calibrated, using only the lower half of its natural register. She could use the chamber pot in her own room now, but as she couldn't wash her menstrual rags and hang them on the public line, she had to smuggle them out in burlap sacks, mixed with basil to hide the metallic smell, and take them to the streets, where she left them, guiltily, in a different alley each month, like a murderer's bloody refuse or some twisted heathen offering. (It was thanks to Fausta's advice that she used the basil, and every time she smuggled out these incriminating sacks she could hear her old bunkmate's voice, *use basil, cover bad things with it, so the evil eye will go away*. But what if Fausta could see her now, creeping into alleys, dressed as a man? Would she see Leda as protecting herself from the evil eye, or as the evil eye itself, a demon to be warded off? And what about Fausta herself—how was she faring with her husband in the wilds of this city? Had she found what she wanted: thyme, coriander, motherhood, pesos for daily bread? Leda longed to know, and yet the thought of running into Fausta filled her with dread.) She could never drop her guard, not even for a moment, because, as it turned out, men sized up other men, not just sometimes but constantly. She'd never realized the full extent of these invisible transactions until she was involved in them. Sometimes they were blatant, sometimes subtle, delivered with pursed lips or darting glances, sometimes behind a smile or coupled with a kiss on the cheek, all the while calculating your odds in case it came down to a fight. Because being a man meant facing possible violence at any turn. If you were helpless, it did not serve, as it could for a woman, to make you seem more innocent, more pure. It would not inspire a gentleman to come to your aid when you were in distress. And she lacked the muscle of the men around her; not only did she know this but the men around her knew as well. There was no way to conceal the narrowness of her shoulders, her lanky build. To make up for this, her persona had to be even tougher. She bought a dagger in a pawnshop—a *facón*, the shop-keeper explained: the kind of knife the gauchos used in the Argentinean countryside—and she wore it tucked into her trouser leg at all times. As she walked, the blade moved against her calf, and she drew comfort from its hard presence. Forward, back. Forward, back. Her small yet potent companion, scissoring a silent rhythm against her skin. Its slim pressure fortified her. In the big city, you had to hold your own if you didn't want to die.

Sometimes, deep in the night, she unbound her aching breasts and sat alone in front of a cracked mirror, staring at herself in the light of a sin-gle candle, amazed at what she saw. A not-man. Not-woman. A fallen-woman-risen-man. She couldn't tell what was stranger: that a man existed inside her, or that the world accepted his existence. She wondered why no one saw through her disguise. Perhaps people could see only what they expected, what fit inside their vision, as if human vision came in precut shapes more narrow than the world itself, and this allowed her to hide in plain sight.

Hidden but not silent. Now she practiced out loud, in her little room. Nobody seemed to mind or even notice in the din of La Rete's days. A wild freedom to let her hands sing tangos, to refine her sound, which grew a little clearer and brighter each day as she practiced in that cramped rectangle where sunlight shone only through the slit beneath the door, that humble stinking space that she could love because it was her own, and where music possessed her, her first lover, her only lover, perhaps forever, since even if by some miracle she managed to keep living on this knife's edge, undiscovered, surviving, besting death at its own game, she obviously could never have a man. She didn't mind the sacrifice. It seemed enough for a life, to give yourself to music the way nuns give themselves to God. To vow. To surrender. Only music, after all, made life bearable. Only with music did she feel—what was it? Free? Happy?

No, it was something else.

Awake.

Music, arrow to pierce all barriers. Music, the great equalizer. Music, invader of centuries. Nectar of demons, whiskey flask of God.

It rained heavily that winter, the winter of 1913. Children got sick and died of pneumonia in their rooms. Brothers and sisters were forced to sleep in the courtyard to evade contagion, in the cold, in the rain. Each time a child died, the mothers wailed and the bachelors shook their heads sadly and returned to their card games. On nights when the central courtyard filled with water, the men huddled in their room and taught young Dante games from France, Lebanon, Andalucía, Catalonia, as well as how to curse and communicate in Spanish. Without realizing it, they initiated Dante into the secret sect of men. The leaning back and sitting with legs spread apart. The space under the surface of their words, suffused with instinctive understanding. The talk of women, low enough to keep out of female earshot because they were good men after all and wouldn't want the ladies to hear what they wanted to do to whores. The vivid language they had for lust. Dante would never have guessed the vocabulary for private parts could be so broad. No food or object was exempted from the sexual imagination. Corncob, carrot, pole, post, spear, knife, sausage, broom, cigar, pestle, melons, apples, fig, cake, cup, pot, slit, cut, hole. Her brain raced to absorb this new cosmology of the body. The men didn't seem to know what to make of this strange young man who was really still a kid, they said, with his face that refused to grow even the smallest semblance of a beard. They called him El Chico, which meant the Kid in Spanish but also the Small One, a nickname she tried and failed to refuse. He was a strange fish in their waters, that Chico, an odd quiet boy with no relatives anywhere in the city, who played the violin behind closed doors and insisted on bathing upstairs in his own room, which required two men to haul the metal tub up the stairs, full of water already gray from a family or two's ablutions.

"Why do you want to do that?" the men said.

"You got a scar you don't want us to see?"

"Moles maybe?"

"Or the size of your pole."

"Like we haven't seen small ones before."

"Or big ones. Maybe that's the secret? Eh, Chico?"

The men laughed. El Chico just smiled and said nothing.

She engaged the assistance of a hale young man, usually Guido, La Strega's son, who at first refused Dante's coin of thanks at the end of the chore, though after a month in which it became clear that this strange tenant's phobia of bathing in front of other men would not abate, he slipped the silver in his pocket with a nod and a mumbled "please don't tell my mother."

From the men's talk, she learned of new places where she could find the tango. Night places. Cafés that stayed lit and loud all night, where decent women never went and where men had better know how to watch their backs.

I can't go, she thought. I have to go.

She'd start with La Moneda, a little place squeezed between a pawn-shop and a bakery, which the bachelors often talked about and which looked innocuous enough, at least by day. It was Valentino's favorite place. She'd keep her dagger close. She'd go alone.

She arrived at one a.m., just as La Moneda was beginning to fill. It was larger inside than she would have imagined from the street, as the store-front was small but let into a long narrow room crammed with little tables over which men drank and played cards and crouched without speaking to each other. The wall behind the bar screamed with bottles. The air was thick and smelled of onions and unwashed mouths. Men everywhere, claiming chairs, leaning against walls, three deep at the bar. There were also women, though fewer of them, interspersed among the men. Women difficult to look at, harder not to look at. These women bared their throats. Their lips were painted red, and pulled back into smiles. They leaned close to men, touched them, draped themselves over them like human shawls.

Music flowed from the back of the room, though it was too crowded for her to see the musicians. Guitar, flute, and one more instrument she couldn't place. It sounded like an accordion, only more subtle and intense, a tempered howl. She recognized the song; it was one of the first she'd learned from Nestore. She moved toward the bar.

"Well?" The barman was impatient.

"Yes?"

"What'll it be?"

She wasn't prepared, didn't know how to order at a bar. She scanned the bottles against the wall, tried to think fast, look certain. "Grappa."

The barman nodded and walked away, returning soon with Leda's drink. The men around her wasted no time in gulping down the contents of their glasses, so she did the same, thrusting her neck back as she drank. The grappa burned. The music swirled and rose to a peak, then ended with a flourish quickly drowned out by applause. Another song began. No one seemed to be fighting, there were no brawls, no brandished knives, though surely there were many that lurked hidden. She herself had her facón in her trouser leg, at the ready. She ordered another grappa and reveled in the hot trail it made through her body as it went down.

A few paces away, a girl in a green dress stood close to two men, one of whom had his arm around her waist. The second man touched the girl's breasts. She pushed his hand away and said something into his ear. The man laughed and stroked her breasts again, harder this time, grasping in a way that surely hurt, although the girl showed no reaction and this time didn't stop him. She stood looking indifferent as though the man weren't there at all. She was a slight girl, sparrowlike, though her breasts were surprisingly full. Leda was staring. She shouldn't be staring. She turned away, toward the dancers pressed into the center of the room. Some men danced with women, but many danced with other men. The reason was obvious; there weren't enough women to go around. Maybe six or seven women altogether, and dozens and dozens of men. And the women: the way they danced. Moving like regal snakes. Backwards in the man's arms. That one in the red dress that's been washed too many times (and she thought of the Red Woman she'd seen in Naples, on the street, the urge to leap out of the carriage and lose everything), she was a good dancer, better than her partner, even though he was leading. Her face was a stone mask of concentration as she glided, dipped, rose, slanted against her partner as if melding to him. When the song ended, her dance partner whispered something in her ear and the woman shook her head and turned away. In doing so she caught Dante staring at her. Smiled. Held his gaze for a few seconds, then made her way to the bar and sidled right up to Dante.

"Do you want to dance?" She had a foreign lisp that Leda couldn't place, flinty eyes, and a great mane of dark brown hair. She barely reached Leda's chin, and she was younger than Leda had thought, no more than twenty. Bolder than that other girl, the sparrow-girl. Unsettling.

"I'm sorry. I don't know how."

The woman shrugged and stepped closer. Her hand landed on Dante's neck, lightly. "Then perhaps you'd prefer to go right upstairs."

"Upstairs?"

"Thirty centavos."

Those fingers. They glided along Dante's neck, lightly, with casual confidence, as if they'd taken that trajectory many times before, as if it weren't the first time for those fingertips, that skin. They arrived at the jaw that would surely feel too smooth to them, no stubble or hint of hairs ever to come. Leda pulled away. "No. No, I'm sorry."

The woman let her hand fall to her side. Her lips pursed with irritation. "Then why did you call me over here?"

"Call you. I . . . I didn't realize—"

The woman looked at Leda for a moment longer, with something between exasperation and disbelief. Then she turned away brusquely and moved back into the crowd.

Leda stood, frozen. She didn't know the rules of this world. She was a fool. She'd tried to prepare herself for the danger that might come from men, but had not prepared for what might come from women. From a woman. The secret language that this kind of woman would speak with her eyes.

Upstairs.

She should leave. She'd been seen by others, and what would they think of her, of a dimwit young man who didn't even know how to talk to whores? She glanced around, but no one seemed to care. The men were too busy drinking or dancing, the women too busy with the men. The sparrow-girl and the man who'd stroked her breasts had disappeared, no doubt up those very same stairs. Leda was alone in the crowded room. A new song rose from the band, ardent, sumptuous. The air was so thick with sweat and liquored breaths that it was difficult to breathe.

That woman. The red dress, lifted. Thighs exposed, allowing touch. The place between that woman's legs, splayed open for thirty cents. The smell of it laid bare.

And then what?

You idiot. You couldn't have done a thing with her because there's nothing in the front of your trousers but an old balled-up sock. If you'd gone upstairs you would have been discovered, your whole new life would have come undone.

A counter-voice rose inside her: perhaps I couldn't have done everything a man could do, but I could have done something.

Oh! Like what?

Look. Touch. Smell.

And why would you want to do that?

. . .

It's wrong. There's something wrong with you.

She thought of Cora, in the hut up the hill, legs open in fear and pain.

You're an abomination.

She needed a drink. She ordered another grappa and gulped it in one quick shot. The music swelled, pushing at the thick unventilated air of La Moneda, making objects swim in her vision.

Later that night, as she walked home on unsteady feet, she could not stop thinking about those stairs.

A letter arrived for Leda Mazzoni, addressed in her mother's hand. La Strega handed it to Dante with a look of deep sympathy, having thoroughly believed the story he'd told her, *I've sent my relatives this address for my cousin Leda, she died last summer in La Boca, and you understand, of course, I haven't had the heart to tell her parents.* As though this new tenant Dante were some kind of hero, striving to protect his relatives back home, rather than the opposite. A liar. A fraud. Perhaps even a kind of killer.

She waited until she could be alone with the letter. Even then, she sat on her pallet for a long time in the dim light of her kerosene lamp, staring at the worn unopened envelope. The letters of the address seemed written at an aggressive slant, the *g*'s and *ʒ*'s and capital *L* brandishing loops of accusation. Her mother. Enraged and potent. Shaping words strong enough to cut the flesh of a daughter thousands of kilometers away. This daughter who had kept the money meant for a boat back home and run off with it, refused to obey, stayed where she was despite the danger and the shame she could bring down on her whole family, because everyone knew that a young widowed girl alone in a city was bound to fall prey to sin. Probably the village gossips had already begun to wag their vicious tongues, spinning tales of vice and disgrace, *that Leda alone in América,* and she could not fight them back on her mother's behalf, nor could she reasonably deny that they were right: she had fallen, she was beyond redemption. Though from what kind of sin, of course, the village gossips would not have guessed.

She put the letter under her pallet, against the cold stone floor. She would open it later, when she could face it, when she had more courage.

The next time she went to La Moneda, she found her neighbor Valentino at the bar, and they had a couple of drinks together. Valentino was astonished to learn that Dante did not know how to tango.

"You've never danced it, not once?"

"No," she said. She didn't dare acknowledge the truth of her dances with Arturo. They had occurred in a past that she avoided discussing at all costs.

"But you must start immediately! Dance with me, I'll teach you."

"I don't know," Leda said. If they came close to each other, he might detect her secret in her scent or motion or in the slight bulge at her chest. "I'm a bad dancer."

"That's all the more reason to learn. This is Buenos Aires, Chico. Every sidewalk crack is stuffed with men. You can't afford to be a bad dancer forever."

He grasped Dante's wrist and placed one hand on her back while his other hand clasped hers. To her relief there was a slice of space between their bodies, they did not touch. He was shorter than she, but this did not seem to faze him; he smiled up at her with an almost paternal reassurance. Valentino began to step in time to the music, forcing her feet backward, to the side, bumping into other pairs around them. He smelled of cigarettes and sweat and cologne. He was more skilled than Arturo; a gentle press to the small of her back was enough to guide her, suggest a step, with gestures so subtle yet assured that her body responded before her mind was aware of them. She was dancing backward into unknown space, and the thought made her tense.

"Let me lead," he whispered into her ear. "Let go."

She didn't want to let go. She fought surrender. But, as with Arturo before, once she let herself relax, the moves began to flow from her or, rather, from both of them, as though a secret tide had caught them both and bore them in gentle circles circumscribed by the legs and arms of other pairs aloft on secret tides of their own. As soon as she began to think again, she stumbled. Stop thinking. The steps come out of nothing, out of touch, hand on back, body speaking, there, there, there. At the end of the second song, Valentino dropped his hands, stepped back, and grinned. She had survived. He suspected nothing.

"Not bad."

"Thanks for the lesson."

"When you start leading, remember that it's you who moves the woman. You have to make her feel like she has no choice but to go where your mind sends her."

Leda nodded, and Valentino kept studying her, as if waiting for something. But what? Had she missed a joke?

"What?" she said.

"You're an odd fellow, you are."

She tensed. "You think so?" She braced herself for questions that she'd have to find a way to dodge.

But Valentino only laughed his wide booming laugh, such a large sound for a small man. "Let's get a drink."

When Valentino went upstairs with a sallow woman with a drooping paper flower in her hair, Leda shot back another grappa and pressed through the crowd toward the band.

They sat huddled in a corner, faces grave. The guitarist and the flautist were no older than thirty, two wiry, lanky men. The bandoneón player was burly, with hair growing from his nostrils and ears. He looked like an overgrown gnome, hunched over the beautiful square instrument on his lap as though hoarding stolen treasure. The three of them played with skill, though not much vigor. There were so many things she longed to ask them. Whether music filled and lifted them—it didn't seem to—or whether perhaps it had once, at an earlier time in their lives. Whether it was true, this dream of hers, that music could keep the soul from shattering. How they'd started making music in public, for pay. How she could find a way to do the same.

It wasn't until the next time she came that she finally dared approach them. She caught them during a break, and offered to buy them a round of drinks.

The musicians looked suspicious, but they accepted. They were quick with their shots. As they were wiping their mouths with the backs of their hands, Leda said, "How long have you been playing?"

"Long," the bandoneonist said and began to turn away.

"I play too," Leda blurted quickly. "The violin. Do you know anyone who needs a violinist?"

The bandoneonist looked him up and down, slowly. "How old are you, kid? Fifteen?"

"Twenty," she said, then regretted the lie when she saw the doubt on the man's face.

"How many songs do you know?"

"Many. And I learn fast."

"Look, *muchacho,* I don't know of anything. You'll have to ask around. Now leave me alone, I've got to get back to work."

Ask around. He made it sound so easy. She burned with embarrassment. She went back to the bar, where she saw the girl from the first night, the sparrowlike one with the full breasts. She was wearing the same green dress, which Leda now saw had a tear along the left seam, near her waist. The girl caught Leda staring and raised her eyebrows in a tired invitation. Leda looked away, having quickly learned the danger and power of eye contact.

Just as the band's next song came to its last, drawn-out note, Leda ventured out into the lamplit night.

But she didn't give up. In fact, just the opposite: the next day, throughout her long shift at the cigarette factory, as the tobacco rolled endlessly into its little white paper prisons, she thought and thought about the music she longed to make. Over the next month, she prowled the San Telmo nights. She opened door after door, following the music that bled through walls onto the streets. Not all of the places from which music poured were open to her. Toward downtown, she found dance halls so exclusive that they had guest lists, where the well-coiffed women in the foyers didn't even deign to address Dante with words, but simply turned their backs and let the menace of their hulking guards do the rest. And there were brothels set up in worn-down conventillos, where patrons could hear music after paying, as they waited for their turn. Patrons who, like Dante, slaved all day at a factory or warehouse or construction site, and brought their worn bodies to this place, she thought, to taste the things for which God had made them sentient. The lust of men fascinated Leda, in its sheer focus, the simple arrow of its aim. I want a woman and when I have her I'll know just what to do and then feel better. In her hunt for tango, Dante went into one single brothel, on a single night, and leaned against the wall in the corner, clutching her zinc token, listening to the mediocre trio and the moans from the closed rooms until the madam gestured toward her and then toward a door—*your turn, in there*—at which point she ducked out in a panic but kept the zinc chip in her pocket and fingered it as she walked until it grew warm from her touch. The best places for an odd fellow like her (too poor for the dance halls, scared of the whores) were the cafés, where she could buy a drink and lurk in peace. There was an astonishing number of such cafés in San Telmo—even more in La Boca, rumor had it, but of course she wouldn't venture there—and all of them burst with tango and with men. Men who came for drinks, men who came for women, men who came to hawk the women whose bodies they sold (and these would arrive in their pristine suits and tilted hats with two or three women in tow, gaze fixed on them all night as they plied their trade), men from the rich neighborhoods in the north (often young men, no more than boys, cocky, bawdy, bright with rebellion, itching for a dance, a fuck, a lawless night on the wrong side of town), men who came for the company of other wakeful bodies staving off loneliness and pain. She, Leda, Dante, was there for the music, and she drank and drank it, still reveling in the freedom to be out at night in a public place without fearing rape or disrepute.

All creatures on earth sleep either through the day or through the night, but Buenos Aires did neither, which made it a beast not of this world. In the night the cafés burst with light, most of them with kerosene lamps and a few with the arrogant new gleam of electricity. Men danced and drank and slipped away with indecent women. (Occasionally they didn't even slip away; more than once Dante saw a couple in a corner against a wall, the woman's skirts hitched up and leg raised around the rutting man. So that's what it looks like. The sight made her burn, whether with shame or thrill or fear or desire she did not know.) When dawn light arrived, men still lined the grimy café walls, hunched around little wooden tables, and took their last swigs at the bar, shoulder to shoulder with strangers. As the night wound down, the brutal grind of the day began: as one man headed home another headed out to brave the factories. Sometimes Dante went to work directly from the cafés. She ground tobacco for infinite cigarettes with her eyelids held open as if by invisible wires. The clang and clatter and stink of the factory saved her, kept her awake, as did memories of the night before, which roused her over and over like shots of coffee. So much to see. So much to absorb. The world under the surface of social acceptance: the *under*world. Roaring with life no matter what good girls were told. After work, Leda would go to her room and sleep for a few hours, until La Strega's daughter knocked to tell her food was ready and she came downstairs for a bite to eat before diving back out into the night.

Her luck turned when, at a café called Il Sasso, at about two thirty in the morning, the violinist was stabbed during his solo.

It was a pimp who attacked him. Lunged for his heart but missed in the scuffle and sank his blade in just below the violinist's rib cage. The violinist fell to his knees, the music stopped, and dancers turned to face the low stage that was quickly being blanketed with blood.

"You son of a whore," the pimp said. His words slurred. "You stay away from her."

The violinist made a terrible sound, somewhere between a groan and a howl.

"Chucho!" a woman wailed. "Chucho, no—"

And then the woman, still wailing, pushed through the crowd, toward the stage, and embraced the violinist for an instant before her pimp pulled her off him, her blue dress now red with blood. She was young, a rail of a girl with a bruised eye, and there was something at once desperate and tender in her gaze toward the violinist as she struggled to escape her pimp's grip and return to her lover until the pimp punched her in the face and she crumpled and her eyes went flat.

The other two musicians had put down their instruments and rushed to the violinist's side. The guitarist removed his shirt to bandage the wound and stanch the flow of blood. The pimp punched his girl again, and Dante wanted to help her but she feared that man's wrath, his muscle, his knife. She could feel both wounds—the blade inside the violinist, the punch on the girl's face—as though they'd happened to her. She flexed her calf so she could feel the dagger rub against it, hard and ready, though what could she do with it against such a large and savage man? It was nothing, really, a cub's tooth in a den of lions. The room was packed with men hunched over scarred tables, smoking at the crowded bar, leaning against the back wall cluttered with dry-good drawers, *coffee, flour, sugar,* each word painted in a hopeful cursive. No one made a move in the girl's defense. Leda had always thought women were to be defended, that this was a basic law among men, but now she was confronted with another of their laws: that whores were not women and so the same rules did not apply. And if she was ever found out, she could be just like that whore up on the stage in her blood-streaked dress, a woman beyond the laws of decency, abandoned to the brutal cold. She drew her shoulders back and kept her mouth shut.

It was the barman who intervened after the third punch. "Now now," he called out. "You either calm down or take this outside. I'm not having this in my café."

The pimp grabbed the woman by the hair and dragged her, now silent, through the crowd and out into the night. The barman went to the stage and helped the guitarist carry the wounded violinist to the storeroom. The bandoneón player was left alone on the stage, arms limp at his sides.

"Is that it, then?" a man called out. "No more music?"

The bandoneonist looked lost, adrift on a suddenly red stage. He was not very old, perhaps twenty-four, a small man whose bulging eyes made him look perpetually mournful. A man cursed with a temperament too delicate for this place. But Dante had heard him play on many nights and knew that, when it came to music, this man was as solid as a mountain. A murmur of complaint began to move through the crowd, spiked with jeers, and when a glass flew to the stage and shattered on the wall behind the bandoneonist, a veil lifted for Dante and she saw her chance.

She didn't think. She didn't weigh the risks. She strode to the stage, picked up the violin from the floor, coated with blood, and said quietly to the bandoneonist, "I can play with you."

The bandoneonist stared at the young man in front of him as though he'd suggested lewd behavior at a funeral. "Play?"

"Just until your friend gets back," Dante said quickly. "Until he's better."

The bandoneonist seemed to weigh this possibility, consider what alternatives he had, and give up on them. He nodded blankly, sat down, and picked up his bandoneón. The instrument was scuffed but elegant, with mother-of-pearl inlay and metal ribbing along the black accordion center. The keys along the sides resembled little stained teeth. "What songs do you know?"

"How about 'El Choclo'?"

They played. The violin was red and sticky with another man's blood and also lighter-weight and more worn in the neck than Dante's own instrument, not to mention that a raw-copper smell rose from its bridge to fill her senses and her fingers were surely getting stained, but it was still a violin and Dante could still could play it, clumsily at first, with a tone more rasping than she wanted it though at least her notes were accurate, her rhythm true, the bandoneonist glanced at her as if in reassurance and added a little flourish to his melodic line, she played through her embarrassment, played through the blood, and when her sound grew cleaner the bandoneonist smiled and that was when they truly merged, the song robust, men dancing again, with each other or with whores and by the third song the guitarist had emerged from the back room and joined back in and it was magic to blend sound with them like this, with strangers, and the sound they made was red red red and stripped of all the lies they told all day and night to survive these Américas, a naked sound that pulsed with everything they longed to be and never would become except like this, alone in a crowd, playing tango.

They played for two more hours, during which the wounded violinist bled to death in the back room and thereby made his position available to the new young man if he would have it, the guitarist said, and what was your name again?

His name was Dante and he would have it. Oh yes he most certainly would.

Before Dante left Il Sasso that night, the barman put a sweaty wad of small bills in his hand. "See you tomorrow, kid."

Dante walked out, exalted, wide awake. It was five a.m. and the street rang with each step as if it craved the impact of her feet. As if the streets themselves were a musical instrument, a vast drum of asphalt and stone. She would play better tomorrow, better still after that, even if it meant she had to practice until her fingers bled. She felt hungry for something: for improvement, for the stage, for life itself. She meant to go home but there were damp bills in her pocket and they insisted on another plan, they sent her around a corner to the left and down a narrow street to La Moneda, where, by the great serendipity of this night, Dante found what she didn't realize she was looking for.

The sparrow-girl. In her fraying green dress. She was just coming back downstairs when Dante's drink arrived at the bar. Dante shot the grappa back and caught the girl's eye. This time she held the girl's gaze and it was thrilling, the way the girl came toward her as though a mere look could hold the power of a magnet over iron.

An easy boy, this one, the girl thought as she approached the bar. He didn't seem violent, not yet, and might even be a little scared. The scared ones were easier, except when fear turned mean, which made for the worst customers of all. It had been a decent night so far. There were no new bruises and the man she'd just left had been quick, rote, muttering in a language she didn't recognize and so easily ignored. In her three years in Argentina, she'd spread her legs for every language on earth or, at least, many more languages than she'd known existed as a little girl. She spoke Spanish now but not the other tongues; she didn't want to know them, wanted the men's voices to wash over her like water over rocks, rushing, senseless, soon gone. She never spoke Polish anymore. Polish was a secret language locked up in a box deep in her mind. She refused to open it—her one rebellion. The worst men were not the ones who beat her, or the ones who tore her that-place and made it hurt for days; the worst men were the Poles who tried to speak to her. She pretended they were wrong, shook her head as if she didn't understand. What are you? they asked. A mute? A Russian? Some gave up, they weren't there to talk after all, but others got angry and tried to punch her into answering but they always lost the fight, she always won, she would not do it.

The box would stay locked up until she died. She dreamed of death the way other girls her age dreamed of marriage. When she died, she'd have to go to Hell—she didn't fear it anymore, she'd seen it already— but first she'd march up to the gates of Heaven and open her Polish, open her mouth, pour words between the golden bars so Yahweh and all the archangels could tremble at what she had to say, because she'd say everything then, she wouldn't hold back, she'd dare to call God by His name and spit through the gates and shout Where were you? Have you seen your cursed América? and if they listened, those archangels, Michał, Gabriel, Rafał, she'd send them down to tear the faces off the men who'd carried her across the ocean.

She'll see the world, the stranger said to her father, and his gold rings glinted in the firelight. Her father stared at his visitor's black suit, tailored in a modern fashion never before seen in the village, no doubt the finest clothing Warsaw had to offer. He seemed proud of the visit and dwarfed by it, a peasant called on by a king. She was at the edge of the room, crushing dried marjoram with a pestle beside her mother. Matka was separating dough into strands, to braid into challah for Shabbat. She looked tired, Matka. She was always tired. She'd borne eleven children. And you, she always said, are the most difficult, you're a colt who needs breaking, your poor husband will have a hard job. But she said none of this to the stranger when he spoke of taking her pretty girl, and so he said it, *your pretty girl,* to the New World, where a husband would be waiting. The stranger paid her father a dowry fit for a princess, or so it seemed, and also promised to pay for her bridal gown, travel, food, and shelter until her wedding day.

Since then she'd seen the ocean from the deck of a great ship and seen, also, many small dim rooms that filled too fast with men. There was no wedding. The first weeks were the worst because the colt still rose in her and forced the men to teach her a lesson and another and another. Lessons that broke the skin and filled every orifice she had, she was a field full of holes, she was a poisoned field where nothing would ever grow again.

That was three years ago. Now it was better. There were nights like this when she felt almost nothing at all. She rarely went outside, but she didn't miss the sun. She didn't want heat, didn't want to be exposed. She missed the cold of home, deep winter, hot red broth, fire crackling in the oven, skins and wool and furs to enfold you, soft layers between you and the world.

When she dared to dream, she dreamed of snow.

Snow casting itself across the fields to hide the broken earth.

Snow alighting on each branch in fragile benediction.

Snow to force the bears into their caves.

Snow on roofs as if to wash them.

Snow before the footprints, before the mud and ice, as far as the eye can see a hush of white.

And when her room became unbearable, she didn't bear it at all: she dissolved from her body and the city and América itself, and reappeared in the most perfect moment of her life. She was eight years old, out to fetch water in the first snow of winter, stealing a glance at the field. It was so entrancing, crisp and pure and quiet, that it took her a minute to see the miracle: a kropiatka bird, perched in the whiteness, so light he left no footprint. Nobody would believe her if she told. The kropiatka migrated in the fall, and were never seen in winter. Surely his brethren were all gone by now. But he was here, and did not act lost; he trilled with shocking joy; she couldn't take her eyes off this brazen little bird, the most beautiful creature she'd ever seen, so full of spring that he sang in the face of everything, the loss of his flock, a buried field, the dark about to come.

The sparrow-girl arrived at Dante's side, looked up into his face, and waited. Dante wondered what to say. Good evening? You've been on my mind? My name is Dante? She wasn't at all sure that she wanted to tell the girl her name, or that the girl would have any use for it.

She settled for the most direct route. "How much to go upstairs?"

"Thirty centavos."

Dante nodded, and the girl turned and walked away. Dante followed her, to the stairs and up them (sway of green skirts, faded and stained but what shaped them no less wondrous) and down a narrow dim hall lined with closed doors through which Dante could hear business being conducted and the last door on the left was theirs. It was a tiny space, just large enough for a single cot with a mattress bearing a stained sheet and no pillow. A kerosene lamp on the sill held a dim flame. The girl turned to Dante, expressionless, and moved to open her customer's trousers, but Dante was ready and caught her wrist.

"No," she said. "I don't want that."

The girl looked bewildered, then angry, the face of a cheated child. She was Dante's age, perhaps a bit younger, sixteen or seventeen. Here we are, Dante thought, two teenage girls in a room, nothing more, though one of us will never know it. She put money in the girl's hand, a whole peso she'd just earned at Il Sasso, the bill still damp with sweat or rum or God knew what.

"Don't worry, I'm paying."

The girl looked at the full peso in surprise. "So what do you want, then?"

Her accent was unfamiliar to Dante, nothing liquid about her Spanish, all firm bones and raw angles. "To look at you."

"Just to look?"

"And touch?"

The girl's stare became mocking.

Dante felt like a fool. She shouldn't have phrased it as a question. She'd thought the girl would be glad to have a customer who asked permission, but instead it seemed to expose something pathetic about him, something laughable.

"I suppose you'd rather have the dress off."

A lump rose in Dante's throat. She nodded.

"Fifteen minutes, just like everybody else," the girl said as she unlaced her bodice and let her dress fall to the floor. She stepped out of it, wearing a brassiere and panties. "What about these?"

Dante nodded again.

"What's the matter?" she said disdainfully as she took off the rest of her clothes. "Don't tell me you haven't seen this before."

Dante couldn't speak, couldn't breathe. The girl was naked now, and

Dante filled her eyes with the sparrow-girl, whose breasts and skin and hips and thatch of hair where her legs met were more glorious than she could have imagined. The sight stirred something in Dante that was fierce enough to break her. This brutal city was full of noise and blades and death and dirt and hunger and also this, a naked girl so beautiful she put the stars to shame. Dante might have fallen to her knees before the sight and reached toward the girl, but suddenly the girl, now clear about her power and her customer's submission, took matters in her own hands: she lay down on the cot and closed her eyes.

Dante, who was also Leda, sat gingerly on the edge of the bed. The girl must be tired. She'd been working for hours. And *working*, what that meant for her was another thing entirely from factory shifts or hours with needle and thread. How had the girl come to this dismal life? She couldn't bear to disturb her. Part of her longed to enfold the girl the way she'd wanted to enfold Cora years ago when the nightmare began, wrap her in a blanket and protect her from the harsh side of lust. But this time she, Leda, was the enemy—sitting here beside the girl she could not deny it: she lusted. That was why she'd come here, what she hadn't been able to admit even in the depths of her own mind. But how could she want such a thing? How could a woman—? She'd never heard of such a thing. It had to be impossible or else demonic, the worst kind of sin, beyond hope of penance.

And yet here she was. Wanting.

She touched the girl, lightly, on her belly. The girl didn't respond. She was either asleep or, more likely, pretending to be so. Dante let her hands move across the girl's skin, a gentle glide along the perfect slopes of breasts and arms and hips and breasts again, her hands amazed not only at the loveliness beneath them but also at their own joy. There was pleasure in her palms and in the rest of her as well, a hot vortex in the space between her hips. A sensation so strange and powerful she could almost have believed it supernatural. In that moment she knew that she'd rather spurn the laws of God and go to hell when she died than let this be her last time near a beautiful naked girl. And then, as if the girl had a clock inside her ticking off the seconds of her task, she sat up and pushed Dante from the bed.

"That's it," she said, reaching for her clothes. "Time to go."

Dante stood, dazed, blood rushing to her head. She didn't know what to say. Whether to thank the girl or beg forgiveness, or tell her she was beautiful. She felt dizzy, unhinged, hot to the marrow of her bones. She tried to gather her thoughts.

"Out," the sparrow-girl said.

As Dante walked down the hall to the stairs, she prayed—though not to God, who, in his wrath, would not understand her—that she hadn't hurt the girl. That the girl had somehow felt the worship in her touch.

But you didn't only want to worship, did you?

No. Yes. I don't know. I don't know what it's called, this wanting, no words exist for it.

She walked home on streets alive with dawn.

Dante-also-Leda played at Il Sasso throughout the spring, each night its own small miracle. There were no more murders onstage, and only a few stabbings in all those weeks. There was one night when a *compadrito* pulled a pistol on another man, but the bartender, a seasoned protector of his small domain, got them out onto the street before the shots began. Dante played without sustaining a single wound. With her own violin under her chin she was able to play better than the first night. The two other musicians didn't talk to her much, didn't ask her questions, and she was glad of it. She learned new songs from her fellow band members, new moves to strengthen her playing. She learned to play loudly, and to square her shoulders, firm up her stance, and push forward her chest so she could sustain the music for a long time. You couldn't play in a timid girl-pose without wrecking your back and neck. You had to hold your violin like you were king of somewhere. She reveled in the boldness of

it. The more tangos she learned, the more at home she felt inside the
form: no two songs were alike but there was overlap in the melodies,
in their favored notes, their essential texture, the build and release of
verse and chorus. It was a simple form, really, the tango: nothing like
those convoluted classical melodies over which her father had labored
for weeks; meant not for the plaza in the light of day but for this place,
these sticky nights, this lit café where the insomniac soul could meet its
match. She played tango after tango, songs that swelled, poured, flowed,
strutted, raced, crept, crooned, sparked, howled, mourned, bragged, and
battled with the air. She embraced them all, played them all. Her joy
grew alongside her skill.

She didn't miss being female, though she would have liked relief from
the dull soreness of her breasts. Her nipples pressed and crushed beneath
the bandages. The pain that Dafne may have felt in her tree-limbs after
metamorphosis, when she became a tree to escape Apollo and take refuge in the freedom only an enchanted world would give her. Pain, there
had been pain in the version Cora had told her as a child—for the hands
now forced into the immobile form of branches, the trunk that had no
mouth with which to speak. That's how Leda thought of the soreness in
her nipples. My Dafne pain.

But the balled cloth in the front of her pants: that she did not find
uncomfortable at all. It seemed to graft to her. She experimented with
different shapes and textures, with socks and napkins and torn rags, with
colors—blue and white-gone-gray and brown—until she finally settled
on red. She felt the strongest and most confident when wearing red cloth
at her groin. It pumped its presence into her. Its slight pressure reminded
her of that place in her body, the place where a male sex would be, so
that, when onstage, she played from it. It didn't feel like an absence.
Something coiled there, a source of heat, and she pictured it spread-
ing through her body, pouring through her arms to her violin, where it
transformed into whipping strokes of sound.

They were beautiful, those first months at Il Sasso. But she did not sleep. And one day she arrived at work so tired that she dozed and almost cut her hand off in the tobacco grinder. She jolted awake to the shout of a fellow worker—*"¡Dante!"*—just in time to pull back from the spinning blade.

She thanked the man. He was a plump Spaniard who scowled through his workdays and rarely spoke.

"Idiot," the Spaniard said and went back to his station.

The blade whirred on. Its sound became aggressive to her ear, *wwhhrrrr, I would have taken you; tobacco, hand, it's all the same to me.* Leda, she thought, you've got to stop this before you lose a limb and then can't play at all. The factory and the music, it was hazardous to do both. But she brushed off the thought: she couldn't quit her factory job, because her musician's pay was not enough to live on. As for leaving Il Sasso, she couldn't bear the thought. Playing at home and at the café were not the same. It was at the café that she stretched the edges of her music, learning from the other men, fusing with the guitar's round chords, the bandoneón's bittersweet drone. They rarely spoke to her, these fellow musicians, and yet she felt engaged in a long wordless conversation with them, one that struck up when they played and wove through spaces she could not otherwise reach. And then there was the place itself. Il Sasso. A visit to the lip of chaos every time. In playing for strangers—hard men, brash whores, the scattered rich boys—in watching them dance to the sounds she made, she felt an incomparable power, as though it were not the music but she the music-maker moving their bodies, propelling them, unlocking their desire.

As for her own desire, she gave it all to her violin, and to the sparrow-girl, whom she visited about once a week and thought about on all the days between. The girl had grown accustomed to her strange new client, the young man with broken Spanish who stared at her and never once unbuttoned his trousers. They no longer spoke to each other: a look at the bar was enough to signal the beginning and send them both up the stairs, to the room, where the girl took off her clothes with quick efficiency, lay down, and closed her eyes, leaving the strange client alone with a beauty that reduced him to mute idiocy, that made him, for fifteen minutes, a gaping fool. Dante didn't dare do more than touch her with feather-soft fingers, not wanting to disturb the girl, burdened by the thought of her just-past hours and those about to come. Touch that wouldn't disrupt sleep, though potent enough to leave Dante's fingertips burning as if she'd dragged her hands through fire.

At home, at La Rete, she took to playing violin in the patio, at first to keep her skills honed and then for the sheer pleasure of it, because now, after a few hours without her violin, her fingers began to itch, craving her instrument the way her lungs craved cigarettes. She'd thought it would annoy people if she played in the patio, in the middle of crowded family life, but it was just the opposite: when she stopped, men and women and especially children asked her for more. Sometimes her neighbors kept on washing and cleaning and smoking, but at other times they took brief breaks to dance: La Strega danced with her son (who towered over her), the Lebanese brothers grasped their wives, the French and Calabrese children tested moves with each other, the childless couple from Spain (the wife now pregnant) glided across the tile floor with silent steps, the air around them crackling with a deeply private exchange. It reminded Leda of when her father used to play the violin when she was much younger, on Sundays after the family meal. Neighbors would come over to listen, or he'd strike up in the plaza and make people smile, sing, dance. A single melodic line can be enough to dance to. One good solid rope of music is enough to pull your body if it's ready, if it's awake. In Alazzano, one lone violin could make people rise and move, clapping the rhythm, kicking their feet: grandmothers, lanky boys, girls dropping their compulsory modesty for a moment, laborers just in from the fields, and in those times Leda had thought her village the most marvelous place on earth. A place you'd never want to leave, not ever, when such magic could be spun out of nothing more than sun and people and a single violin. She tried to bring some of that feeling to her playing in the conventillo, turning the patio into a kind of plaza, despite its crush of bodies and endless damp and stink you could not run from. She tried to play the far green hills into their midst.

And she had loved them, those green hills, she truly had. They had been beautiful—they had been home—before Cora's madness. In her new San Telmo life, Leda tried not to think of Cora's madness, but it was no use: anytime her village entered her memory, the madness spilled in too and flooded everything, drenched her mind.

Cora's madness reached the public eye on three occasions. The first time took place three days after the afternoon by the river, the one on which Leda had failed to lift her cousin's spirits with sun and grass and tales of old Pompeii. Leda had spent those next three days weighed down by shame. She had not healed her cousin. She had failed. She would try harder. They would find a way to run away and make a new life, somewhere, anywhere, she would follow Cora's heels down the path out of her village and not ask questions or stop even if her soles bled, walking and walking until her soul-cousin said *now look! look! we've arrived*.

But she had missed her chance.

She was at the washing tubs on the plaza with the other women, scrubbing her brothers' clothes, when the screams began. They were coming from the church, and all the women left their dirty linens and crossed the flagstones, hands dripping with soap.

"Stop it!" a woman's voice shouted inside the church, into the screams. "Stop, you devil-girl!"

The women crowded the church door, so that Leda had to crane her neck to see over them into the chapel. Cora stood in the aisle between the pews, a few paces from the altar. On the altar lay her crumpled dress. She was naked except for a white cloth that Sister Teresa of the local order was struggling to keep around her shoulders, but Cora was younger and stronger and kept writhing to push it off, keening in protest.

"Sister Teresa!" the women said.

"I'm—trying—to cover—her up—"

Cora bent down and bit Sister Teresa on the wrist.

Sister Teresa screamed, and the cloth came loose and fell to the floor. At that moment, Leda saw that it was an altar cloth, adorned with an image of the chalice and the host. A collective sigh of horror rose from the women in the doorway at the sight of the holy embroidery on the floor, and of Cora's nakedness, her bared teeth, the unnatural twist of Sister Teresa's arm.

Within seconds the baker's wife was beside them. She was a burly woman who lifted great pans of loaves from dawn to dusk, and she pulled Cora from the nun with one swift gesture. Cora screamed and Leda felt the women of the village tense in anticipation of more fighting—and there was surely pleasure in the anticipation, Leda felt it though she knew none of them would ever dare admit it—but then, to all of their surprise, the scream ended abruptly as Cora fell limp against the baker's wife, her head against the woman's ample breasts.

"Get her clothes," the baker's wife instructed Sister Teresa, who obeyed.

When the dress arrived Cora shook her head wildly against the baker's wife's chest and made a sound, *Eeeeeeeeee.*

"Get dressed!" said the women at the door, swarming toward her.

"The nerve."

"How dare she?"

"Sacrilege!"

"Someone get that girl into clothes before—"

"I'll see to it—"

"Oh just wait, let me past, I'll slap her so hard she won't recall her name!"

"Not if I get to her first, you won't—"

There were several women around her now, struggling with the dress and with Cora's limbs, trapping her in a human cage that grabbed and slapped at her while she kept droning *Eeeeeeeeee*. Leda stood frozen at the door. This was not her soul-cousin Cora, the bright one, the brave one. This could not be.

"Get her out of here," said a man's voice. The priest's voice. He had entered through the door from the sacristy.

"You heard him," the baker's wife called out. "Let us through!"

The women made way and Cora and the baker's wife came to the door, the girl still naked and still in the matron's arms. They walked in unison like a strange four-legged beast, crossing the sun-drenched plaza, slouching their way toward Cora's house, Palazzo Mazzoni, with a crowd of women in their wake that grew as more women abandoned their washing and their hearth fires to murmur aspersions and shake their heads and stare and clutch their hearts and hold up evil eyes and crucifixes with a pageantry that made Leda think of a saint's day procession, turned inside out.

When they arrived at Palazzo Mazzoni, Cora's mother took her by the wrist, slapped her for all to see, pulled her inside, and slammed the door. The crowd waited at the steps, hoping for shouts to leak through the regal windows or for more heinous sounds from the girl. But there was only silence. The crowd dispersed and Leda stayed alone for a long time, watching the windows of the upstairs rooms for hints of what had happened next. She even knocked on the front door but got no answer. By the time she returned to the washing tubs the light had left the village and it was too dark to finish. Mamma would scold her for coming home without the laundry done, but at that point she didn't care. She could think only of Cora. Her bony wrist in the nun's clasp. Her wilt against the baker's wife. Cora, *carissima,* what has happened to you?

The next day the story was all over the village. Cora had walked into the church in the middle of the day, when not even old widow Fiora was in the pews. She was so quiet, at first, that nobody had known she was there until Sister Teresa came into the sacristy to mend the father's alb and heard humming in the chapel. When she went to look, she found

Cora on her knees behind the altar, completely naked, humming with her eyes on the tall crucifix on the back wall. Her clothes were on the altar. The melody she hummed was so familiar that the words sprang right into the nun's mind. *Kyrie eleison. Kyrie eleison.* In her shock, Sister Teresa reached for the closest thing at hand that could dispel the sacrilege, a folded altar cloth, and tried to wrap it around the girl and drag her out of the church at the same time. That was when the girl began to scream.

The following Sunday, Cora missed church again. Leda felt the disappointment of the gossips as surely as if they'd given it voice. There would be no spectacle, no blasphemy, no chance to tear down the girl. Still they savored the delicious horror of the story. Madness alone would have been enough of a crime to delight them. But to have it come from the daughter of Mateo Mazzoni, landowner, exploiter of poor men, cause of so much suffering that Christ himself would have flinched to meet him—to see him shamed by his own daughter seemed too good to be true. A revenge sent down from heaven for all the denizens of Alazzano.

Cora Matta, they called her. Crazy Cora. Over the washing tubs, at the outdoor market, the bakery, in the apothecary's shop. Days and weeks of Cora Matta this, Cora Matta that. She carried the brunt of the sins of her father. Two months passed before the second public sighting of her madness. It took place on a Thursday, when Leda was at home making dinner with her mother. She saw nothing of the incident and only heard about it later. This time Cora was found in the woods east of the village, naked again, her dress nowhere to be seen. She had covered her body in dirt and caked her hair with it, so that she looked like some sort of swamp creature risen from a realm beneath the earth. She had dug a hole in the soil with her bare hands, a low shallow bowl in which she knelt, eating dirt by the fistful. It was the blacksmith's son who found her this time, a boy of eleven who ran screaming all the way back to his house and dragged his father out to see the earth-witch, or so he called the apparition he'd seen. The blacksmith tried to talk to Cora but was met with nothing more than a silent gaze that he later said would haunt him to his dying day.

That's no earth-witch, he told his son. That's Cora Matta.

He sent his boy for help. It took four grown men to restrain Cora and bring her home.

The third and final occasion took place a month after that, two and a half hours after midnight. Cora was found in the central plaza of Alazzano, under a full moon. The whole incident might have passed unnoticed if the blacksmith's wife had not woken from a nightmare and stepped out for a breath of air, only to hear a melody borne on the dark breeze. She'd followed the sound out to the plaza, then rushed back home for her crucifix, the best protection against the kind of devil-work she'd seen, and in the process she woke half the village and drew them out of their beds to wallow in the spectacle. Leda woke to the sound of footsteps on the street below her window and voices muttering their alarm.

Cora Matta, Cora Matta.

Dirt in her—

The devil—

Shhhp! The horror.

Leda's gut clenched at the sound of her cousin's name. She snuck out of her house despite the absolute certainty that Mamma would beat her if she heard of it. To her surprise, the rest of her family seemed to sleep through the noise. She walked the two blocks to the plaza in her nightgown. The night air chilled her skin, an exhilarating, unfamiliar feeling that might have caused her pleasure if she hadn't been so scared for Cora.

She expected to find a tight knot of women and men around her cousin, beating and attacking as they had inside the church, but instead she saw a wide circle of figures around the plaza. In the light of the full moon, the townspeople looked like silhouettes of Death, their crucifixes held out before them, their Our Fathers and Hail Marys a low blanket of sound. At the center of the human ring, many paces away as though no one dared get too close, lay Cora. She was fully clothed this time, splayed out on the ground with her limbs extended in the shape of a five-pointed star. She must have gone to the woods first, because her hair and dress and exposed skin were matted with dirt. She was droning the same tune she had the first time, *Kyrie eleison, Kyrie eleison, Kyrie eleison.* It was not a hum but an openmouthed sound, a wordless *aaaahhh* somewhere between a song and a moan. Her voice skulked under the surface of the town's muttered prayers, almost but not quite drowned out.

Leda walked toward the center of the circle. "Cora," she said. "Cora."

Cora kept on droning and ignored her.

Before Leda could reach her cousin, someone came up close behind her and held her back. "There's nothing you can do, child," the person said. It was the baker's wife. "Come on. Step back."

Her arms were kind but firm and Leda struggled against them. She called out. "Cora!"

Cora sat up and met Leda's eyes for the first time since the madness had begun.

And it was what Leda saw in those eyes that took the fight out of her. It was not madness in that gaze, but something else she'd never seen before. In that moment, standing in the moonlit plaza restrained by the baker's wife, Leda felt something inside her come undone, the fragile hooks that give shape to the mind and keep it from devolving into chaos. She knew nothing, could do nothing, had nothing to hold on to except the melody that Cora had spun and spun without its words, *Kyrie eleison,* whose meaning now swallowed the night.

Lord. Have mercy.

She might have stayed at Il Sasso forever if not for Santiago.

He arrived one night in December, when the first hot breaths of summer were forcing men's jackets off and sweat onto every forehead. He was an elegant man. His clothes were not fine, but they were ironed and the trousers creased. He wore his hat at a confident tilt. He seemed to be in his late thirties and had a sensuous face, the black curly hair of a Sicilian or what the Spaniards called a Moor, and eyes so large and liquid that women surely drowned their hearts there of their own free will. He did not dance. Instead, he leaned at the bar and watched the band intently, eyes fixed on Dante. It made Dante nervous to have someone watching her so closely. Who was this man and what was he looking for? Did he suspect her secret? But how could that be? Nobody had suspected her until now, to the point where there were moments she herself forgot that she was not a man. What if he'd been sent by someone who had known her as Leda? Fausta. Arturo. Nestore. Someone who had caught her trail and sent a man to track her down. There was no logic to this fear—none of these people had any reason to bother, except perhaps Arturo, and surely he had moved on by now and found another bride?—but still it caught Dante by the throat and made her stumble through the rest of the set.

When her band took a break, she tried to avoid the stranger, but he followed her to the far end of the bar. "Dante?"

"Yes."

"Santiago."

She started to turn away.

"Let me buy you a drink."

"What do you want?"

"Just to talk to you."

Dante hesitated. If this man was in fact spying on her for someone who'd known her before, she didn't want to hear what he had to say. But it might be worse not to. "One drink," she said.

They stood at the crowded bar, and when their grappas came they shot them down in unison.

"They said you were good," Santiago said.

Dante wondered who *they* were.

"And they were right."

She almost thanked him but didn't want to seem soft. She nodded briskly.

"I came to hear you." He leaned closer. There was something electric about his presence; the air around him came alive. "I'm forming an *orquesta* and I want you to join us."

Not what she'd expected. For a moment she couldn't speak. Santiago waited with an unreadable expression on his face. She collected herself. "Where?"

"There's a dance hall that wants to contract us, where customers know how to pay. Nothing like this place. Well heeled." He gestured to the bartender to fill their glasses. The bartender, pouring whiskey to a loud fistful of men at the other end of the bar, waved back in exasperated assent. "But there's more than that. There are cabarets opening up downtown, as fine as anything in Paris, and I'm telling you right now, one day my orquesta will play there."

"How do you know?"

"I know."

"And you need a violinist?"

"I need you."

Something swelled open inside her. She tried not to show it. "What's your instrument?"

"The bandoneón. There'll be three of us, soon four."

The bartender returned, filled their glasses, and disappeared again, picking his hairy ear as he went. Dante had said one drink, but here she was, another shot, more warmth as it went down.

"When would we start?"

"Tomorrow."

"Tomorrow!"

"Or else I lose the contract. Dante. Quit this sad place and come play some real tango."

Dante fingered her shot glass. Her fellow musicians were starting to head back to the stage. The fistful of men were on their third round of whiskey, their voices rising, banter on the verge of aggressive. There might be blood tonight.

"Listen," Santiago said, and his eyes glittered with the reflected flame of a lamp, "you're a young man and you seem new to the city. Am I right?"

Dante raised her eyebrows and didn't answer.

"Right. So you may not realize that the tango is changing. Transforming. This winter, all those months we were huddled in the rain, it was summer over in France, and guess what those Parisians were doing?"

"Sitting in the sunshine?" Dante asked, imagining white parasols, a sculpted green park, cuff links that glinted with light.

"Dancing the tango."

"Our tango?" Dante said, amazed, both at this news and at the *our* that had just escaped her mouth.

"Of course, yes, our tango. What else? You ever seen the rich boys who come down here for a drink and an easy girl?"

"Of course."

"Well, seems some of them took the dance on their Paris vacations. Showed off to the French girls. It sparked a fire. Now all the fancy ladies in Paris want to dance the way these whores are doing it here at old Il Sasso. Can you imagine?"

Dante shook her head. She couldn't. The Old World, Europe, ignited by songs from the grim conventillos of New Babel. To think she'd crossed the ocean to find this Argentinean music, only to find it sailing back to Europe, closing a vast loop around the world.

Santiago went on. "We still have no idea what the tango can become. It wasn't long ago that there was nowhere you could dance it in public. There's a whole high-class side of this city where, a few years back, they'd sooner have swum in piss than danced the tango. You probably haven't seen that side of Buenos Aires yet."

Dante shook her head.

"I didn't think so. Well, it's there, and let me tell you something about the rich: they follow Paris. And with Paris dancing tangos, everything will change. It's not just about making money. This music of ours is going to rise up into something."

The guitarist was starting to glare at Dante. Time to get back to the stage.

"What kind of something?"

"A mark on history. Even if nobody knows about us, even if no one remembers our names. Music that sings after we die."

The way he was speaking. The thrill of it. "I have to get back to work."

"Don't go back up there. Forget this place. Walk out with me tonight, right now. I'll pay your night's wages, we'll practice until dawn."

He was staring at Dante now with a look that flustered the woman in her, a look that would have seemed seductive if she weren't disguised as a man. Behind him, the whiskey men were arguing now but there were no knives out, she couldn't make out their words. A whore came over and draped herself between the two ringleaders, smiled like her mouth was a weapon all its own. Distraction. God bless the whores.

"Where do you work, other than here, Dante? At a cigarette factory?"

Her spine went tight. Had he been spying on her after all? What else did he know? "Who told you?"

"Nobody. I can smell the tobacco."

She went hot with embarrassment.

"Don't worry. We all smell like our jobs around here, whether it's metal, tannin, bread, or shit. If you come work for me, one day, I swear to you, you can quit the factory and then you'll just smell like music."

Dante laughed. "Really? What does music smell like?"

"You tell me."

Dante met Santiago's gaze. He was serious. She had never met a man who talked this way. He loved music as recklessly as she did. It seemed madness to trust a stranger in this city. He could be tricking her, luring her into some sort of trap. Naïve new immigrant, easy to stab for a few coins. And yet his vision pulled at her. It made her want to follow him anywhere, out into the night, like the children in the story of the pied piper, blinded by an irresistible song.

"*Che,* Dante." It was the guitarist, come up behind her. He grabbed Dante's shoulder. "You coming or what?"

Santiago waited, watching them.

Dante rose. She meant to walk to the stage. She meant to ask Santiago for more time, to come back tomorrow, in a week, when she'd had a chance to think. But the guitarist's grip was too tight on her shoulder and what if this stranger didn't come back and found another violinist for his scheme and together they played music that sang after they died? She would never forgive herself. This man had opened a portal in the chaos of this city, and if she didn't step through it now she'd never know what lay on the other side.

"I'm coming," Dante said.

The guitarist let go of her arm. "About time."

She strode up to the stage and grasped her violin and bow. She felt Santiago watching her from the bar. Her instrument case was backstage, but there was no time for that; no matter, she'd get another one, a new skin. "I'm leaving," she said and headed down to the bar.

"What!" the guitarist shouted behind her. "You can't just leave, you—"

"Quickly," Santiago spat when she reached him. He grasped Leda's wrist and pulled her through the crowded café. The guitarist was close on their heels, pursuing them through the thick crowd of men, and when Leda turned she saw the glint of his dagger and the red rage of his face. She wasn't sure what she'd expected but she hadn't expected a knife.

"Don't look back, you idiot," Santiago said. "Come on, come on—"

This is madness, Leda thought as she ran to the door with him, spilling across its threshold, heart pounding as they made their escape into the night.

CINQUE

Ladies and Gentlemen!

She wanted it always, every bit of it, the blistered fingers and sore feet and arms aching from holding up that damn blessed violin, the long endless chain of nights performing until the sun came up as if only their music could make the light return. Her new orquesta's sound tightened over the months, fusing into a shape that could curl and soar and sting. They played and played for arrogant and easy crowds alike. Then she'd walk home on streets dipped in the liquid gold of morning, looking around, dazed, amazed at the city that had taken her in and given her a way to survive. At least so far. Because no day was promised, nights even less so; it was not a soft city, it was full of edges on which you could cut yourself or trip and fall quick and lost right down to hell. Which made each breath of Buenos Aires air an act of grace. There were mornings when Dante came home to her matchbox of a room and lay her head down in wonder, one more night, one more stony dawn, a gift so large it almost seemed untenable. She earned her bread with her violin, a miracle that seemed as large as loaves and fishes. She was able to quit the factory, as Santiago had said, and live in a manner she hadn't known was possible: from music. And *for* music. For what happened when bodies filled the dance halls and the tango gripped them like a beautiful curse, propelled them around the room in pairs, bodies caught in the fierce language of dance, the room disappears, the world disappears, all things give way to a single bright circuit of light between two dancers. She knew how it felt, she'd danced it too. She also knew that the feeling of the world reduced to two, and two alone, was an illusion. Because no couple generated the dance on its own. There was no tango without music, and the music came from her, from them, the music makers: she pressed her strings and fifty women's shapely ankles moved in time, fifty lovely backs arched, fifty thighs lifted along trousered legs, oh, blessed kick, hook, sliding. Oh, bodies pressing as she pressed the sweet neck of her instrument and watched from the stage. Hold her close, *compadre,* Dante would think, flick your leg between hers, press her so gently to the left that she believes the turn is born from her own will, hold the small of her back like it's the core of every pleasure on this earth, and I will give you my sound, over and over, night after night, my sound will move you, my sound will guide you, my sound, through you, makes love to her.

The orquesta was called El Cuarteto Torres, after their leader, El Negro Torres, whom Dante still called Santiago because this was how he introduced himself, always as Santiago, a given name that quickly disappeared behind the Negro that stuck to him and called from every mouth and every crowd, nothing to be done about it, a man does not name himself in a city like this one, the city names the man. In this city you didn't even have to be a black man to be called El Negro, but if you were indeed black, even the way Santiago was, with the wide curls and olive skin Dante had at first mistaken for Mediterranean, then you were El Negro this or El Pardo that and there was no escaping, just as short men became El Petiso, fat men El Gordo, bald men El Pelado, on and on. The nickname becomes ravenous and swallows your first name whole. At first, Dante occasionally forgot and called him Negro, like everyone else, but she noticed that, although he didn't seem to mind his nickname, when she remembered to call him Santiago there was something else in his reaction, a flicker of glad surprise. She knew what it felt like to want to define yourself. It was a slippery goal, never fully secured. She gave him what she could by using the name he chose.

Pedro was their second bandoneonist, not as agile on the keys as Santiago but always solid, a keen rope of sound. He often played with his eyes shut, wisps of his overgrown hair sticking to his sweaty skin, giving him the appearance of a strange amphibian creature, neither animal nor human, wet, transformed. Then he'd open his eyes and step offstage and the toughness would return to his face, the clenched jaw, the defiant chin, like a seasoned gangster or a boy who's been roughed up one too many times. He was young, twenty-three at most, a drifter from the rural cattle lands outside the city. No one knew how he'd gotten himself to Buenos Aires, or why (though that was easy to imagine, as of course everybody did: the noise; the music; the work; the broader selection of whores; who wouldn't come if they could?).

El Loro was the fourth member of the group, and played the violin alongside Dante. He became El Loro when he was three years old because, as translator for his parents—Jews arrived from Russia—he was forced to chatter and repeat himself incessantly in both languages. Just like a parrot, *un loro,* his conventillo neighbors said. El Loro was younger than Pedro, at twenty-one. He was born on a ship halfway across the Atlantic, which, according to a busybody matron who'd insisted on attending the birth, doomed him to roam without anchor for the rest of his life. What the hell, he said, laughing as he told the story over whiskey and stew after work at six a.m., what's an anchor anyway? Just a chunk of metal to drag around. El Loro lived with his parents and sisters and brother in a small room, and shared all his earnings with them. He was friendlier than Pedro. When he talked, he swept the air with arcs so wide they seemed to enlarge the room. As a violinist, he was undisciplined, exuberant, bringing an energy that drove the group and was well tempered by the steadiness of Dante's sound.

"You lose the tempo when you get excited," Santiago told El Loro. "Control yourself. Come back to the bones. Follow Dante."

"Of course. He's like a rock, that Dante," El Loro said, a little sulkily. "He is."

"How does he do it?" El Loro said. "A kid like him?"

El Loro and Pedro glanced at Dante for an answer. She shrugged and turned away to busy herself with her instrument case.

"Don't worry about how he does it," Santiago said. "Just be glad he does."

She didn't know how she did it, where the steadiness came from. Everything in her life was unsteady: pesos, bread, work, her hole of a room, the intense proximity of neighbors who must not under any circumstances discover what she was. Her life could be upended in an instant, and this truth often made her feel fragile, brittle-boned. And yet, when she stood on a stage (or in a corner when there was none) and played, something else awoke in her, a sureness so vast it seemed to belong not to her but to some mountain, some monster, some ancient thing. Not a sureness of survival—never that. A sureness of motion. A sureness of rhythm. A sureness of sounds bound together by desire.

Santiago was a mystery; he seemed driven by forces beyond the human world. There was no other way to explain the singular intensity with which he worked. He talked little about himself, and yet Dante felt as though she'd known him for a long time, as though she could tell him anything and he'd at least listen, if not understand. Thanks to him, she was no longer alone, but part of a group, a foursome floating through the world on a shared raft, and she trusted it, trusted where their leader was taking them even if he himself had no rudder and no map. She couldn't say exactly why she trusted him. His assurance, perhaps, or the pure vigor of his vision. Santiago didn't want to just play tango: he wanted to vault it into rarefied realms where its existence still went unacknowledged. His orquesta couldn't just be good; it had to become a legend. This made him a harsh leader sometimes, demanding, though not ever cruel as she had heard other orquesta leaders could be. He never insulted or lied to his musicians, never attempted to cheat them of their pay. But he rode them like a ghoul. There were no breaks in rehearsals; mistakes onstage were crimes. Sometimes Pedro and El Loro grumbled and threatened to leave, but the truth was that they knew they could be replaced, that there were many men who'd taken up instruments recently with dreams of conquering the tango world. Yes, granted, Pedro and El Loro had a unique combination of rough talent and the kind of dedication that suggests insanity, which gave them good chances, but even so, they wouldn't risk it. Dante never thought of leaving, never questioned the bright conviction in Santiago's voice when he said, We're going somewhere, I'm telling you, keep with me and keep the faith. In any case, she didn't care too much where they were going. The luminous present moment was enough.

They played everywhere. They played where they could. There were lush times when El Cuarteto Torres had two or three offers at once and could choose the best venue among them and, more often, leaner times when they had to fill in with the kind of place where they left at dawn sticky and tense and relieved to have made it out alive. There were gleaming dance halls where tips for the musicians slowly filled a crystal bowl; cafés whose candlelight hid the stains on tablecloths and whores' clothes; bars where old bullet holes riddled a web of cracks in the walls, the work, perhaps, of a violent and furious Arachne. They played through the night, played to push the sun up over rooftops. They played for poor men and for rich men out for adventures among the poor, for women paid to dance and women paid to dance and fuck, and, when they were really hard up, for women paid to fuck so much they never came out to dance. For all her months and months of this work Dante could not get used to the women. They plagued her. Plagued her dreams. She woke up hot, gilded with the sweat of lust and grief and shame because so many of the women had eyes like those of dead fish and the other men seemed not to see this, or not to care, thinking, perhaps, she's already broken, it doesn't matter what I do, or simply look at that can't wait to fuck her. But she herself could not get past the thought of these women's pain. It seemed a crime to want them. She lay in the dark trying not to think of them, trying not to think of Cora on her back eyes shut against the shadow of her father. Dante could not stand the thought of hurting a woman.

Oh, you liar. The beast inside you. Waking you in sweats like this, what do you think it wants?

Not to hurt, no, no—she fought the voices in the fetid darkness. To see yes, to touch yes, to sink inside of the way men do, God, if only— but not ever to hurt.

You think they'd know the difference, those girls? After all they've been through? You'll just be one more monster to them.

She fought these voices night after night, could not find resolution. She was guilty. She railed against her own guilt. She tried not to lust, to stop wanting the women, and failed. She came to an uneasy truce with herself: she could look at the women from a distance but not touch them; she'd protect the whores from her touch. The only exception was the sparrow-girl, to whom she returned as though to a secret shrine until the day she arrived at La Moneda to discover that the sparrow-girl had disappeared. Nobody knew what had happened to her, or was willing to say.

"Find yourself another one," the bartender told her, shrugging, "and either buy a drink or let me do my job."

Dante tried not to think of the sparrow-girl racked by illness, stabbed in an alley, or simply worn to death by long nights. Girls like her got swallowed up and spit out by this city every day. Perhaps that wasn't what had happened; perhaps she'd run away, escaped on a boat across the river or a train to the pampas, those yawning plains that supposedly arose beyond the city. Dante hoped it was true. She wished she'd known the girl's name; she hadn't wanted to give it and Dante had been reluctant to press her for it. *Find yourself another one.* An easy fix. Already the other whores were looking her way, angling for centavos, but Dante could not face them, so she ducked out and walked quickly home.

The men in her band all had girlfriends, though these came and went and in any case didn't stop them from enjoying visits to the brothel on the side. Just the opposite, she learned: serious girlfriends were often virtuous, and the more virtuous a girl was, the more necessary visits to the brothel became. For the first few months she made excuses not to join them, but with each time they grew more incensed and bewildered at her refusal.

"You can't say no again," El Loro said. "What's your problem?"

"He's just a boy," Pedro said, in a mocking falsetto.

"I'm not," Dante protested. "I'm just focused."

"On what?"

"On my music."

Santiago was watching intently. She couldn't read what she saw in his eyes.

Pedro laughed. "Right. Music. You know what helps a man focus on music?"

"He's right, Dante," El Loro said. "If you're not careful your nuts might explode."

"You'll join us tonight," Santiago said, in the same tone he used to demand that they appear at work on time or practice for another hour, and it was this tone above all that was Dante's defeat. She shrugged her assent and, to avoid looking at the men, picked up her violin to tune it. Her hands shook at the pegs.

"Oh, look at him blush!" Pedro laughed. "He really needs it."

Dante didn't answer. The words *I can't do it I can't go* were on the tip of her tongue, and she imagined herself opening her mouth and letting them slip out, followed, surely, by more words, confessions, an unmasking. But then it was time to perform, and she followed El Loro up three ramshackle wooden steps to a raised platform that, though worn and tawdry, still placed her in a magic realm, the realm of the stage, her secret refuge. Her hands gradually stopped shaking as music caught her up in its great tides.

After work that night, they went to Lo de Amalia, a dance hall where they'd played in the past with several back rooms that almost verged on clean. They arrived at six thirty in the morning, when the dancing public had mostly dispersed and left the working girls to focus on the back-room side of business. The hall was crowded, dimly lit, and smelled of beer and kerosene. Dante found it difficult to breathe in the close air, or perhaps because of her own fear. She followed the musicians to a little table and sat down stiffly. A whore soon slung her arm around her neck, and, fortunately, she had plenty of life in her eyes. She was pretty in a moonfaced, thick-bodied kind of way. She was older than most of her fellow prostitutes, thirty or perhaps even older. A seasoned woman who'd seen a thing or two and hadn't let them break her.

"You, pretty boy," she said, "you'll be coming with me."

She said it with the tone a mother might use to tell a child to wash his face. She sat down in Dante's lap and pushed her ample breasts against him.

"There's a good boy."

She smelled of sweat and cinnamon. Dante felt dizzy. This woman, so much of her, so very close. She'd sworn she wouldn't touch a woman again, no one but the sparrow-girl, but she wasn't the one touching, now, was she? when this woman had come over of her own accord and didn't seem fragile, either, just the opposite, she was solid as an oak. Santiago cast Dante a look and raised his eyebrows, as if to say *there are other girls here, you don't have to accept, is that really what you want?* Dante strove to answer with her eyes, with the look of a satisfied man. Santiago looked like he was stifling a laugh, and Dante felt herself flush with embarrassment at being mocked. But then Santiago tipped an invisible hat in Dante's direction and turned back to the girl on his lap, whispering something in her ear that made her smile. Not mocking. Just laughing. Relieved that Dante, the youngest of their tribe, would be taken care of, would have his good time. The gesture seemed paternal, even tender in a way, and maybe that was exactly what it was, maybe this was a known rite for fathers and sons, she didn't know, she'd never been a son to her own father, but in any case, despite her guilt over the girls, she found herself moved by Santiago's gesture, his care for her, for all of them, these almost-boys he'd pulled from the gutters of Buenos Aires. The men soon headed to the back rooms. Dante followed them, right behind the moonfaced woman, hoping that the walls weren't too thin (though they were bound to be) and that her silence wouldn't raise suspicion. Her whole body felt tight, and she fought back waves of panic with each step. She just wanted to get through the session without being discovered. It was a long hall, she thought, a long way to run if she was found out, and a far longer way to find a corner of this land where she could hope to start again.

When Dante and the woman arrived in the dim room, Dante whispered, "Lie here with me."

"Silly boy. What else would we do?"

"No, I mean, just lie down. Nothing else."

"What's the matter? Is it sore? Got the clap?"

Dante shrugged. The woman laughed and lay down. The walls were thin. El Loro was next door, already grunting. Dante lay down on the thin mattress next to the woman. "What's your name?" she whispered.

"Everybody calls me Mamita."

She was a lovely woman, even more so now, relaxed against the bed as if about to dream. Leda didn't mean to touch, but her hands ran along Mamita's body, lightly. Loosened her bodice. This didn't count, did it? No touching, no— "You're warm, Mamita."

"That's just the first of it. Does it hurt?"

"Does what hurt?"

"Your tool."

"It—uh—no, not much."

"You sure? Don't want me to kiss it and make it better?"

"No, thanks, really."

"I made you shy!"

"No." Her hand was inside Mamita's bodice now, stroking her breasts, returning over and over to the miraculous nipples. She was not allowed. She had to stop. Every fiber in her body blazed with pleasure.

"I did." Mamita was laughing. "You're just a boy, aren't you?"

She was looking at Dante with wide brown eyes, half-mocking, half-nurturing. She's joking around with me, Dante thought with a shock. She even seems like she might—stranger than strange!—be enjoying herself. Imagine that. A whore who was alive inside, who laughed and seemed to mean it. The breasts were freed from their bodice now, right in Dante's greedy hands. "I'm not hurting you?"

"Hurting me! With those little paws?"

"I don't . . . I don't want to hurt you."

"Oh, you poor dear. You don't know a thing. Look, you've only got a couple of minutes left—you hear your friend finishing up in there? And you've been paddling in the shallows like a baby. So I'll give you a little something: I'll tell you a secret. Come here."

Dante bent close to Mamita and met her eyes.

"Are you listening?"

Dante nodded.

"Now I'm doing you a big favor telling you this, because most ladies, they won't ever admit to it, not directly. It's just something you have to be a man about. Understand?"

She nodded again.

"It's fine to pet them softly like you're doing. But it's also boring. A lot of ladies like a little bite. Take the nipple between your thumb and finger, give it a good long pinch."

Next door the groaning had given way to silence.

"Do it."

Dante obeyed, gingerly.

"No, harder."

She did it a little harder.

"Pathetic. You call yourself a man? Harder, hard as you can."

Dante did as she was told, and Mamita arched her back and shut her eyes and made a long sharp sound, as pure as it was beautiful. For an instant it even seemed that the artifice between them, the distance made by the roles they were acting, had dropped away, and that they were elsewhere together, on a great sea, Dante a raft, Mamita the bright water itself. Then the room returned. Mamita opened her eyes and stared vacantly for a moment at a point on the wall. Then she turned to Dante with a look of amusement. "Well, look at you. Little devil."

Dante didn't know what to say. Her mind groped for words. Stumbling.

"Your time's up."

"Oh. Yes." She rose, shakily, and reached for her hat. "Thanks for the secret."

"Don't forget it."

How could I? Dante thought, and would have said, but Mamita was already closing up her bodice with businesslike gestures that made Dante feel thrown out like a dog. She walked out on unsteady legs. The hall shimmered strangely. Pedro and El Loro were leaning against the wall, waiting. Santiago had not yet returned.

"What did you do to her, Dante?"

The question she'd dreaded. El Loro staring, waiting for an answer, and if they knew that she hadn't—that she couldn't—the world would crumble all around her.

"To make her scream like that? Come on, tell us how you did it!"

It was not suspicion on El Loro's face but admiration. His girl had been silent the whole time. Even Pedro was looking at her with an expression of grudging curiosity.

A new Dante smiled now, cocked his hat on his head, and drew himself up tall. "Boys, you know what they say. I'm a gentleman, I'll never tell."

————

On some mornings Dante fell into sleep like a dead weight, but on others she lay awake, restive, aching. Loneliness wrapped tightly around her throat, a thin wire, fatal. There was nobody who saw her as she truly was. There was no end to the disguise, to the invented story. It was not that she did not want to live as this new Dante. But in hiding half of her story, she became unseen, or half-seen, like the moon when it veils one side of its face in darkness. And there were times when she wanted to be seen. Even touched. But these things were not possible; she brushed them off. She was glad no one could see her, that she was invisible in full view. It was her salvation. People cannot see what they can't imagine, and she was unimaginable, even to herself, a kind of rip in the fabric of reality. Women had never done such things before. Had they?

One rainy morning, as she lay down on the dank floor to sleep, arms sore from a long night's work, she thought of Joan of Arc. Fat drops roared in the hall outside her door. Water leaked in through the threshold of the closed door and soaked her pallet. Downstairs she heard La Strega calling to her daughter to move faster with the peas or she'd still be shelling when the archangels announced the end of the world. What about Joan of Arc? In the dank unbreathable air of her little room, she recalled Cora's stories of the saint's life. A girl in armor. A fight for justice. Well, she thought, I'm not fighting for justice or to free a whole people; my fight is unseen, I'll be buried by the clamor of a million untold lives, a speck in the avalanche of history. No one will ever know that I was.

Joan of Arc, unlike her, was remembered. Even held up as a hero.

But she was also burned at the stake.

Better not to look too deeply into old stories.

Only the violin accepted her fully, without question. She sometimes imagined that she was making love to it. She gave it all her force and longing, and the violin received it all in its fine curves, its secret hollows, utterly sensuous, neither male nor female, complete. I can live without romance, she thought, as I clearly must (although a crack of doubt had appeared in this thought, Mamita's arched back, her flashing pleasure, what if she could make that happen in other women?—no, don't think about that), I can live without being seen, I can even live knowing that heaven will close its gates to me when I die and force me down to hell, but I cannot live without my violin.

At times she would imagine that, when she played the violin, someone or something else was playing her with the same fierce care, using her to fulfill its inscrutable vision. She, nothing more than an instrument, of the divine perhaps, though not the god of priests and the Bible from whose embrace she was surely excommunicated by her sins; there had to be some other force that also was divine or at least felt so, perhaps originating among lax angels or bold demons or some creature that fused them both within itself, an angeldemon, a spiritual hermaphrodite, exiled from heaven just like her, entirely awake. Only that kind of god would deign to fill a vessel like Leda-who-was-Dante, pour in through the crown of her head while she played and rush down her arms through her fingers to strings that moaned beautifully not for her alone but for all the secret exiles here on earth.

Home stilled pulled at her ankles. A riptide strong enough to drown in. She tried not to think of it, tried not to miss Alazzano, tried to ignore its imprint behind her eyelids when she blinked, but it was there, always throbbing beneath the surface, always beckoning to her, threatening the ground on which she stood. The letters continued to arrive, and now she read them and even, occasionally, answered. In an effort to soften the blow of her absence, she wrote of a happy false life in which she lived from her needle in a bustling and charming city where chaste and honest immigrant women came together to sew and protect each other in a tenement whose walls kept the world's dangers at bay. She didn't know whether her parents believed her or not. They kept writing. They finished every letter with the same request, *And please, Leda, come home, come home,* but even this seemed like an incantation spoken out of duty, robbed of power through bland repetition. It was her father who wrote

the letters now. They were doing fine, he said. The little ones were growing at a startling pace. Tommaso had a son now, another on the way. The
harvests had been good. The war in other European countries had them
worried that Italy might join in, but war, her father pointed out, was like
the weather: it comes upon you and seeps in everywhere and can't be
stopped, there's nothing that an ordinary man can do. Leda strained to
read between the lines. Was Tommaso happy? And Mamma? Would her
father ever forgive her for staying in Argentina without his blessing? To
disobey your parents was to commit the worst treason. She was a bad
daughter, worse than they would ever know. Staying was a betrayal, but
it protected them from ever learning of the larger one.

This was her only home now, Buenos Aires, La Rete, where she
sometimes played in the patio, working out the kinks of a new song,
watching her neighbors dance. Feet moving, couples dancing as the
laundry fluttered over their heads like a disparate collection of flags;
the inhabitants of La Rete danced even when the air was cold, the job
lost, the belly empty, the baby dead. La Strega took to singing tangos.
Her voice was large and raspy and climbed the walls with an avid reach
toward the sky.

Sometimes, Leda dreamed of Vesuvius, that she was climbing its slopes
on bare feet. Her feet bled but didn't hurt her. She walked and walked
until the volcano erupted with what looked at first like lava but, on her
arriving closer, revealed itself to be a glowing river of people, pouring
down the mountain on all sides, droves and droves of immigrants flying
past her with startled expressions on their faces as the victims of Pompeii
might have had, except unlike those ancient victims these people were
alive, completely alive, arms outstretched in a futile attempt to hold on
to something, anything—a branch, a rock, a memory—as they soared
down slopes and out to the horizon, which swallowed them by the thousands, leaving not a single trace.

———

El Cuarteto Torres had many successes and only occasional humiliations, such as managers who sent them off without pay, which happened
only twice: once at a grim little brothel and once at a clean hall whose
owner flashed a menacing smile and simply said, "I already paid you."

"You didn't," Santiago said, his face a wall of calm.

"You're trying to cheat me."

"Sir, we agreed to payment at closing time."

"Listen, *negro de mierda,* get out of here before I call the police."

Santiago did not flinch and did not move a muscle in his face.

El Loro spat on the floor and said, "You can't do this!"

Dante stared at El Loro in surprise. She'd never seen him act this
way. He was always mild-mannered, even sweet, the kind of immigrant
boy who respected his elders and strived to keep the world free of fric-
tion. She was seeing another side of him now, the side that flared up
at injustice, a brave side or a stupid one, perhaps; she couldn't decide.
The dance hall owner leaned forward. He was a small man with enormous ears and too much grease in his hair. Even I could take this bastard,
Dante thought, and only the specter of almost certain prison stopped
her. "Get this kid out of here."

"Let's go," Santiago said.

"But no, Negro—" El Loro protested.

"You heard him," Pedro said. "Let's go."

They walked out into the night. The street blared at them, raucous,
hostile. They walked to the corner and paused under a streetlamp to
light their cigarettes. It was five a.m. and men spilled out of the bars and
dance halls, filling the sidewalk, humming or bantering with each other
or striding off alone into the darkness.

"You should have punched him," El Loro said. He was sulking now,
his spark turned to ash.

"We'll have our revenge," Santiago said.

"Oh yeah? How? By reporting him to the police?"

"Don't be stupid," said Santiago. That silenced them for a moment.

Obviously the police would never take the side of a fistful of *tangueros* from the tenements over a business owner.

They started walking again, toward San Telmo, smoking, their instrument cases in hand or slung over their shoulders. The sky to the east grew pale. On a broad avenue, a lamplighter had begun to extinguish the streetlamps, raising up his pole to flames enclosed in glass high above his head, snuffing them out with a swift flick of the wrist. His face was tired, expressionless. How many lamps did he put out in one morning? Hundreds? Thousands? How many little fires burned in this city? Dante felt dizzied by the thought.

"We could break in and steal his money," Pedro said. Dante wondered how serious he was. His tone was light but his eyes glittered.

"No."

"I'd like to smear my shit all over his pretty walls," El Loro said.

That made Pedro laugh. El Loro laughed too. There was a unity between them then, a boyish ease, that Dante couldn't help but envy.

"No," Santiago said again. He was walking in front of Dante, she couldn't see his face.

"I was joking, Negro."

"I'm not taking any chances. I want things clear."

"I thought you said we'd have our revenge."

"Not that way."

"No? Then how?"

The four musicians' steps drummed softly beneath the din.

"By succeeding."

Dante gazed out at the street, at a carriage drawn by a horse the color of garbanzos. The curtains at the carriage's window were closed; anything could have been happening inside there, anything at all. She felt a chill at Santiago's words, a strange mixture of dread and hope.

"What about our pay?" said El Loro.

"Don't worry." Santiago stopped to flick his cigarette butt into the gutter. "We'll have another job before you know it."

And they did.

There was, after all, a need for bands like theirs, with a strong sound and men willing to break their backs to keep the crowd dancing. Every day, it seemed, there were larger crowds, new halls. The tango was changing: everybody, not only the poor, wanted to dance it. Not only that: the sound itself was changing, some instruments rising into prominence while others began to disappear. By the winter of 1915, as the Great War raged across Europe and shook the immigrants of Buenos Aires awake at night with terror for their loved ones across the ocean (and Leda learned in a brief letter from her father that Alazzano was safe from bombs and guns for now, though what the *for now* meant for the months ahead she didn't dare to wonder), the tango without the bandoneón was no longer considered true tango. That strange German instrument had been absorbed into the music, altering its essential texture and slowing its pace, because there's only so fast that fingers can fly across the bandoneón's keys and press the air within it. The bandoneón brought a velvet longing to the tango, and made it slower and statelier than when Leda had first heard it. And at the same time, other instruments—flute, guitar, mandolin—were falling out of fashion. They were becoming part of the old sound, the old tango, quickly fading into oblivion, into the abyss of the past, while the new tango rose, a luxurious sound, featuring more musicians—five, six, seven—and, if a venue wanted to be truly chic, a piano to give the sound complexity and finesse. The introduction of the piano changed everything. Pianos could not be slung over your shoulder or tucked under your arm. Each venue had to provide its own, and that took space and money. In turn, if a venue obtained a piano, the bands it hired had better have a pianist in their ranks.

After all, you couldn't have the piano bench sitting there looking empty and alone like a jilted bride while the orquesta played.

That's what La China Irene said when she told Santiago she'd bought a piano for her dance hall.

It was a good hall, larger than most, and quite clean. It had no windows. The walls boasted exotic tapestries and stained-glass sconces. The stage looked like the work of an erratic, fevered carpenter. There were women for hire, but only to be danced with, and they dutifully kept up the pretense that they weren't for sale in any other way. The men who came to this place to dance were, after all, often gentlemen from across town. If you wanted to rut like a common animal, La China would say, you'd come to the wrong establishment. If a man and his dance partner slipped off early, whether for a drink or perhaps a walk in the park (and here she'd meet your eyes as if to dare you to suggest there could be any other reason) then that was their private business and had nothing to do with her. La China's establishment was so respectable that she had a man guarding the bathrooms at all times to ensure that couples did not slip in together. She managed the place for an owner who never showed his face; as long as she kept the clients and the pesos pouring in, she reigned freely, a queen in garish necklaces whose laugh could infect your dreams.

El Cuarteto Torres had been playing at La China Irene's for three weeks when she announced the piano.

"For the best clientele," she said, "it's necessary. You understand."

"Of course," Santiago said. They were in the tiny curtained space La China referred to as *backstage*. El Loro and Dante were tuning their violins, close enough to hear each other's breath. Pedro sat on a crate beside them, wiping his bandoneón in the semidark.

"I'm sorry to have to let you go," said La China.

"But you don't have to let us go."

"You have no pianist!"

"Yes we do."

She raised a painted eyebrow. In her youth, as a newly arrived Andalusian immigrant, La China had worked the back rooms; Dante thought of this with amazement, unable to picture this woman as anything but stout and formidable, bedecked in plumes that rose from her dress like soldiers at attention. "Ah? Where?"

"We'll have one in— When does your piano arrive?"

"In two days."

"We'll have our pianist then."

"That's absurd, Santiago, you won't have time to practice—"

"It's enough time. Don't you worry."

"Santiago," she said, "you know I'm fond of you. But I won't have my clientele forced to dance to your rehearsals."

"Chinita," Santiago said, "I promise we'll be ready, we'll be everything you dream of, and if we're not I'll give back all the money you've paid us these past three weeks."

El Loro didn't take his eyes off his tuning pegs, but his face went tense. Pedro flicked his rag in noisy protest. All that pay had already been split between the four of them, and it was likely that each had already spent his share on rent or bread, as Dante had herself. How could Santiago put that money on the gambling table? What if he lost?

"All right," La China finally said. "But you'd better be good."

"I promise, we'll have the crowd by the balls."

La China left through the red cotton curtain, leaving a trail of rose perfume.

"What were you talking about?" said Pedro. "You don't have a pianist!"

El Loro leapt in: "How are we going to—"

"Shut up, both of you!" Santiago said. "Just leave it to me."

He left La China Irene's that night for the bars and cafés of Buenos Aires, trolling for a pianist, just as a couple of years earlier he'd gone diving for a violinist and found Dante. Who knew how many bars he went to or just what he did there. Dante pictured him scanning each stage, searching for pianos, slipping cash to bartenders in exchange for information, listening and moving on, over and over.

The following day, when Dante arrived at Santiago's home on Calle Defensa—a front room in a conventillo that his family cleared out of during rehearsal time—there were not one but two strangers in the room.

"This is Amato." Santiago glowed with triumph as he gestured toward the man perched on a stool in the corner. "Pianist."

Amato nodded at them all. He seemed older, in his late twenties, with an unshaven face and a slight paunch that gave him an air of authority. Pedro, El Loro, and Dante nodded back, in that manner that was not so much an affirmation as a flinch of the chin.

"And this is Joaquín. He plays the bass."

Joaquín was a tall, lean man, standing guard over an enormous black instrument case. His face seemed at once mournful and refined, as if he'd made a home for himself inside of sadness and elevated it to an art.

"He's joining us too?" El Loro said.

Santiago nodded. "We'll be a sextet."

"I've never seen a bass in a tango group before," El Loro said.

"We don't need one," Pedro said.

Santiago turned to gaze at Pedro, and the air grew tense. Pedro did not say, did not need to say, that more musicians meant less pay for each of them, that he didn't want to share his cut with this Joaquín, who watched the exchange without a sound, his face solemn, unreadable.

"It's not about what we need," Santiago said evenly. "It's about what we can become." He let those words land in the middle of the room, where they hovered, daring anyone to contradict them. No one did. "Joaquín has something to bring us that no one else can. We'll be original, a band like no other. The tango is for dancing. Rhythm matters. That's why there used to be drums."

Dante felt a jolt of surprise. She had never heard of, and could not imagine, drums in the tango. She had so many questions, but was too embarrassed to ask.

Fortunately, El Loro was less inhibited. "Drums! Are you joking?"

"No."

"What kind?"

"African drums," Amato said. It was the first time he'd spoken, and his voice was deep and rich, the voice of a man twice his size.

"And what happened?" El Loro asked.

"It changed," Amato said.

"Everything changes," Santiago said quickly. "Nothing wrong with that. Tango is still changing and we'll be part of changing it."

Pedro looked doubtful, but he said nothing. El Loro seemed curious and a little bewildered. Amato tapped his thigh as if playing imaginary piano keys and, when he caught Dante looking at him, flashed a warm smile, as if they'd been friends for a long time. Joaquín studied a spot on the far wall. Santiago took a moment before he spoke again.

"We could be part of something bigger—much bigger. Don't you want that?"

The question was for all of them. No one answered aloud. The question swelled open and filled the space between them.

"Let's get to work," Santiago said.

There was no piano in Santiago's home, so Amato sat on a stool and watched the other musicians as they played, fingers roving across the empty air. Joaquín's bass notes grafted to their sound with startling ease. They did more than graft: they dug a deeper well for music to inhabit, pushing open low foundations for the high flights of violins, the smooth wails of bandoneóns. He was a firm yet agile player; Santiago had chosen well. A genius, really, that Santiago, he'd brought them all together and now they formed something they could never have shaped in isolation, a thick bright sound all their own. Inside that sound, Dante felt close to the other men, almost fused to them, in a manner more immediate than sex, or so she imagined based on what she'd gleaned from the matrons of Alazzano and from brothels and bars. There was nothing husband-wife, nothing man-and-whore, about this communication. No one yielded and no one conquered. Each musician penetrated the others and was penetrated at the same time, each man exposed: you, you ache like this, you spark like that, here is what drives you. And as for me, here, this, ache, spark. Every human being has unmapped regions within, hidden from view, but lock rhythms and the secret parts spill out and gleam.

———

Ladies and gentlemen! shouted La China as she spread her arms wide onstage. *El Sexteto Torres!*

Their sound exploded into the hall. It was wider, rounder, more lavish than ever before. Amato's intricate trills and rhythmic chords on the piano filled the space beneath the soaring violins, sustained their flights, and meshed with Joaquín's rhythmic spine. The bandoneón's melodies traversed a richer weave than ever, growing bolder, holding dramatic pauses worth weeping into, swirling out sumptuous lines to pierce you and push you into motion at the same time, make you forget your unpaid bills or lonely heart or even your dying mama, make the whole world collapse into a single sphere composed entirely of La China's dance hall, warm with music and all of life compressed into its walls. Santiago had been right: they had the crowd by the balls or by whatever other part they wanted. Men gripped their dance partners more closely; the bar sold more drinks with every passing night; La China, to her delight, had to hire more girls to keep up with demand. She had offered them a three-month contract by the end of the first week. They celebrated at a neighboring bar, where Santiago insisted on paying for their chorizo and whiskey and even for the girls.

"You're sure, Negro?"

"It's a special night."

"Morning, you mean."

"If it's morning, that's all the more proof of how hard you've worked."

They had descended on a large round table in the corner, and already the whores were smiling their way, though they stopped short of coming over, having plenty to attend to, for the moment, in the rest of the crowd.

"Is it really work," Joaquín said, "when we get to spend the whole night with the tango?"

"That's like calling it work to spend the night fucking your wife," El Loro said.

"That *is* work," said Pedro, and the men laughed.

"What do you know about it? You've never been married," Amato said, and Pedro glanced up nervously, afraid he'd offended the only married man at the table.

But Amato was smiling crookedly.

Pedro looked relieved and kept on. "Why would I get married? Music is enough of a ball and chain."

"True," said Amato.

"Oh, but she's beautiful," Santiago said.

Music as lover, Dante thought. *I feel that too. But what kind of lover? A woman? A man?*

"And she doesn't talk back," said Pedro.

"Oh yes she does," said Joaquín, nodding solemnly as if referring to a great mystery.

"All right," said Pedro, "but she doesn't expect you to be home at this or that time."

"That's because you're out with *her*," Amato said. "Doing her bidding and treating her like a queen."

If the tango itself could dance with me, would it lead or follow?

"She lets you have plenty of other women," said El Loro.

"True," said Joaquín.

"Only half-true," said Santiago. "She lets you as long as she always comes first."

"Oh yes," said Amato. "She's a jealous one, that music."

"But sexy, right?" El Loro said cheerfully. "The sexiest!"

What are you, tango, and what on earth am I?

"Now you've gone too far," Amato said. "Music doesn't have a pussy."

"Or tits," said Pedro.

"Tits," said Joaquín.

And then, just like that, the six men reached a place of unity. The air between them brightened. They all laughed. Santiago refilled their glasses and raised his. "To music."

"To tits."

"Music."

"Tits."

"Music!"

"Tits, tits!"

They quibbled and laughed and Dante laughed along with them, at first to blend in, although at some indiscernible moment her laugh stopped being false and became something real. They toasted, in the end, to tits, and for an instant as the whiskey poured fast down her throat she felt like part of their tribe, a tribe of men, all of whom, in unison, loved tits and music; she was just like them, and not alone; she wiped her mouth on her sleeve just as the rest of them did, amazed to feel a kind of lightness in her body, in her shoulders, a fleeting liberation from shame.

When shame pressed on her she sometimes heard the old voices as they'd rippled out one afternoon years ago, while she hid behind a tree at the plaza's edge:

Shameful, shameful.

Pfft, that girl.

Cora Matta.

A disgrace.

Covering herself with mud like that.

Like a rutting animal.

Like a whore.

Drat, I'm out of soap and all these sheets still left to wash.

Here, use mine.

Or mine.

Or mine.

I will, God keep you for it.

Cora.

It's witchcraft, I tell you.

Devil's work.

And that last night in the plaza.

Was she chanting? Were you there?

I was there. All I heard were the demons.

What demons?

A flock of them, circling her. The sound of them flying drowned out everything else.

What are you talking about?

Yes, tell us. What do flying demons sound like?

I don't want to repeat the sound, it's terrifying.

Come on, we have to know.

It's like this. *Whoooooooooosh.*

Do it again.

Whooooosh.

Ha ha! Again.

Oh, shut up.

Well, I don't know about any demons but I certainly heard Cora. She was muttering.

Ah! Muttering what?

I don't know. It didn't sound like Italian.

The devil's tongue.

A curse no doubt, a curse on Alazzano.

I saw her levitate.

No!

Yes. Right there in the plaza.

How high?

Higher than a tall child.

No!

Evil, evil.

She hovered above the stones like a witch.

She's cursed us.

Our church is marred forever by what she did there.

Shhp! Don't even mention that. The poor nuns doing their best.

I heard they scrub it down three times a day now.

I heard that too.

But what can scrub out a thing like that, a naked screaming girl?

I don't know.

Nothing.

They don't let her out of the house anymore.

They weren't letting her out before, she still got out.

But now she can't escape.

Why not?

I heard they've got her tied down and someone watching her at all hours of the day or night.

You can't tie down a demon. They can fly anywhere, right out of the body.

In the name of the Father, the Son, and the Holy Ghost.

Thank God they've started the exorcisms.

Not a moment too soon.

I've seen them going into the house, Father Domenico and the nuns.

I've heard the chants.

I've heard the screams.

Demon-screams.

Of course.

Holy Mary, mother of God, help them with what they must do.

Summer arrived on a brutal heat wave that felled dogs and old men alike. In the peak months of January and February, the Torres Sextet traveled to outlying towns to play the outdoor stages of Argentina's Carnaval. They took the train together, through the long flat countryside. They slept three to a room at tiny country hotels, some with dirt floors, some with hand-laid tiles, some with rooms where a single small window let right into the chicken coop. The first time they arrived at a hotel, Leda's heart constricted when she saw the washbasin in the corner with the large pail: everyone to bathe in the same room. She couldn't bathe in front of them, but if she didn't bathe, all summer, in this demonic heat, what would they think? Fortunately for her, the musicians slept like the dead all morning. They lay down at about seven or eight a.m., just back from work, and didn't wake till lunchtime. She willed herself to wake up first, prayed for it, set the tension in her body like the spring of a clock. And her body complied: she always woke first. She crept out of bed and washed herself without removing her underwear or the bandage from her breasts, scrupulously keeping her back to the sleeping men. For the first two weeks she managed this before anybody stirred, and by the time they did she was already dressed, shrugging casually, *go ahead compadres, I've already bathed.* El Loro and Amato stripped easily, baring their bodies: El Loro's lithe, muscular back, Amato's hairy chest and paunchy belly.

"How do you do it, Dante?" El Loro said. "Don't you sleep?"

She shrugged. "I wanted a cigarette."

"That's not what it is," Amato said, and, as always, his voice rang with authority.

El Loro turned to him, expectantly, for the answer. Dante, for the ten thousandth time, went tense with fear of being unmasked.

"It's that he's young," Amato said. And he laughed.

El Loro looked perturbed. "But I'm young too."

Amato slapped El Loro on the back. "Sorry, my boy. But Dante's younger."

One morning, in the third week, in a small town outside Rosario, Dante put on her shirt after bathing and turned to see El Loro, eyes wide open, staring at her intently.

"What's the bandage for?"

Dante had imagined such a question might come one day, and she'd had a few years to think of an answer. "For the scar on my chest. It never healed right."

Loro didn't seem to blink. He was completely awake. He was a sweet-faced boy, really, the kind mothers doted on beyond reason. He'll make a bride very happy one day, Dante thought. "What's it from?"

"A knife wound."

Loro said nothing. He watched Dante thread her belt through her pant loops, buckle the belt, sit down to put on socks. The day was blistering. If only musicians could wear sandals. Even barefoot would be better than this. Finally, El Loro said, "Did it hurt?"

Dante busied herself lighting a cigarette. The tobacco scratched at her lungs. "I'm alive."

El Loro closed his eyes and slept or seemed to sleep for another half hour. He never mentioned the conversation again.

She also couldn't urinate the way the men did, on dirt roads or up against the walls of buildings. While their venues in Buenos Aires had always had a private bathroom, however small and filthy, these country bars relied on the fields behind them. She tried to stop drinking, but the men protested: it's hot, you're crazy, have a beer. And so she took to pretending to drink, then sneaking outside at intermission to pour beer into the dirt. Her heart pounded with the fear of being caught, but she never was. She grew accustomed to playing the second set with the ache of a full bladder, and holding her pee until they made it back to their hotels, which always had outhouses where a man, it could be agreed, had decent reasons to squat.

"You sure do shit a lot," Pedro teased her.

The other men watched her, curious, as if they'd noticed the same thing.

She smiled, every muscle on alert, and looked Pedro full in the face. "Better than staying full of it."

The men laughed, Pedro smiled grudgingly, and Dante felt a wash of relief.

It was beautiful to travel with these men. She came to know each of them better, Amato's snores, El Loro's sweat, the warm spike of Pedro's laugh, which came rarely but stayed a long time when it did. Sometimes, on long dull train rides, they told stories about their lives. Amato told them about the many orquestas he'd worked with, and the singers he'd played behind, because, you know, he said, it's happening more and more, this business of singing along to tangos, and the best of them all is that Carlitos, you know the one, Carlos Gardel? All the men had heard of him, but none of them had heard him sing. He sang in a duo, Gardel-Razzano, and had come up from the same streets and conventillos they all knew. Amato had backed him during a stint at a dance hall, and swore the man had a voice like sweet fire that he knew just how to calibrate and he was a smart bastard, too, courting café owners like they were village girls, though now that he'd hit the fancier circuits he'd become more deferential. Just last year he'd toured Uruguay and then Brazil and been received like a prince, his face on flyers plastered all over the cities, interviews with all the best papers, only to come back to Buenos Aires and get shot last month, in a fight at a party, you know the kind, Amato said, our kind of party. From the highest high to the lowest low. That's tango for you, said Pedro. Maybe, Amato said. But anyway, I went to see him as he was healing up, just a few weeks after I joined all of you, and I sat beside his hospital bed and told him, in no uncertain terms, you have to heal, Carlitos, you bastard, you can't take that voice from us, and do you know what he told me? He said that, in Montevideo, at the end of the show, the audience—well dressed and fine—had leapt to its feet and demanded an encore, shouting his name, *tocate otra, Carlitos,* shouting and clapping and roaring until he returned to the stage and gave them another song he had to come up with quickly because he hadn't planned for this, he'd never done an encore in his life. And when he went back to his dressing room, do you know what he did? His voice went very quiet when he told me, because, you know, the wound was delicate and it hurt his chest to talk. He said to me, I wept, Amato. I wept like a baby.

Amato's stories opened room for others. Dante was amazed to learn that she was not the only one who'd broken with expectations to become a musician. El Loro had, in his own words, broken his parents' hearts; they were grateful for the money he brought home, but had hoped that he'd become a doctor and support his family, marry a good Russian Jewish girl, not spend his nights out in dens of sin—on Shabbat, no less, making his forebears in the Old Country turn in their graves—and his summers playing a fiddle on dirt roads. What decent Russian girl would take him in this state? He laughed as he told the story, but Dante heard the catch in his throat. And then Joaquín spoke up: I think I know what you mean. Joaquín had never talked about his life outside music, and all the men looked at him in surprise. Joaquín told them, as wheat fields sped by outside their window, that he was a lawyer's son, groomed from a young age for a life of classical music. His father loved music more than anything, and had grown up playing piano as if galaxies depended on its sound to keep on spinning, but he had studied law at the insistence of his parents, who were immigrants from Spain. His greatest dream was to send a son to the conservatory, and he did, never expecting that the son would drop out of school to play a wholly different kind of music that, for all its popularity, would always be the music of the lower classes, of those who had no culture, who didn't know Handel from Bach. Dante, listening to this story, bristled at the worlds *no culture*, and wondered for a fleeting moment how Joaquín saw her, and the rest of the members of the band. But then she brushed the thought away. Joaquín had come to the tango for the same reason they all had: out of passion. The other men weren't bothered by this part of the story, or else they didn't let on. El Loro nodded as though grateful for another tale of parental pressure. Pedro listened intently, not saying, not needing to say, that he had no parents to pressure him into anything, orphan that he was. Amato roved invisible piano keys across his lap as he listened, always practicing, halfway out of the conversation; Santiago rolled a cigarette and lit it, seeming unperturbed—this was nothing, after all, that he hadn't heard before. He'd surely heard much worse things said about the tango, his tango, their tango. His hair had grown out a little, and curled black and wild against the rapid sky outside.

These talks, these moments, made Dante feel like part of something larger, a long tradition of wandering musicians who gave a little joy in exchange for a coin or bit of straw on which to sleep. She had heard, back in Alazzano, of minstrels through the ages who lived simply, close to the ground, eating on some days and starving on others, existing at the world's edges and bringing music to the center with relentless hands. She felt part of their ancient nameless ranks, and this moved her. It also moved her to play outside, in the quieter lands outside the city. Green. For the first time since she'd come to the New World, Dante's eyes could feast on boundless green again, in the low hills around them, the long flat fields, the groves of great old trees whose sumptuous branches dripped with tiny lights like wayward stars that shone all night as wealthy couples, on vacation at their families' estates, danced and forgot themselves—and the stubborn mosquitoes, and the dark of the surrounding land—in the arms of tango. The women wore heavy ruffled dresses that buttoned primly all the way up to their necks, and elaborate hats that looked, to Dante, heavy enough to cause perpetual headaches. Their dancing was just as prim: their feet dutifully stepped back or to the side in response to the man's moves, but rarely attempted a *gancho*, rarely slid a calf between a man's legs—an unseemly act—and even when they did it was a quick and timid motion, obscured by floor-length skirts. Even so, the women looked thrilled to be dancing. It seemed to Dante that the dance floor gave them permission they didn't otherwise have: permission to move, permission to touch a man in public, permission to breathe a slightly looser breath.

"Would you look at that." Pedro whistled. "Ladies dancing tango. I never thought I'd see it with my own eyes."

The rich were infinitely fascinating to Dante. They were good to play for in many ways. They gave money freely, tossed their bills into the musicians' bowl without a second glance, as though it were not money but old rags they were casting to the side. She'd never seen this kind of wealth before; in her village, her family, the Mazzoni family, had always been the richest, and her uncle Mateo had accepted his aristocratic status like a debt owed to him. But these people made Mateo Mazzoni look like a pompous country fool. Their clothing dazzled. Their posture spoke of majesty, or at least of a kind of virtuosic arrogance. They had books, they had paintings of themselves in cavernous houses, they had educations that grasped the heights of human thought, at least the men. Their gaze flicked across musicians on a stage as it might across a cadre of servants. Everything in order, yes, nothing more to care about or see. And yet, Dante would think: you don't see us but you need us. You need this tango. That is why you came here, to this summer theater, in your gleaming carriage and polished shoes. You need the tango and we're the ones who have it, so take this, bastards (line of melody spools out under her fingers) and take this too (staccato notes that mesh with the piano's snarl) and this and this and if you think for an instant I don't own you then it's you who are the fool.

The men never looked twice at the musicians, but some of the ladies did. Young wives, solid matrons, virgin girls. When their husbands or fathers were distracted, they stared at the musicians with expressions of curiosity or longing or discomfort, as if the coarse men onstage were wolves on the loose, rarely seen in their own confined lives, keen to maul them if they weren't careful, and as if they, the ladies in question, weren't at all certain that careful was what they wanted to be.

The musicians of El Sexteto Torres were entirely proper with these ladies, except for a few long intermissions when Joaquín or Pedro or Amato disappeared at the same time as a lady who returned with a ribbon of mud at the hem, a single unclasped button at the throat. These moments were discussed among the musicians with the silent language of looks: amusement, envy, admiration, and, from Santiago, disapproval— one feminine complaint and they'd be out on their ears—mixed with an almost paternal resignation, *boys will be boys*. Most of the time, however, the musicians saved their lust for the town brothels or, sometimes, an easy chambermaid, kitchen girl, or innkeeper's daughter. Pedro, in particular, seemed to make a new girlfriend in every place without trying. Girls would follow him from room to room with young-fawn eyes. He neither encouraged them (as Joaquín did, for himself, with mixed success) nor turned them down. Sometimes they fell away, chastened by their fathers or Pedro's tepid response or their own goal of chastity. At other times Pedro took them to a barn, a yard, a rooftop, and left town with a lock of hair, a tear-filled goodbye, a promise to wait for his return. He put these promises in his pocket like small change, quickly accepted and forgotten. Dante pretended to share the other men's admiration. She kept her own ventures to the brothels, ramshackle sheds nailed to the backs of town bars where she cashed in her chips like all the others, so as not to draw attention to herself, but, once alone with a girl, did nothing more than stare at her sublime body—sometimes fully naked, sometimes breasts, bared thighs, a rump bent over with the skirt thrown up—as she raged inside with a thirst she could not slake.

Except with the tango. The music itself. It seemed to carry something of this land in it. It seemed a strange thought, absurd, that music could somehow contain the pulse or imprint of the earth where it began. It seemed like the kind of thought that got people carted to insane asylums. And yet, some nights, as she played on those torchlit summer stages, she felt the continent beneath her feet—the bedrock buried far under the wooden planks—moan in grief. Or perhaps it was pleasure. She didn't know. But the moan was there; it wrapped itself around the backbone of Joaquín's bass, those solid notes that formed a skeleton around which the melody could flex and breathe. The moan sailed along the underside of the bandoneón's warm howl and echoed between the piano's restless notes. It rose and fell around them, a ghost-sound in their midst, a disembodied echo, a throb of untold wounds and glimmers and urges and colors; the throb of América; the continental heartbeat, unleashed.

She kept this secret along with all the others.

She played for herself.

She played for no one.

She played for América.

El Sexteto Torres returned to Buenos Aires in March 1916 with a new fame along the edges of the tango world, which itself had continued to expand: new cabarets were opening, riding the wave of the dance's growing popularity in the upper classes, competing to create the most lavish havens for the form.

Their first job back in the city was at La China's. Santiago was in a buoyant mood that night; he'd found a cabaret that wanted to hire them, and that told him to come back two days later to sign a contract. The news sent sparks through all the men. A cabaret would mean the other side of town, more pay, a vaulting leap from the ill repute of dance halls into the polished glamour of the Argentinean elite.

At intermission, a young woman approached them in their cluster beside the stage. She wore a simple yellow dress, and her short black hair curled richly around her face. She was pretty in a plain way, easy to pass over in a crowd. You had to look close to see the delicacy of her features, the feline intensity of her eyes.

She didn't say anything at first, simply stood there and watched them until their conversation ebbed to silence and they turned her way. Roosters, Dante thought, ready to pounce, waiting to see whose prize she'd be.

"You could use a singer," the girl said.

"Is that right?" Joaquín said, cigarette barely moving between his lips.

"You should audition me."

Amato laughed, then Pedro, then the rest of them.

"I mean it. I'm good. And I know a lot of tangos."

The men went silent as they saw her seriousness. They stared at each other, then settled on Santiago.

"Women can't sing tango," Santiago said.

"Of course they can," said the girl. "And they do. Look at Linda Thelma. Pepita Avellaneda. Andrée Vivianne."

The men took a good look at her, slowly, toe to head. The girl did not blink. Behind her, two men were vying for the attentions of a dance hall girl who accepted a cigarette from one and a light from the other, her face a mask, just another night's work.

"What's your name?" Santiago said.

"Rosa."

"Well, Rosa. You're right, some women do sing tango. But they can't sing the entire repertoire, because most lyrics are from the men's point of view. Their loves, their troubles. So the songs wouldn't make any sense. I'm sorry."

The girl stood very still, her back straight. Dante marveled at her courage. If it had been her, standing there in a dress and lipstick, she might have turned and run the other way by now.

"You haven't heard me yet," Rosa said.

"We could find a private place for that," Pedro said.

She glared at him.

"I'm sorry," Santiago said, "but we're not looking for a singer."

Rosa hovered for a moment, then turned and walked away.

Dante watched her go. Delicious from behind.

The other men were watching the same thing.

"She had some nerve," Pedro said.

"She might be good for other things," said El Loro.

"She's all right," Joaquín drawled. "I've seen better."

"We all know *that*."

"Well, I'd do her."

"Loro, you'd do anything that moves."

The men laughed. El Loro blushed and pushed his hair away from his face. When it fell back over his eyes, he let it stay there.

"Boys," said Santiago, "three more minutes. Last chance for a piss or a drink."

Two days later, when Santiago went to sign the contract with the cabaret, the waiter who answered the service door didn't let him in. The owner had signed on a rival orquesta, he said. Santiago protested that they'd promised him the job already, that his orquesta was better than those idiots and everybody knew it, until finally the waiter took pity on him and told him the truth: the owner had balked at the sound of the group's name—not its formal name, El Sexteto Torres, but its underground, tip-of-the-tongue name, El Sexteto del Negro Torres. On hearing this, Santiago had stood for a moment in silence, then turned and walked back down the alley without another word.

He told his men about it that night, behind the curtain at La China's, in a dull monotone they'd never heard from him before.

"Bastards," said El Loro, and again Dante was struck by his indignation in the face of wrongdoing, the intensity of his voice.

"We'll make them sorry," Joaquín said. He was tuning his bass in the far corner, and didn't take his eyes off the strings.

Amato slapped Santiago's back in reassurance. "Something else will come through."

"I don't want 'something,'" Santiago said. "We're better than just 'something.'"

Dante heard a catch in his voice that sounded like despair. Just a hint of it, but more than she could stand.

"We're the best," she said forcefully, "thanks to you. One day everyone will know it but you can't give up hope."

All the men stared at her, at him, Dante, the skinny kid who always watched conversations with eyes wide and mouth shut.

Santiago blinked.

"Well, Chico, listen to you," El Loro said.

"So the kid's got something to say," Amato said.

Dante shrugged.

Santiago was still staring at Dante, with a mix of pride and surprise. His mood seemed lifted. A warmth spread through her solar plexus at the thought that she'd helped.

La China was glad to extend their contract. They were her pride, her special power, an emblematic offering in an ever-growing world of tango. Her hall had become what she'd most dreamed of it being: a fashionable underground destination for rich men who wanted to get away from their ladies, rather than take them out as they might do at a cabaret. Here at La China's, they could dance the tango the way they most wanted to: not with the woman held at a modest arm's length, but with her pulled in so close that their two torsos almost fused, so close that the scent of her hair could dominate his lungs and mind. They could slide into ganchos with abandon, not worrying about too much skirt to get lost in—the dancing girls at La China's wore short dancing dresses of the kind upper-class ladies would rather die than wear—or the impropriety of tangling thighs. Best of all, with the right whispers into the girls' ears, they could persuade their dance partners to continue the party off the dance floor, at a dingy hotel or in the back of their carriage while the driver sat quietly outside, holding the reins in the lamplit night.

Sometimes, the musicians struck up romances with these dancing girls, though it was clear that they were not serious girlfriends, let alone future wives. You seduced her with sweet words and songs and flowers and saw how much you could get out of her for free or, at least, for the indirect cost of flowers, dinner, little gifts here and there. El Loro had a romance with a girl called Raquel with a mare's build and black hair you could drown in. Dante watched them together with hunger, though not with envy, exactly, as you can't envy the impossible, and romance was impossible for her. Until, one day, El Loro told Dante he'd caught the eye of Raquel's friend.

"Alma, you know the one, short? Great legs? Don't tell me you didn't know. She's been trying to get your attention for days now."

Dante stared at him, blankly.

Pedro laughed and wiped sweat from his forehead with a handkerchief, elbows at rest on his bandoneón. "If that girl were flirting with me like that, I'd have her in bed in seconds."

"Oh, please," said El Loro. He was rubbing resin on his bow and swatted it through the air in a mock reprimand.

"I could do it, you know."

"Without your own girl finding out?"

"Why not?"

"Well anyway, forget about it. Alma doesn't want you. She's only got eyes for Dante."

"No kidding?" Dante said.

"Dante," Pedro said, "you can really be an idiot sometimes."

"Hey, he can't be too much of an idiot," Amato cut in. "You're not the one who's about to bed that Alma."

"Point taken. You win, Dante."

"Come on, boys," Santiago called through the curtain. "Intermission's over."

Dante went to the stage and took up her violin. Alma. Alma. Where was she now? The crowd was thick tonight, music and liquor already doing their work. No sign of her. She was a slight girl with rich black hair who danced like a mellifluous dream. She wore bright red lipstick and kohl around her eyes in an attempt to look more mature than her years, or perhaps to make up for her size, though it seemed to Dante that her size didn't keep her from getting noticed: men flocked to her precisely because she was so small, a slim bird you could almost tuck into your pocket or cradle in your palm. She awakened a ferocity so pure it was almost tender. So it seemed, at least, to Dante. There were customers who arrived early to reserve her time, and she made them look large on the dance floor in comparison, yet weightless, caught up in her light, avian glide.

Was it true? Could it be? Was Alma thinking of her? And more important, was it possible to have a real girlfriend? Three years now of living as a man and the loneliness had become like a second skin, indistinguishable from her own essential self, an automatic cost of being alive. You live, you breathe, you are not caught, and in payment for this vast gift you are alone. You look at girls and do not touch them—no one but Mamita, and even that is just a loosened bodice, a few minutes, little more—so as not to harm anyone. And anyway, brothel women kept their souls locked tight. It was not love. She knew that much. She didn't know what love was, and without realizing it she'd given up on ever finding out.

Then she saw her: Alma: toward the back, in a gray-haired man's arms, eyes closed, face solemn, as though she'd just taken communion and the holy bread were dissolving in her mouth as she danced.

To be with a girl who really wanted you. Who let you get close to her mind along with her body. And if it were Alma, that delicate girl, that lithe girl. To be near her, to—Dante's fingers tripped over a note, Santiago tensed in front of her, she had to concentrate.

It took her a week to gather the strength to approach Alma, as she waited for the bathroom in the back hall. She opened with a stupid compliment. "You dance beautifully."

Alma's smile was almost mocking. Those red lips.

"Let's go out sometime." Dante meant for it to come out as a question, but now it was too late.

Alma studied her. "Why?"

"Because I want to be next to you."

She laughed. Bright honey in that laugh.

"We could go dancing."

"Dancing!"

Dante rarely danced, as she was always onstage, creating music for others. In fact this was how she preferred things; dancing felt dangerous, a test of her masculinity, and anyway she didn't have to dance when she could experience the tango from the inside, by making the music itself. "If you like."

"I'm here dancing every day."

"Well, where would you like to go?"

"To the park. In the daytime."

"Which park?"

"The one in Palermo."

"Tomorrow?"

"You mean today?"

Dante was confused for a moment, then remembered it was three in the morning. "Yes. Today."

The following afternoon, at three thirty, Dante arrived at the door of Alma's home, a conventillo four blocks from hers. The front door was gray and worn, and Alma had her wait on the street until she was ready to emerge, which made Dante wonder about the state of her quarters, how many people shared her room. Then they set off across town, in a tram to the north side, to the park in Palermo. Sunshine glistened on the grass and winked on the smooth surface of the lake. Trees raised their arms over decadent shade. There was a park in San Telmo too, Parque Lezama, and Dante had wondered why Alma hadn't wanted to go there, but now she understood. On Sundays, Lezama was crowded with innumerable rowdy bodies. Here, in Palermo, rich ladies guarded themselves with parasols and were trailed by maids who carried their things, while the gentlemen strutted in perfectly ironed suits, brandishing canes before their feet. The ladies and gentlemen glared at Alma and Dante, clearly interlopers from the tenements. Though not the only ones: there were families on benches, sharing a single loaf of bread; young couples escaping the crowded rooms of home to hold hands and stroll; a lone girl in a maid's uniform gazing sadly at the water. And nobody was telling them to leave. You can glare all you like, Dante thought at the rich, this city is ours as well and there are more of us every day. She felt large in a manner that surprised her. It seemed that the city could belong to her, that she could one day belong inside it; that she could make a life here as an immigrant man, playing tango, eluding danger, and not die young, perhaps—radical thought—not even die alone. She felt a swelling in her chest, something warm and dangerous, akin to hope.

They chatted as they walked. She made Alma laugh, though in a coy way, face at a slant. Flirting, thought Dante, this is called flirting. She'd seen the other men do it, charm a girl and keep her guessing at the same time. Alma was no stranger to this game. Every gesture of hers felt expert, even the modest ones, especially those. And yet there was a sparkle to her that felt sincere, and that reminded Dante of Palmira, with her whip-long eyelashes and bright smile. Of course, this girl was not as sheltered as Palmira. She'd seen some things. And done some. How many times? With how many men? Lust opened under Dante like a vast rip in the ground. She had to step carefully to keep her balance.

At dusk, they took the tram back to San Telmo and had beers and a grilled sandwich at a bar. After the north side, their neighborhood seemed at once shabby and familiar, welcoming and cramped, warm with voices, rank with garbage, devoid of trees. Soon it was time for both of them to go home and get ready for their night's work. Dante walked Alma home, and on the walk Alma flashed her a look of annoyance, or disappointment. What was she, Dante, doing wrong? All day she'd tried to be respectful.

"You're beautiful, Alma."

"You think so?"

"Isn't it obvious?"

"That I'm beautiful, or that you think so?"

"That I think so."

"No. Not really."

She felt like an idiot. She hadn't been forward enough. How far would a real man have gone by now? She gathered her courage, stopped on the sidewalk, pulled Alma close, and kissed her. They stood in the shadows at the edge of an alley, and anyway no one tried to stop them, no one even slowed their walk, this was the big city after all and to each their own sin. The gutters smelled of horse piss and citrus rinds; in the distance, a motorcar droned and faded away. The kiss was gentle at first, a soft pulse between them. Dante hadn't kissed anybody on the mouth since those nights in Italy under the olive tree. Did she kiss like a woman? Taste like a woman? What did men's mouths taste like? Alma's mouth tasted like cigarettes and cognac and pure brutal life. Her tongue was plush and surprisingly strong. Her body stayed relaxed; she seemed to suspect nothing. Dante began to kiss her with more force, and Alma didn't resist, she snaked her arms around Dante's neck. Dante pulled her into the alley and pressed her against the damp stone wall, kept kissing her, a hand in Alma's hair, against her scalp, her chest was heaving, she mewed softly. Dante kept one hand free and close to her own sex in case Alma made any attempts to touch her there, an unnecessary defense because Alma's hands were still clasped at the nape of Dante's neck, she hung from him and let herself melt, she was rocking softly against him and Dante knew exactly how that felt, the urge to rock and rock and press against something anything or else explode and so she put her thigh between Alma's legs. Alma moaned. Not loudly but fiercely, a kind of hiss, so close to Dante's ear that the sound drowned out the noise of the street. *Make her do that thing. Do it.* They were rocking against each other, Alma pinned to the wall and draped around Dante's leg and were her feet still touching the ground? or was she floating? Alma suspended, Alma rubbing beautifully against Dante's thigh and making rough unscripted sounds—*this too is tango, isn't it*—until she drew in her breath as sharp as talons and fell limp in Dante's arms.

Drunken voices, oblivious voices, the creak of wheels, the whinny of a tired horse pulling its owners home.

"You . . . Dante . . ."

"Alma."

Her hand began to slide down Dante's chest, toward his sex. Dante caught her hand, brought it to her lips, and kissed each finger.

"Don't. You don't have to do that."

"All right," Alma said, "I don't have to."

Her tone was coy, her hand tried to pull away and travel down again. Dante held it tighter. "Don't," she said again, more firmly.

Alma pulled back to stare at Dante, who resisted the urge to escape her gaze. Curiosity and suspicion and a slash of relief.

"You're a very strange man."

There was nothing to say to this, no place to begin.

The rest of the walk home was beautiful, lit by far too many stars.

At Alma's door, they kissed again, more fiercely this time. After Alma went inside, Dante walked home, elated. Heat surged through her hands, her limbs, the bowl of her hips. She felt an overwhelming urge to press against Alma again, harder this time, with every centimeter of herself.

And then what?

The way Alma had looked at her, just before they kissed: that expectation. Men needed to take the lead, to know what to do. She had to prepare.

That night she went to work, and in the morning, instead of going home to sleep, she went directly to another dance hall, Lo de Amalia. Once inside, she had to wait twenty minutes until Mamita was free. The back room was close and stuffy and smelled of overripe vegetables and a thin veneer of lavender oil.

Mamita sat down on the bed and smiled at Dante. "Nice to see you, sweetheart."

"You too."

"What shall we do tonight?"

"I want to see it."

"See what?"

Dante gestured.

"Oh, my God. You've been here how many times, and you haven't been in there yet? What am I going to do with you, Dante?" She had her skirts hitched up in fistfuls, and she sat down on the bed and spread her legs. She was not wearing underwear. "Take a good look now."

Mamita seemed amused and a little bored in a manner that loosened the ache in Dante's chest. It had taken her three years to ask a woman to spread her legs, partly from her own shame and partly to protect women from her lust. But this woman, this Mamita, was not fragile: she was strong and vast, the mother of every poor lonely man in Buenos Aires, a role that kept her making a living at an age when other prostitutes had disappeared from brothels and sometimes from the face of the earth. Nothing could break her or, at least, not this, a clumsy lusting boy. It was safe—she hoped it was safe—to look. Dante looked. It was nothing like what she'd imagined. She fell to her knees. Mamita laughed.

"Go on," she said, not unkindly. "Touch it."

Such warmth, such damp, such utter softness. And the scent of it: bay leaves and copper and fresh bitter dirt. Dante moved her fingers along the folds, exploring, staring, touching, bursting with amazement and desire, possessed by the smell of this woman's secret place, her central place, this place that was the subject of endless songs and jokes and humiliations and warnings and blood feuds, and look at it, look at this, look at her, here, Mamita full of grace and yes you among women—and then Mamita let out a small moan.

"You liked that?"

"Mmmm."

"Really?"

"Really."

"What else do you like?"

"Whatever you like, *corazón*."

"No." Dante sat up. "Don't lie to me."

"Now, now, don't get upset—"

"I want you to teach me."

"Teach you what?"

"How to make you feel good."

Mamita lifted herself up onto her elbows and studied Dante for a long time in the dim light. "Why?"

"I'll pay extra."

"Where would we start?"

"You tell me."

"How experienced are you?"

Dante didn't answer.

"Oh, child," Mamita said.

"I'll pay for the whole night."

Mamita studied her. No part of her was laughing anymore. "You have that kind of money?"

"How much?"

"Seven pesos."

"I've got four pesos and sixty cents. I can get you the rest on Thursday. Or I'll give you what I've got and stay however long you let me."

Mamita was silent for such a long time that Dante began to feel the cold enter her feet. "You've got a girl now, haven't you?"

She almost nodded, but then shook her head.

"Not yet. You hope to have her. But right now you wouldn't know what to do with her."

Dante looked at the floor. Wood planks, scuffed and tired, worn down by all the things they'd seen.

"And you want to make her happy. Yes, you do." And what Mamita did next shocked her: she reached out and stroked Dante's face. "You're a good boy," she said. "Such a pretty little mouth." Her hand gripped Dante's face, thumb on one cheek, fingers on the other, so hard it seemed she might bore a hole right through the flesh. "Now put it to work."

Dante surrendered to Mamita like a twig in an ocean storm.

You don't know, when they start to call you Mamita, that the name will come to subsume all other names, that the name you were born with will drown in the great noise of your life, but that's how it is in this city, Buenos Aires, it renames you, rebaptizes you for better or for worse. You don't know any of this at first. You work because you have to, because your human body keeps insisting on a crust of bread and a place to sleep and another place to shit and some way to stay alive, even when your mind rails against it all and fantasizes about death as though it were one of those sweet desserts that flaunt themselves in the windows of fancy pastry shops like exuberant clouds you'll never be able to touch. Just as your mouth craves those pastries, your mind craves death. But not the body. No matter what happens, the stupid body wants to live. It insists on breath and food and so you live. And to live means to fuck, and to fuck means to open up your body to whoever shows up at the door and there is always someone at the door, always another hungry man in this city in which night has no beginning and no end. The men keep coming and coming and they—not you—are the ones who find Mamita inside you and start to call you that, present you with her name. They give it to you because they need it, because Mamita is what they want of you whether they know it or not: they are all boys inside still desperate for their mothers' skirts—and so many of them are thousands of kilometers from their mothers and cannot abide this, can't stand the thought that their mammas or muttis or ommis or mères are aging on a faraway continent and will die without ever seeing their sons again, that they, the sons, will never again touch their mothers' hands or eat their stews or wear clothes their mothers mended with needles sharp enough to draw blood, these grown men lie awake and weep over this loss of their mothers, even the rough ones, especially the rough ones—so when they find a spark of their own mothers inside you they come groveling for it and can't see or even call you anything else. You play along and let them have their games. You don't realize that the games they play are changing you. The years pile up and one day you wake up and realize two things: first, that you have become Mamita and barely remember being anyone else; second, that, with the passing years, your odds of survival have slimmed and being Mamita just might save you, might allow you the miracle of a long career as a whore, continuing to work when all of your contemporaries have starved or disappeared or run off with evil men because there's nowhere else to go. And so you stay. You last. You work. There is nothing left of your original self, the whore-self looms larger and there's power inside her as long as you can stomach the cost. And you do stomach it. Your body is an empty cup they fill with whatever they want to. On your best days you are able to erase sensation, to curl away from your own body while it is doing its job. Sometimes there is pain. More often there's only irritation, like the feel of harmless cockroaches walking across your skin. Every once in a while, it's true, there is pleasure here or there, but it is always an accident, a stray flash that ends as quickly as it began. Except for now, on this night, with the boy. Dante, he calls himself, though you suspect he, too, has other names he's hiding behind the one on everybody's lips. The tension with which he holds himself tells you he's afraid, the way a thief on the run is afraid, though it's hard to imagine this boy committing any serious crime. It doesn't matter. He's a child and he reminds you of your own boy, your gone boy, the one whose age you count as the seasons pass and whose face you try to imagine on sweltering days of restive sleep. You were fourteen when you conceived him, fifteen when he was born, and the men you worked for let the other whores stand around you in a circle as you labored, then gave you a few days to hold your little boy and give him milk—you gave him your milk and in the hardest times you say that to yourself over and over, *there's that at least, he had my milk*—before the men who owned you took him away. After that you used the herbs the other girls did, every time you needed to, so you'd never have to say goodbye like that again. And every day you think of him and God may punish you for thinking of that boy of yours when young ones come to you but to hell with God, he's the one who invented hell in the first place so how about he just go live there like the rest of us? The young boys tear at your heart because any one of them could be him, could be your own. Your child is a man now, eighteen and a half, more than old enough to visit whores and you hope that, wherever he is, he's one of the gentler ones. This Dante, this boy now with you, he's a gentle one all right, he wants to please you so he can please other girls and nobody's paid for a whole night with you in eleven years and even then they certainly didn't pay seven pesos, what an outrageous lie, poor naïve boy, you just want to crush his face between your thighs, you want to swallow him whole into your cunt all in one piece just the way your little boy came out of you, all at once slipping whole through your cunt slow slow slow at first and then with shocking speed, out into the world, out into the light, he shot out of you and it's the most radiant memory of your life, and now with this boy you want to do just the opposite, namely, swallow him out of the world and out of the light and right into the core of you, stealing him inside to where you can possess him forever—but you can't. You don't. Instead, you teach him. You are not patient. If he wants to learn he'd better flex his muscles. If he wants to learn he'd better get over any fear of his skull getting crushed between two thighs. If he wants to learn you can just put him to work for *you,* and let him pay *you* for it, because why not—? That's right, little boy, do as you're told, I'll slap you if you get it wrong or if you miss the spot or use your teeth or stop paying attention. Get the rhythm right, the pressure. You pretty little boy. You say you want to make me feel good, you want to know how. How about you find my baby boy for me? no, you can't? you young pretty boys don't all have some secret telepathic bond to help me reach him through you? then you'd better work that tongue until all the words it's ever spoken are wrung out of it, you'd better follow my instructions to the letter, you'd better stick fingers to make me feel good yes but also for your own sake, so you can have some kind of anchor when I burst, a yoke to this world so you don't get flung into the next.

Dante spent three nights with Mamita—nights that whipped and lit her, dismantled what she thought she knew—before taking Alma out again. It was the following Sunday. They returned to the park. Just as the deep gold of afternoon light was starting to fade into dusk, Dante whispered in Alma's ear, "I want to be alone with you."

Alma leaned against Dante for a delicious instant, then lifted away, her profile calm as a queen's. "Where?"

Dante had thought about this. Home was a minefield: thin walls, screaming children, La Strega's all-seeing eyes, families bickering in many languages and surely casting stares of disapproval at a young woman who disappeared behind a closed door with a man. A single glare from the conventillo women could make this delicate thread between her and Alma shrivel away to nothing. Not to mention the unromantic stench. And so, the night before, she'd done her research with El Loro, who was happy to instruct her in how to find a private place for, in his words, a fuck you earned with something other than pesos. "I know a place in San Telmo where we can get a room."

Alma looked away, kept walking. To keep up appearances, she couldn't say yes. But she hadn't said no.

Dante grasped her arm and steered her in the direction of the tram. "Let's go."

The room was dingy and smelled of mold and vinegar. The sheets on the bed had been hastily arranged. But, on a slender end table, there stood a hopeful bowl of water with a single red rose floating on the surface. The rose's petals were wilted and brown at the edges, but with luck Alma wouldn't notice. She didn't look at the bowl when she walked in. She stood in the center of the room, her back to Dante. A graceful creature from another plane, wings folded in wait.

The street murmured at them through the window. Dante closed it, trapping the twilight heat inside. Then she leaned against the wall and lit a cigarette.

"Strip," she said.

At first, Alma did nothing. She didn't move, didn't look at Dante, didn't say a word. The room crackled with silence. Dante blew slow, controlled smoke toward the ceiling. If the game could not be played according to her rules, then she couldn't play at all. Perhaps this had been a mistake. There was still time to put an end to it, turn around, leave this place and walk this woman safely home.

And then Alma reached around her back and unzipped her dress.

The body, exposed, arms and thighs and waist a unified song.

Fabric pooled on the scuffed parquet, around high-heeled feet. Spine straight, gaze steady on the wall, a dancer's focus.

Dante couldn't breathe. Power and fear of her own power. Thrill. A shivering.

Where was her voice? She summoned it. "The bra too. Panties. Everything but the shoes."

Is this my voice? Mine?

Alma complied.

The song of her, perfect.

Her body the song that commands the dance.

Dante, who was also Leda, put her cigarette out on the windowsill and came to Alma from behind. She pressed her fully clothed body against Alma's naked one, careful to keep her groin at a distance to hide the lack of a hard sex (and she remembered how her cousin Dante had felt, back in Italy, under the fig tree, against her thigh, the press of someone else's lust) and let her hands and mouth lead the way, to the nape of Alma's neck, the arms, breasts, waist, and neither of them made a sound just as two tango dancers move without a word, shut up and let your body do the speaking, like this, this, this. Alma stood still, arms at her sides, encircled. Her stance relaxed slowly, butter lifted toward the sun.

Alma beneath her hands. Alma at her lips. Alma everywhere, inescapable, the scent of her, the warm flesh offering itself to her tongue, teeth, hunger. The crescendo of her breath. Staccato pain—or was it pleasure?—making her tense and soften in alternating waves. Dante led her to the bed and pushed her onto it. Kissed her hard. She was ready to fight if Alma tried to undress her, but Alma didn't try: she lay with her eyes closed, willing to be taken, willing to ride the river on a current not her own.

Her legs opened without resistance. But when she felt Dante's face at her sex, she let out a sharp sound and her body went tense. "What are you doing?"

"What I want to do."

Alma opened her eyes and lifted her head to stare at Dante as though she'd suddenly grown two heads.

It's not what you want? Dante wanted to ask, but couldn't, as it seemed out of keeping with what a man would do. Instead, she said, "Shhh, lie back, don't be afraid."

Alma stared at her a little longer, then lay back. She tasted brighter than Mamita, a hint of bitter orange mixed with copper and fresh-turned earth. She had a different shape, elongated, taut. Unlike Mamita, she gave no instructions or advice; there were no words to guide Dante, nothing but the raw and blinding moment.

She stayed there a long time. She could have stayed forever.

Twice, Alma tried to get up, but Dante pushed her back down. Finally Alma's hips began to shake. She made sounds as though she were fighting something back—a jaguar, a shark, a sword of joy. Then she lost the fight, and as sensation stabbed her Dante held fast to Alma's hips to keep her own mouth fused in place, as she'd learned to do with Mamita, accompanying the storm, swallowed by it, lit up in every centimeter of her body.

Once Alma had fallen back again, gilded with sweat, Dante lay down between her open legs, as men do; their heads were together, their hips were together, her hand was at Alma's sex, two fingers now inside her and Alma's eyes were closed, she was lost at sea, she was in no state to look down and discover—and even if she did, Dante miraculously had no fear because there was no room for fear in this moment, only a shocked sense of rightness, of being vital and alive and completely in her skin as she did to Alma what men do.

The pleasure of it, immense, enfolding. Woman all around her. Heat in the marrow of her bones. Washing her skin. Pouring through her arm into her hand where it rocked right in front of her own sex like an extension of it, rocked into Alma, over and over, a ragged rhythm, primal, unrehearsed.

Afterward, Alma turned to the wall and lay still for a long time.

Now the fear poured in. If she suspected. Then she would—it couldn't be.

"Alma. Are you all right?"

Alma finally turned to face Dante. She was crying.

"I'm fine."

"Did I hurt you?"

"No."

"Did I—"

"Shut up, Dante." Alma reached out and stroked Dante's cheek. "Just promise me we can do that again."

"I promise."

"Your skin. It's so soft, it seems impossible."

Dante said nothing.

"So much about you seems impossible."

"What do you mean?"

"I have to go." Alma rose and reached for her clothes on the floor. "I'll be late for work. And so will you."

Dante walked to work that night on feet that seemed to levitate, stepping on pure air. Was this love? Was this what it felt like? A sweet hollowness deep inside you, desperate to be filled. A joy that bites and slashes. The urge to be with her again, right now, immediately, doing it and doing it and to hell with the rest of the world.

Backstage at La China's, she found the musicians clustered expectantly around Santiago, who surveyed them like a captain assessing his crew. He nodded at Dante. "There you are."

"Sorry I'm l——"

"Never mind that," Santiago said. "I wanted us all to be here for the news. This is our last night here at La China's."

Dante was flanked by El Loro and Pedro, and felt them tense.

"We've broken through. We've got an engagement at Leteo."

"Leteo?" El Loro asked.

"It's a cabaret, you idiot," Amato said congenially.

"One of the finest," Santiago said.

"Where is it?" asked Joaquín.

"Downtown. Right on Calle Corrientes."

The men stared at each other.

Here it is, thought Dante. They were about to cross a border into another world. A world where men like her—or any of the men she knew here—didn't go, didn't belong. How quickly life could dwarf you. How vast the world. She felt terror, coupled with a rush of excitement and a sense of possibility.

"Do you understand what this means?" Santiago went on. "We're rising to the top. We're going to be a real orchestra, making real money. Tuxedos and everything."

"Tuxedos!" said El Loro, pushing stray fronds of hair from his face.

"You'd better believe it."

Dante tried to imagine herself in a tuxedo. A new costume of maleness. Would it be easier or harder than what she now wore?

"Leteo," Amato said, slowly, as if savoring the sound.

The other men were silent for a moment, as the weight of that word hung between them. They stood close in their curtained backstage corner, close enough to breathe each other's breaths.

"It's run by a certain Señor Carrasco and his sister," Santiago said.

"What?" Joaquín said. "His *sister*?"

"I know it's strange. She's a widow. Rumor has it they used her money to open the place. But he's the owner, of course."

This seemed to put Joaquín slightly more at ease.

"They just opened six months ago, and I met with Señor Carrasco himself today. He's ambitious. He wants to stake out new ground. We're going to help him do that." Santiago looked around at each of his musicians, one by one. "There are to be no mistakes. Make a mistake and get your balls cut off."

Pedro and El Loro laughed.

"And you'll be fired from the orquesta."

No more laughter.

"Anyone who doesn't like it can leave right now. Understood?"

All the men nodded.

"Anyone leaving?"

The men shook their heads.

"We have to be perfect," Santiago said. "Better than perfect. We have to play so beautifully they forget their own mothers, forget their own names."

"We can do that," Amato said.

"Of course we can," said El Loro, flashing his bright boyish grin.

The men voiced their agreement, and Leda loved them, every single one of them, for their obsession, for the tribe they'd created, a silent pact between the mortal souls of men. For just a moment, standing behind the flimsy curtain at La China's surrounded by musicians, her body still glowing with sex, she had the most incredible feeling, one she wouldn't have thought possible: the world felt hers.

A Cup of the River of Forgetting

Never, in the history of the world, had there been another place like Cabaret Leteo. Dante was sure of it. When she stepped through its doors,
the city fell away: all the noise and bluster of Buenos Aires disappeared,
not only from her senses, but from her thoughts and, almost, from her
memory, replaced by the lavish atmosphere of a contained world. She
and her fellow musicians came in through the service entrance, which
led to a vast kitchen with enough pans and knives and cooks to set a
banquet fit for the gods. And as they quickly wove their way past crates
of high-piled vegetables and great boiling pots to reach the white double
doors that led to the great hall, Dante thought of them, the gods, the old
ones Cora used to tell stories about—one born from her father's forehead, another from the ocean foam, others on a hidden island shrouded
by their mother's exile—and she imagined them gathering at the front
entrance of this tango cabaret, ravenous, itching for a dance. The front
entrance seemed designed to entice them. Dante had seen it: the tall
ornate double doors opened into a foyer of mirrors and polished brass.
Low light from the crystal chandelier played and wept perpetually, a
subtle song of flame and shadow. Plush red carpet covered the floors.
The coat check was flanked by crystal vases, each the size of a large
dog, their long-stemmed flowers watching the room like a many-headed
beast.

Whether one entered through the front doors or the back, all roads
led to the great hall. It was circular, with ceilings so high they evoked

a sense of sky, and a stage raised a full meter from the ground. A wide clear space opened below the stage, reserved for dancing and ringed with round tables sheathed in white linen. White napkins fanned artfully in wineglasses. At the height of business hours, waiters glided unobtrusively from table to table, elegant in their black and white uniforms, discreetly taking orders and disappearing through the double doors to the kitchen.

Paintings of nymphs and satyrs hung along the walls, and naked statues of them stood watch as well, scattered across the room, towering between tables, so that patrons could enjoy their wine or *bœuf au vin* almost within reach of bare breasts. Flocks of multicolored birds—toucans, starlings, ravens, thrushes, jacamars—hovered close to the high ceiling, frozen in mid-flight, the strings that suspended them invisible to the mere mortals below. But the decoration that most stole Dante's gaze was a mirror right across from the stage. It was four meters long and painted with a giant peacock, its blue and livid green feathers fanned in a great half circle that gleamed, majestic, flecked and rimmed with gold. Whenever Dante glanced in the mirror's direction, she glimpsed shards of herself caught between the long bright feathers.

She learned to walk quickly through the slice of the great hall that led from the kitchen to the door backstage. The hall scared her; it was too sumptuous; it was made for old gods and rich men, not for her. She held her breath as she walked, exhaling only when she'd arrived in the musicians' dressing room and closed the door behind her. The air was more familiar there: cigarette smoke and sweat and the sticky thickness of men in an unventilated space. It had none of the polish of the great hall or the foyer, but to the musicians, after the curtained corner they'd crammed into at La China's, it seemed the height of luxury. There were two velour sofas, only marginally stained. The parquet flooring was not missing a single piece. The wallpaper bore a red, yellow, and orange fleur-de-lis pattern, which, along with the fact that there were no windows, gave the room a dim and cave-like feeling, as though they were not so much musicians as lions gathered in their lair, as Pedro said one night, joking, and that's what they called it from then on, the Lair. They met there six nights a week, just before midnight, and opened their instrument cases as though undressing beautiful ladies. They tuned their instruments and discussed the lineup of songs or simply spoke to each other without speaking, as men do, as musicians do, itching with silent excitement and the stiff fit of their borrowed tuxedos. They were not gentlemen but they would be as elegant as if they were; they'd put the real gentlemen in the audience to shame. Look at us as we step out onto the stage, as we bow to your polite applause; see how immaculate our suits are, how painstakingly polished our shoes; you may laugh at us, we see the condescending smiles, but we are not down there with you in the hall where you mock us, we are here in a separate realm entirely, a realm we call the stage, and which is neither palace nor tenement, neither your space nor that of the poor; it is our space, the space of music, and music is a thing which we will make for you out of thin air and send pouring out to your fine tables where your ears and minds and blood will be invaded by our sound.

It was not that the rich men who came to Leteo were so different from those at La China's. In fact, Dante recognized a few faces from the dance hall. Here, though, those same men acted proper, and brought women on their arms. The women wore fine gowns and pearls and drank champagne and, when they danced, kept their paces modest, did not press into the embrace. This was a civilized tango, after all, and these were civilized ladies. They were chaperoned and danced only with men from their own tables. They came in groups, or with their husbands, but they never came alone.

Except for one.

Every night, an exquisite woman occupied a small table at the hall's edge. She wore daring evening gowns, lower-cut at the collar in that Parisian style just coming into fashion to the alarm of the Buenos Aires elite; only, unlike the bright colors imported from Paris, her gowns were always black. Her black hats were extravagantly decorated with black velvet bows or tall black plumes. Even sitting down, she seemed tall. Ageless. Impenetrable. Back straight with the posture of an arrogant dancer. She sipped her oporto and watched the crowd.

"Who's that woman in the back, alone?" El Loro asked, in the Lair, at intermission.

"That," Santiago said, "is La Viuda Ruiz. Don Carrasco's sister."

"Viuda?" El Loro looked up from his violin in amazement. *"She's a widow?"*

Dante, too, was surprised, even though she herself was a widow and hardly looked the part. But all the widows she'd known in Alazzano were stout, veiled, resigned down to the slouch of their spines. This woman was the opposite of resigned. She exuded power. She seemed to know that she turned men's heads. Her very dresses made a mockery of the widow's duties; they drew the eye right to her bare flesh and whispered *stay.*

Pedro whistled and played a long, languorous chord on his bandoneón.

El Loro smiled and opened his mouth.

"Shut up," Santiago said.

"I didn't say anything."

"Don't start. Not a word about Doña Ruiz. Don't even *think* of her, you hear? Doña Ruiz is not a woman. She's your boss's sister. Understand?"

They complied. But even so, the next time Dante went onstage, she snuck a glance at Doña Ruiz. The widow was watching them with the calm alert gaze of a general just before battle.

The money was good, damn good. Amato gave his wife a Singer sewing machine and his mistress a Parisian coat. El Loro rented another room for his family in their conventillo and, in a flush of optimism, got engaged to a sweet Russian girl who lived across the hall. Pedro appeared wearing gold rings that flashed as he pressed music from his bandoneón. No one knew exactly what Joaquín did with his money; he said nothing about it, and seemed unchanged. So did Santiago. All of them, at Santiago's insistence, bought new tuxedo suits from a tailor on Corrientes, a gentlemen's tailor, who received them with a kind of shock but served them nonetheless. Dante held her breath when the tape measure approached her groin, but there was no close touch, she was not discovered, she was safe. If the tailor noted anything suspicious about her proportions, he didn't say a thing about it, the picture of discretion. When the suit was done, it was as supple as a second skin. She hadn't worn such well-fitting clothes since La Boca. They made her feel powerful, potent, the world in her reach.

The money had a similar effect. Money opens many kinds of doors in a city. You can go into a restaurant and dine right next to respectable couples, never mind their stares. You can buy five kilos of meat at a time if you want to, or a strand of pearls, or perfume bottled on the other side of the world. Dante bought all of these things: the meat for La Strega, the pearls and perfume for Alma. She saw Alma once a week, on Sunday afternoons. The biting winds of autumn cut short their walks on the promenade. No matter. Dante took her to a fine salon that served high tea, complete with scones in the British style, fresh jam, delicate cakes, and whipped cream that glistened in a polished silver bowl. Alma fingered each pastry as though on the brink of some incomparable communion, and her eyelids fluttered closed with pleasure as she ate. Dante watched her raptly, her whole body on fire. After tea, they crossed town to San Telmo, to that dingy room with the bowl of water and its single wilted rose (sometimes it was red, sometimes white or pink or yellow, but it was always wilted). There they stole hours of visceral wonder. Alma was always naked, Dante fully clothed. She always put her mouth on Alma first, to make her delirious, to make her surrender, to make her believe, as she seemed to believe, that the thing Dante did next was what any man would do. As an added safety measure, she sometimes blind-folded Alma with a handkerchief and tied her hands together behind her back. Why? Alma asked the first time, and Dante, reaching for a reason, said, Because you look beautiful this way. Which was also true. In any case, it was an unneeded precaution. Alma took what came and gave no sign of wanting to reach down or undress her lover or do anything other than ride the waves. All week Dante thought about seeing her again. She even dared to dream into the future, about days with Alma, hundreds of them, strung forward into the great fog of time. Since becoming a man, she'd thought about the future only in immediate terms—Tomorrow, Next Week, Next Month If I'm Still Here—so deeply did she believe that she'd die young, if not at some knifepoint, then struck by the light-ning of God's vengeance for her sins. But none of that had happened. God was bored or distracted or rationing his bolts, and, as for knives, at Leteo there were fewer of them in trouser legs, more of them on linen cloths, it was a different life now, almost civilized. If she could live into the future, how many nights of music, how many days with Alma, months and years of tango and sex, enough to live for.

Then, one gray June afternoon, as Alma lay naked in the crook of Dante's arm, she said, "I'm pregnant."

She hadn't heard right. She couldn't have heard right. "What?"

"I'm pregnant," Alma said again, more quietly this time.

The walls weren't solid anymore. Nothing was solid.

"Maybe your . . . time, is simply late."

"I'm never late."

"This could be the first time."

"It's not."

"How do you know?"

"I know," Alma said, her irritation palpable. What did men know of these female matters, after all?

"Whose is it?"

"Whose else would it be?"

"I don't know, Alma, you tell me."

"How dare you?"

A stain snaked down the wall by the window, brown, menacing. Dante had never looked at it before.

"Why would you doubt me?"

She couldn't say why. Her tongue silenced. Alma had believed it, all of it, Dante's plan had worked, better than she'd dared to hope. Perhaps too well.

Alma was pouting. Waiting.

"What are you going to do?"

"What are *you* going to do?"

Dante opened her mouth to say something but nothing came out.

"I thought you were different from other men." Alma sprang up from the bed and reached for her clothes. "How wrong I was."

Dante watched her dress, paralyzed. If Alma was really pregnant, she wanted to help her. But then, she was lying about there being another man—or other men. Deceit either way. Deceit at every turn. It hurt her head.

Alma was dressed now, hair unkempt but elegant already. Her belly gave no hint of what it contained. "Well? Is that all you have to say?"

What if she wasn't pregnant at all? What if she just wanted money? What if this was what she'd gone to bed with her for—with *him* for—in the first place? How could she have been so stupid, so trusting?

"Bastard. Faggot. Coward."

Dante rose to her feet. Alma flinched but didn't step back.

"Alma," she said.

Alma looked into Dante's eyes and ran out of the room without closing the door.

For the next seven days, Dante thought—in the depths of night, on the gleaming stage, on walks through the early winter rains—about what to do.

Only one thing was clear: she could not be the father. She could not make a woman pregnant, could not even lie naked with her; she knew how those things worked, what it took, and she knew she didn't have it; she was a farce, an aberration masquerading as a man. Even so, Alma must be suffering. She didn't want to be cruel. She didn't want to be one of those men who turned their backs on women when they were vulnerable. The thought of it pushed at the pit of her stomach, an aching fist. She should offer her money, or marriage. Marriage! She tried to imagine it, the rest of her life hitched to a lie. It seemed a nightmare, a false life, an interminable cage. Of course, she, too, was lying; but her lie freed her to live her truth more fully than she otherwise could. Perhaps, for Alma, this lie felt similar, a key to her best authentic life. Dante strained to imagine this. She didn't know, couldn't know. It shocked her to realize that, for all the raw hours they'd spent together, for all the intimacy she had with Alma's body, she knew very little about her mind.

On some nights, she woke suddenly in the darkness, enraged at Alma for trying to trap her. On other nights she lay awake consumed with thoughts of Alma's lovely belly, swelling with new life, miraculous, vulnerable. Emotions tore at her from all directions. There was no precedent, no example she could turn to for guidance. She had never known or even heard of anyone in a similar predicament. Joan of Arc's ghost haunted her nights, standing in the corner of her dark room like a prison guard, wearing dull armor and a crown of flames. *You're disgusting*, the ghost whispered, *unspeakable, like nobody else in the history of the world. I am not with you. No one is with you, you're alone.*

She saw Alma one more time, the following Sunday, at the usual hour, at the door of her home. Alma came out dressed for the park, wearing a sleek blue hat that Dante had bought her a few weeks before. She looked equal parts wary and hopeful.

"You came back," she said. "I didn't know whether you would."

"Listen to me, Alma."

Alma waited, somewhat sulkily.

"I want to help you."

Alma didn't blink.

"I just need you to tell me the truth."

"I already have."

"The whole truth. About the other man. Or other men."

Alma said nothing. She stared out at the street, where a carriage laden with coal was making its noisy way toward the boulevard.

"I know I'm not the father. I can't be the father. Just be honest with me, and I'll help you."

"Why don't you believe me?" She said it in a child's plaintive voice.

Dante lowered his voice and glanced away in a gesture of shame. "Because I'm sterile."

Alma flinched. "You're lying."

"It's the truth."

"How do you know?"

"It's a long story."

"Look me in the eyes and tell me you're not lying."

Dante held Alma's gaze. She opened her mouth. But then, she found the words wouldn't come, because she was in fact lying, though not in the way Alma thought, and not in a way Alma could imagine. She stood for a few moments, mouth agape, hands empty. Finally, she said, "It's the truth."

But the silence had been too long and spoke more volubly than her words. They both knew it. Alma shook her head in disgust. "I hope you rot in hell," she said, and then she went back inside and slammed the door and Dante stood looking at it for a long time before he turned and walked down the street, past clusters of immigrants spilling from their doors, grasping at Sunday, drinking grappa from the bottle, laughing too loud or grimacing as they tightened their shawls against the wind.

———

"Good riddance," Pedro said when he found out. "The last thing you need is some knocked-up slut to chain you down."

Winter shrouded the city in cold thunderstorms. Leteo's owner, Don Carrasco, had feared the rain would keep the clientele away, but it did not. Santiago composed new music that the sextet played at Leteo for the first time, melodies that rippled with energy and flourish, and that spread across the city that winter, bringing prestige to both the band and the cabaret where they'd had their debut.

The news from Europe became worse each day. All the time there were new battles. Her father's letters were short and grim. A munitions factory had opened in nearby Salerno. The chickens were laying smaller eggs. Able-bodied men had been taken from the village to go fight in the distant war, among them Tommaso, the baker, and all the blacksmith's sons. *The baker's wife,* her father wrote, *won't leave the church, she has to be dragged from the pews in the evening by the nuns.*

Her brother Tommaso. Off at war. The word *taken* made it sound as though he'd been packed into a burlap sack and carried like so much fresh-ground flour. He'd always been a sensitive boy, her brother, drawn to storytelling and games of the imagination. He fought with the village boys because he had to, coming home scratched up by fists and brambles, but they were amicable fights, no broken bones, no end to friendship, and most of the time he lost. The thought of him in a war zone turned her stomach and made her mouth sour.

She wasn't the only one at La Rete affected by the war. The German bachelor had two brothers and an uncle on the battlefield, a fact he kept extremely quiet about to stave off the smoldering rage of his neighbors, because their nations were enemies back in the Old World. The French family in the back room on the right lost all their relatives, twenty-four of them, in a battle that destroyed their village. La Strega's two brothers, three nephews, and eleven male cousins had all been conscripted as soldiers. "Half of Scylla went," she said quietly, in Italian, out of respect for the French wife who was wringing linens at the other end of the patio (it was the first time she'd left her room in three weeks; the other women had done her laundry and brought her meals without a word for all those days and hidden all the rope and knives and never asked her to stop weeping or be quiet, not at any hour of the night). "And for what! A battle that's far away from us. What do they want with some poor Southern fishermen? They cast nets. They gut fish. They'll be no good with a gun."

In Argentina, another kind of war seemed to be afoot. The anarchists continued to roil and organize. In July, an anarchist attempted to shoot President de la Plaza. The bullet grazed his head during a parade and did not harm him, but panic rippled through the government and the upper class.

"He had it coming to him," El Loro said. He'd become a fervent anarchist, often arriving at rehearsals directly from meetings. Several of his friends and two of his uncles had been arrested in the past week.

"If you were part of that attack," Santiago said, "for God's sake don't let me ever find out. Much less Don Carrasco."

Don Carrasco was intensely against anarchists, and had already fired two kitchen boys for their involvement with a collective.

"So that's all we're doing here now? Catering to the rich?"

"We're here for the tango," Santiago said. "Our music will reach far more people because we're here."

"And the workers? The tango came from us, it belongs to us!"

"The tango belongs to everyone."

"There are children who don't have enough to eat! And these rich patrons—"

"—are helping you put bread on the table," Santiago said. "Or hadn't you noticed? You can do a lot more good with a stage to play on and cash in your pocket. Look, Loro, I'm not saying you can't go. Just be careful. You could get us all fired, and that doesn't help anyone."

El Loro brooded the rest of that night, but he didn't leave the orquesta and continued to abide by Santiago's rules. Dante wasn't sure what to believe. The anarchists always made her think of her husband-cousin, shot dead on the street, brains on the pavement. She recoiled from the movement that had brought this about. At the same time, the anarchists seemed brave to her, and their dream seemed noble, at least the way her neighbors at La Rete and El Loro—ever passionate, ever ignited, outraged—spoke of that dream: good pay for all, a decent life for any-one who worked. She had good pay now and she knew how incredi-ble it felt, the lightness of knowing how you'll eat tomorrow and the next day, the thrill of a new suit, the happiness in helping someone else with needed pesos. She could afford to leave the conventillo now, if she wanted to. But La Rete sustained her, with its bursting noise, its chaotic smells, La Strega's affection; it had become the closest thing to home she could hope to have. Rather than leave, she moved into a larger room that stank less, with a window where she could sit and practice on her violin for all the street to hear.

This left her with money for other things. Like her parents, to whom she sent short vague letters with guilty clutches of bills. And women, too, because there was always a dance hall girl happy to go out with you if you fed her a nice hot meal. She took them out to ease her heart-break about Alma, to help her forget, although she doubted, in those first weeks, that she'd ever love again. She didn't want to love. She wanted to gaze at these women, sit close to them, watch them eat steak and knock back whiskey and arch their bare otherworldly necks. She didn't push them to come back with her to the room of wilted roses. What a gentle-man you are, they'd say, surprised, relieved, bemused, and then she'd go home alone and think of them as she touched her own body in the dark, rubbing her sex, rippling with lust. Every once in a while, a dance hall girl would herself suggest they go somewhere private, and Dante would try to resist, but instead she'd find herself in the room, often drunk, the girl naked—what was her name again, what was her own name, what did it matter—she let her hands and tongue dissolve along the plains and curves of the girl's body, marvelous body, mortal, perfect, vast enough to hold the world, she roved it until there was no Dante, no Leda, only lightning pleasure and a voice begging for mercy or for more. Sometimes the pleasure shot through all of her, all the way to her own sex, a crest that matched theirs; at other times it was enough to watch their ecstasy, revel in making them burn. She didn't put her hips close to theirs when she fucked them, so they'd know it was her hands, so they couldn't trick her later. Afterward some girls sprang into their clothes and others gazed at her (at him, they thought) with curiosity shot through with hope, but no matter what they did, Dante knew she'd never bring the same girl to the room again. That way they'd never ask too many questions or invade the hidden cellars of her heart.

Perhaps it was a monstrous thing to do.

But she was already a monster. There was no escape from that.

The months turned, sloped into spring. Leteo gleamed and hummed to bring down the mortal sky. Dante forgot herself there, forgot sadness, war, the dangers of the city. At Leteo she was large; she was invincible; her instrument was restored to its true place, a royal place, fit to charm the ears of kings.

Or queens.

There was one uncontested queen at Leteo. The widow. It was difficult not to look at her, even more difficult to tear her eyes away. She was always the most elegant woman in the hall and, to Dante, the most beautiful. Not that there weren't other women with fine features and delicate necks and a pristine glow to them, the glow of modesty and innocence and of never having washed a rag or hauled a bucket of water in their lives. You could tell from the way these women danced that their legs had been trained to stay shut. They had the careful beauty of porcelain dolls. But La Viuda Ruiz had the beauty of smoke rising from a wood fire: roiling, unpredictable, strong. Bursting at the seams of her own body. Desperate to escape all constraints.

She danced with many different men. She danced with all the men she could. She was the only woman in Leteo who did so, the only one who could turn such scandalous behavior into a business strength. Male patrons had come to anticipate a dance—no more than one—with the mistress of the hall. They took it as a ritual of welcome, though it could just as well have been a test. Leteo, Dante gathered from the rumors among the waiters, was quickly gaining a reputation among the Buenos Aires elite as, if not the best cabaret, certainly the most eccentric, featuring not only excellent food and music and decorations as lavish as they were strange but also the possibility of dancing with a beautiful widow, all in black, so graceful on the floor that she made even the clumsiest men seem like they knew a thing or two. Dante tried not to stare but sometimes couldn't help it. Watching her dance was like glimpsing a shred of the tango's soul, unbound. And yet, for all her flagrancy, Doña Ruiz was untouchable. She never spoke to the men afterward, never smiled or thanked them. She retreated to her small back table and sipped her drink, alone, surveying her domain.

One October night, Doña Ruiz caught Dante staring at her.

The widow's face opened in surprise, who is this boy, who does he think he is? Dante looked away quickly, ashamed, alarmed, she'd crossed a line, she'd get them all fired. She glanced at the peacock mirror at the far end of the hall, but the sight of her own face between the bright blue feathers unnerved her, so she focused, instead, on the back of Santiago's head, where he sat right in front of her, moving slightly in time with the music. Perhaps Doña Ruiz would think she'd misread the look. When the song ended, Dante looked for the widow. She was staring back. The surprise had given way to something else, controlled, focused, intense, either intrigued or furious beyond reason. They held each other's gaze in the gap between songs. Let no one notice. Let no one see. Soon they were playing again and Dante kept her eyes on her instrument, as though she were some crude beginner who couldn't find the notes without looking. If the violin was like a woman's body, the place where it rested at a musician's throat would be its sex. How had she never thought of this before? Her instrument seemed warm now. Steady, steady with the bow. She'd been reckless. She broke into a sweat, her skin felt damp and hot and achingly alive.

There was no retribution, not that night or the next. She began to think she was safe, that she may even have invented the exchange in her mind, which was a relief, of course; there was no reason for the prick of disappointment.

A week later, a waiter came backstage with a sealed note for her on a silver tray.

"Who's it from?" Amato asked.

Dante opened it.

I wish to speak with you. After your work. Upstairs, in my office, second door on the left. If anyone asks, you were called upstairs by Doña Ruiz.

"From no one," Dante said. "It's nothing."

But her heart thumped loudly in her chest.

What could it mean?

The punishment she feared?

Or—

The second set sped by in a haze. When she finally dared look over at Doña Ruiz's table, she was not in her chair but on the dance floor, with a regular patron, a portly man whose wife watched helplessly from her table, fidgeting with the cuff of her prim blue gown.

That night, Dante began leaving with the musicians, and when they were halfway through the kitchen, she said, "I forgot my scarf backstage. You all go ahead, I'll see you tomorrow."

"What! No drinks?"

"No girl?"

"We'll wait for you."

"No, I'm tired tonight. I'll just get my scarf and go home."

They protested amiably, then let her go.

She meant to go backstage, to get the scarf she'd left behind on purpose. But all she could think of was the office upstairs. She'd never seen it, never scaled the curving, regal staircase that led to the upper floor. Its rich red carpet made no noise beneath her feet. She was ready to tell anyone she saw—a maid, a waiter, the boss—that she'd been sent for by Doña Ruiz, but no one stopped her, no one was there.

Second door on the left. She knocked on its pale, grooved surface.

"Come in."

The room was more spacious than she'd imagined, and surprisingly bare compared to the opulence downstairs. No paintings graced the ivory walls. A fine Persian rug covered the parquet flooring. To the left stood a divan and an armchair, both upholstered in a sapphire-colored velvet. At the center of the room, a wooden desk gleamed, dominating the space, larger and more elaborately ornamented than Dante had known desks could be.

Doña Ruiz stood in front of the desk, half-leaned against it. Behind her a great window framed the Buenos Aires sky, the inky blue of early dawn.

"Close the door."

Dante complied. Doña Ruiz did not offer her a seat, so she stayed standing at the center of the room.

The widow took a cigarette case out of her small purse and opened it. She did this slowly, methodically, with keen focus. She put a cigarette between her lips and lit it. She inhaled, let the smoke out slowly, and extended the case to Dante.

Dante took a cigarette and bent forward for the light of the widow's match. She'd never seen a woman light a cigarette for a man before. Nor had she ever seen an upper-class lady smoke.

"You can put your violin down."

She'd forgotten she was holding it, as she often did, so familiar was its weight. She put the instrument case down, and inhaled. The cigarette had an unfamiliar flavor, smooth and flecked with something other than tobacco.

"You're Dante."

It wasn't a question. "Yes."

"Italian."

"Yes."

"From which part?"

"Campania. South of Naples."

"You're a village boy?"

She was not a village boy. She'd never been a village boy. She'd been a village girl and now she was a man or a not-man of the city. "Some might call me that."

"I see."

Doña Ruiz said nothing for a while. They smoked their cigarettes until there was nothing left but ash. Dante was just starting to think that she should leave, that she had no idea why she'd been called here and little hope of finding out, when Doña Ruiz said, "You play beautifully."

She looked right at him. It was not a coy look. Nor was it the look of a woman lost in perfumed dreams of romance. She did not slant her head or smile. The gaze was direct and as limpid as crystal. There was desire in that gaze, matter-of-fact, unveiled. And there was a question. A searching. Dante gazed back and felt her sexual edifice crumble, all those walls and rules of *no touching* and *no second nights* and *never the widow, never* that had no possible bearing on a force like the one inside this room, inside this woman's open stare.

She was defeated and willing to be so. She would melt, fall on her knees, do this woman's bidding.

But before she could summon any movement, Doña Ruiz broke the spell.

"You may go."

Dante hovered for a second, disoriented. The floor unsteady beneath her feet. Then she picked up her violin. "Good night, Doña Ruiz."

"Call me Carmen."

Dante blinked. The widow seemed amused. It was the first time she'd seen her smile. "Carmen. Good night."

"Good night, Dante."

Six days later, Dante received another sealed note.

The office tonight. C.

She could decide not to go. It was not too late, she told herself, to escape the danger.

But she didn't want to escape. She'd spent the last six days in a fever, unable to stop thinking about her encounter with Carmen, and by the time she took the stairs again she found herself rushing up them, two at a time.

Carmen was in the same place, standing in front of the desk. The band had finished a little later tonight, and the sky behind her was pale, the buildings visible in sharper relief. Two long black plumes sprang boldly from her hat. Feathered hats were the height of fashion in the upper class, but Dante had never seen any as large as Carmen's; they had the effect of transforming a compact woman into a giant presence.

Carmen took out the cigarette case, unclasped it, and offered it to Dante as a greeting.

They smoked. Their smoke entwined in the space between them. It was not such a large space after all.

"What do they say about me?" said Carmen.

"Who?"

"The musicians."

"They don't say anything."

Carmen raised an eyebrow in rebuke. "You don't want to tell me. I know what people call me. But you know what? I'm done with the rules. No one knows what I've endured."

"No one ever knows that about anybody else."

She hadn't expected to say it, and, apparently, Carmen hadn't expected to hear it. She didn't mask her surprise. "True." She studied him. "I suppose you've been through a thing or two yourself."

"Yes."

"Tell me."

Coming here on a boat alone, losing Cora, losing my husband, having nothing to my name, losing my name, living with the terror of being discovered. "Why did you call me here?"

"You think you're going to ask questions?"

"Why not?"

Carmen looked amused. She put her cigarette out. "Do you know what I love about the tango?"

"No."

"Two things. First, it is flight. Gliding across the floor with someone, especially if he's good, there's no gravity, there's a lightness you can only get in the tango or by dying."

"Are we light after we die?"

"What do you think?"

"I don't know." The very subject felt subversive. To conjecture about life after death was to question heaven, not to mention hell and God and soul and darkness. She'd never spoken about such things, except with Cora. "What's the second thing?"

Carmen stared at Dante, searching. She stepped toward him until there were only centimeters between them, a slim finger of space. "Dance with me."

Dante reached for Carmen, quaking inside, amazed at the steadiness of her hands. One of them clasped Carmen's hand as the other landed on the small of her back. There was no music but Dante didn't need it, the music was always inside her, etched into her bones, where it was impossible to lose. She picked a tune in her mind—"El Llorón," the one which most made her wish she could step down from the stage and take a woman in her arms—and began.

Carmen danced as though she, too, heard the music. She was lithe; she was strong; she had balance; there was no ripple of tension at the start of a move or at the end of it. Her responses seemed to guide themselves. The illusion of a single body on four legs, following commands that came from neither mind, from no mind at all, from something beyond any realm the mind could touch. Raise and lean and glide and hook and turn and back again to the center, always back to the center, then out again to edges where the soul can ache and stretch and make an arc out of its longing, sweep its secret shape into the air where it will leave no mark, because that is the dance, it leaves no imprint, has no owner, gleams and then is gone without a trace.

She couldn't stop the song. They kept dancing. They were closer now, in a pressed embrace. Dew on Carmen's forehead where it grazed Dante's jaw.

End it. End it. You have to end this dance.

The last move: Carmen leaned into Dante's body, like falling. Dante held her up, steady, in a slanted line. They stayed there, still, both breathing hard. Time stretched and slowed and revealed a drop of infinity and then Dante gently drew Carmen to her feet. But when she started to pull away, Carmen tightened her hold on Dante's hand to keep her close. Now they were still, now everything was still. The scent of her hair. Sweat and bread and Parisian cologne. Tightly groomed hair that caught the light of the growing Buenos Aires dawn.

Don't fall in, Dante thought desperately. Don't fall in.

Her mouth fell to Carmen's neck and she fell in.

Kisses rained down on so much supple skin. Carmen's noises, beautiful noises, not loud exactly, but bold, inhabited, ethereal and growling all at once. The fine black couture unzipped and peeled slowly down to reveal a shape finer than any of the Greek statues in the great hall below. Carmen, naked, standing. Dante on her knees fully clothed. The shock of looking up to find Carmen's eyes wide open. The shock of gazing back. Into her eyes, at every curve of her. Lean her back against the desk and move her gartered legs apart—they open smoothly—and go inside, inside, inside.

How long was she there? She didn't know. There was no time. There was no danger. Or there was, but it didn't matter. Even if she was killed for this it wouldn't matter. My life for this, my mouth on you, speaking an ancient language it was never meant to learn.

The arch of Carmen's back. Her screams. She will wake the whole city!

She will wake all of América!

A stab of fear, a pulling back.

"More," Carmen said.

The sun poured clear and vigilant from the square of sky cut by the window. Carmen finally pulled Dante up and leaned her head against his chest. "Ah," she said, and then went quiet.

How to leave? Dante pictured the hall and stairs as a gauntlet of possible spies. Was anyone here? Had anyone heard?

Carmen seemed to read her mind. "No one's here at this hour. Don't worry. The first employees don't arrive until two o'clock. My brother comes in at eight in the evening, at the earliest, if he comes in at all. You're safe to walk out. No one will know." She kissed Dante's mouth. "And no one can know. You understand?"

"I understand."

"I mean it. If you tell anyone I'll have to kill you." She laughed, a little wildly, the way a drunk sailor might laugh at a good yarn.

"I won't tell."

"But you'll be back?"

"Yes."

"Or else I'm not letting you go."

"I'll be back."

"Promise."

"I promise."

It was true: the hall was empty, the stairs deserted. Dante's legs had not yet returned to her, they seemed made of a hot liquid and she did not walk but poured down to the ground floor and out into the brash light of day.

The following night, she came to work terrified. If Santiago found out what she'd done, she could be expelled from the band. They would know. They would smell it on her despite the several times she'd rinsed her face at the washbasin at home, despite the cologne. If they didn't smell it on her body, they'd smell it in her thoughts.

But nothing was different. The musicians gathered backstage, in a jovial mood. During their first set, they played another new song of Santiago's—he'd been composing feverishly for weeks, with shocking ease because, he told Dante in a rare moment alone, between you and me, the melodies wake me in the night and make me grab my bandoneón and teach my fingers to sing them—and it was a lovely piece, luxurious, seductive, couples crushed onto the dance floor eager to glide to its beat. Carmen came to her regular table and sat with the same alert severity as always. Her eyes grazed across the stage, across all the men including Dante, with such impersonal attention that Dante for an instant wondered whether the night before had been a dream, a fevered one, as fevered as the visions of those bathing maidens in Pompeii.

At intermission, and after the second set, Dante waited for a note from a waiter on a silver tray. But none came. And so she went home to her conventillo room and lay in the early morning light and touched herself furiously, thinking of Carmen, naked, pushed back against the desk, making sounds that could rip the world in two.

———

Five nights later, the summons came. Dante went upstairs after work and found Carmen in the same place, in front of her desk, no cigarettes this time. They didn't speak. All the words Dante had gathered, all the *why did you make me wait so long*s and *what is this we should stop*s dissolved in the face of seeing—in the widow's posture, in her face—a raw open lust. They kissed, roughly, and when Carmen's hands began to roam toward Dante's crotch, Dante pinned her wrists behind her back with one hand and touched her everywhere with the other. Mark the rhythm. *You* mark it. Don't let her do it, you'll be lost. Devour her, lift her, see how light she is and carry her to the divan where to your surprise she does not fight but lies back with a feline sigh. Push her dress up her thighs, to the tops of her garters and beyond them, uncover her sex which is bare beneath her gown and which you have been craving since the last time.

Afterward, they lay on the divan, both breathing hard, Dante's head on Carmen's belly, the wrinkled pillow of her raised skirts.

"Fuck me," Carmen said quietly.

Dante tensed.

Carmen must have felt it. "Don't worry. I want you to."

She didn't know what to do. She had to obey. She wanted to obey. But it was past dawn, the sun was high, the room was full of light and this was not the sort of woman to keep her eyes closed. Dante pulled out her handkerchief and moved to blindfold Carmen.

Carmen made a sound of surprise and pulled back.

"If you want it"—Dante stroked her face—"you will have to"— cloth bound over her eyes—"trust me"—a tightened knot.

Then she was between Carmen's thighs and inside her and the sun was a river that swept them both.

There were no more notes after that; none were needed; Carmen would wear a particular ruby necklace when she wanted a visit to follow the evening's work. The rubies sparkled with light borrowed from the chandeliers. From across the room, they formed a bright red slash at Carmen's throat. These secret invitations came three or four nights a week—or rather, mornings, since the dawn's first rosy fingers always beat her upstairs—and Dante always complied, always slunk right from work to that office, whose air they soon thickened with the scent of sex. Sometimes they spoke; often, they said nothing until Dante had collapsed on Carmen, head on her damp breasts, and they'd had a few minutes to catch their breath. Then they'd murmur or laugh or do both at the same time, understanding everything and nothing.

There was less time for sleep. Dante didn't care. She lived off sex and music, drank them in the way she imagined that the old gods had sucked their nectar: greedily. She was constantly half-drunk, wakeful, taut as a wire. When she was not with Carmen, she craved her, thought of her, itched to feel her under her hands, around them. The musicians knew Dante had something going on, as he rarely went out with them after work anymore for "a drink and a poke," as they put it, and they teased him for this—"oho, our Don Juan! At last! So you've found yourself some high-class lady, have you?"—but the tone was admiring, approving, exaggerated: he couldn't really have found a lover among the linen tables of Leteo.

Could he?

Santiago seemed to wonder. He studied Dante quietly, as he surveyed all his men, only, it seemed, with even more intensity, a focused stare that made Dante want to tell him everything, to confess the way you might to a gentle father whose arms were strong enough to embrace you no matter what you'd done. But she feared that if she started telling, she wouldn't be able to stop: that she'd start with the trysts with the rich widow and end up spilling out the secrets of her aching bound breasts, the sock in her pants, the unspeakable shape of her lust, the ways she'd found of giving women joy (did men do the same things? some of them?), the radiant cramp in her hand when Carmen finally begged for mercy, the tense fear in her gut that never went away, the loneliness of banishment from heaven. If there was anyone she could tell these things to, it was Santiago. But this very fact made talking to him dangerous, and so she didn't dare.

Leteo, home of luxury and ecstasy and danger.

"I had no idea," Carmen said one morning, naked, blindfolded, sated and glistening with sweat, "that this was possible."

"This?"

"So much pleasure in one moment. In one life."

Dante felt a rush of happiness. "A woman like you? How could you not know?"

"What does that mean, 'a woman like you'?"

"I mean—you seem—"

"Careful, now." Teasing.

"No, not that. It's that you can have anything you want. And you're confident. Able to *say* what you want. I've never seen that in a woman before."

"Well, I've never seen this in a man before."

"What do you mean, 'this'?"

"This."

"The blindfold?"

"Much more than that."

"I'm sure your husband—"

Carmen laughed, a sharp bark. "You're not serious."

They were silent for a while.

"Release me."

Dante untied Carmen's hands and removed her blindfold. Carmen gazed at her.

"I can't have anything I want," she finally said. "If only I were so free."

"But you are free," Dante said, and in her mind the sentence continued, *freer than any of my neighbors, freer than any poor San Telmo soul.* "You have money. You built this cabaret."

"It doesn't matter. Money doesn't free a woman. You don't understand because you're a man."

Dante bit her lip *shut up shut up don't answer that.*

"You're right about one thing, though. I built this cabaret."

"How?"

"How did I build it?"

"Yes."

"You really want to know?"

"Yes."

The story came out in fits and starts, beginning with Carmen's marriage, which was, in her words, its own private circle of hell. Don Ruiz had been a mean old man who stank of stale soup and never smiled. It was her brother who'd forced her to marry him. Her brother became her guardian when she was seventeen years old, and he was twenty-five. Their father had just died of a heart attack; their mother had already been gone for years. At their father's death, they discovered he'd squandered the family fortune, which had taken four generations to amass in the cattle ranches of Entre Ríos, and left a trail of unpaid debts. They were destitute; they let go of all the staff except the old housekeeper who had been Carmen's nanny when she was small. When old Don Ruiz started to call on Carmen, his footman bearing rose bouquets large enough to lose a child in, her brother, Felipe, saw an opportunity.

You'll marry him, he said, and we'll get our standing back.

Carmen tried to fight it, but her brother was firm. One night she tried to escape through a bedroom window. The old housekeeper, suspecting a burglar, cried out and woke her brother, who dashed out into the little garden before she could make it over the fence.

You stupid child, he said, grabbing her by the arm, where were you going?

Away.

To become a whore.

No—that's what you're trying to make me.

He raised his hand to slap her but she glared him down.

Carmen, he said in a steadier tone, you're being ridiculous.

Am I?

I'm sorry. This isn't what you want. But it's not—what you called it. It's a respectable marriage. And you'll see, you'll grow to love him.

There was real hope and real tenderness in his face. He wanted to believe his own words.

And if I don't? Carmen said.

He took her into his arms and she felt the low thrum of his heart. You will, I promise.

She tried to believe him.

After Carmen married, Don Ruiz arranged a plum job for Felipe Carrasco at a railroad company where he owned shares. Felipe lined his pockets and attracted an aristocratic bride. Carmen tried her best to squeeze happiness from the dry fruit of her marriage. The first six months were tolerable. Don Ruiz was not kind, exactly, but he kept to himself much of the time and seemed to enjoy Carmen's beauty or, at least, the way others responded to her beauty when she stood beside him. But after six months, Don Ruiz became ill—the doctors found no malady to speak of, except that he was old, until finally the fifth doctor to replace his predecessor supplied a list of diagnoses and useless pills— and angry. The more she tried to soothe him with words or caresses, the more briskly he slapped her away. Everything became her fault: his aches and pains, the maids' laziness, the rainy weather. By their first anniversary, he'd stopped speaking to her except to spit insults or commands. In bed, he treated her like a mule to be slapped into acquiescence if necessary. He liked to urinate on her. He liked to see her cry during the act. There was no pleasure. She became obsessed with obtaining caged birds and watching them throw their bodies at the bars for a few days before releasing them into the Buenos Aires sky. She strained to memorize the exact slant of their wings as they soared off so she could call it back to mind in times of despair. She bought and released thousands of birds, and it was never enough, would never be enough until the sky became so crowded with finches and parrots and jays that she could grasp their feathers like ladder rungs and rise up to the clouds.

After three years she went to her brother and said, I'm unhappy, I'm horribly unhappy.

I'm sorry, Carmencita.

He is cruel to me.

I'm very sorry. He looked sincerely pained.

Then help me.

Marriage can't be undone. What can I do?

Help me escape.

What?

Across the border. I'll go to France, Morocco, anywhere.

Morocco. You're crazy, Carmen. What would people say?

I don't care.

It would ruin us.

Ruin *you*. I'm already ruined.

You're not. You're a lady, a respectable wife.

I am nothing. I'm a stain on the bottom of his shoe.

Things will get better with time, *querida*.

You're wrong.

More firmly, he said, You have to go back home.

I'll kill myself.

No, you won't. You wouldn't shame us that way.

What do you know?

But he was right—she couldn't kill herself. She tried: she kept poison close at hand and put her lips to it several times over the years. But some phantom force always brought the vial back down. She wanted to leave, yes, but not by dying. She wanted to live. *But,* she sometimes asked herself as she lay beside her husband, *for what?*

Bird after bird lashed at its cage with frenetic wings.

Ten years into her marriage, her husband took her, only once, to see tango at Club Armenonville. It was the first luxury cabaret for tango in Buenos Aires, and that year, 1913, all the people of their class went at least once between trips to the opera to see what the commotion was about. Carmen both loved and hated the opera: loved the soaring grief and passion of the characters, which spoke directly to her soul, but loathed the crowd at Teatro Colón, which clapped primly after each act as if they gave a damn about heroic love or tragic loss but then spent the intermission hissing petty gossip. Still, the opera had been a comfort, before she found tango. At Armenonville, Don Ruiz looked on at the spectacle, impassive. They did not dance. But even so, Carmen was amazed: the dance was like nothing else she'd ever seen, a couple's dance that was not a series of predetermined steps but, rather, improvised. The bodies of the dancers had to talk to each other. A secret communication flowed between them—how did they do it? how did they know what they knew? The dance and its music shot through her skin and right into her blood, where it woke a part of her that had been in a stupor, a kernel full of rage and joy and claws and dreams, livid with life, biding its time.

Then her husband died, suddenly, in his sleep. Age and a weak heart, the doctor said; his cluster of maladies had finally overwhelmed him. Carmen was free. She put on black clothes and went right to her brother.

You owe me, she said. I did all of this for you.

You're right, he said, I'm sorry. I do owe you.

She was so surprised that for a moment she didn't know what to say.

What can I give you? he went on. I could send you to Paris.

No. I have money now. I can send myself to Paris.

Then what?

I want a cabaret.

What are you talking about?

It was the first time she'd said it aloud. There was nothing she wanted more than a place where she could not only dance tango but dance it on her own terms, be in charge.

Listen, she said. I want a cabaret, but I need you to run it with me, or else no one will take it seriously. I'll put down my money and make you the owner. It'll be good business for you. All I ask is that I get to name it, decorate it, spend as much time there as I like, and have the final say on anything concerned.

The brother agreed, and seven months later Cabaret Leteo was born.

Dante was listening with her head on Carmen's naked breasts, fondling the nipples, drunk on their shape. She thought of what they had been through, these breasts, this body. She thought of the multitude of birds hanging from the ceiling in the great hall. "And the name?"

"What name?"

"You named the cabaret, right?"

"Yes."

"Why Leteo?"

"For the river in the underworld. You know the story?"

She did. Cora had loved the stories of the ancient underworld. "It's the river people drink from when they die, to forget their lives."

"To forget their suffering."

"Yes."

"That's what I want this cabaret to be. A river to drink from. Each dance is a cup from the river."

"A cup of forgetting?"

"Forgetting is joy."

Forgetting. The elixir of forgetting.

The thought of it stayed with her for days. She pictured a great chalice at the center of Leteo, presiding over the dance floor, overflowing with mystical waters. To forget. Ever since Cora's death, she had longed to forget; that longing was part of what had driven her across the ocean. Because, while she still lived in Alazzano, there were things she had tried and failed to cut out of her mind. Like the sounds of Cora's exorcisms, screams from the grand old house where all the doors and windows were shut tighter than the fist of God. Like the nuns trooping in and out like black-robed armies, faces stern, determined to destroy their enemy at any cost, although they failed in their attempts and finally surrendered to the devil-girl, a hopeless case, nothing for it but to send her to live far up the hill in that dilapidated hut as though she were a mangy dog, or worse than a dog, because strays could roam the village plaza in search of scraps to call their own while Cora was locked in by several bolts and forbidden any company save the monk who brought her meals twice a day and checked to make sure she had no way to hurt herself (and her father, her father visited as well, the only one allowed, but forget, forget, forget). Leda was a coward, a shameful coward, which was why it took her four months to sneak out in the night and make her way to the hut through a forest that even in the light of a three-quarters moon (she didn't dare go at the full moon, the most wicked time) terrified her, absolutely terrified her, each crackling leaf and whispering branch reminding her of old stories in which girls were eaten by monsters, stolen by witches, swallowed by holes that opened to pits of endless darkness. I'm not afraid, she lied to herself as she walked, over and over, not afraid. She saw the hut at long last in the low defeated light. She looked at it and looked at it and did not approach. She'd knock the next time.

The second time she came, she heard weeping. It was Cora. Still her voice. The same voice that had told her the most luminous stories the world had ever carried on its back, the same voice that had drawn her to the river, mothered her more than her own mother, urged her to be brave. Now she hesitated at the door. What if Cora didn't want to see her? What if she bit and scratched her like an animal, as the village gossips claimed she would? In the end, she slunk away. Next time, she would knock.

But the next time she went, she did not knock; she couldn't because she heard something, or maybe she didn't, there was no reason or all the reason in the world for her to run the way she did, racing home so fast the trees blurred as she sped by them. When she woke up the next morning she couldn't remember what had made her run, she'd forgotten what it was she'd heard, forgotten everything except this: she would never go back to that hill.

November unfurled its brazen spring throughout the streets of Buenos Aires. By December, the air was a thick hot brew you could get drunk on. Dante lived for the moment, in the moment, as though there were nothing but the cabaret, the upstairs room, nights with tango and mornings with Carmen. At home at La Rete, she was El Tanguero, the one who played in front of gilded crowds, envied and revered. La Strega's daughter married and Dante paid for her crisp white dress, never worn by anyone else, as fresh as a wordless page, and for the feast that took place in the central patio. La Strega thanked him with tears and copious blessings on his future progeny, should he ever have them, and he should have them, good boy that he was, you, Dante, like a son to me. She embraced him so heartily that Dante had to close her eyes against the hallucinatory power of her breasts.

El Sexteto Torres did not travel that summer, deciding instead to stay on at Leteo, where the crowds continued at a steady pace. They'd been a sextet now for a year and a half, and Dante could no longer imagine their sound without Amato or Joaquín, the chords and ornaments of piano, the bedrock of long deep strings. Their sound had grown lavish, as well as tight: they meshed with each other, knew each other's sonic shapes, nested together without thinking.

For the New Year, 1917, Carmen planned a lavish party, complete with rare wines, towers of French pastries, several piglets choking on the polished apples in their mouths, and trapeze artists to slice the air between acts.

The musicians toasted with champagne in the Lair, half an hour before midnight.

"Here," Santiago said, raising his glass, "is to the best year of our lives!"

"Which one?" Amato said, grinning. He'd grown portlier that year, and had a fourth child with his wife, and one with a mistress, all of whom he talked about with pride. "The one that's ending or the one to come?"

The men laughed.

"The one to come," Santiago said, his expression serious.

"I don't know, Negro." El Loro raised his violin into the air with a triumphant flourish. His wedding was just a couple of weeks away; the entire band had the day off work to attend the ceremony at a synagogue in San Telmo. "This year's been pretty good!"

"Hear, hear!"

"At least on *this* side of the Atlantic."

"At least for us."

"I mean look at us!"

"Look at this!"

"Can things really get better from here?"

"Just you wait," said Santiago. "You won't believe your eyes."

They played beautifully that night, and the trapeze artists flew and sparkled and did not fall (the blond one, Pedro later told them, made pretty little sounds in bed and bent the way you dreamed she would), but much of the pork and pastries went uneaten, as crowds did not appear in the droves that had been hoped for.

"Where was everyone?" Carmen moped, upstairs. "Why didn't it work?"

"It worked just fine," Dante said, tying her blindfold.

"It could have been better."

"Shhhh—"

"Why didn't—"

She trailed off into incoherent sounds.

Three days later, a new sensation hit the tango world. That young singer Carlos Gardel, of whom Amato had spoken with such warmth and admiration, had presented, as part of his appearance at the Esmeralda Theater, a new phenomenon called a tango canción: a tango that revolved around vocals rather than instruments, in which the lyrics not only accompanied the tune but told a story; in this case, in the song "Mi Noche Triste," the story was of a man whose woman has broken his heart and left him to face the sadness of night. The audience had roared with applause at the end, enraptured, transported, sold. One reviewer called it the start of a musical revolution: *the soul of the tango can be sung!*

"As if we didn't know that in the conventillos," El Loro grumbled when Santiago read the article aloud in the Lair.

"It's not the same," Joaquín said, with a haughtiness that sent a prickle down Dante's back. "They're talking about art."

"Art does happen in the conventillos, you know," El Loro said, an edge to his voice.

Joaquín squinted at El Loro and opened his mouth, then hesitated.

"One thing's for sure," Amato said. "If Carlitos keeps going with this, and he will, the world won't be able to turn away."

Don Carrasco was beside himself. He wanted a singer. Now he understood why their New Year's party hadn't worked; they'd failed to keep abreast of a rising trend. All the most important cabarets would now have a singer; he could see the wave, and they'd join it. He pulled Santiago aside just before intermission to tell him his new vision. There would still be dancing but there would also be a show. People could sit and sip their wine and watch the spectacle; it was clearly what they wanted, so it was what they'd get.

"If we find the right man," Santiago told his musicians, back in the Lair, "we can make this work. Who knows, it might even be a great way for us to expand."

"These rich people," El Loro said as he rubbed resin along the length of his bow. He always treated his instrument with tenderness. He must be a good lover, Dante thought, though perhaps a little tentative. "They don't have the guts to dance, and now they want to change our music to suit them."

"I don't think it's just them," said Pedro. His hair had grown even shaggier and gave him a wild look. "There have always been lyrics."

"That Carlitos." Amato shook his head. "He deserves the good luck. Smart bastard."

Joaquín lit his cigarette. It hung from his mouth like a dead bird. "The real question is, how do we find the right man?"

"Don Carrasco will help us," Santiago said. "He's arranging auditions. We can take our pick."

Four days later, at seven in the evening, long before the first set of the night, the musicians gathered at Leteo to hold auditions. They sat in the front row of tables by the stage.

A waiter brought them a full bottle of grappa and six glasses, poured for them, and stood by as they raised their glasses in a toast.

"Here's to the right man," said Santiago.

"The right man," the men echoed.

The grappa burned Dante's throat as it went down. A delicious burn, how had she ever lived without it? She felt an undercurrent of nervous excitement between the men, about who this Right Man was, how he might change the band. Every member of the group deeply affected the whole. Their leap from quartet to sextet had transformed them, thickened the delicate webbing of their bonds, put pressure on their tribe and ultimately strengthened it. This new change, a singer, could enrich them or pull them apart.

The waiter cleared his throat. "Don Carrasco wishes to know whether you're ready to receive the candidates."

"Send them in."

Amato went up to the stage and sat at the piano, ready to accompany songs. The singers entered. There were more of them than Dante had imagined; they kept coming and coming; twenty of them, thirty, forty, in a muted stampede. The band members exchanged glances of surprise, *so many!*

"Line up against the wall, please," Santiago said.

They did so, jostling for proximity to the stage, each out for himself, young men with jet-black hair slicked back in tidy place, old men whose bellies strained at their tuxedos, poor men torturing their smiles to hide their missing teeth, men with money or at least enough of it to polish up their shoes and add a flash of gold to their cuffs, men lit up with ambition, men struggling to hide their desperation, men fidgeting with nervousness, men who moved as if they did the air a favor. They stared in amazement or hunger at the hall, its opulence, its marble, its brass, its birds hanging from the ceiling, frozen in a travesty of flight.

Dante's fellow musicians, she realized, were looking at the back of the line, where an applicant had been pushed by the throng of singers.

It was a woman.

She wore a man's suit and a dark bowler hat. She held a briefcase at her side. Her breasts and hips were obvious under her clothes; she was much too curvy to ever convince the world she was a man. And she was making no attempt to do so. The suit seemed tailored to her round hips. She wore bold red lipstick and black kohl around her eyes. A woman's face under the arrogant slant of a man's hat. A woman's shoulders squared like a man's, legs farther apart than a woman should ever stand. Dante stared at the apparition, her human echo, her worst nightmare—her face was pretty in a frank, pragmatic way, and she knew that face, didn't she, think, think, Dante, search your mind—and then she knew: it was Rosa. The woman who'd approached them at La China's and asked to sing. What was she doing here? How dare she? She had no right to do this, a young upstart from the dance halls, toying with the border that Dante had risked everything to cross, flaunting it for all to see, anyone could look at her and get to thinking about men and women and the lines between them and drop the blinders from their eyes and then how long would it be before they looked at Dante and saw what she really was?

She glanced furtively at her fellow musicians. Their eyes were on Rosa. They spoke to each other in whispers.

"My God."

"Is that really a woman?"

"You can't call *that* a woman."

"What, then?"

"I don't know. A thing."

"Who is she?"

"What does she think she's doing?"

"She looks familiar . . ."

"Never seen her before."

"She must be crazy."

"It's disgusting."

"It's a joke."

"Kick her out, Negro."

"Oh, come on. Let her embarrass herself."

"It'll be distracting."

"It'll be fun."

"She can't be here. She's got to go."

"No, wait." Santiago raised his hand, a gesture which never failed to part the seas of chatter and open space for him to speak. "I want to hear her."

The other musicians' looks ranged from surprised to amused to annoyed, but no one argued. Dante wished that someone had. She couldn't relax in that woman's presence, couldn't let the knot at the pit of her stomach untie.

It took three hours to get through all the applicants. Santiago gave them all a chance to sing, no matter how scuffed their shoes or gray their skin. A lesser man, Dante thought, would have sent the most pathetic ones away on sight, as they'd clearly never be presentable to the audience at Leteo, but under Santiago's direction everybody had their few minutes onstage. Some were mediocre; many were good; a few were excellent. After a while they bled together in her memory. Halfway through, as one exited, shoulders hunched in the sense of his defeat, Dante saw that Don Carrasco and Carmen were sitting at the very back of the hall, watching. How long had they been there? Carmen did not meet her eyes, but still, when Dante turned back to the stage she felt Carmen's presence as a prickle at the nape of her neck.

Finally it was Rosa's turn, the last one. She rose to the stage in absolute silence. The musicians did not clink their glasses or shuffle their feet or twitch an eyelid.

"Name?" called Santiago.

"Rosa Vidal."

"Song?"

" 'El Terrible.' "

Next to Dante, Pedro let out a sharp sound of disbelief. And Dante herself was shocked at the chosen song, a bold celebration of male bravado—how could a woman ever sing it?

Amato, onstage at the piano to accompany the singers, froze with his fingers over the keys. He looked at Santiago for explanation or reprieve. Santiago only nodded, slowly, *go on, play.*

Rosa opened her mouth, and her voice made the world fall away. It was full-bodied and potent, large enough to fill the stage, the cabaret, the entire city. She seemed to grow twice as tall as she sang, and your ears were made to hear her, your eyes were made to watch her strut and flash, hands hooked loosely in her pockets, chest puffed out because she was, she told us, a man who knew what he liked, a man who went where he pleased, a lover of women, all women, *criolla* women, the best dancer and best knife man at any party, lover of guitars and food and may the noble audience listening now forgive him, he must be frank, he must be true, he must tell them who he really was, El Terrible. Rosa caressed every word on its way out. She was pure vitality. She was the compadrito from the brothels, from the cafés, rebellious, good-natured in his obscenity, unabashed. She swaggered like a man and sounded like a woman and the combination caused a clash inside that could wake the depths of a person, monstrous depths. She leaned into the suggestiveness of each line, eyeing her audience from below the slanted rim of her hat, winking at her audience as if to encourage them to dirty up the meaning of her words, as if to rope them right into her story. El Loro laughed despite himself, turned it into a cough. Dante could not breathe. She wanted this woman to evaporate. She wanted her to become the world. She clutched the table in front of her, groping for stability.

Finally, Rosa finished. Silence returned to the hall. She stood, expectantly, small again, dwarfed by the heavy velvet curtains.

"Thank you," Santiago said. "That's all."

Rosa walked off the stage, picked up her briefcase, and left. Santiago motioned for the musicians to follow him to the backstage Lair.

"What was that!" said Pedro, flinging himself onto the sofa.

"I've never seen anything like it," said Amato.

The men settled themselves on the sofas and chairs, poured whiskey, lit cigarettes.

"Really, Negro," said Joaquín, "I can't believe you let her sing."

"Oh, come on," said El Loro. "It was entertaining. You have to admit."

"And the song? 'El Terrible'?"

"She must have given Don Carrasco a heart attack!"

They all laughed. Dante laughed with them.

"She wasn't the only one who embarrassed herself."

"True!"

"Some of those men!"

"Thank God for the good ones."

"I liked the one who sang 'Brisas Camperas'—what was his name?"

"He was good. But not as good as the compadre near the beginning, you know, the Russian."

"He wasn't Russian."

"How do you know?"

"His name wasn't Russian—what was it, Pérez?"

"Well, he looked Russian to me."

They chain-smoked, refilled their glasses, and kept talking, comparing and contrasting the different candidates, the debate soon locking into the Russian versus the Brisas Man. They were both excellent singers; the Russian had a majestic quality to him, while the Brisas Man was a natural charmer sure to win over the ladies. The Russian had the best voice. Not true. The Brisas Man was agile in his phrasing. The Russian seemed more trustworthy. The Brisas Man seemed like more fun to have around.

Dante argued for the Russian, though she could easily see both sides and would be happy either way.

Finally, they noticed, as if of a single mind, that Santiago had not yet said a word. He sat in his armchair, listening, bandoneón on his lap, fingers roving the keys without pressing down as if holding a quiet conversation with his instrument. They turned to him and posed the question without opening their mouths, *and you?*

Santiago looked at them through the gauze of cigarette smoke. "I want the girl."

"The girl!" El Loro looked stupefied.

Joaquín leaned forward in his chair and spread his hands open. They were enormous, his hands, long-fingered, muscular, disproportionate on such a lanky man. "You can't be serious."

"She's good," Santiago said.

"But she doesn't have balls," said Joaquín, and the other men laughed.

"Yes," Santiago said, "she does."

Silence. Dante was afraid to look at Santiago, afraid her mask might slip.

"We'll be the laughingstock of the tango world," said Pedro.

"Maybe we will, maybe we won't." Santiago's fingers still flew across the keys, more quickly now, chasing a tune with an urgent drive. "But we'll be doing something new. That's good for tango, and good for the cabaret."

"Or disastrous," Joaquín said.

"Maybe."

"They'll never allow it."

"Maybe not. But I'll tell them I want the girl."

"With all due respect," Joaquín said, "it's a mistake."

"I say it's not," Santiago said.

"And if we vote?" Joaquín pressed.

Santiago's fingers went still. "There's no voting here. This is my orquesta. Anyone who doesn't like it can go."

No one moved. The air itself seemed to prickle.

"Negro," said Pedro, "you'd trade us for some girl?"

"I'm asking you to try something different."

"Different," Joaquín said, "isn't always good."

Santiago lowered his bandoneón into its case and said, in a measured tone, "That's what people said when I hired you to play bass."

Joaquín looked both astonished and furious. He opened his mouth as if to protest, but nothing came out.

Santiago shut his instrument case with a crisp click.

"Is this even tango anymore?" Pedro muttered.

"What do you know," Santiago said, "about what the tango is?"

Pedro flinched as though he'd been slapped.

"Anybody else have a grievance?" Santiago said.

Silence.

"I'm with you," Amato finally said. "She's one hell of a singer."

"I'm with you too," El Loro blurted, looking amazed at himself.

Pedro glared at El Loro, who raised his arms in a gesture of helplessness.

Dante felt her tongue cut in two: half of it wanted to cheer for Santiago and for the arrival of this strange talented girl, but the other half burned to defame her, crush her, push her out of the world to keep it safe.

"Good," Santiago said.

And he was gone.

Santiago braced himself for battle as he crossed the great hall. If it had been that hard to persuade his musicians—they were good men, but they didn't risk, they didn't try to look past the damn patch of ground in front of them to the horizon let alone beyond it—it would surely be near impossible to persuade Don Carrasco. He took the stairs slowly, counting them as a trick to calm his mind.

But Don Carrasco's office door was closed. The headwaiter stood beside it like a sentinel.

He's not here, the waiter said. He went home.

But we were supposed to meet.

Yes, he left a message for you.

Ah?

He says to go arrange your business with Doña Ruiz. The waiter gestured across the hall. She's in her office.

His sister? Santiago thought. *He left his sister in charge?*

The waiter marched down the stairs, duty fulfilled.

Santiago knocked at the widow's office door.

Come in, a voice called.

The space was dim and made him think of forbidden steeples, places never meant to be entered. It was larger than Don Carrasco's, which surprised him, and made him wonder, as he often did, about the mysterious arrangements of this family. There was a blue divan in the corner, and high windows that made stark rectangles of the night. The widow sat behind an ornate desk that had surely cost as much as Santiago's annual earnings. She looked up at him with an inscrutable expression that did not change as he launched into his argument for the woman-singer, Rosa Vidal, who, though unconventional, had, he felt, a talent that could not be ignored.

When he was finally done, she said, You're sure that's what you want?

I'm sure, he said.

People will talk.

And let them, Santiago thought, but all he said aloud was, I can understand, señora, if this worries you—

Oh no, I'm not worried. She fixed an even stare on him, her face a sculpted fortress. And it looks like you're not either.

No.

You're a smart man, Señor Torres. She's the best of the lot.

Santiago nodded, startled.

I've already told her to come back tomorrow night.

Unsteady. His legs were unsteady. The floor seemed to be moving, too quickly, beneath his feet.

It's fortunate, she went on, that we agree.

My band this is my band not yours you don't—he forced a smile. Yes, señora.

You may go.

He lurched out of the office and down the stairs to the street. He had half an hour before the orquesta's regular time to gather and prepare for the night's work; his men were probably still in the Lair, stewing and chafing, waiting to see what came of his request to hire the girl. He would not go back in there. Not yet. The avenue seethed with noise and traffic; he hurled himself into its flow. Walking never failed to clear his mind, and he needed it now, the clearing. That woman. That sleek anaconda of a woman. Lurking behind Don Carrasco as though the man were nothing more than a flimsy paper cutout of authority. Once, incredibly, Santiago had wondered about the widow, about whether she and Dante—but how ridiculous, it couldn't be, what an absurd suspicion, a single encounter would have broken that quiet lanky kid in two. He couldn't stand the thought of anything hurting Dante, the boy he'd scooped up from the gutters, lost, reeling with talent, aching with pain he thought no one could understand. Santiago walked on. The streetlamps poured their light over cars and kiosks, old men and young fops, sleek boutiques and damp gutters. That woman, the widow: who knew what she was capable of, sitting up there in the turret of her castle, acting as if she owned him, Santiago, or, more accurately, as if her grandfather had owned his grandfather as in truth he might have and this meant that anything he, Santiago, did or felt or *was* belonged to her even now. It rose in him then, the great red rage, bright, familiar, a whipping flame of it that burned to shout out of his mouth or pour down his arms into the world as violence or else through his bandoneón, how many times the bandoneón had saved him, cleansed him, his fingers itched for that now. That smirk on her face, as if she could buy not just a cabaret but his orquesta—*his* orquesta, which he'd slaved to build up all these years—and, beyond that, as if she could buy the soul of tango itself. These rich bosses treated the tango as if it were a flimsy amusement, nothing more, easy to mold to their whims. And the tango was changing as a result, he couldn't deny it, the piano would never have been added without the rich, this was the world now, the world of tango, and if he didn't play the game by its current rules, it would continue without him, and that was a thought he could not stand. And so he would embrace change and keep tango alive. *Is this even tango anymore?* Pedro's voice in his head. Pedro, of course, was an idiot: he was good enough with his instrument and a hard worker but he was too sullen and talked before he thought. But the question rattled. Not because of the singer-girl, not because of the widow, but because Pedro had no idea—nor did any of them in the Lair—how much the tango had already changed, how much of its history was unsung, erased, in danger of being lost forever.

A music born among the children of slaves is like an orphan: it will never know its real parents, will never hear the full visceral story of its birth. That's what his uncle Palo had told him. Palo used to drum when Santiago was a boy, every night after dinner and for hours on Sundays, on drawers turned upside down, on barrels salvaged from the port, drumming as if the slap of palms on hard things could fill his children's bellies for the night (though it could not), as if the dead gathered in a circle around him listening and reveling and stepping in time. And there were so many dead. Palo's three older brothers had died in the Paraguayan War, conscripted by the Argentinean government, taken off by force along with all the black men of their generation, because, Palo told young Santiago, they needed a way to not only win their war but also rid this country of us in the process, two birds with one stone. Buenos Aires was too black for them, one third of the population, that's enough blackness to swallow you up! to get strong on you! and so they sent our fathers off to war and opened floodgates to European steamships so that white men would pour into the city to replace us, and their plan worked, the bastards, look at our city now. Look at San Telmo. It's like an outpost of Italy around here. Not that I'm complaining: your father was a good man and if he hadn't come here from Florence, he wouldn't have met my sister and you wouldn't have been born. History is dirty but you're a good thing to come out of it, one of the best.

When Santiago was six, his father died in a construction accident, and after that Palo always kept him close. Uncle Palo lived in the room next door, and played candombe—three drums of different sizes locking rhythms to form a complex throbbing whole—as well as tango, in those earliest days when the music was just beginning to assume the name. He played with other men in the neighborhood, in the patio of the conventillo as the women washed plates and pots and clothes and as boys sharpened knives and made rope to sell in the plazas and girls shelled beans or wrung out linens in tubs the size of coffins. In the 1880s, when Santiago was small, Palo had played with El Negro Casimiro and El Mulato Sinforoso, who were among the first to take the tango out of tenements into bars and cafés, playing a couple of songs and passing the hat, happy to gain a coin or two and warm men's spirits in the process. They became famous in San Telmo and La Boca for the exuberance of their violin and clarinet, back in those days when the tango was still joyful and unkempt, still riddled with the old dances of Africa and rhythms that sped your blood. Palo's wife didn't like it when he went out with Casimiro and Sinforoso—all those sailors and whores, she said—so, after a few years, Palo stopped going. Santiago started on the drums with his uncle Palo, but, when he was twenty, he heard an old German neighbor's bandoneón and immediately fell in love with its velvet voice, its sweet piercing melancholy sound. He began helping the old neighbor with errands in exchange for lessons, and soon came to love everything about the bandoneón: its steady weight on his lap, its elegant inlay, the complex navigation of all those tiny keys, the strength it took to press the air out, compressing, expanding, pushing music out of hidden darkness.

But you're not German, a neighbor said. What are you doing with that thing?

I like it, he said, lacking words for the whole truth.

His uncle Palo rose to his defense. Leave him alone. It's an odd box, sure, but he sounds good playing it, and anyway, new instruments aren't to be feared if they help keep music alive.

He has a point, the old German neighbor interjected, lighting a cigarette.

And in any case, Palo pressed on, look at Sebastián Ramos Mejía!

He said the name with sunlight in his voice. Santiago had never met Sebastián, but he knew that he was an old man, the son of slaves, who performed in cafés and, rumor had it, had brought the bandoneón to the tango as never before. That his uncle Palo would place him in a category with this man made Santiago feel hot and large inside.

Over the years, Palo drummed to Santiago's bandoneón, and the sounds they made together were more beautiful than anything they could have made on their own.

Uncle Palo lived to the age of sixty-two, when pneumonia tore through the conventillo and took many small children and old men. Santiago was thirty-three then. At the burial, as the men of his family shoveled redolent dirt over the coffin, he thought of Palo Torres and the world that would soon forget him, forget his name, the sound of his voice, his drumming, his steps on cold flagstone. Palo, a giant of a man, condemned to erasure from the books of time. Santiago pledged, then, spade in hand, to take Torres as his stage name, and to make music with such ferocity that his name would force itself into the world of tango, or, if not his name, at least his sound, which carried Palo's sound under the surface.

This was the commitment that fueled him still, kept him striving even when the odds seemed insurmountable. He never married and now, at thirty-nine years old, he still couldn't think of marriage, for fear a wife might split his heart away from music, blunt his hunger. Sometimes, when he was tired and the other members of his band had gone back home, he wondered why he was doing all of this and whether he should give up the fight, maybe find a wife and settle down into a life of nights by the hearth with a full belly and feet up, children other than the scattered bastards he suspected might be his but had never seen, children who could climb all over him and accost him with shouts of delight—and in those moments of doubt, he called up his uncle's voice, saying, the tango is ours, remember that, remember where it came from. For every person who knows the roots of tango there will be one hundred people who do not and maybe one day those who do know will all disappear. But the secret lives on, it beats in the drum, and in these syncopations even when the drum is gone, in the steps of dancers who'll never know they're mimicking the steps of an old religion that arrived here in the festering bellies of slave ships like the only bright thing left in hell: a god and goddess dancing side by side the way they used to do before the tango made them face each other and embrace. Then those white people wonder why the dance makes them feel so alive. Don't worry about that. Don't ever try to tell them. Just give them the music and let music take care of the rest.

It was time to go back to Leteo. To face his musicians with their countless fears. The new girl, this Rosa, she had a new way of keeping tango alive, and he welcomed it, even though he had no idea what it would bring. You can't cage the tango, he thought, and as he approached the service entrance he suddenly was not thirty-nine anymore, but six years old, scrubbing rat shit off crates in the conventillo, hearing Palo argue with Casimiro and Sinforoso in the warm way of good friends.

Tango, Casimiro said, is the sound of Africa.

No, said Palo. It was born here. Tango is the sound of América.

But it has the sounds of Africa inside it.

Look at us: we have the blood of Africa in our veins, but we were born here. Are we African?

Of course.

And our children? Are they African?

Why not? Argentina will never accept them as her own.

Sinforoso shook his head. Listen, he said. You're both wrong.

What!

What!

But they leaned in close to listen.

The tango began with drums, and drums are prayer, they're still underneath the rest of it.

Yes.

All right.

And so?

And so, my friends. Tango is the sound of the gods.

A NEW ACT! the posters shouted. LIKE NOTHING YOU'VE SEEN!

ONLY AT:

CABARET LETEO.

No names. No more description. Even "Orquesta Torres" was left off the leaflets, the posters, the marquee. The strategy worked: on the designated night, the crowd was so thick the waiters rushed to nearby restaurants and rented their chairs to line the walls.

Because what on earth, for a Buenos Aires gentleman, is like nothing else he's seen?

The musicians came out first, at half past midnight, and played an instrumental song. Dante, in her stance at the center of the string players, between Joaquín and El Loro, felt the crowd hum with disappointment. A few couples got up to dance, but their movements were halfhearted, rote, was this all there was, El Negro Torres's band, solid and predictable? By the second song, a few more couples were on the dance floor. By the third, the crowd fidgeted, whispered, smirked with disappointment.

After the third song, Don Carrasco came to the stage. The crowd went silent in expectation. Don Carrasco had tucked a red rose in his lapel for this occasion. He was unaccustomed to the stage and his hands shook as he spread them wide in welcome.

"Ladies and gentlemen! I present to you, the star of our evening, the best kept secret of Buenos Aires, a lady like no other, a legend about to be born: Rosa Vidal!"

The crowd responded with polite applause.

She came to the stage.

The applause stopped abruptly, as if swords had just severed hands from wrists.

She stood at the center of the quiet, shoulders squared, in her vest and jacket and trousers and hat, smiling into empty hostile space.

At Santiago's nod, the band began to play "El Terrible."

Rosa opened her mouth and sang. She strutted. She boasted and cajoled and belted out the words, and, when she turned and Dante glimpsed her profile, she gleamed with sweat under the stage lights. Her stance was masculine in its vigor but female in its curves, a glorious sight.

At first, at the end of the song, no one clapped. Then a smattering of applause began at the back, shot through with murmurs and the sound of chairs pushing back, clusters of people rising to leave, walking out as the next song began and Rosa assured two hundred stricken faces that she'd gladly give everything away for the woman of her dreams, who was the night, who was laughter, who was dangerous.

"Well," Rosa said after the second song was done, "it seems that some good people had another place to go."

Dante glanced at the other musicians. There was no script or plan for this. They were supposed to launch right into a rendition of "Mi Noche Triste." Joaquín looked tense and was just starting forward from his bass toward Rosa as if to restrain her, but Santiago, seated in front of him, raised a surreptitious hand to stop him. Rosa reached into her pocket for a cigarette and lit it, unperturbed. She exhaled smoke. Smiled.

"Listen," she said in a confiding tone, "I understand." She gestured widely at the audience. "Not everyone is like you." She shrugged. "Or like me."

Nervous laughter. The room was still. Not a single wineglass or lady's fan moved. Even the waiters stood frozen in place. Only Carmen, standing in the back near the kitchen doors, turned her head to survey the great hall with the air of a captain at the helm of a deadly voyage.

"But now that it's just us"—Rosa took a slow drag on her cigarette—"can I tell you what it's like to be me?"

No answer.

"Good," Rosa said and nodded at the band.

She sang "Mi Noche Triste" and every word of it was true, she was a devastated man with a spine in his heart, abandoned by a woman and now his home was an empty shell in which even the mirror was streaked with tears and he could not close the door in case she should return to him, even the lamp refused to shine light on his sad night and every syllable was true, the tragedy was complete, the singer knew the greatest and most delicious pain the human soul could possibly withstand and shared that pain with the full force of lungs that were made to bring this very melody to this very crowd, which sat, rapt, amazed, confounded, awash in Rosa's song.

The next day, Leteo was in all the papers.

A sensation.

A perversion of nature.

An embarrassment.

A miracle. You won't believe your eyes. This señorita has all the melodiousness—and all the bravado—of Carlos Gardel.

Such things should not be permitted.

Such things are not to be missed.

Leteo should be shut down.

Leteo is the cabaret of the summer.

You'll never see the tango the same way again.

That week the crowds swelled and spilled over as the gentlemen and ladies of Northern Buenos Aires crushed in to see the new act for themselves. They were outraged, they were curious, they could not turn away. Don Carrasco purchased more chairs and pressed the tables closer together. Even so the shows sold out and they had to turn people away.

Backstage, in the Lair, Rosa spoke very little. She arrived early to give herself plenty of time to change into her men's suit, which she brought to work in a leather briefcase. The waiters hung a curtain from the ceiling to create a simple little changing area, though most nights, by the time the other musicians arrived, Rosa was already in her suit, ready and pressed, her face masked with a smile.

They knew almost nothing about her. She was nineteen years old, one year younger than Dante. She was from Uruguay. They didn't know where she lived, how long she'd been in Buenos Aires, how she'd gotten here or with whom. Nobody asked her. The first few nights were painful. The men could not talk as freely as before, about women, about whores, about anything, without fear of offending the gentler sex. And it was more than that: a woman, a stranger, had invaded the Lair, their very brotherhood, the mesh of their souls when they played. A silent pact ran beneath the surface of their music, and that pact felt shaken if not shattered. Everyone felt it though no one spoke of it aloud. El Loro fidgeted and lowered his usually exuberant voice to a mumble. Pedro sulked and kept his distance from Rosa, eyeing her occasionally with a mixture of lust and condescension. Amato made a few too many jokes that landed flat at the center of the room. Joaquín brooded in a vague rage that was difficult to interpret. Santiago became more formal, careful to pay equal attention to everyone, focused on the work, torn between trying to ease the tension and sticking to his guns, straining, Dante thought, to keep a cool appearance and not let his frustration show. As for Dante, she didn't know how to react or what to do with herself. Part of her wanted to offer Rosa something: friendship, admiration, sympathy for the constant exhausting battle to be here, to occupy space. But she could not afford to arouse suspicion, and, beyond that, it would have been a false camaraderie, stained with rage and envy at Rosa's ease, the way she toyed with the trappings of manhood as if they were so many game pieces and not the hazardous tools of survival.

Rosa did not let the silence buckle her. She sat quietly on the sofa during intermission, waiting for the next set to begin, as though saving all her noise and fire for the stage, where she unleashed enough power to light up all the city's new electric lamps. When the night's work was done, she disappeared almost immediately behind the curtain at the far edge of the Lair, which came to feel like the border of a separate and hostile nation. The men poured out drinks and busied themselves with their instruments while Rosa changed (Dante tried not to think of the stripping, unhooking, the slide of fabric, the writhe of limbs, but she couldn't help it and from the way the men glanced over she guessed she wasn't the only one), and though they sometimes spoke to each other, they never addressed the veiled side of the room. When Rosa emerged, skirted, fully female, the men didn't look at her, didn't speak to her, didn't pour her a whiskey, acted as though she were not there. At first she'd stand, still as a hungry bird, and watch them before picking up her briefcase and heading out with a quick goodbye. After a few weeks, she simply left, as though acting out her part in an unwritten but unrevisable script.

Carmen, for her part, was delirious with triumph. Upstairs, she raved to Dante about their success—"we've shown them, that's what, now everybody wants to come here, even the prudes, especially them, I don't care what they say, we beat them." She laughed more than before. She became bolder; spread her legs wider; unfurled a larger appetite than Dante had ever seen in a woman (and she suddenly thought of Alma, lying still with her eyes closed, weeping afterward; the baby must be born by now, if there had really been one, was it a girl? a boy? how were they doing? stop, don't think about that, come back to this sweat-thickened room, these salted thighs), Carmen wanted everything now, to see Dante naked, to put her hand down her lover's trousers.

"Why won't you let me?"

"Because—no."

"Come on, I want to see you. All of you. It's not fair that I'm always naked and you're not."

"You don't like what happens when you're naked?"

"That's not what I said."

Smiling, coy. Hands traveling to buttons. Dante pushed them away, sharply.

"No. No."

"Why not?"

"Because I don't want you to."

"You are one strange man, Dante."

Dante sat up and lit a cigarette. Its smoke coiled in the air, made a gauzy veil for Carmen's nakedness. If only she weren't so beautiful.

Carmen resumed with a gentler voice. "What do you have to hide—some kind of scar?"

She might almost have gone with that lie—it seemed a good one—but Carmen added, "Because then I really want to see."

And then she pounced like a puma at its prey and Dante fought back, Carmen laughing, Dante wrestling at her until Carmen leapt back with a howl of pain.

"You burned me!"

Dante stared at the angry red mark on Carmen's wrist. "I didn't mean to."

"You're an animal."

"You don't attack a man holding a cigarette."

"So it's all right to hurt a woman if you're smoking?"

"Shhhh, Carmen, don't shout. I told you, it was an accident."

"You're nothing but a dirty *conventillero*."

Dante stared at Carmen in the stark morning light. She shouldn't be here. She should never have been here. But when she rose to leave, Carmen grasped her arm.

"Don't go."

Dante froze, at war with herself.

"Look at me."

Dante turned. To her shock, she saw tears in Carmen's eyes.

"You can't leave me."

"I didn't mean to hurt you."

"I know."

"I'm sorry about your arm."

"I know."

"You can't—you can't break my rules, Carmen. You have to accept them if you want me to stay."

Carmen stared at Dante for a long time as though there were some cosmic puzzle trapped beneath her skin. "I will. Now stay."

Dante softened and fell to her knees to kiss the tender wounded skin at Carmen's wrist, as if kisses could keep wounds safe from harm.

Months passed and they kept making love, almost always with rope, not only for protection but also for the thrill because Carmen's joy was more brutal with a blindfold, her body more ferocious when lashed down, and for all the danger of their time together, for all the sense that This Is a Mistake and We Must Stop and for all the galaxies of space between their worlds, Dante couldn't stop coming back for the wild arch of Carmen's back as she raised her breasts to heaven, straining against the cords that held her down.

Carmen decided to hold a masked ball. The notion came to her in a gauzy dream that, she told Dante, woke her from her siesta in a delicious sweat. It would take place on the spring equinox, to welcome the fresh September sun, and would rival the best costume parties of Carnaval.

She was lit up by her idea, and orchestrated every detail. She ordered Venetian masks of every color for the Grecian statues in the hall. For the musicians, she bought matching black masks in the Neapolitan style, with long black noses that made El Loro joke about having grown a new appendage for the ladies (and it was good to hear him try to lift the men's mood, though they didn't all laugh, the atmosphere was tense between them still). Everyone was to wear a mask at the party, from waiters to statues to clientele—except for Rosa, who would sing with a naked face.

On the night of the party, they were all to arrive at ten o'clock, to rehearse.

At ten thirty, Joaquín still wasn't there. They began without him, running through a few of their newer songs onstage. Their sound reached out to the carved nymphs of the decorated hall, whose glittering green and silver and purple masks drew attention to their nudity. After rehearsal, they retreated to the Lair, still without Joaquín. No one spoke. No one dared ask what would happen if he didn't come. They put on their masks, and sat, paced, stood, sat back down again. Rosa sat quietly, in her vest and trousers, studying the parquet flooring with great focus. Santiago seemed to smolder, though Dante found it difficult to read his masked face. She felt unsteady. Joaquín had been angry ever since Rosa joined the group, and though she'd thought he'd calm back down after a while, as the others had, he showed no signs of doing so and, if anything, seemed only to grow more bitter with time. It suddenly occurred to her that the orquesta was more fragile than she'd thought. She'd come to think of it as solid, permanent, the way a family or a village is permanent—or seems to be. Because, in truth, even families could be scattered to the winds: look at all the immigrants in this city, blown about by fate, far from their roots. This band itself was made, in part, of such men, brought together by music to form a new family, the only one she had. Now fighting. If she lost them, she didn't know what she'd do. She looked up and, to her shock, found Rosa staring at her with a curious open gaze. It seared her, that gaze, she had to break it. When she glanced back, Rosa was looking away, at the fire-colored pattern on the wall.

The headwaiter poked his head into the doorway, wearing the green face of a grinning satyr. "Ready?"

"We're ready," Santiago said.

"You're not all here, though?"

"We are." Santiago looked grim. "This is all of us now."

"We promised El Sexteto Torres."

"It's still us."

The waiter sighed. His mask grinned on. "All right. Five minutes."

He left, and Santiago reached for his instrument. The others followed suit.

They were all on their feet, on their way to the door, when Joaquín appeared at the threshold, his giant instrument case slung over his shoulder.

"Where were you?" Santiago said through his black mask.

"Around."

"What happened?"

Joaquín shrugged. He seemed drunk.

"We were about to go on without you."

"You can't play without me."

"We can. In fact, I shouldn't let you on the stage."

Joaquín pushed past Santiago to the side table where his black mask lay waiting, put it on methodically, and turned back to Santiago. "It's not your stage," he said and then, slowly, deliberately, "Negro."

The men froze. They all heard the underside of that tone; Dante heard it too, the slithering attack, though she didn't want to believe it. Santiago stood unmoving, alert as a soldier. The two men stared at each other through their masks, with their ridiculous long noses, an unspoken transaction taking place between them. Dante realized, as she watched them, that she did not know Joaquín, for all the long nights they'd spent together making beautiful and intricate sounds. Staring now at his masked face, she glimpsed a deeper seething place that rarely surfaced, that swirled below the haughty sadness he usually displayed to the world. She strained to see. She did not want to see. And then Santiago picked up his bandoneón and walked right past Joaquín, to the stage.

The other men followed him, not looking at Joaquín, who came to the stage a minute later and took his place at Dante's right. No one stopped him. They launched into their first song and the doors burst open, crowds burst in, the masked and costumed gentry ready for their Spring Equinox ball. The band played but couldn't mesh. Their rhythm was right, their pitch was right, the untrained ear would suspect nothing, but Dante could feel, under the surface, the aural web that bound them fray and strain. They played for a delighted, oblivious crowd. The party grew wild, as wild, at least, as the upper crust got: champagne poured; couples danced more brazenly than ever before, as if the cramped quarters left them no choice but to press together and tangle legs; voices spiked and fell, laughed and howled, sang and sobbed; whiskey poured; gin poured; men licked Chantilly cream from the fingers of masked ladies; a male figure in a full boar's head tore through the room grasping women's behinds; a drunk woman vomited on her fine silk gown. Rosa charmed the audience, shone as always, received whistles, hoots, roses thrown from lapels, a few slurred proposals of marriage shouted at the stage. Where was Carmen? Wasn't this her party and, even more, her dream? Dante looked but couldn't find her. At intermission, the men retreated to the Lair and drank shots to ease the tension, barely speaking to each other. They did not take off their masks. Santiago was silent throughout the intermission, except to say Easy there, Dante, at the sight of her downing another quick glass. It did not make her stop. The liquor flushed her with warmth and calmed her nerves. In the next set the stage spun a little, but she played the first song with perfect steadiness.

And then Carmen appeared.

She was not wearing black. Her dress was red, blood red, to match the ruby necklace at her throat. Her mask was golden and left her mouth exposed, that red mouth, smiling, triumphant. Soon she was dancing with a tall young man and Dante itched with jealousy: it should be her down there, on the floor, holding Carmen in her arms, not that man, not anyone else. But how could that be when no one knew what was between them? And what was this thing between them, anyway? Carmen a flame in the crowd, gliding, dancing, living the tango, and Dante forgot the troubles in the orquesta, the rift in their sound, Joaquín, Santiago, what was said and what was not, as she pictured herself falling into Carmen's redness, against her breasts, and disappearing into this new woman who could wear any color and do anything she wished, what a woman, that Carmen, blinding like the sun. Dante played like a demon, horsehairs broke out of her bow and swept the air as her violin sang the way it had long ago for a soon-to-be-exiled king in a voice that had now become her own, exquisite, resonant, blanketing the crowd.

By the time the ball was over and Dante could escape upstairs, dawn already glowed in the windows.

Carmen was waiting for her, standing in front of her desk, still wearing her glittering golden mask. "Well? Did you like it?"

"Yes."

"Everyone did."

"You've come out of mourning."

Carmen smiled. It was a languorous, drunken smile. "Keep your mask on."

Her voice was commanding, flush with the night. She took her dress off before Dante could make it across the room and it was better this way, no more talking about the night, to choose instead the present moment as though there were no other, to choose this woman with her whiskey skin, for now, at least, another swig of life. The lust that rose in her was harsh and bright, she grabbed Carmen and carried her to the divan, flung her down and took her with more force than ever before, their masks colliding, Carmen writhing in what could be outrage or thrill, she didn't say stop, she didn't say yes, she didn't say a thing in any language known to man unless you counted the languages of monsters and wolves.

Explosive pleasure, as if she'd touched herself. As if semen could burst from her hips right through her hand.

Afterward, she collapsed on top of Carmen, who wrapped her arms around her. "Dante. Dante."

"Are you all right?" Dante murmured, but before she could hear an answer, she fell into a pitch-dark sleep.

She awoke to a hand between her legs, inside her trousers, where it grabbed—she shrank back in panic—and darted back as though it had touched a viper. Dante opened her eyes, all muscles tense. Carmen stumbled off the sofa and across the room, where she stood with her back against the wall.

Dante stared at her. The fog of sleep unfolded to the fog of horror. It was a dream, it had to be a dream. She stabbed herself with a fingernail. No waking. She scrambled to button up her trousers.

"What are you?" Carmen said.

Dante couldn't stand what she saw in Carmen's eyes. The sun had risen higher now, and drenched the room in a terrible light. "I told you not to touch me."

Carmen reached for her dress from the floor and held it up to her body to cover it. "What. Are. You."

"What do you think I am?"

Long silence. The room spun. The world, crumbling, faster than she'd known was possible.

"My God," Carmen said. "My God."

Dante wanted to say but did not say *you had no right how dare you* words stuck in her throat.

Carmen made a keening sound, at once pure and pained. Then she set her stare on the great window, on the slice of gray sky above the buildings. Here it was, the moment Dante had dreaded these four and a half years, and to her shock the walls were still in place, the sky still vaulting over buildings. She'd thought, somehow, that discovery would break everything around her, the walls, the window glass, her limbs. She couldn't tell which outcome was worse.

"Carmen."

"Get out."

"Let me explain." An empty promise. What was there to say?

"Out!"

Dante ran out of the room, down the stairs, through the kitchen, and out of the service entrance into the wailing city.

Heartbreak of Mountains, Lust of the Sun

She could not go back. She had to go back. She had nothing in the world if she did not have Leteo.

She sat inside all day, in her small room at La Rete, listening to La Strega sing as she washed clothes in the patio. La Strega, smasher of ships, wringer of linens, song always ready to rise from her throat. Dante's head throbbed with pain. She should sleep, she had to work that night, but she could not lie down, could not take off her shirt, could not move.

What was this thing pouring through her at a boil?

Shame.

Loss.

Fear.

The urge to die.

There was nowhere else to go.

And she *should* die. Didn't deserve to breathe the world's air into this revolting body.

She looked around her room for methods. No beams at the ceiling for hanging rope. No poisons. She had her facón, that was all: it would be enough if she slashed the blade across her wrists.

Carmen's face. The look on her face.

Santiago, waiting tonight for a violinist who never appeared.

The orquesta, all five men, backs turned to her.

Her secret spilled out to the musicians, would they beat her? rape her? spit on her? these men whom she'd come to see as her brothers.

Her secret spilled out to a shocked crowd.

The service entrance guarded by a cook with rough hands.

Or by dogs. Claws and teeth ripping her apart in the dank alley.

Her body—traitor body—torn to shreds.

She couldn't go. Better to cut herself open before the rest of the world got a chance at her.

She took the facón out of her trouser leg and passed the blade along the inside of her wrist, a practice stroke. And then she heard Carmen's voice in her head: *I tried but I couldn't do it, I couldn't bring myself to die.*

For three hours she sat with the blade in hand, looking at it, looking at her wrists. La Strega's songs continued outside her door, Italian folk songs, a ballad of a fisherman's wife whose heart is broken, her husband leaves to fish one morning and never comes home, and she sits at the shore and waits, and waits, and waits, and the sea does not change, the sea has no end, the sea swallows everything. Her voice was pebbled with sorrow. She repeated the chorus, over and over, as the water in the laundry bucket sloshed in time. I'll die, thought Dante, I know I have to die, but first I just want to hear the song, one more time, one more, one more, and then light had fallen and hunger began to rise. A shock that she could still be hungry. That she could still want food, want anything. Rebellious body, determined to lust, determined to live.

The day's light faded. Dark enfolded her. And when her throat was dry and her back sore and her stomach growled into the silence, she heard what she didn't know she'd needed.

Cora's voice.

Wait, Leda. You can kill yourself tomorrow. Go to Leteo tonight.

I can't, *carissima,* my almost-sister.

Why not?

They won't let me in.

And if they do?

———

There was no monster at the service door, no cook to stop her. Backstage, the musicians welcomed her as if nothing had changed, no second looks, no different treatment. They could not possibly know. And in any case, their minds were elsewhere: Joaquín and Santiago sat next to each other, warming up on their instruments, Joaquín's posture contrite, Santiago's forgiving. There was no exchange of words. The others watched them with careful optimism.

Dante played that night with fingers clammy with dread, but Carmen didn't appear in the great hall. Around her the musicians, above her dead birds, before her the great hall with its vast peacock in which she couldn't bear to see her own reflection and its statues still wearing masks as if refusing to believe the revelry was done. After work, she followed the other men to the brothel, to drown her sorrows, if her world was about to be destroyed why not wallow in a bit of pleasure? She lay down beside a lovely naked girl and hummed her a slow tango while the girl pretended to sleep. But Dante's sorrows were not drowned. She went home and slept and woke up still alive, bewildered at the fact.

She returned to Leteo, prepared for her doom. But again Carmen was not there. A spike of relief, the joy of another set. At intermission, Don Carrasco came to see them.

"Doña Ruiz," he told them, "is resting after the great ball."

"Of course," Santiago said politely.

"She has gone to the baths in Salto, Uruguay."

Dante felt something unlock within her.

"Ah," Santiago said.

Ask how long she'll be away. Ask how long I have.

"I hope she feels well?"

"Indeed." Don Carrasco looked confused, as if his sister's state of health were a puzzle he was failing to decipher. "She's left detailed instructions for everything. The decorations are to stay up in the great hall. And you are all to continue as before."

"Thank you," Santiago said.

Don Carrasco nodded and left.

"Well!" said Amato. "What was that all about?"

"He seemed to know as little as anyone," El Loro said.

"She's an odd one, all right," said Joaquín.

"Probably ran off with some lover."

"God help the man!"

"He'll be eaten alive!"

Laughter.

They returned to the stage. Carmen, far away, across a border. The thought made Dante feel light enough to almost float away. Once Carmen came back she had the power to rip open the ground under Dante's feet, divest her of everything she'd become. What would she do then? Run away, or fight back with weapons of her own? What were those weapons? She could threaten to expose Carmen as having an illicit affair with a dirty conventillero. Surely that could cause some embarrassment in her world. But the embarrassment of an aristocratic woman, especially one with her own money and cabaret, not to mention a track record of flouting convention, was nothing compared to the ruin Dante faced. It would not be an equal fight. Better to run, she thought as she lifted her violin to her neck and launched into song at Santiago's cue. But until then, she had this: a stage, these lights, wine, fire, music.

She became bolder. She played fiercely, night after night. She had nothing to lose and so she held nothing back, spent all of herself while she still had a self to spend.

She'd lost hope and that losing made her free. How hard we all work to hold ourselves up, she thought, to play the role we've chosen or that's been chosen for us and we fall asleep right in the middle of our days with our eyes open, we talk and laugh and shit and fight and walk around fast asleep, caught in a dream in which the part we're acting threatens to devour the hidden self. And maybe after a while it succeeds. Maybe the parts of us that never come to light get eaten over time and disappear. The parts of me I no longer am—village-Leda, skirts-Leda, never-ever-touch-a-naked-woman-Leda—I don't know where they are, they're gone, and now parts of the Dante I've been are also threatening to go, careful Dante, fearful Dante, El Chico, the Kid. Always vigilant like a thief who knows he's done for if he's caught out in the night. But now I'm done for anyway so why not wake up from the dream and take a good look at the world around me before it falls apart?

Colors were keener. Lamps were brighter. At times she wanted to kill something, anything, whatever lay close, a rage that blurred into the urge to kill herself. At other times she burned with love for everyone, even the arrogant customers who looked at her with scorn or condescension, they just didn't know better, didn't know how to see, but every single one of them had once been a small child who needed help to wipe his face, and the tango sang for them, too, didn't it? It sang for everyone, no matter how closed or broken. It sang for her, Dante, for her bruised soul. It sang for Santiago, keeper of music, stoker of its flames. It sang for Rosa, sang through Rosa, who onstage was neither man nor woman, or perhaps was both at once, a hybrid creature privy to the heartbreak of mountains and the lust of the sun, or so it seemed when you stood inside her voice.

She was a powerful singer. A brilliant singer. Nobody could deny it anymore, though the musicians still didn't treat her as one of them, not even Santiago, not even Dante herself. Santiago may have taken this way out of politeness, afraid to intrude, but still the effect remained: Rosa slunk out as soon as her women's clothes were on, as if she didn't belong to their tribe, as though she had no place with them offstage. But wasn't she a part of their sound, just as much as any other? Didn't they have her to thank for the new reaches of their fame? All this time Dante had accepted the dynamic, acted the same as the other men, but their behavior had come to disgust her. She disgusted herself. In her new clear sight, she looked like a coward.

One night, she gathered her courage and, just as Rosa came out from behind the curtain, called out, "Rosa! Have a whiskey with us."

The room went quiet with surprise.

Rosa looked like a hunted deer. "No, thank you. I should get home."

Dante had already reached for the bottle and poured a glass. "Come on, have a seat."

Rosa sat. The musicians stopped talking, their irritation palpable; they'd planned to head to a brothel after the bottle was done, and this would have been their time to argue over where to go as they all had favorite girls in different places. The air grew tense. Rosa didn't say a word as they finished their drinks quickly and got up to leave: first Joaquín, then Pedro and El Loro and Amato, who turned at the door and glanced at Santiago: "Coming?"

Santiago looked angry. "No."

Amato shrugged and was gone.

The room seemed empty, just the three of them, Santiago and Dante and Rosa.

"You did the right thing," Santiago said to Dante. And then, to Rosa, "I'm sorry."

Rosa knocked back the rest of her whiskey. Santiago refilled her glass.

"Why did you do that?" She said it with eyes on her drink, so that it took Dante a moment to realize she wasn't talking to Santiago.

"You deserved it," Dante said. "You're part of this band."

"I'm not," said Rosa.

"You are," Santiago said.

Rosa leveled her gaze at Dante. "I don't need your help."

That gaze, it punctured her, she was defenseless against it. "All right."

They sat for a long time in a silence that started out taut and eased with each passing moment, each sip of whiskey, the three of them pulled together and apart and together again by the room's breath.

When the bottle was empty, Rosa stood. "Thanks for the drink," she said and walked out without looking back.

Santiago crossed the room for a new bottle, then sat down and refilled Dante's glass. They knocked the shots back quickly.

Santiago said, "You did the right thing."

"It didn't do any good."

"Don't give up." He filled her glass again. "You're important to this group, Dante. Don't forget it."

She didn't know what to say. His words took shape inside her, formed a tenuous glow, fluttered. They drained their glasses more slowly this time, not looking at each other. In that moment, she felt strangely close to Santiago, as though the air between them could hold anything, even her secrets. For the first time she was aware of his body, planes and angles in the dark space beneath his clothes. It wasn't possible for her to love a man, not anymore, not with everything she'd become and all the things she'd cast aside that men needed from women—but if she could ever love a man again she could see it would be a man just like Santiago. The whiskey had gone to her head. Her hands itched for naked skin. She wondered what Santiago was thinking. He was gazing intently at the wall.

"Sometimes," Dante said suddenly, "I want to swallow the world."

"All of it?"

"Yes."

"And then what?"

"I don't know. Swallow it again. Or let it swallow me."

"I know exactly what you mean."

"That happens to you too?"

"Of course. That's why I'm here." He gestured broadly at the room, the bandoneón case at his feet.

"It's too much sometimes."

"It gets easier with age."

"I'm glad to hear it."

"Unless, of course, it kills you first."

Dante laughed.

Santiago laughed with him. Their laughter rose and glowed and rippled, reaching every corner of the Lair.

The next night, after the show, when Rosa changed and left quickly as usual, Dante got up to follow her without thinking, without saying goodbye to anyone. The musicians called out to her, but she ignored them. She followed Rosa at a distance, through the kitchen and out into the dark back alley. Rosa walked quickly, to the wide street and then a sharp right toward San Telmo, where she lived only four blocks from Dante, why had they never walked together? Why was she speeding up? And then Dante realized that Rosa didn't know who she was, and that a strange man tailing a woman on the street was a threat. What an idiot, she'd forgotten. She ran to catch up with Rosa, who herself began to run.

"Rosa, it's me!"

Rosa slowed. "You scared me."

"I'm sorry. Can I walk with you?"

"I don't own the streets."

They walked side by side. It had rained earlier that night, and rivulets poured quietly in the gutters, flecked with cigarette butts, a few dead rats, shards of light from the iron lamps. The sky hummed with clouds.

"Whatever you want, the answer is no."

"I don't want anything from you, Rosa."

"Then what are you doing?"

Step, step, step against the cobbles. What a question. She had no idea of the answer. "You just seem so alone."

"I like being alone."

"I understand. I like being alone too."

"Really?"

"Yes."

"Then why did you follow me?"

"I don't know. I really don't."

Rosa said nothing. They walked in silence, listening to the creaks and horse clops of Buenos Aires on the brink of dawn.

"Maybe," Dante ventured, "there are different ways to be alone."

"Maybe."

"Some are nourishing and some are poison."

"There's poison in being with others too."

"That depends on what the others are doing, no?"

"It depends on who they are."

At her door—a conventillo whose façade was chipped, stained, exquisitely wrought—Dante said, "Thanks for letting me walk with you."

Rosa nodded, still wary.

"I don't want anything from you. But I'd like to walk together again."

"We'll see," Rosa said and slipped inside.

The next night, Dante followed Rosa again; she felt pulled toward her like a magnet, she didn't ask herself why, her body sprang up from the sofa and she followed the urge without thought. Rosa didn't stop her, not that night, or the one after that. They began to walk home together regularly. They spoke in ellipses; they spoke of God and grappa, stars and horseshit, odd thoughts that floated in from nowhere to puncture each other's consciousness. They never spoke of their work together, the stage, their music. Long silences stretched over the rhythm of their steps. Dante found herself looking forward to their walks almost as much as to the hours onstage. She didn't know why, except that, as she counted the disappearing days of her freedom, she craved the company of people who woke her. And Rosa woke her. She was a mystery, a puzzle with no solving, frank and labyrinthine, distant and honest all at once.

"Do you want to go for a drink?" Dante said once, as they passed a bar.

"You know I can't go in there. I'll get treated like a whore."

"Not if you're with me."

"Then I'll get treated like *your* whore."

Again she'd forgotten. In her time as a man so much of her had gone to sleep. "Let's just walk."

They started walking a little longer, some nights, passing Rosa's door and Plaza Dorrego and the San Telmo marketplace with its great fortress walls, chained shut for the night, walking on past peeling doors where workers were emerging for their early factory shifts and women nursed babies at windows, squinting at the sky for clues of what the day might bring. The more they walked, the more their silences spoke and hummed, knitting them together, turning their steps into a single percussive song. Because they were walking, they barely looked at each other; because they barely looked at each other, Dante began to feel at risk of saying more, too much, saying almost anything to this woman who was like no one else. Be careful, Dante. Don't let it spill, not any of it. After two weeks of walking—during which Carmen had not come back and Dante stayed free, the world intact—she asked a question she'd been holding on her tongue.

"How did you do it?"

"Do what?" Rosa said.

"Become this. What you are."

"I auditioned, you were there."

"No, before that. How did you become yourself?"

Silence, the low pulse of their steps. They approached a boy, five years old at most, sharpening knives in a doorway. He stared at them as they passed, blade still swinging. "I just did."

"There's more than that. I'm sure there's more."

"There's always more. Every person has a story as long as the ocean."

"Yes! You're right! I've crossed the ocean—"

"I've never seen it."

"It's beautiful. It's terrible. It goes on and on. That's the version of your story I want."

Rosa laughed. Dante could get addicted to the bite of that laugh. "Well, you can't have it."

"Why not?"

"I can't tell it."

"Of course you can."

"Anyway, there's nothing grand about it."

"I don't care."

"I don't have the words."

"Try."

"It would take hours."

"I have hours. We'll walk. The city is big enough for that."

Rosa seemed shaken for the first time since Dante had met her. She was quiet for so long that Dante thought she'd failed, that she should find something else to talk about. Then, in a circling way, Rosa began.

She'd come to Buenos Aires by herself just two years before, with cash given to her by her mother to soften the blow of exile. Her mother hadn't used that word, *exile*, but Rosa called it that in her own mind. When Rosa left Melo, the town of her birth in the rural north of Uruguay, she was eighteen years old and had never traveled further than the fields just across the river that ran a half hour's walk from her home. Those fields beyond Melo were green and rich and rolled out in all directions to infinity. When she was a little girl, her mother had been mistress to a wealthy *estanciero,* a landowner, who had kept them both in a pretty blue house on a clean street where Rosa's mother was spurned by the decent families but always kept her head high and her dresses fresh and elegant, buttoned to the neck. Rosa knew, growing up, that the estanciero was her father, but that she should never call him that, should never call him anything other than Señor, which she rarely had the chance to do because when he visited she stayed quiet in her room as she was told and didn't come out no matter what she heard, and, on some visits, she heard many things. Her mother always made sure that Rosa had a plate of food and an empty chamber pot when Señor came, unless he came unannounced, at which times Rosa went right to her room and didn't ask for a thing and held her pee as long as she could (and only sometimes did she fail). Still, it was a good life: she went to school through the third grade; their house had a little garden where she sang for hours to fairies she saw clearly in the specks of light on grass; she got to sleep in her mother's bed when Señor wasn't there, which was often, because he lived with his real family in a big white house on his *estancia* (she had no way to prove the house was white but she knew it was, it had to be). Then, when Rosa was thirteen, Señor stopped coming and stopped paying for their pretty blue house, and Rosa and her mother had to move in with her mother's brother, a good man of course but there was never enough space, they were always a burden, as his wife never hesitated to let them know no matter how many floors Rosa scrubbed or meals she cooked or bones she had to steal from the dog. Rosa and her mother started washing laundry for the wealthy families of Melo, enormous baskets that they hauled down to the river at the edge of town, which every day received flocks of women wringing linens against the rocks and filling the shallows with the shining, fragile bubbles of their soap. She learned to carry great baskets of laundry on her head as the black women did, even though her mother told her not to, you look like a slave when you do that, *hija,* you are not a slave, never forget it. The black women weren't slaves either, though Rosa knew some of them had been before they escaped across the border from Brazil, and in any case they looked powerful to her with their baskets up high like enormous woven crowns. But she didn't tell her mother this. Her mother was prone to mood changes so quick they made you dizzy. She was still beautiful, only sixteen years older than Rosa, and determined to find a man to care for her again. When she did, Rosa was happy that she and her mother would have a house of their own again. The new house was not blue, nor was it pretty, but it was enough—until, two months after they moved in, Rosa's mother sat her down and put more cash on the table than Rosa had ever seen at once and said, he doesn't want you here. I'm sorry. This is for you. Take my advice and get as far away from Melo as you can. Rosa was not a child anymore—she had just turned seventeen—and so she didn't shed a single tear on the whole train ride south to Montevideo, the great capital, which startled her with its size and its river so wide you couldn't see the other side and had to wonder how long a boat would have to sail before you'd see land again. Buenos Aires was the city on the distant unseen shore, even larger, it was said, than this one. City of tango. Montevideo was a city of tango too, as Rosa soon learned from the washerwomen at the shore of the Río de la Plata. One of the women took pity on her and shared her workload in exchange for a few centavos. A girl like you, she said, should never be alone in a city like this one, where is your mother? Dead, said Rosa, because it was easier than the truth. The women clucked and shook their heads. Rosa rented a tiny room in a run-down building where several families shared a long hall and a single bathroom, and it was there that she first heard tangos played and fell in rapture with the music. She danced with a vivid joy she paid dearly for when, a few nights later, one of the men, a guitarist, a factory worker, father of five, broke into her room and gave her reason to sleep with a knife on her nightstand for the rest of her days. She left that building and found another, and in her first night in her new room she lay on her hard bed and thought of her mother, of the estanciero, and of the father of five, all asleep right this moment in different beds. She made a vow not to rely on any man. She would survive alone, or die. There were good people in the new building, and tango. The knife stayed close, she did not dance, but she did sing. And in the singing she found an even greater joy than in the dance; when she sang, she led rather than followed, pushed open the walls of sound and made room for her voice in the raw world. She earned a reputation as the songstress of her street. In Buenos Aires, people said, you'd be famous, on fancy stages, can you imagine? She began to imagine. She began to dream an absurd dream.

"And now I'm here," she said, and stopped. During the telling they had reached the port at La Boca. It was a shock to see it again, the great warehouses, the slapdash houses built from salvaged wood and corrugated iron, painted in a bright patchwork of colors that announced their hope and chaos. Dante and Rosa stood at the rail, the water below them a dark mirror under the growing dawn. There was no moon. Dante had broken her own rule of never coming to this neighborhood, dangerous as it was to her disguise, but Rosa had set the pace and she hadn't dared do anything that might interrupt the story. Words like water to a parched man. It was her own story and not hers at all.

"I've never told that," said Rosa.

Dante thought of the man, the father of five, his hands stained from the factory. She struggled not to think of Rosa, under those hands, alone with him in the dark. She didn't know what to say, but Rosa seemed to be waiting, so she said the first stupid thing that came to mind. "Do you miss Uruguay?"

"I don't know. Do you miss Italy?"

"Yes, but I can't bear the thought of going back."

"Why not?"

"A lot of reasons."

"You'll have to tell me."

"I can't."

"You didn't let me get away with that. Tomorrow it's your turn for the long story."

She'd made a mistake. She was an idiot. There was so much of her story that she couldn't tell, it wasn't possible. "I'd rather listen."

"Dante." Rosa was looking out over the water, keenly focused away. "I love the orquesta. I love that stage. I don't care what the other musicians think of me."

"They respect you," Dante said quickly.

"I'm not stupid."

"They're afraid of you."

"Maybe." Rosa seemed to consider this. "They'll always see me as a woman first, then as a singer or a person."

"They think you're beautiful."

"I'm not beautiful. You're not talking about beauty, you're talking about conquest."

Startling, such directness. Dante felt a prick of shame, though she couldn't have said why.

"Look, Dante, what I'm saying is that the stage is everything. It's life to me."

Dante nodded, though Rosa kept her gaze on the water and did not see.

"And I won't do anything that jeopardizes that life. Not even with you." And then Rosa did something incredible: she reached for Dante's hand, where it perched on the rail, and held it for a moment before moving away.

Dante stood frozen. Her whole body hummed from the touch of that hand. She didn't know what to say, and it seemed that there was no room to speak, that a portal between them had closed, and so she stayed in place beside Rosa, looking down at smooth black water that revealed nothing.

She thought about this conversation for days. She could not stop. Rosa's words, *not even with you,* rang over and over through her mind. Rosa thought that she, Dante, was pursuing her. She was wrong, of course. But Dante could not shake the warmth of Rosa's hand on hers, its stinging power. Maybe Rosa had not been wrong. Maybe Dante had followed her all this time with hopes more complicated than she'd realized. Lust, after all, was a prismatic thing, refracting differently with different women. Alma, Carmen, Mamita, the dance hall girls, the sparrow-girl. Rosa was unlike any of them. She was honest in a rare, unsettling way. She was a universe, glittering with the stars of her own thoughts. Dante wanted to swim in the space between those stars, to swim in Rosa's laugh, in her voice, in her silence. Friendship, that was called, wasn't it; Rosa had no reason to fear. But then there was that hand finding hers on the rail, the duet of their touch, brief, searing. Now, as she rolled cigarettes and oiled violin strings and unbuttoned her shirt for bed, Dante could not stop thinking of that hand. The arm it led to, the body. What she could do with that body. She started touching herself in bed at the thought. She'd touched her sex hundreds of times before, thinking of this or that woman, but when thinking of Rosa she touched more of herself: the length of her waist, her pelvic bone, the breasts that sprang out of captivity every night, stubbornly resuming their shape. The delicate inner thighs that no one else had ever felt. She wondered at it all, this secret body, warm, insistent. The pleasure was as strong as it was frightening. She should not pursue Rosa. Rosa did not want to be pursued. That radiant moment between them had been a warning. And in any case, it would be an enormous mistake for reasons Rosa could not yet know. She, Dante, was a liar, an impostor, poised to run away at any moment (to where? to Uruguay, perhaps, this nearby land that Rosa spoke of with a prickly kind of longing?) and an entwining would be hazardous to them both.

She vowed to stop thinking of Rosa. But it was too late. At work, at Leteo, she could hardly look at Rosa for thinking about the body beneath that men's suit, the breasts that pushed the shirt out, the hips defiant in their trousers. Her singing voice had become the most lambent sound in the world. When she changed behind the curtain, after the show, the thought of every move back there consumed Dante.

Sixteen days since Carmen left. Seventeen. The baths at Salto must be wonderful; stay away, Carmen, stay a long time. Dante didn't leave. How could she go? She didn't know how much more time she had, or how her story would end, and it was bound to end badly but it wasn't over yet. The nights at Leteo were beautiful. Rosa's act had staying power, the crowds continued, and she'd begun to receive offers from other orquestas and cabarets, each of which she'd turned down.

"She'll leave us one day," Santiago said.

"Oh yeah?" Joaquín said. "For where?"

"For the stars."

"You owe me," Rosa said on a walk home together.

"What do you mean?"

"I told you my story of becoming, or whatever you called it."

"Yes."

"And you still haven't told me yours."

"I can't, I really can't."

"Why not?"

"A man has his secrets." She tried to make it sound witty.

"And a woman doesn't?"

"That's not what I meant."

"They can't be bigger secrets than what I told you."

She longed to tell herself to Rosa. To have a person, a single person in the world, who knew who she was. She longed for it so much it made her bones ache.

"I know what your problem is."

"Oh really? What?"

"You think you'll shock me. But I can't be shocked."

Dante laughed.

Rosa stopped and took out a cigarette. She was not laughing. She handed a cigarette to Dante and accepted a light. "Why don't you start with your big secret."

Dante took a long, slow drag of her cigarette. Across the street, a grocer was setting up crates of his wares with the help of a small boy. The man looked haggard, the boy half-caught in dreams. "I'm going to run away."

"When?"

"Soon."

"Where to?"

"I don't know."

"Why?"

"I'm in trouble."

"What did you do? Kill somebody?"

"Worse."

Rosa met her gaze, completely calm. "I'm listening."

"It's La Viuda Ruiz. She left because of me."

"What did you do to her?"

"What do you think?"

Rosa flicked ash from her cigarette. A light rain had begun, and tiny drops caught in her hair. Across the street, the grocer grimaced at the sky. "And she didn't like it?"

"No, that's not the problem."

Rosa flashed a smile at Dante so direct that she blushed and looked away.

"I'm sorry," Rosa said. "I know this is serious. You want to run. But maybe you can work it out—apologize, send her flowers, lick the mud off her shoes, she'd like that."

"It's too late."

"Why?"

"She holds power over me."

"She holds power over all of us. So what?"

"She holds more power over me."

"Do you love her?"

The question unsettled Dante. This damn rain, wetting her forehead, darkening her sleeves. "I don't know."

"Then you don't."

"I don't know what love is."

"Well, whatever it is, you can't have it with her."

"Why not?"

"Because she'll never *see* you."

Dante thought of Carmen, wearing nothing but a blindfold, crying for more *dirty conventillero*, shrinking back from a cigarette burn. She thought of Rosa as a girl, locked in her room, listening to her mother with the man she called Señor. "Nobody will ever really see me."

Rosa focused on lighting another cigarette, cupping her match against the rain. "That's up to you."

"No, it's not."

"I'm waiting."

Dante looked into Rosa's face. The hiding of the past four almost five years crashed over her, and she felt she'd trade all the careful safety of her life for just one moment of being fully seen. By Rosa. By this clear-faced peerless woman standing in front of her. She almost spilled her secret, but then Rosa shrugged in resignation. "It's getting late," she said and resumed their walk.

Another week passed. The urge grew, to reveal herself, to tell Rosa everything: the whole of her, the ocean-story, all of it rushing to the sur-face whenever she saw Rosa, demanding air and light. Maybe Carmen would never return. Maybe she could live forever inside this space, a life that swung between the two poles of the stage and these walks home, requiring nothing more.

They did not touch again, but, sometimes, when silence swelled languorously between them, Dante thought she felt the hum rise up between their bodies as it had in La Boca. Surely Rosa felt it too. At times she seemed to reach the verge of saying something and then change her mind, close her mouth, close her face, rein herself in.

"You're beautiful, Rosa," Dante ventured one night, in one of those moments.

"Shut up."

She didn't push it any further—didn't dare.

The world seemed too small for them, for her and Rosa. If they weren't careful they might make it explode.

She buried her desire but couldn't kill it. The urge sat beneath her skin, like the urge to tear a scab off and damn how it heals, damn the scar it leaves, better to let the broken flesh hit air, to tell the truth of your life no matter the cost so that even if it kills you, at least, after you die, the story of your days won't completely disappear from the earth. Just one person can do that, can, by listening, make your story exist beyond your skin. The power of it thrilled her, terrified her. At night she dreamed of riding horseback in Joan of Arc's armor, through a forest in the dark, tearing branches as she went, following a voice that sang tangos with the immanence of a ghost, Rosa's voice, and she searched for her in tree after tree but couldn't find her; the voice seemed to come from one direction, then another, then from nowhere and everywhere, and as she rode the armor rusted and broke off in slabs that took her skin with it, leaving chunks of flesh along the forest floor, she was almost there, but where?—she reached a river where a body lay, bloated, the face mangled, it was her own face.

She woke from that dream and decided to do it. To tell Rosa the truth, open her world to her. As she dressed for work, she gathered her courage.

But before she got her chance, that very same night, Carmen returned.

She stood at her small table, in the back of the great hall. She wore red again, and she looked radiant, freshly scrubbed somehow, though there was also something brutal about her, in the set of her jaw and her general's stance. Incredibly, the ruby necklace draped her throat.

They were performing "El Terrible," which had become one of Rosa's specialties, and never failed to shock and delight the crowd. Rosa sang with one hand slung in her pocket, the other raised toward the chandelier. Her curved backside in those men's trousers, her voice rippling into the hall—she, too, was beautiful, and more than that: a miracle, a creature that, like dragons or unicorns, could exist only in realms of invention like the stage. In that moment, the stage, that rectangle of illuminated space on which Dante stood, felt like the only safe place in the world. She could not believe the ruby necklace. It could not possibly be for her. She looked past Rosa, past the elegant couples dancing and sipping wine, at Carmen, straining to read her expression across the hall. Carmen gazed back, unwavering, ferocious.

Dante didn't know what to do. She was terrified to go upstairs, and terrified not to.

She still wasn't sure five hours later, at the end of her shift, in the Lair, as she closed her violin into its case and smoked a cigarette to calm her nerves. When Rosa emerged from behind the curtain in her dress, she glanced a question her way: *coming?*

It had become their routine, to leave together.

Dante found herself shaking her head.

The other men were busy putting away their instruments and didn't seem to notice. Only Amato, smoking on the sofa, watched out of the corner of his eye. The look on his face was not unkind.

Rosa nodded quickly—did she look stung? did she know? but even then why would it sting her?—and ducked out of the Lair.

Dante went upstairs. It was five in the morning. Carmen stood behind her desk at the window, her back to the door, looking out at baroque roofs and balconies. This woman, fearsome, larger than life, how did Dante ever imagine that she knew her?

Carmen did not turn. Dante stared at her exquisite back, framed by the red V of her dress. She shuffled to make her presence known. Waited.

"You lied to me."

"Carmen," Dante said.

Carmen stood still, impassive.

"I didn't lie."

"How can you say that?"

"I never said I was a man."

Carmen laughed, quick, sharp, almost a bark.

"You never asked."

"Then I should ask now."

"You know the answer."

"Who else knows?"

"No one."

"Only me?"

"Only you."

"Well, then. I am asking."

"I don't understand."

Carmen turned. Such hard elegance, it hurt to look at her. "What are you?"

Dante had no answer. The question was a door into madness.

"The things you did. How could you possibly have fooled me?"

"I don't know."

"I'm not the first one?"

"No."

Carmen flinched. "What kind of woman does those things?"

"A woman like me."

"So you're a woman?"

"I don't know." The purity of madness, the limpid air. "I'm a tanguero."

"That's why you do it? To play tango?"

"That's why I started." That, and to survive, she thought—but that second part exposed another gulf between her and Carmen, as wide as the first one, wider than words could reach across.

"I can't imagine you in a dress." Carmen's face contorted. "I've tried to imagine, and it disgusts me." She walked to the front of her desk and lit a cigarette without offering one to Dante. "I don't—I'm not one of— those women. You know what I am saying?"

"Yes," Dante said, though she'd never heard it spoken in her life.

"Maybe you're one of them. But I'm not. Understand?"

Dante didn't. She took out her own cigarettes and lit one.

They stood smoking together, quiet for a moment. Lust brightened the air between them, it couldn't be but there it was, an electric pulse that urged them closer together, resist, resist. Carmen would not look at Dante. She took a drag of her cigarette and studied her fingernails with intensity. Dante had never imagined that she'd see this brazen woman in such a state, unsure, at war with herself.

"You, as a woman—I hate you. You, as a man—I need you. I tried to stop thinking of you. Believe me, I tried. But I can't do it. I don't know what you are, but if you say that you're a man, you'll stay."

"And if I don't want to stay?"

"Don't test me."

Dante swayed a little, against her own will.

"Don't worry." Carmen flicked ash into a small brass tray. "I'll tire of you one day." She took a last drag from her cigarette, put it out, and looked up. "Well? Are you a man?"

She should say no, escape while she could, avert disaster. But it was already too late to come out unharmed. She was trapped, a moth before the lamp of this woman, transfixed, drawn in, forgetting all reason in her urge to touch the fire. "Yes."

"Then come over here," Carmen purred, "and show me."

Carmen closed her eyes this time, and did not use her hands; Dante's clothes stayed on, she stayed intact, *he* stayed intact, the ravenous man, the ravaging man, an animal from the dirty conventillos, words that rang through her mind as she spread Carmen's thighs, roughly, and for the first time she turned Carmen around and pushed her to her hands and knees and Carmen's pleasure went savage then, and Dante wondered what it was, this roar in her own body, this aching force, how much of it pleasure and how much of it pain.

Rosa knew without being told, searched Dante's face for what she wanted to know and then turned away and, for the rest of the night, wouldn't look at Dante, not in the Lair, not onstage, not when the work was done and it was time for her to leave, which she did without saying goodbye. She shut the door of the Lair behind her and Dante stood staring at it with an empty feeling in her chest.

"Here, Chico." El Loro handed her a shot glass and filled it with a smile.

The liquor stung on its way down. The air roared around her. Rosa. Before she could think about what to do, Dante was running out of the great hall and through the kitchen to the service entrance, out into the alley and to the boulevard, where Rosa had almost disappeared into the crowd. There she was, a lone woman with an incongruous briefcase, weaving past revelers on their way home. Dante ran.

"Rosa!"

A wealthy couple at the door of a motorcar turned their gray heads, but Rosa didn't slow. Even when Dante reached her side, Rosa kept walking, briskly, eyes straight ahead.

"Rosa."

"What do you want?"

"To walk with you."

"Why don't you walk with Carmen?"

The bite of her tone. Dante felt shamed. The truth was that Carmen had not worn her ruby necklace that night, and that, if she had, Dante might well be in the upstairs office by now. "She won't be seen with me."

"Then why should I?"

"You're angry."

"I'm not, why would I care?"

She fell into step beside Rosa, a familiar rhythm, now tense with words unspoken. Their footsteps were drowned out by the song of the city, the growl of cars, the clop of horseshoes, a fight between three drunks too tired to do more than shout, a whore's thorny laughter, the last tango sets at cafés loath to end the night, the cries of babies through conventillo windows, which were swinging open one by one, it was a new day, after all. At Rosa's door, Dante tried to think of something to say, but wasn't fast enough. Rosa stepped inside and closed the door without a word.

For the entire day that followed, Dante thought about Rosa's face as she closed the door. It haunted her. She wanted that face to open to her again. She wanted it more than she'd imagined, more than she'd ever dared admit to herself. But she could not allow these thoughts, could she? They were dangerous. She was not free. She was trapped in the penumbra of Carmen's power. She went out for a walk alone and the city growled at her, hostile, *who do you think you are?* She was nobody. She had nothing. She'll never *see* you, Rosa had said. The ruby necklace hovered in front of her eyes, on the street, in the courtyard with her neighbors, in the Lair when she arrived for work: not a necklace but a chain, oversize and garish, a collar for a well-groomed dog. By the time she got onstage and played and saw Carmen in the back, wearing the necklace, she felt repulsed by it. Meanwhile, here was Rosa, the woman who strode in front of Pedro and Santiago, where they sat playing their bandoneóns to hold up her rebel songs. A woman whom the world should never have allowed to be. And if she can be? and I? Too many thoughts to hold inside one skin. Dante's violin spun them all into a fine thread of sound. Horsehairs burst from her bow and danced around her as she played, they were true to themselves, to the air around them, completely wild, free, broken. She, too, would break. She would not obey the ruby necklace. She would go where she needed to go, whatever the cost.

When the night's work was done she ran after Rosa, sooner this time, and caught her at the service door. "Rosa, wait."

"What do you want?"

"To talk to you."

"There's nothing for us to talk about."

"There is." Dante took a deep breath. "I owe you a story."

"You owe me nothing."

They were out of the alley now, on the boulevard. Dante fell into step beside Rosa, who did not slow her walk, not even to cross the street, not even when a carriage almost hit her and the driver swore and yanked his horse aside.

"I don't love her," Dante said, catching up to Rosa.

"It doesn't matter."

"I want to tell you about me. Please, stop, let's smoke a cigarette."

They stopped at a corner. Rosa took a cigarette from Dante, accepted a light. "Well?"

Dante put her violin case on the ground and lit her own cigarette. Her hands shook so hard that she burned her fingers with the flame. The pain felt good to her, a spike of life. "Carmen knows my secret, that's her power over me. She found out the night before she left. She's threatened to destroy me if I don't do as she says."

Rosa's lips were tightly pursed, but she was listening. "Your secret."

How beautiful she looked in the pale morning light, a creature between worlds. Soon the sun would rise and pour its light over the streets of this city, bright and harsh, revealing what the night had shielded, what Buenos Aires had lost, stolen, perhaps never wanted to see. If she could only freeze time, she would stop it here, right here in this moment, standing with Rosa in the dusty light of dawn just before the telling, the smoke from their cigarettes twining and vanishing with the dark.

"Rosa," she said, "I'm a woman."

Rosa stared at her for a long time. Confusion first. Then shock and understanding warred for her face. She took a slow drag of her cigarette. It was her turn, now, for her fingers to shake. "My God."

Dante tried to speak but had no words or too many words to say.

"How long have you been——?"

"Four years. Almost five."

"And no one else knows?"

"No."

She studied Dante's face as if remapping it, as if giving it new form with her gaze. "I'm listening."

"I have to walk."

"Let's walk."

They began down the block, and Dante told her, slowly, elliptically—as she could tell it no other way—about the ship from Italy, the nervous bride on deck, the cousin-husband whom a bullet made a hero in the eyes of workers; the ache of hands that sewed from dawn to dusk;

the violin that, if her nonno could be believed, and perhaps he could, once belonged to the King of Naples; the blind man in the courtyard who played like a demon and the armoire full of a dead man's clothes; the transformation of a village girl into a rootless city boy who poured his soul into the tango as if music could save his soul or at least stave off hell with a few hours of joy, and then a few hours more, a few more; the constant possibility of death. Somewhere in the telling they reached their neighborhood of San Telmo, already awake with factory workers on their way to another day's grind and wives sweeping the bad spirits out along with the grime, the way their grandmothers had done in distant lands now lost to them. Rosa said nothing until Dante's voice trailed off.

"You're brave," she finally said.

Not disgusting, evil, shameful. Dante found it difficult to breathe.

"I've never heard of such a thing."

"Me neither."

"But you can't be the first."

"I don't know."

"And . . . with Carmen . . ."

"I kept it from her, too, for a long time."

"Even when—?"

"Yes."

"I can't believe it." They arrived at the corner of Rosa's street and, by mutual and unspoken agreement, did not turn there, continued on. "And then she found you out."

"Yes."

"And she still wants you back?"

"I'm her toy."

"So why are you telling me?"

Dante stopped and placed her hand on Rosa's face.

They stared at each other in the broadening light of day. There were passersby, the street was not theirs alone, but perhaps it belonged to them as much as to anyone. The ornate run-down buildings flanked them like quiet sentinels, keeping watch, it seemed, just for them. The kiss began gently, a brushing of lips, and then, to her shock, grew strong; still no disgust; Rosa leaned in with surprising force. The world tore open along a hidden seam. It was not the same street, not the same San Telmo, but a much larger place, raw, aching, alive with possibility.

"What is this?" Dante whispered. "Are you sure?"

"Shut up, Dante."

She shut up. More touch, more kissing, up against the wall, in the doorway of a conventillo whose door could be opened any moment by a disapproving matron ready to sweep them away. Her violin and Rosa's briefcase had both fallen to the ground to free their hands, which ran along each other's bodies, each plane and curve a revelation. "Rosa."

"Mmmmm?"

"Come home with me."

They were lucky: as they slid into Dante's room, no one spied them from the courtyard except the French wife, who returned calmly to her sewing, absorbed as she no doubt was in a conversation with her village dead. They kept the shutters closed. Slats of morning light fell across Rosa's blue dress and across Dante's hands as she unzipped the dress, slowly, as though unwrapping an infinitely precious work of art. They took their time. There it was, Rosa's body, rich heavy breasts, delirious curves, thighs fierce enough to sink a thousand ships. So much wonder. So much to rove. And then, finally, after a long sweet time, the hot sublime place that could swallow a lover whole, secret axis of the world. Rosa's pleasure spiked and crashed and surged again and you, father of five, in your Montevideo room, you did not break her, go rot in the hell of your own nightmare, this woman is flagrantly alive.

She fell against Rosa's soft belly, catching her breath. They had tried to keep quiet, had they been quiet? The neighbor women's chatter bled through her door, on the rise with the day, while, outside her window, a horse cart creaked and clopped. Rosa's hands were in her hair, tracing delicate paths across her scalp, almost too tender to bear.

Rosa sat up languorously and reached for Dante's trouser buttons.

"What are you doing?"

"What do you think?"

"I've never done that before."

"Well, here's your start."

"I can't."

"Of course you can." The trousers were open now, the shirt unbuttoned to reveal the binding below. "I want to see you. Take them off."

Dante complied with trembling hands. Rosa watched intently as though memorizing every move, every centimeter of flesh as it unfurled. She touched the sheet binding Dante's breasts with the gentle curiosity of a child. "Does it hurt?"

"A little. You get used to it."

Rosa nodded. Dante unwound her binding and sat naked and exposed. They looked at each other in the dim light of the closed room, two women in the wilds without a map or compass. Rosa pushed Dante back on the bed.

"Teach me."

At first Dante was too stunned to move. Then, slowly, she began.

To open. To surrender. To taste it from the other side.

To speak of it—like that, now here—until you can't speak anymore, until words melt in the hot crucible of your mind.

To unfurl, to be unfurled. No need for map or compass, the land is new and ancient and we learn it and are lost in it, become it, we break in glittering pieces and need nothing more.

Carmen, you were wrong: forgetting is not joy. Joy is this. A truth with open skies, sweeping all of it up, shadows, music, hunger, beauty, pain.

———

Afterward they lay together, entwined, breathing air made plush by the day's heat.

"Rosa?"

"Mmmmmm?"

"Never leave me."

"Mmmm."

"I'll never leave you."

"No?"

"No."

"What about her?"

"I'll free myself."

"How?"

"I'll tell her. I'll just tell her." In the glow of this moment it seemed that simple.

"And then what?"

"We'll be together."

"Where?"

"Here. Or anywhere."

"And make music."

"Yes—music."

"And do this."

"Lots of this."

"Forever?"

"Forever."

"Are you proposing?"

"What do you mean?"

"You know what I mean."

"Marriage?"

Rosa sat up in the slatted light and her breasts hung close to Dante's face, manna, heaven. "Yes."

"I can't marry you, Rosa."

"Why not?"

"I'm not a man." Then, laughing, "Didn't you notice?"

"You don't want to be a man?"

"That's not what I said."

"Do you want to go back to women's clothes?"

"I didn't say that either."

"But do you want to?"

Dante ran her hand over Rosa's hip and closed her eyes for a moment. "No."

"Then don't. If you want to, you can call yourself a man forever."

"And be with you?"

"And be with me."

"But, what you just did to me . . ."

Rosa's voice was low, shy. "Did you like it?"

"Yes. Yes."

"We can still do that and you can still be a man."

"How can that be?"

"Because we say."

Dante tried to stretch her mind wide enough to hold these thoughts. She tried to picture her own future, beyond the simple question of *will I live or will I die?* to which the future had been reduced for so long. Outside her door, the children were bickering over their chores, and La Strega had begun to sing.

"So many of them out there," Rosa said. "They'll see me, I'm trapped."

"You could stay here. All day. I'll bring you food, we'll sleep and eat without putting on our clothes."

Rosa shook her head. "If I don't go home the shame there will be worse."

"Then what will you do?"

"I'll wear my costume." Rosa gestured toward her briefcase. "If I lower my hat and hide my face, your neighbors won't guess."

Dante watched Rosa dress in her men's trousers, shirt, and vest, seeing the transformation for the first time. A strange mirror. Unthinkable. And yet the simplest action in the world. Rosa was soon dressed, not as a man, but as a woman in male clothing, holding everything inside one skin.

"See you soon, Dante."

Rosa kissed her on the lips, pulled down her hat, and was gone.

The room hummed with heavy light. Dante lay naked and alone. She thought about her future. She thought about truth. She thought about what it could possibly mean to be true. She thought about madness and kindness and the chance before her. She thought about losses without measure, volcanoes she would never again see on the horizon, a river that would never again enfold her feet, a husband-cousin's brains spattered on the ground, a broken father, a shut door of a mother, and then suddenly she was running in her mind, running fast, running away, down the hill from the monk's hut where Cora lived her final days and running also away from a truth that overtook her and forced itself in, she knew, she remembered it all and this time she would not turn away.

She heard it clearly now, the sound that came from Cora's hut. It was a baby. Crying. Not an evil spirit as the village gossips came to say. The woods are haunted, they would claim, it's all Cora Matta's fault, she brought this evil down on us—a twisting of the story, proof that they knew, others knew, they'd heard the same sound in the woods and told a version that was easier to swallow than the truth.

A human baby. That was what she heard the night she stole her way up the hill to the hut, hoping to talk to Cora one last time but running instead as fast as her twelve-year-old legs would take her, away from the untenable sound which was not a scream, not a wail, but an infant's whimper, as though it had already spent its strength and given up on reprieve. All these years the sound had hidden in a corner beyond memory, furled into itself, waiting for the chance to unleash.

Rumor hid the story and revealed it at the same time. A ghoul haunting the woods. A weeping in the leaves. Evil spirits brought down by the crime of Cora's madness. One story obliterates the other. The tongues of the village wagged, whipped, cursed Cora's name, and, strangely, told the secret of what happened to the baby without ever acknowledging its existence.

Bless the nuns, they did their best.

Cleared the woods.

For the good of all.

The nuns did so many good works. They exorcised demons from bad girls, or tried to. They cleaned altars and dishes and the dregs of their own souls. They also owned a stone building in Salerno that, it was said, had been a medieval prison, and then a stable, before becoming an orphanage with barred windows and moldering walls. As for the priests, they had always bent like saplings under her uncle Mateo's will; all it would take was a gift to the church, and the priest would talk to the nuns, who in turn would make a baby disappear.

Where was that baby now? Was it safe? Happy? She longed to know the child's name, its face, the shape of its soul. If the child lived it would be nine years old now, but Leda, who was also Dante, lying naked in her bed on a hot Buenos Aires day, could not think of it as anything but a baby, still crying in that hut, calling out for help that she had failed to give. *Because I couldn't.* A knot of shame tore open. She would have saved them if she could have, but she was twelve years old then and, she now saw, so much smaller than her world. The knot unraveled further, acutely painful, stabbing. Cora *querida, carissima,* my almost-sister, forgive me, I would have liked to save you both but I did not have the power, not then, not yet, I long to see your face as you bent over your child in the moonlight, the face of a mother however young or mad or broken. Did you love your baby even though it was your father's child?

Can such a love be? I am glimpsing love now, Cora, it's a vaster force than I ever thought and more mysterious, don't despair, I'm coming for you, can you see me rising from this conventillo in the New World and flying back over the ocean, back in time? I am bringing all the strength I wish I'd had that night when I approached your hut and that I had to cross the wide ocean to gather, this strength to see you clearly, to come up to the door, to break the lock with my bare hands and find you both inside, holding each other by the light of a fire, both of you pure, and beautiful, and you won't be surprised that I'm wearing men's trousers because you'll know my face, you'll know it's me, arriving with the King of Naples's violin in one hand and reaching out the other; you'll brighten when you see me and the baby will sense the change and stop crying, a miracle, and when I say Cora, are you ready to go? you'll stand up tall and your smile will be a star to guide us all.

Dante dressed and went out for a walk without thinking of where she was going or why she'd stuffed her pocket full of pesos before she left. She had not slept, she was not tired, the streets seemed to murmur to her in a stony tongue. She wandered for a long time without purpose or direction, or so she thought before her feet arrived at a gray door.

It was slightly ajar. She entered without knocking.

The courtyard was crowded with children and a few women wash- ing linens and hanging them on the line. The children thronged around her quickly, examining her with bright eyes and grimy hands that roved her trousers for pockets from which to steal. She held her pockets down tight—no coins, not one, or there would be no end to it. For an instant she thought of her first day in Buenos Aires, when she'd entered the conventillo that became her first home, with Arturo, a thousand years ago, or so it seemed.

"What do you want?" a thick-bodied woman said.

"I'm looking for Alma."

The woman snorted. "She doesn't live here anymore."

"Where can I find her?"

"We don't know."

"She didn't leave an address?"

"No," the woman said coldly and turned her back to Dante. The other women tightened their faces and kept to their work.

Dante gave up and was almost all the way down the hall when a voice said, "Pssst, mister."

She turned.

It was a girl, tall and skinny, somewhere in the hazardous space between child and woman. She glanced behind her to make sure no one saw them together. "Alma left because they threw her out." She mimed a large, pregnant belly and widened her eyes.

"I see." Dante kept her voice to a whisper, following the girl's lead. So it was true, then; she'd been pregnant. At least that much was certain. "Do you know where she is?"

The girl nodded. She pursed her mouth closed.

Dante pulled out three coins and handed them to the girl, who stared at them in wonderment.

"Well?"

"It's a place called Lo de Julia."

Dante felt punched. She knew the place. The women lived there and worked all night in their own beds. She thanked the girl and walked over there immediately.

At Lo de Julia, she persuaded the madam—a woman reminiscent, in her size and force, of a city tram—to let her in even though it was off-hours and, for a few more coins, to call Alma out to the courtyard. Alma emerged from a back room on the right. She looked much older than when Dante had last seen her. Her skin was drawn and pale, her jaw set like that of a boxer between fights. She'd lost weight from her already thin frame, and her bare arms hung like brittle twigs. She balked when she saw Dante.

"Alma," she said.

"What do you want?"

"I have something for you."

Alma put her hands on her hips, waited.

Dante wanted to ask how this could have happened, what the downward slide had been. The madam had returned to her end of the patio and was pretending to attend to her embroidery, as if madams cared about such things. "What happened to the baby?"

"Born."

"Boy or girl?"

"Girl."

"She doesn't live here, does she?"

"What does it matter? I thought you were impotent." She spat the word, loudly, and the madam turned to stare, all pretense gone.

"Not impotent, Alma. Sterile."

"Fine. Sterile. Anyway, if you can't be the father, why do you care?"

Dante lowered her voice. "You can't raise a child in a place like this."

"Then you fucking raise her."

"Please, calm down."

"Fuck you, Dante."

The thought pushed in with brute force: this could have been me. If I hadn't put on trousers, I might have fallen off this same edge and the face I'm looking into would resemble my own. She was not so very different from Alma, though Alma would never know. There was no use trying to explain herself, so she said nothing as she handed Alma a chaotic wad of pesos, making sure it stayed hidden from the madam's line of sight. Alma looked shocked but quickly tucked the bills into her corset. The madam, eyeing them from behind, seemed not to have noticed.

Alma leaned in and lowered her voice. "So you admit you're the father?"

Real hope in her face. Perhaps it had never been a lie, not a complete one. Perhaps Alma truly believed Dante was the father, or wanted to believe it so much that she was making it true in her mind. Maybe she had no idea who the father was. Maybe she was groping in the dark, not lying exactly, but searching for a story to hold on to, as so many people do.

"I just don't want your girl to suffer."

Alma said nothing, her face a granite wall.

"I have to go," Dante said and kissed Alma on the cheek, pretending not to notice the way Alma flinched at her touch.

That night, when she arrived at Leteo, instead of reporting directly to the Lair, she went upstairs to Carmen's office, uninvited, full of resolve. She knocked on the pale door. No answer. Perhaps Carmen hadn't yet arrived. Dante wasn't sure; she'd never come so early in the night and didn't know the routines of this hour. She was an interloper. She should leave. But first, she tried the door handle, which turned and gave way.

Carmen sat at her desk, drinking whiskey from the bottle. She was wearing red again—it seemed that, in coming out of mourning, she'd traded one color for another—and stood up quickly when she saw Dante. "You," she spat.

"Carmen."

"You can't come here at this hour. My brother could have seen."

"I'll be quick."

"Where were you last night?"

"I came to say it's over."

Carmen swayed a little, and her mouth tightened. "It's not over, Dante, until I say it is."

"You don't own me."

"How dare you?"

"I'm not your dog, Carmen, to come whenever you call."

"Is there someone else?"

"That doesn't matter."

"Who is she?"

"There's no one."

"Rosa Vidal?"

Dante startled; she couldn't help it. How had she known? "No," she said, too late.

"That whore! She exists thanks to me."

Dante couldn't begin to imagine what Carmen meant by that. She didn't dare ask. "Carmen, please, calm down."

Carmen stared at her with wild, vulnerable eyes, and Dante longed to enfold her in her arms, strip her naked one last time. This beast of lust, she thought, how it refuses taming. She still wanted Carmen. But she wanted Rosa—and the new life opening for her, for them both—even more. She reached for Carmen's hand and kissed it gently. Carmen watched and waited with an indecipherable expression. They'd done so much together. There had been, if not love, at least passion between them. There still was. Of all the things she could say, an appeal to that passion seemed her best chance at getting out unscathed. "Set me free, Carmen. Like one of your caged birds."

Carmen sneered. "Or like my husband?"

Dante didn't understand at first. Hadn't Carmen's husband died? How had she put it? *Suddenly, in his sleep. The doctors said. Weak heart.* And then Dante recalled the poison Carmen had fingered before that, contemplating death. Her own death. Unless. She shook her head. It couldn't be that Carmen had— No. This woman whose face in pleasure would melt Eros himself.

The danger she was in came into sharper relief.

She thought fast: don't ask, don't take the bait, try a different course. "Carmen. You're so beautiful. There are thousands of men who'd give anything to be with you."

"Then stay. Don't go."

She was pleading now, her face naked, about to break. Dante could see the scared girl in her, the forced bride, the hurt wife, the woman scratching her way out of an abyss. And, also, the rich child who always got the doll she wanted. She took Carmen in her arms and felt her collapse against her chest. Her smell was so familiar, tart, refined.

"You'll be all right," she whispered into Carmen's hair.

Then she pulled away and found she had to pry Carmen's arms from her and block out her sobs in order to escape the room and descend the stairs without looking back.

I'm free, she thought as she flew downstairs to the Lair, where the musicians were tuning their instruments and warming up with stray arpeggios. We're free, we can start over. Rosa emerged from behind the curtain, resplendent in her men's clothing, and Dante beamed news of her victory in a glance they both quickly broke away from. They took the stage and played a glorious set, with Carmen nowhere to be seen in the great hall. Rosa sang with fresh abandon, made the audience laugh harder than ever between songs, strutted as if the world belonged to her, and maybe, tonight, it did. Dante's violin sang into the band's collective sound, more keenly than ever, an extension of her body and her soul.

But then, at intermission, when they were all gathered in the Lair, the headwaiter arrived and announced that the rest of the night was canceled.

The men stared at each other.

"What do you mean?" said Santiago.

"Leteo is closed," the headwaiter said.

Dante felt her limbs grow cold.

"Furthermore," the headwaiter said, "I have a message from Doña Ruiz. For men only."

Silence spread across the Lair as all the men looked at Rosa, who stood as still as a statue, hat in hand.

"You don't have to go," Santiago said.

Don't go, Dante thought at Rosa. *It's a trap, we're not her pawns, don't do it.*

"It's fine," Rosa said, placing her hat on her head. "I'll see you all tomorrow."

She picked up her briefcase and left in her men's clothes.

The headwaiter pulled a piece of paper from his pocket. "The message," he said, and read. *"I consented to one woman on my stage, but only one. Fire them both or don't come back. Doña Ruiz."* He cleared his throat and gazed intently at a point on the far wall. "Any questions?"

Silence. The men looked too stunned to speak.

"Good night," the headwaiter said and was gone.

The six musicians stared at each other. Dante looked into their eyes, one after the other, feeling her face burn; she had to mimic their reactions to survive; she watched them all make furious calculations as her world fell apart in slow motion. Shock on all their faces, one after the other, until she reached Santiago, who studiously avoided her gaze and that was when she realized that he knew. Santiago knew.

"Good God," said Amato, and he crossed himself.

"Who is it?" said Joaquín.

"How dare she?" said Pedro, crushing out a cigarette with unnecessary vehemence.

"She's crazy," El Loro said, his voice tight.

Joaquín said, "So it's you?"

"No!"

"Stop it, both of you," Santiago said firmly. He stood and opened his hands, as if they held an unseen, combustible sphere. "We're not firing anybody. We'll stay together."

"And leave Leteo?" said Pedro.

"There'll be other places."

Joaquín sprang up from his seat on the sofa, tight as a wire. "But someone here is lying, Negro."

"We don't know that—it's the widow who's—"

"It's not me." El Loro raised both hands into the air like a man in a police raid.

"Nor me," said Pedro. He let out a laugh that came out too sharp.

"Oh yeah?" Joaquín said, to them both, to all of them, to no one. "Show me your dicks."

"You show yours first!"

Joaquín was already unbuckling his pants.

"Stop it!" Santiago shouted.

Joaquín's sex lay in his hand, a limp flag. "Who's with me?"

Pedro laughed at the absurd sight, but no one joined him, and the sound quickly ebbed to nothing.

"I don't need to do that shit," Amato said.

"You, Amato, are not a suspect," Joaquín said, glaring at El Loro.

"I have a wife," El Loro said weakly.

"You haven't knocked her up yet, have you?"

El Loro went pale and took a step back toward the wall. He began to unbuckle his trousers.

"Loro," Santiago said, rushing over to him, "stop—"

Dante's mind roared and roared as she said, "It's me."

The men shrank back as if they were one amoebic being. El Loro made a disgusted sound that hurt Dante more than if he'd stabbed her.

"You," Joaquín said. "I should have known."

Dante met Joaquín's eyes and felt the world reduced to a single point of hatred. Nothing could have prepared her for it. It aimed to knock her off her feet but she did not fall, did not even sway.

"Show it to us," Joaquín said.

She would die here tonight. She would die before she let him strip or rape her, if she had any say *just let me have a say* in the matter.

"Leave him alone," Santiago said.

"You still call that thing a *him?*"

"Joaquín," Amato said, "maybe we should all calm down—"

Joaquín reached into his trouser leg and a knife flashed in his hand.

The air in the room shifted, tightened, turned all eyes to the weapon. It was not a facón but a larger blade, a butcher's blade that flashed with reflected light. "Show us," he said, in the calm voice of a man ordering a drink.

Dante reached for the facón in her trouser leg and rallied all her strength just as Joaquín pounced and slammed her against the wall— she prayed for a quick death—another body lunged between them, Santiago, wrestling Joaquín back and gasping, arching, crumpling to the floor. Joaquín sprang back, knife red, and stared in horror at Santiago on the floor in a growing pool of blood, holding his side, struggling for breath.

Dante fell to Santiago's side and felt for the wound. Her hands filled with blood at an alarming rate, warm blood, she tried in vain to stanch it. The smell of sickly metal overpowered her, she could not bear it, he could not die, not for her, not for anything, Santiago—a slow red explosion filled her mind.

Joaquín dropped the knife on the floor, made a low moaning sound, and was gone.

Amato fell to his knees, tearing his shirt to make a tourniquet. El Loro kneeled beside Amato, spread open his hands as if to perform a magic trick, and left them open, helpless, hovering in the air. Pedro stood frozen, his back against the wall, staring at the pool of blood, or perhaps at Dante, she didn't know, she couldn't look up, she couldn't think, her hands were nothing, useless, she cursed her hands as the blood leaked out around them.

"Loro," Amato said, "run for a doctor."

El Loro did as he was told. Pedro ran out behind him. Now it was just the two of them, Amato and Dante. Together they wound the cloth around Santiago's body without exchanging a word, and Dante felt a stab of gratitude for this man whose love for Santiago overrode the disgust he must feel at kneeling by her side. She could not feel her fingers as they worked, they were a stranger's fingers, sticky and agile, immune to the screams inside her. Santiago's eyes were twisted shut and his breathing rasped and wheezed and for a few moments she actually thought he'd make it, but then, after one last glissando moan, the breathing stopped.

"No," Dante said. The room spun and spun and refused to stop.

"Chico," Amato said, breathing hard, "we'd better get out of here."

"No. No."

"You don't want to be here when the cops come," Amato added as he vanished through the door.

Dante stumbled home with her coat drawn tight and her hat pulled low to hide the stains, but still, when La Strega saw her stumble in, she shrieked in alarm.

"What's happened to you?"

Dante fell into her arms and wept for the first time since arriving in Argentina. She streaked La Strega's chest with blood and snot and tears, and it enfolded her, that ample chest, it smelled of sweat and onions and animal warmth. La Strega asked for no explanations and, once she'd established that Dante was not wounded, held and rocked her like a baby until the tears subsided. Then she demanded to know what had happened. Dante told her about Santiago's death, leaving out the original reasons for the fight.

"He saved my life."

"It's still in danger." La Strega wiped Dante's face with her skirt. "You have to hide."

She installed Dante in the little closet upstairs, her first room at La Rete, now a storeroom again. La Strega brought her a chamber pot and a plate of bread and cheese, and insisted that Dante stay inside and not make a sound and not come out for anything, not for water, a cigarette, or a breath of air. Then she left Dante in the dark. Dante fumbled for space to lay her body down. She felt sacks of grain, broken crates in a pile, empty washtubs stacked one inside the other. Something rotted in a forgotten corner, she couldn't tell what. Voices wafted up from the courtyard through the closed door, the ordinary lives of the living, continuing on. She crawled into a washtub and curled up inside it, still caked with blood, clutching her violin as though it were the flotsam of a shipwreck, her only hope for staying afloat.

She woke at dawn to the sound of men stomping through the courtyard, opening and closing doors. Official men. Police.

"Where's Dante Di Bacco?"

"I don't know, sir. He's not here." La Strega, her voice innocent, ignorant, verging on stupid. The perfect act.

"When did you last see him?"

"Before work last night."

The slam of doors.

"Why? Did something happen to him?"

"Show us his room."

They marched to Dante's room and she gave thanks for the good people of La Rete, who formed a shroud of protection around her, not one of them giving her away. The police spent half an hour in her room and then left. Two hours later, La Strega knocked on the door and entered, bearing coffee, gossip, and the morning papers.

"It's not good," she said as she lit a candle.

Dante looked at the papers.

BLOOD AT LETEO, the headlines read.

THE DEADLY CABARET
TANGO AND MURDER! POLICE ON THE TRAIL

The articles featured photos of Santiago's bloody body and the incriminating knife on the ground. They bemoaned the lurid violence of the tango world and described the corpse in greedy detail. La Strega had more to add, having trawled the street with the great prodigious net of her connections, catching one slippery fact here, another there. The police were beside themselves, desperate for a suspect. They obviously didn't care about El Negro Torres from the conventillos of San Telmo, but they were under pressure to arrest someone for the sake of the cabaret. They'd spoken, so far, to a bandoneonist and a Russian violinist— Pedro and El Loro, Dante thought—because they'd returned with a doctor and found the dead body. No one was sure what they'd said to the police, but rumor had it that the Russian claimed the bassist was the murderer, while the bandoneonist had accused Dante. Meanwhile, the bassist and the pianist were nowhere to be found.

"The bandoneonist. What's his name?" La Strega said.

"Pedro."

"Why would he accuse you?"

It was easy to imagine why. Pedro was surely disgusted by Dante's secret, and he no doubt blamed her for everything that had happened in the Lair. But it seemed that none of this had leaked out, not yet, not if La Strega knew nothing. Relief whipped her on the inside. "It's a long story."

La Strega squinted at Dante in the candlelight. "It must have been quite a fight."

"Yes."

"Well. Dear boy, you're in trouble. Those policemen this morning, they wanted your hide. And if the one who did it disappears, as it seems he has, they'll pin it on you faster than a fly can blink."

Dante thought of the Buenos Aires police, the same ones who'd killed her cousin-husband at the strike years before, who cared nothing for lowly conventilleros, and everything for clearing Leteo's name. "You're right."

"You can't stay in this city."

"No." Buenos Aires seethed around her, garish, unforgiving. "I'll leave tonight."

"Where will you go?"

She could find only one answer in the great swirl of her mind. "Uruguay."

La Strega nodded, satisfied, and reached for the chamber pot. "I'll miss you terribly. You're like a son to me."

She'd said it hundreds of times before, but today Dante heard it with all of her being and stashed the words where they'd never be lost.

"Can you help me escape?"

"Dante, *carissimo,* I already am."

She tried not to think of her losses, the life she'd made, this beautiful hazardous city, Santiago vibrant onstage, the orquesta, its tribe of men, shining Leteo, moonlight in gutters, dawn over rooftops, Santiago crumpled in a red pool, Rosa, Rosa, Rosa. Don't think. If she started to count her losses she'd get tangled in their numbers and might not survive the bridge to exile. Rosa. To live without her, a punishment. And yet, to subject her to danger was even worse; there was no choice; she had to escape without saying goodbye.

But that afternoon, when La Strega brought Dante a clean chamber pot and a bowl of soup, she said, "Someone's come twice now to see you."

Dante's heart pounded.

"A woman."

"What was her name?"

"Rosa."

The room glowed in the light of La Strega's candle, not decrepit anymore, a dim chapel where any prayer was possible. "What did you tell her?"

"What I tell everyone. That you're not here."

"Please. If she comes back, I have to see her."

La Strega pursed her lips and studied her.

"She can be trusted."

"My God," La Strega said. "You're finally in love."

Dante looked up. There was so much she could have said in that moment, so much left to be said, but there was no time, there could never be enough time, and, she now realized as she took in La Strega's face, there was no need.

"Oh, my boy," La Strega said. She reached out and stroked Dante's hair, then was gone.

Rosa came an hour later. La Strega brought her to the door, then closed it, shutting them into a shared dark. Rosa groped for Dante and, when she found her, fell into her arms. They held each other for a long time without speaking. Rosa's body sparked a riot in her, joy and grief and pure bright lust.

"You're all right?"

"Yes," Dante said, though she wasn't sure.

"I can't see you."

"I can light a candle—"

"No, it's all right."

"Rosa."

"What happened?"

Dante told her about the note from Carmen and everything that rippled out from it, until Santiago's death.

"My God. I will kill that Joaquín."

"There's been enough killing."

"I can't believe Santiago's gone." Rosa's voice rasped with pain. "He was good to me."

"He was good to all of us."

"And now they're after you."

"Yes."

"What are you going to do?"

"Leave."

"Where to?"

"Uruguay."

Rosa filled the dark with silence.

"I'll cross the river. Make a new life." Dante tried her best to sound hopeful. "Maybe even play some tango."

"Of course you'll play tango."

"Don't forget me," Dante said, trying to keep her voice from breaking.

"You're an idiot, Dante."

"What?"

"Light the candle."

Dante did as she was told. Rosa's face appeared, determined, sublime, how had she ever thought this woman was less than beautiful?

"I'm coming with you."

"You can't do that," Dante said, too quickly, belying the hope that pierced her chest.

"Why not?"

"You're not on the run."

"But you are."

"Your career. You're on your way to the stars." She could still hear those words in Santiago's voice.

"I can sing in Uruguay."

"You shouldn't have to give that up."

"Do you want to give me up?"

"No. No." She was weeping now. "This is all my fault."

"It's not. You didn't wield the knife."

"But Santiago—"

"—defended you. As he was right to do."

"The orquesta, it's destroyed now."

"To hell with the orquesta."

"Don't say that."

"Why not?"

"The orquesta is life."

"No, *mi amor*. Life is life. The orquesta was only people playing music."

"I don't know the difference between the two."

"There is a difference."

"The stage is life for you too. You said so yourself. And if you leave with me, that life will end."

Rosa leaned forward. "We don't have the least idea what life can be."

"We don't?"

"No."

"Then how do we find out?"

Rosa wiped tears from Dante's face with her fingers. The gesture was as firm as it was tender. "We plunge."

That night, three hours before dawn, two figures slipped through the shadows of San Telmo and onto a boat that waited for them at the La Boca port. One carried a briefcase, the other an instrument case just the right size for a violin. A fishing boat stood at the docks; its wooden body welcomed them without question, as did the fisherman who palmed more bills at once, that night, than he ever had in his life. The two figures went belowdecks and huddled together on a net whose ropes were still wet from yesterday's catch. As the boat launched onto the Río de la Plata, they held each other close, humming tangos to mesh with the slosh of waves and, finally, falling into a gauzy, dreamless sleep.

Meanwhile, Buenos Aires continued, awake in the night. In a public morgue, the body of a bandoneón player was prepared for burial by two men who remarked to each other on the corpse's hands, which were stronger than any they'd seen before, fingers muscular from years of music, now clasping each other stiffly across a chest cleansed of blood. They gave up on taming the cadaver's curls and let them spring in a lush black crown around his face. While they worked, in the cemetery, a tired old gravedigger prepared the hole for the bandoneón player's final rest. A few meters away, in an unmarked grave, a Polish girl lay buried, her flesh blending slowly with the earth, becoming food for worms that would one day be food for birds.

At that moment, in San Telmo, a woman known only as Mamita sat on her bed, a gray-haired man suckling at her large breasts like a baby. The top of his head was bald and shiny, and there was nothing hard about his touch. She pitied the old sod and gave him five extra minutes, rocking gently back and forth, humming an old tune in her boredom. Nine blocks from Mamita, a young man from the Cilento Coast woke with an ache in his arm, which had broken in his youth and never set right. He'd just dreamed about his dead friend again, first the moment when the bullet blasted open his head, then the two of them together, whole, laughing on a great red ship. His wife felt him stirring and turned to massage the limb, groggily, gently, preparing it for the day's labor to come.

Two houses down from them, a blind old man who sensed his time to die was close, but not yet here, dreamed an intoxicating dream. He was walking barefoot on a road that led to Naples, or that he hoped would lead to Naples, thinking to his dream-self that, the world being round, all roads could lead to Naples if you walked them long enough. He walked and walked. His feet throbbed with pain. And then he realized that he was not walking on a road at all but on the neck of a violin, long enough to stretch out before him to infinity. The land on either side had fallen away, leaving only blackness. If he fell, he knew, there would be no return. The violin strings cut the soles of his feet but made soft sounds beneath his steps, odd sounds, ghost sounds, sounds to carry a man beyond this world.

Three blocks from him, a woman woke. Her name was Fausta. Her son was crying for her milk. She pulled him close and opened her nightgown at the collar. As he nursed, he locked eyes with her and reached his small hand to her face. They caressed each other in the moonlight, and then, because he did not seem tired and she, too, felt wide awake, she whispered a story to him, an old story her grandmother had told her, the oldest story she knew. There was a time, she told him, when the gods were many and they destroyed the earth with a great flood to make it new. All the people died in the vast rising sea that covered the land, except for two, a brother and sister, who rode a little raft to a tall mountaintop that kept them safe and dry. They watched the devastation until, finally, the sea receded, and they found themselves in a land they did not recognize, strewn with the corpses of the drowned. At first, they despaired. Then they found their way to the temple of a beautiful goddess, where they kissed the cold stone of the ground. Help us, they said, restore our people, tell us how to make this world ours again. The goddess said: when you leave my temple, throw your mother's bones behind you. At first the couple balked. Defile our mother's corpse! How could we do such a thing? But then they realized that they had two mothers, just as everybody does. We have the woman who gave birth to us, as I gave birth to you, but we also have a greater mother, the earth. This mother's bones are everywhere, in the form of stones. And so, as the brother and sister left the temple, they threw stones over their shoulders and the stones grew and softened into people, until soon the land was full of men and women made from material strong enough to endure this harsh life, and then, my boy, my light, my angel, they filled the air with their song.

PART THREE

◆

Bright Jagged Thing

Rosa and Dante lived together in Montevideo for fifty-one years.

They settled in Ciudad Vieja, the city's historic center, which jutted into the Río de la Plata like the thumb of a stalwart hand. The river was a marvel, a different color every day: blue, brown, silvery gray, sometimes smooth as a mirror, sometimes whipped into waves full of white tongues. The water stretched out to the horizon as though it were the sea itself, and perhaps it was the sea, wide as it was, an estuary, a mixing place, not yet the Atlantic but shot through with its salt. The waterfront reminded Dante of the Bay of Naples, only without the volcano on the skyline. Home and yet not home, known and unknown. In those first ecstatic and uncertain months, they took long walks along the shore, talking or moving in silence, looking out over the water, searching it for secrets of the deep. The day they married, they celebrated with a long stroll from their apartment in the Old City down to the Punta Carretas lighthouse, where they climbed down the rocks and laughed as waves crashed up to them and swallowed their bodies to the thigh.

They soon found that Rosa had been right about the tango: it was thriving in Montevideo, there was more than enough room for two performers fresh from Buenos Aires cabarets. They joined an orquesta that played at hotels and bars and theaters—at Politeama, Artigas, Stella D'Italia, even at the elegant opera house, Teatro Solís. Rosa's act shook the stages of Montevideo. There would be no lack of work.

In their first summer, Rosa and Dante hung a mosquito net over their marital bed, and when they made love beneath it they were no longer in Uruguay, no longer on earth at all, but weightless, suspended, shimmering like cosmic beasts aloft between stars.

"Never take that thing down," said Rosa. And they did not.

The Argentinean police never came to their door. They were free. And they were happy, almost obscenely so, aware of the enormity of their luck, as if the gown of reality had torn and they had managed to worm their way out through the hole. But there were also sorrows. For a long time, Rosa was haunted by the father of five, who lived, as far as she knew, in this same city, and whom she sometimes glimpsed in crowds until the stranger would turn and reveal himself to be another man, and who invaded her dreams until she found, by word of mouth, a healer in the dusty neighborhood of Punta Carretas, a tiny woman who sat in the back of a butcher shop and listened with the stillness of an owl, then dispensed remedies that gradually expunged the nightmares from Rosa's sleep. In 1919, news from Argentina told of a Tragic Week, so it was called, in which the police shot down anarchists and tens of thousands took to the streets to protest, resulting in riots and massacres, hundreds dead, thousands wounded, tens of thousands imprisoned. For weeks, Dante could not sleep, thinking of her cousin-husband's exploded skull, thinking of El Loro and Arturo, two anarchists who might have been at those very riots, though really any of the others from the conventillos— Francesca, Carlo, Valentino, Fausta, La Strega, Palmira, any of their uncles or daughters or children—could have been on those same streets, and so she pictured all of them, one by one, vivid against her dark ceiling as she wished them safe from harm. (Years later, she would meet El Loro again on a tango tour through Montevideo and be thrilled to find him alive; he came to their apartment for dinner and they reminisced warmly over Rosa's gnocchi and a long slow bottle of whiskey; it was marvelous to see him, he seemed genuinely happy for their marriage and never brought up Dante's secret, never even seemed to flicker, as if there had been no secret at all, as if that moment in the Lair had never happened. They drank and talked until dawn, swapping stories about Amato's life in Paris with the same wife and a new mistress, it seemed, and Pedro's successes in New York, both men riding the waves of the tango's stratospheric rise across the globe to make new lives on distant shores, like tango exporters, El Loro said, or tango missionaries, Rosa said, and they all laughed, and then they mused over what the hell had happened to Joaquín, who had never been seen again, and toasted to the old days and above all to Santiago's memory, his immeasurable imprint on their lives). The letters from her father trickled down to once a year after her mother died. Even when they came, they told her almost nothing. It was to be expected, but still, it shredded her inside to think of her mamma buried in a tomb she'd never see, to be left wondering about Tommaso's life after he lost one of his legs in the war, to never meet her many nieces and nephews. To never again see or hear or breathe the air of Italy. On some days, this seemed an impossible sacrifice. On other days, it seemed no sacrifice at all, a mere illusion, as Italy was not far away but deep inside her, in the pulse of her veins, the shape of words in her mouth, the volcano dreams that still greeted her in sleep.

A few times a year, Dante sent Alma money for her daughter, whose name, it turned out, was Miriam. In return she received occasional brief notes, not of thanks but of acknowledgment: *your envelope arrived, Miriam is well, growing quickly.* No photographs, no anecdotes or details on how the money was spent.

"Why do you do it?" Rosa asked her, gently.

Dante could never fully answer the question. It was too tangled in the briars of lost Italian hills and the sticky labyrinth of the past. "Because I want to" was the best she could manage, and Rosa accepted this as answer enough.

As the 1920s unfolded, they watched the tango rise into an unimagined glory under Carlos Gardel's explosive fame, and with the advent of the radio and its power to amplify a single human voice across invisible waves into thousands of homes. Gardel's voice spilled from windows and invaded every sidewalk, as did the voices of other singers, even women, because now women could not only sing tango but do so in evening gowns fit for queens. Tango singers were no longer purveyors of vice; they had become the height of glamour.

"Well look at that," said Rosa. "Who would have believed it?"

"Santiago," Dante answered. "He always knew."

Santiago surged in her mind then, as he did every time she said his name and also when she didn't; he hovered in the room, mocking her grief, demanding life, demanding music, urging on her fingers as she played.

They were among the first in their neighborhood to buy a gramophone. With it, they could dance tangos in their living room, Dante leading, Rosa supple in her dress, their bodies fused in motion, moving, not just to the music, but inside of it.

Now Rosa could sing whatever she wanted, however she wanted. New songs came out every day, scripted with female singers in mind. The freedom was dizzying. She experimented with singing in a feminine dress, but she never abandoned her suit and trousers. Together, Rosa and Dante wrote their own tangos, coded with their passion in secret, slanted verse, and recorded them, as sung by the one and only Rosa Vidal. Soon her voice had enthralled not only the radio listeners of Uruguay but audiences in Brazil, Argentina, the United States, and a Europe just returning to its shaky feet after the war. She began to tour. Dante occasionally went with her (though not to Argentina, where she was wanted by the law), but most of the time she stayed home. She didn't mind; she had no need for crowds. Her favorite way to play, now, was standing at the window of her second-floor apartment in the center of Ciudad Vieja, on Calle Ituzaingó, just her and the violin and the strip of sky above the buildings, pouring music down to the bustling street for anyone who cared enough to catch it, and, often, many did. Men slowed their walks, craned their necks up, peered out through the polished windows of Café Brasilero. Women hanging laundry on the flat rooftops swayed their hips. Children appeared on balconies, jostling for the best view, forgetting their fervent little battles for a moment. She gave them songs, played for all of them, for no one.

Sometime in those years, the Shift occurred, though Dante would never be sure of the exact moment, just as one can't know precisely where the river ends and the great Atlantic begins: but one day he simply knew it, simply found himself a he, at home in the pronoun the world gave him each day, not because his body had changed, not because his story had changed, not even because he didn't see himself as a woman, but simply because the gap between inside and outside, self and disguise, truth and pretense, had narrowed and thinned until it became invisible to the human eye.

When Rosa turned forty—in 1936, the year after Gardel's plane crash wrapped all of tango in a shroud of tragedy—she asked for a special gift. "I want to dance with you, and play the part of the man."

Dante balked. "I haven't worn a dress in over twenty years."

"You don't have to wear a dress. You can still be you, still be Dante. I just want to lead you."

Dante closed the shutters, checked them over and over.

Then he let Rosa lead.

It was still, at the root, the same dance: the same two bodies, connecting, gliding together, two aching souls reaching for each other and finding more than could be told. And then, in the fourth song, or maybe it was the fifth, they switched roles, without speaking, their bodies deciding, hands moving from waist to shoulder or shoulder to waist and pouring the dance in the opposite direction, which was, they discovered, not an opposite at all but a continuation of the very same dance, the same

essential language of the body, of two bodies wishing to be one, forming a kinetic poem out of longing. They switched again, again, until
their bodies knew before their minds did which way the dance would
flow. This malleable secret tango became their truest. They danced it in
private for the rest of their lives.

Later that same year, when Rosa was away for an engagement in New
York City, where her voice would join an enormous orquesta and fill a
hall normally reserved for the solemn symphonies of old Europe, Dante
received an unexpected visit. He almost didn't answer the knock on the
door. When he did, he came face-to-face with a girl with a round face, a
prim bonnet, and a frank gaze.

"Good morning. I'm looking for Dante Di Bacco."

"Yes, that's me."

The girl stared even harder. "Can I come in?"

Inside, the girl looked around at the tidy living room, the potted gera-
niums in the windowsill, the warm little kitchen down the hall as if she'd
just arrived from another planet. Then she blinked and gathered herself.
"My name is Miriam."

Dante felt the air stop in his lungs. He stared at the girl, tried to drink
her in, as though she might dissolve any moment.

"Miriam Di Bacco." She said the last three syllables with the extra
emphasis of a challenge.

Had Alma given her the last name? Or had the girl claimed it? Questions galloped into his mind, hundreds of them at once. "Would you like
to sit down?" he said.

They spent the afternoon drinking *mate*, and talking. Miriam told him
that, when she was nine, she'd intercepted an envelope from Uruguay
and opened it to find a wad of cash and a brief note: "for Miriam, as
always. D." Until then, she'd always been told that her father was dead,
though the two other children in the brothel told her that her father must

have been a customer, just like their own. She confronted her mother and, after a fight that lasted several days, was able to learn that the D. in question was a certain Dante Di Bacco, who lived in Montevideo. *And is he my father?* Miriam had asked her. *Is he? Is he?* Alma had stared at her for a long time before finally saying, *yes, Miriam, he is.* From then on, the money had gone directly to Miriam's upkeep (before then only God knew how it had been spent) and helped her to go to school, as well as, ultimately, to escape her mother's profession when she ran away at fourteen, a wad of Dante's cash in her pocket, intercepted from the mail. She found her first job across town, in Palermo, with a Lebanese rug merchant who let her sleep on the storeroom floor because he believed in giving the wretched a chance in this world. The storeroom floor was better than her mother's room, she said, though she stopped short of saying why, and Dante didn't ask. She worked hard and dreamed of meeting her father one day. She saved money for years before setting out to look for him. The name change had been her own idea, not yet legal but, she said, real in her mind.

"How long will you stay?" Dante asked, his heart in his throat.

Miriam eyed him, equal parts defiance and hope. "How long can I?"

She was still there when Rosa arrived the following week, still there a year later, part of their family for three precious years in which they came to know her coppery laugh and her quick temper and her wildly generous soul—and in which Dante came to know the dizzying joy of being called Papá, never saying anything to the contrary, allowing Miriam's truth to define their world—until, in 1940, she completed her studies in nursing and returned to Buenos Aires to minister to the poor of her old neighborhood, San Telmo. The day she left, Dante and Rosa stood in the Montevideo port and waved and waved until the boat disappeared at the horizon, and even then they held hands for a long time, saying nothing, staring out at the great river in amazement.

———

The tango reached a Golden Age. Orchestras grew to dizzying size, and traveled all over the world to grace the best of stages. Musicians with classical training or years playing jazz, or both, pushed the tango's edges into new terrain, to the outrage of some and the thrill of others. Rosa and Dante were now considered part of the Old Guard, a term that amused and bewildered them, as they remembered so vividly a time when their sound and everything they did was radical and new. Some of their peers, over drinks in Montevideo, bemoaned the changes, claiming that what people now called tango was not tango at all, and sometimes Dante, too, worried that the soul of tango as it used to be would be lost in the cacophony. And perhaps it would. But then his mind always returned to Santiago, his embrace of changes—the loss of drums, a woman's voice, the advent of piano and bass—because, in his words, *change keeps the tango alive*. And alive it was, throughout the 1940s and into the 1950s, riding the tide of Juan and Evita Perón's nationalistic fervor until the generals took Argentina into their iron hands in 1955 and clamped the tango down as though it were the very soundtrack of rebellion. As if music could be crushed like a condemned building or a stubborn anarchist. But it could not. It always rose and returned, vital, immense, fortified by new instruments, new shapes, new musicians crazy enough to give their lives to it like underground, unsanctioned priests. Dante played on and Rosa sang on as the tango rose and fell and flowed and ebbed with the decades, with the times, with those who grasped the songs and carried them into rebirth.

As Dante grew old, he looked around him, at the life he'd built, the friends he'd made, the city he'd come to love, the man he'd become. It was a good life, one he often wished he could wrap in a blanket and carry back in time to the girl he'd been, to show her what was possible, to watch her mind break open in shock. In his sixties, he took to talking to his cousin Cora, on walks along the waterfront, in the shower, in his sleep. He started thinking about the grave, the things you couldn't take with you, and the things you could. That was when he bought the coffin, a simple construction of solid Uruguayan oak, and kept it in his living room, shut and empty, a bench for piles of sheet music or for guests. Word spread among their friends, and throughout the city, of the eccentric old tanguero in Ciudad Vieja obsessed with death. Only Rosa understood the real reason for the coffin, an obsession not with death but with narrating your own life, because if you don't script your own way once and for all, your story will be written by someone else, and your actions will be guided by other people's dreams of who you should be rather than by the bright jagged thing you really are.

Dante died when he was seventy-two years old. Rosa found him in the kitchen, facedown on the morning paper, which featured photographs of a huge funeral procession in the United States for Martin Luther King, Jr. Dante's morning *mate* had been knocked to the floor, and the shredded leaves had spilled out of the gourd onto the tiles. Below the article about Martin Luther King, Jr.'s funeral was another about the Tupamaros, a guerrilla revolutionary movement in Uruguay. Dante would not be there to watch that movement expand and then be crushed by the government as it hurtled toward dictatorship. It would be Rosa who would see those changes; she would hide revolutionaries in her basement and as she did she'd think of Dante's cousin, the first Dante, the way he'd died as an anarchist martyr—and she'd think of El Loro's youthful passion years ago—the eternal march of outsize dreams. She would harbor these young Tupamaros, not because she was one of them or because she believed them for a second when they said the revolution was right around the corner, but because she was moved by their fresh faces and the fever in their eyes. It's unstoppable, this fever, she would think, and not so different from other fevers I've known. Rosa would survive until democracy returned to Uruguay as well as to her other nation, Argentina, the giant across the river, and when it did she'd write a tango celebrating freedom, but she wouldn't join the public marches, wouldn't let her song reach other human ears. She would sing it quietly to the houseplants, and they, the plants, would absorb her old-woman crooning with glad hunger.

But all of that would come later.

Now, at Dante's death, she washed the body herself and clothed it so that no one would discover the secret her beloved had carried all his life, following his instructions to the letter. Only you, Dante had told her, more times than was necessary, if I go first I don't want anyone to see me but you. I see you, you bastard, Rosa thought as she sponged the wrinkled body, I see you, all of you, this corner and that curve, that flap of skin that was so taut when we were young, I watched it pucker and stretch over the years and after all this time I still want to touch it, how could you leave me, selfish brute, you should have bought a coffin with room for two. She lay her head down on Dante's naked chest and closed her eyes, as if that could lock the tears in. It could not. When the sobs subsided, a strange feeling settled over her, a vast and preternatural calm, and she rubbed the tears into Dante's skin and finished her task with steady hands.

By the time the doctor arrived, the corpse was dressed and laid out in its coffin. Rosa had taken care of everything: neatly groomed hair, hands clasped gently over a crisp tuxedo, the bow tie perfectly straight, a letter from Dante on the kitchen table, requesting that his remains go undisturbed. The doctor, a good friend of Rosa and Dante's who'd seen them through two decades of winter flus, was happy to confirm the cause of death without violating the unusual wishes of the deceased. The funeral was crowded with well-wishers from the tango world, their neighborhood, from all of Montevideo, and all of them agreed that Dante made a good-looking dead man. How about that, Dante? Rosa thought at the corpse as the coffin lid closed for the last time with a tidy click like the clasp of an instrument case. Just what you wanted.

The corpse remained silent.

But silence, Rosa thought an hour later as she watched the coffin sink into its tomb, is a kind of music too. It was a clear cold day, the sky so blue it might be outlawed any moment for its beauty. Music is composed of silence too, and now her Dante was wrapped up in a shroud of it, I did that, Dante, I wove the shroud for you. Go home, *querido*. You should have stayed longer, I want four hundred years with you and more, but fine, all right, you can go and I'll stay here, not four hundred years but for however long this aging body lets me, and while I'm here I'll remember everything that's wrapped in there with you and won't ever be spoken—the shape of you, what we did, what we made, our songs and you bastard you sweet bastard how we sang them, how we laughed at the Fates, wildly, madly, as if the world were ours, what a sound, Dante, can you still hear it?

Acknowledgments

Huge thanks—I mean truly roaring waves of thanks—to all the people and institutions named below:

In Italy: the staff of the Rhegium Julii Prize—especially Giuseppe Casile, Josephine Condemi, and Mario Musolino—for their marvelous hospitality in Reggio Calabria, including that unforgettable trip to Scylla. Domenico Chieffallo, historian of Italian migration to the Americas, for so generously opening his home and sharing his books. My relatives in Salerno and Prepezzano, for opening their arms and lives to me, for everywhere they took me, for their exuberant support of my research: Alfredo and Rosanna Grimaldi; Alessandro and Nicola Grimaldi; Giuseppe, Stella, and Mariolino Grimaldi; Liana Basso; and all their partners and children.

In Uruguay, where I lived for a year and a half while writing this book: the Fulbright Commission, for opening doors to my wife and, by extension, our whole family. Patricia Vargas at Fulbright, for her grace and unflagging support. Gabi Renzi and Zara Cañiza for their generosity, their profound friendship, and the many revelations over *mate*. Tomás Olivera Chirimini, who is a living, breathing encyclopedia of Afro-Uruguayan and Afro-Argentinean history, as well as a remarkable man. Alejandro Giussi, my violin teacher, whose passion for tango history is matched only by his generosity in sharing it. Mario Gulla, violinist for the band El Club de Tobi, for his time and his deep insights into his instrument. Darío González Galeano, for the best private tango dance lessons a girl with two left feet could ever ask for. Sergio Ortuño and Patricia Fernández of Triangulación Kultural, for their work, welcome, and vision. Ramón Farías, Jr., Ramón Farías, Sr., and Movimiento de Integración Afro Arachana for the invitation to the town of Melo. The National Library, for access to essential texts. My aunt Mary Marazzi for the unending love and support.

In Argentina: my cousins and aunts and uncles, who accompanied me on investigative expeditions, engaged in sprawling conversations, advised me, loved me, inspired me, and brought Buenos Aires to life in a thousand ways. Daniel Batlla, Diego Batlla, Guadalupe López Ocón, Ester María López Ocón, Mónica López Ocón, Claudio Batlla, Graciela Uribarri, Susana Rodríguez, Carlos Salatino, Héctor Bonafina (you are missed), Horacio Bonafina, Gabriela Bonafina, Lucía Salatino, Sebastián Batlla, Malena Batlla, Fernando Batlla, Cecilia López, Mariana Hilbert, Ricardo Dubatti, and all their partners and children.

In the United States: I am deeply thankful to the National Endowment for the Arts, for its generous support during the writing of this book. Marcelo de León, historian of unparalleled talent and generosity, for probing facts and sources. Malena Kuss, for being kind enough to contribute her vast musicological expertise. Susan McClary, for opening the world of musicology to me so many years ago. Shanna Lo Presti, for the many years of creative support and exchange. Jessica Strauss, for reading deeply and for sparking so much. Others who read drafts, or did other things that mattered: Joyce Thompson, Luna Han, Alex Bratkievich, Micheline Aharonian Marcom, Laleh Khadivi, Margaret Benson Thompson, Pablo Palomino, Mũthoni Kiarie, Ed Ntiri, Jenesha de Rivera, Aya de León, and Joan Lester. And, of course, for so many reasons, my U.S. extended family, including Ceci De Robertis; Alex, Meg, Maia, and Henry De Robertis; Margo Edwards; John Harris (you are missed); and Carlos and Yvette Aldama.

In France: my aunt Cristina De Robertis, for her wonderful support, and for the inspiring work she and her husband, Henri Pascal, do on behalf of *ríoplatense* culture and a better world. Alfredo De Robertis, for everything he's shown me about music, Buenos Aires, love, and the human soul.

In the world of publishing: Victoria Sanders, my beloved and peerless agent, as well as Chris Kepner and Bernadette Baker-Baughman for the miracles they work behind the scenes. Chandler Crawford, foreign agent, doer of many amazing things. My editor at Knopf, Carole Baron, for the sheer joy of our collaboration, and for her wisdom, skill, and generosity. Sonny Mehta, for his steadfast support. Kathy Zuckerman, Brittany Morrongiello, Ruth Reisner, Lexy Bloom, and Jaime de Pablos, for everything they do. All my international publishers, to whom I owe a great debt—particularly Susanne Kiesow and Julia Schade at Fischer Verlag, in Germany; Kjersti Herland Johnsen, Anne Iversen, Trygve Arlind, and Vebjørn Rogne at Schibsted Forlag, in Norway; and Elisabetta Migliavada and Francesca Rodella at Garzanti, in Italy.

In the historical ether: I am indebted to many, many authors and texts, particularly Juan Carlos Cáceres's *Tango negro* and Francisco Canaro's *Mis memorias: mis bodas de oro con el tango*. I am also indebted to Billy Tipton, jazz musician, for passing as a man for fifty years, and to his biographer, Diane Wood Middlebrook, for giving his story an eloquent voice. I bow humbly to Azucena Maizani, early tango singer, whose ground-breaking drag performances have been denied their place in tango history for too long (a taste can be found at www.youtube.com /watch?v=WJPfhwJur5k). And I also bow to all the musicians who made the tango what it is today through their sweat and passion and invention, in the Old Guard and before that, in the mysterious decades when the tango first formed. Many of these tangueros' names are lost in time, but their contribution to world culture endures.

Finally, home. My two children, Rafael and Luciana, teach and inspire me every day. And if it weren't for Pamela Harris, my first reader, soulmate, co-conspirator in matters large and small, this book would simply not exist. *Gracias.*

A Note About the Author

Carolina De Robertis is the internationally best-selling author of two previous novels, *Perla* and *The Invisible Mountain* (a Best Book of 2009 according to the *San Francisco Chronicle; O, The Oprah Magazine;* and *Booklist*), and the recipient of Italy's Rhegium Julii Prize and a 2012 fellowship from the National Endowment for the Arts. Her books have been translated into sixteen languages. Her fiction and literary translations have appeared in *Granta, Zoetrope: All-Story,* and *The Virginia Quarterly Review,* among other publications. De Robertis grew up in a Uruguayan family that immigrated to England, Switzerland, and the United States. She lives in Oakland, California.

A Note on the Type

Pierre Simon Fournier *le jeune*, who designed the type used in this book, was both an originator and a collector of types. His types are old style in character and sharply cut. In 1764 and 1766 he published his *Manuel typographique*, a treatise on the history of French types and printing, and on what many consider his most important contribution to typography—the measurement of type by the point system.

Composed by North Market Street Graphics,
Lancaster, Pennsylvania

Printed and bound by Berryville Graphics,
Berryville, Virginia

Designed by M. Kristen Bearse